THIEVING WOMEN ALWAYS LOSE

TALES OF THE UNDEAD & DEPRAVED

ADRIAN J. SMITH

EREKA PRESS

THIEVING WOMEN
ALWAYS LOSE

CHAPTER 1

The smooth white pill left a chalky texture as it slid down Jerry's throat. The thing was barely bigger than a squash seed, but it was all she needed to keep her head in the game to get more. Gripping the wooden wheel tightly, her knuckles white, she spun it hard to starboard, her small ship turning through the air under her skilled command as they hovered meters above the poisoned sea.

Azar stood at the second wheel, his tall, muscular form holding firm, steering with her as they maneuvered *Yarrow*. Jerry's heart pattered a steady thrum as she followed the ship in front of them at close range. The sleek white medical vessel was rumored to have exactly what she wanted.

Gritting her teeth, she took a sharp turn to port when the vessel they followed tried to out-maneuver them. If Jerry's mouth hadn't been so dry with the flavor of ass, she would have laughed. She was one of the best self-taught pilots out there, and she had been flying the seas far longer than any pilot who had gone through the government's training program.

Azar grunted when something in their engine chugged loudly before sputtering. Scrunching her nose, Jerry scanned the dash to see if she could quickly figure out what had made the noise and if they were going to be able to continue the chase. She didn't want to lose another shipment of drugs. She needed them. Hell, her crew needed them more.

"What is it?" Jerry called to Azar, knowing he was staring at the same readouts she was.

"Don't know yet. Hoping a loose screw."

"Screw loose." Jerry sneered. A screw had been loose in her head since she was conceived. Hats off to her mother for that one. "We can't lose them."

"Pick up speed."

Jerry leaned forward and gripped the thruster, forcing *Yarrow's* engine to work overtime. Again, the medical vessel tried to twist out of their way, but Jerry easily followed them. "Do they think they're really going to get away?"

"How are you going to board them?"

"Wait until they're dead in the water."

"Chase them until they run out of steam? What if we run out first?"

Cursing, Jerry glanced at their fuel stores. They didn't have much left. They'd gotten the tip on a whim when they were working their regular job, and she hadn't waited a second to call her crew of two back so they could take a shot at finding exactly what they needed. "Fine. Get on top then, and I'll jump."

"You're insane. If you miss—"

"Then I guess you'll get to be captain." Jerry turned *Yarrow*, guiding her ship above the medical vessel and bearing down. It forced them to slow their speed since they had no idea what she was planning. Jerry ordered, "Take the helm."

Goal One—get on the ship.

Swishing her black leather jacket behind her, Jerry raced out to the deck then the edge of her ship. She looked down, her stomach in knots as she stared at the distance below her.

"Shit."

"Shit is right!" Azar's voice reached her from the wheelhouse.

Jerry jerked around to glare at him through the front window. She would never live this down if he was right. "Lower us down!"

Azar did as he was told, even though she knew he disagreed with her. She was the captain, and he worked for her, her second only because she allowed it. It had been much that way for the last year since they'd become infected with the virus that was the bane of her very existence. Gritting her teeth, Jerry leaned over the edge of *Yarrow* and held on as tight as she could to a rope.

When they got closer, she let go, pushed off the ledge with her feet and spread her arms and legs out as she dropped. Her stomach rose into her throat, and it was next to impossible to take a deep breath. Clenching her jaw, Jerry waited to be able to reach the boom of the medical vessel below her, flying through the air. She thanked the heavens they hadn't moved or jerked to the side yet.

She wrapped her arms and then her legs around the large boom, sliding down it to the first lookout for the mast that was never used anymore. At one point in the past, it had been useful. Now it was just for show. Jerry relaxed in relief as her feet touched the surface. She'd made it.

Ignoring the fact that Azar would likely yell at her for it later, Jerry flipped over the lookout and jumped to the main deck of the medical ship. As she stood up, she grabbed her gun in her left hand and her short sword in her right. She didn't hesitate as she dug her boots into the white deck and ran for the wheelhouse.

Goal Two—take control of the ship.

Two officers guarded the wheelhouse. Jerry kicked open the side door and pointed her gun at one and her sword at the other.

"Surrender and you'll live." Cocking her head to the side, she gave them each a hard, determined look.

One put his hands up, but the other continued to maneuver the ship, losing Azar for a brief second, but Jerry trusted him to find his way back to her. In the past year, they hadn't been just crew mates. They had become family. Jerry trusted him and his sister, Yafe, with her life.

Jerry fired her gun, shooting the captain in the shoulder. He collapsed onto the ground just as the other one came at her. Ducking down, she swiped her sword across his belly and sliced into his skin. He cried out, falling to the deck. Glancing around, Jerry found a rope and tied them quickly so they couldn't move, though she'd have to go back and make sure it was better as soon as she had a minute.

She grabbed the thruster and jerked it hard, stopping the vessel dead only feet above the water. Azar brought *Yarrow* around and tied the two ships together while Jerry went belowdecks, knowing Yafe would follow soon.

Each person she met was medical, and instead of fighting, they put up their hands and surrendered. She tied them as she went, Yafe joining in and taking the deck below. The ship was filled with patients and medical staff. The tip they'd received hadn't been about a large shipment of drugs, only a small one, but it would be enough to help her crew last a week—maybe two if they were able to stretch it out and not take as much.

That chalky flavor of ass in her mouth was a strong reminder of exactly what she was looking for. As the tension calmed from the initial sting of attack, Jerry rolled her shoulders. They brought everyone topside and lined them up. Yafe watched over them, walking back and forth with two guns holstered on her hips and one in her hand.

She had changed so much in the last year. They all had. The lessons Yafe and Jerry had learned while in Joab, a supposed rehabilitation center for criminals, came in very useful since the world had turned on them. Azar came aboard after tying the vessels together. His dark skin glistened in the fading sunlight as he eyed Jerry.

"We're going to need a new manifold."

"Fuck," she muttered. Turning to Yafe, she nodded at her. "You good here?"

"Yeah, Cap."

"Good." Jerry jerked her head toward the wheelhouse while staring at Azar. "Come with me."

Goal Three—find the fucking drugs.

They went through every single room, combing through to find the drugs rumored to be on the ship. They found nothing. Her heart ached at the thought of all that work for zero results. At least they could pillage what they could from the rest of the ship, but without those drugs, they wouldn't have long to enjoy what they reaped.

In one of the medical storerooms belowdecks, Jerry kicked a cabinet door shut as anger boiled in her belly. *What the fuck was it all for anyway?* Sometimes she wondered if it would be better to die than to live, but the thought of death scared the living daylights out of her.

Azar leaned against the doorframe. "Nothing."

"Same here." She wrinkled her nose. "Take what we need and what we can sell. I'm going topside to see if I can wring it out of one of them."

Azar said nothing as Jerry stalked out of the room. She left him to work as she climbed the steep stairs level by level until she reached the wheelhouse and went out again. They were outside the border of Raegina, meaning the authorities had no jurisdiction there. Jerry found the captain and put her sword under his chin, raising his gaze so he had to look at her as he cowered while bleeding from his shoulder.

"Where are you coming from?"

He didn't speak.

"Where are you going? I assume Raegina."

The captain didn't respond, just stared at her blankly. But the first officer's eye twitched, which told Jerry he might be the better of the two to interrogate. Still, she stayed with the captain, really hoping she wouldn't have to kill him in order to get the information she wanted.

"Why bring them to Raegina? It's not like our healers are any better than healers elsewhere."

"We're going home." A small woman, with bright blonde curls and bright baby blue eyes stared up at her. She was young, far too young to be traveling on her own, especially with what the world had become. Though before the virus raged, women rarely traveled alone even though they had the same right to do so as men did.

Jerry spun on the toes of her boots. "Home? From where?"

"Potelia." The woman looked scared, but she was answering questions, which Jerry appreciated.

She hated the scoundrel she'd become–hardened, thieving, nothing better than what she'd been born into–no matter how hard she'd tried to escape that role of her life. An unsightly creature to the bone. "Where is the vestigen?"

The captain's face didn't change, but the woman's did. One of the healer's eyes widened, and he shook his head as he softly spoke, "We don't have any."

"I know you do. Don't lie to me."

"We don't."

Jerry jerked her wrist, digging the edge of her sword into the captain's jugular. She could so easily kill him. One swift flick of her hand and he'd be lying at her feet, bleeding out. She could leave these people stranded, with nothing, with no hope of getting home to Raegina. Except, she wouldn't do that.

Pursing her lips, Jerry walked over to the healer who had spoken. "I know you have some."

"We don't," he whispered. "I swear. We didn't bring any because no one here was infected."

Tightening her grip on her sword, Jerry eyed Yafe, giving her a silent jerk of her head. The two of them walked toward the wheelhouse, lowering their voices so no one could overhear them.

"What if he's telling the truth?" Yafe asked, her sweet voice filled with worry.

"I suspect he is about the vestigen. I doubt he is about no one being infected," Jerry answered. "Go help Azar. We're taking what we can sell but keep looking for the vestigen. I want it if they have it."

"Are you going to leave them?"

"I haven't decided yet, but I won't kill them."

Goal Four—steal what they could to survive longer.

Yafe reached up and squeezed Jerry's arm, a silent gesture of approval before she vanished belowdecks to help her brother. Jerry stayed put, crossing her arms and leaning against the wall as she stared at each of them in turn. Some of them looked so scared but the trained officers didn't. They were as bad as the authorities, thinking they had all the power in Penum to do whatever they wanted.

Jerry watched the captain for any sign he might try something. She suspected he wouldn't. The training had changed since the virus rampaged through their planet. The protocol now was not to fight, especially if they had nothing to lose. And he had put up very little resistance.

The woman with blonde curls moved, shifting in her seat on the hot deck. Jerry swore her eyes turned a cold steel-blue instead of baby blue, that her face morphed from round to longer and thinner, her lower lip plump and her upper lip thin. She was so small sitting there, wrapped in the traditional garb for a coming-of-age woman that would no doubt be too hot to wear topside for long.

Jerry swallowed, blinked, and closed her eyes while drawing in a deep breath. It wasn't *her*. This woman may look like *her*, but she wasn't. She was someone else entirely. Her hair wasn't long enough. Her face was round, not thin. She was far too young, younger than Jerry herself instead of more than a decade older. And even sitting, Jerry could tell she was far taller than *her Arloa*.

Opening her eyes again, Jerry stared straight at the woman, seeing her for who she truly was. Not Arloa. She just had to keep reminding herself of that. Azar and Yafe went back and forth taking crates of what they wanted to keep and bringing them on board *Yarrow.*

It took close to two hours before Yafe stopped and whispered, "We're nearly done. Still no sign of the vestigen."

"All right. Tell me when you're done, and tell Azar to knock out the ship so it can't move."

"Got it."

Jerry stayed put, eyeing her captives. They didn't move or speak, but the woman kept oscillating before her, changing from the one who was there to the one Jerry wanted to see. She had to stop doing that, she had to see her for who she truly was.

Perhaps the sun and lack of vestigen and water in her own blood stream was affecting her. She'd taken a pill, but it had been her first one in days as she'd tried to ration their store, and still she couldn't function without it. Glowering, Jerry held her place as she watched them.

Eventually, Yafe reemerged. "This is the last, Cap."

"Take it over."

Yafe did as she was told, the beautiful woman always loyal even to the point of Jerry's dragging her into piracy from the life track she'd been on. They'd both been on it, actually. Legal work, a ship all her own, no hints of ever going back to Joab. Jerry was pretty sure if she was caught now, she'd be skipping Joab and going straight to the death chamber.

Azar showed up next, his hands covered in grease as he wiped them on a cloth. Jerry pursed her lips and looked up into his dark eyes. "Take the manifold by chance?"

"Of course, Cap."

She loved that they could think like that, without words, and that they were on the same page. It made living, working, and stealing that much easier. "Get home then."

Azar left, and Jerry was on her own with the captive crew. She did hate to leave them so absolutely stranded, but her crew needed the time to escape, especially if that odd noise had been the manifold malfunctioning. Jerry straightened her spine, squared her shoulders, and walked the line, staring at each of them as she figured out which one she was going to untie. She'd already made up her mind, however, if she truly thought about it.

As soon as the woman had spoken, Jerry had known she would be the one. She reminded her too much of Arloa to leave her stranded in the heat with no hope of escaping it quickly. Jerry walked back down the line of captives, then up it again, giving Azar the time he needed to untie *Yarrow* and get her ready to leave.

When she heard *Yarrow's* engines hum more forcibly, Jerry bent down in front of the young woman. She was at least twenty years younger than Arloa, only a few years younger than Jerry herself.

"What's your name?"

"Whitney." Her eyes were a definite baby blue, not steel-blue, no hints of gray and black flecks in there.

Jerry nodded at her. "You've shown real resilience today."

Swiftly pulling her sword, Jerry held it to Whitney's chin much like she had the captain's, only she didn't push in. She didn't want Whitney to feel as though she was truly threatened. She would be scared enough after what had happened today.

"Which is the reason I've chosen you to save this lot."

Jerry brought the sword down, cutting the rope at Whitney's wrists and ankles. She stood up as Whitney stayed planted exactly where she was, her eyes wide as she stared up at Jerry. Sliding her sword into its sheath, Jerry backed away with her hands out to her sides and toward the far end of the ship where *Yarrow* was still docked waiting for her.

"Don't make me regret it."

Turning on a dime, Jerry raced for the edge of the vessel. She stepped up on the ledge and launched herself over it, landing squarely on *Yarrow's* deck. Without waiting, Azar took *Yarrow* up and above the medical ship and flew straight south, back to where they had originally come from. Jerry went belowdecks, cleaning her sword on the edge of her jacket as she went to the galley, the place they always seemed to gather when they had down time.

Azar wasn't as good a pilot as Jerry, but they had a routine. They'd done this so many times in the last year that they knew what each of them needed. Yafe sat at the table, going through some of the smaller items they'd brought on board and taking an inventory. Jerry swiped a cold drink, downing half of it and getting rid of that awful ass flavor that was stuck on her tongue.

She stared down at what Yafe was inventorying. "That at least made it worth it."

"Jumping off the side of the ship was quite a risk."

Jerry raised a single eyebrow in Yafe's direction. "And an adventure."

"You don't have to be so close to death to feel, you know. There are other ways—"

"Yafe," Jerry said, a warning in her tone. "We're already close to death. We're barely alive."

"But we *are* alive."

"You can believe whatever you like. But we're not living."

"Perhaps you aren't, but I'm not really sure you want to."

Jerry paused. Where had the meek woman she'd met in Joab all those years ago gone? The world had hardened her. Hell, the virus had hardened them all, which only proved Jerry's point. They weren't living anymore. They were surviving, and even then Jerry had to wonder what world it was they wanted to survive for. There wasn't much left.

The economy had plummeted. Real, legal work was hard to come by, and while she had a legal job she ran most days, it barely brought in enough credits for her to fix her ships and pay her crews. It certainly didn't bring in enough for her to buy them the drug they needed to continue on living. They were no longer just unsightly creatures people didn't want to see and ignored most of the time. They had become the scourge of the earth, the unmentionables, the ones who disappeared and were never seen again.

Goal Five—die a worthy death.

CHAPTER 2

The flight to Raegina was quick after they stopped at the salt mines on Beren Island to load up. Jerry's muscles were sore after a long day and night of work. Returning to Beren Island hadn't been her first choice, but with no vestigen to bring to the rest of her crew there was little point in avoiding work that would bring them consistent income.

After they off-loaded their haul of salt, Jerry showered and changed. She pulled a loose tunic over her head, tying it up the front with the long laces and around her wrists. She couldn't get the image of Whitney out of her head, a young and beautifully innocent woman—someone so unlike her Arloa.

Jerry hadn't seen Arloa in over a year, and yet her image still haunted Jerry daily. It had been Jerry's choice, of course, to not see Arloa, to shove her out of *Yarrow* one fateful night over a year ago and to ignore every communication Arloa had sent. Still, she regretted it even though she upheld her decision. She couldn't drag Arloa down with her into the underbelly of Penum.

Braiding her dark hair down her back, Jerry made sure she looked clean and presentable. She had the list of items they were going to sell, provided to her by Yafe, thankfully. She didn't know what she would do without that woman. She was the organizational strength behind their operation—on all fronts.

She checked in with Azar and Yafe before she left, sending Yafe to the exchange to get their money for the haul of salt they'd just brought in. They needed more credits so they could buy vestigen if they couldn't steal it. Stealing was her preferred method of getting it, since buying it from the underground was very likely going to cost five times more than it legally should be sold for—not that she could buy it legally either since it was no longer being manufactured.

Sighing, Jerry flicked her hair over her shoulder, grabbed her jacket and top hat, and bowed her head to hide her eyes so she could walk through the city as inconspicuously as possible. She hated going in broad daylight, but they were going to have to make a fast turnaround to go back to Beren Island. Credits were credits. Sometimes Jerry wondered if life was even worth it. Then she remembered it wasn't, but for some reason—one she couldn't name—she kept on going.

The walk to the bar where she would meet her contact was quick, and she knew it by heart. Jerry slipped through the cobblestone roads, dipping her head as she entered the bar and walked straight to the back after nodding at the barkeep. She moved to the door where only certain patrons were allowed to enter and went inside, down the stairs to the basement, and to a third door. Jerry knocked this time, waiting to be permitted inside.

She hated coming down here. She'd grown up in this world, her mom dragging her into it from the day she was born. It had taken her a hell of a lot of self-control and years of practice to leave it, only to be tossed right back in. Jerry clenched her jaw as she waited for the door to open, for her life to once again be in the hands of the underground so she could survive for whatever reason—and she couldn't even name that.

The room she entered was filled with smoke, creating a gentle haze that she had to narrow her eyes to see through. The lights were so soft against the dark painted walls, that it always took her a few minutes to adjust and be able to see—and breathe—down there. She'd gotten used to it after the first few times, when she'd come desperate for vestigen. She'd be lucky if they had any for her to buy since it was so hard to find.

Jerry paused as she walked through the room, weaving her way through whores and addicts as she went. This was where her mother had thrived for years. Staying in brothels like this one or bouncing between ships when they paid enough to make it worth it for her to leave. She dragged Jerry with her wherever she went, listening to her mother fuck sailor after traveler as she tried to sleep under the bunk.

Shaking the memory, Jerry moved deeper into the room. That was one crime Jerry was certain never to commit. She couldn't be a whore like her mother. She would fuck when she had to, use sex to get into and out of situations if necessary, but she was never paid credits for it. Information, time, resources, yes, but it was all on her own terms.

Miriam stood in the corner, watching the scene unfold around her. She was Jerry's point of contact, a woman who was more than twice her age and had been in charge of the underground in Raegina for longer than Jerry had been alive. Stepping up close to her, Miriam moved in and grinned.

"May I?"

Jerry nodded her affirmation, knowing that she had to agree to allow Miriam to touch her in order to get what she wanted. Touching without consent may be illegal on all of Penum, but that didn't mean it wasn't useful to give in more times than not.

Miriam stepped closer, placing both hands on Jerry's cheeks and pulling her in for a quick and friendly kiss. She tweaked Jerry's cheeks like she was a small child and grinned as she leaned against the wall, her arms crossed and the slinky dress she wore revealing more of her breasts than it had before.

Jerry dragged her gaze away, staring only into Miriam's dark brown eyes that matched her skin. "Got some time?"

"For you? Always."

Convinced it was the only reason Jerry ever got a fair price for what she brought, Jerry nodded. They moved to a smaller room in the back, one far less filled with smoke, but also colder since it was deep underground and farther away from the raging fire that warmed the building. Miriam shut the door and took a seat at the small desk.

"What did you bring me?"

Jerry handed over the small device with the list of items Yafe had given her for sale. Miriam skimmed them, making a few noncommittal noises as she went, and handed it back. "I can sell all of that, though the jewels won't get you much right now. The drugs, however…" Miriam trailed off.

Nodding, Jerry agreed. She'd known that coming in. Since the economic downturn from the virus, anything medical was at the height of cost. Jewels were worthless. It amused Jerry how the times changed in terms of what was worth credits and what wasn't. At one point, in her young life, she'd thought about studying the market more deeply, learning the trends and the ups and downs, but circumstances had prevented that, and she wasn't about to go to school to learn now that she was an adult on the run.

"What do you think you can give me for them?"

Miriam clicked her tongue against her teeth. "For the jewels, no more than two hundred credits for all of them."

"Are you serious?" Jerry's eyes were wide. "They can't be that low. You have to do better."

"Sorry, Jeraldine," Miriam apologized as she snagged the device back, dragging her finger over the list again. "Take it or leave it. You can always try another buyer."

Jerry snorted. She knew if she betrayed Miriam like that she would never get another sale with her. It was part of the deal of buying and selling with the great mistress of the underground, and since Jerry had this connection, she was going to use it as often as she could. "What about the drugs?"

"This one…" Miriam pointed to the small device in her hand. "The loripril will be a nice sum. So will the gauze, surprisingly. It's been in short supply lately."

"Glad we took it, then. I almost told Yafe to leave it."

"Don't. If you see it, I want it."

"I'll remember that for the future." Jerry waited to hear a final price. She was hoping to get at least two-thousand credits for the whole lot. That could buy her enough vestigen for two days if she could manage to find any.

"Fifteen hundred."

"No." Jerry clenched her jaw, her answer so quick she hadn't had time to hold it in. "That's ridiculous."

"The market is tight."

Sighing, Jerry crossed her arms and glared at Miriam. "You need to do better or I will try out Paradise."

"Don't even think about it." Miriam glared. "Seventeen, my best offer."

"Deal." Jerry didn't put her hand out to shake on it. She wanted to collect her credits and get out of there as fast as she could. Except, she knew Miriam was going to offer her a drink, and likely even offer her a woman. She would have to accept the first. Jerry wasn't sure she wanted to accept the second. Another day perhaps, but with the memory of Arloa so close to the surface, she wasn't sure she could bear to fuck another woman.

Miriam handed the device back, and Jerry shoved it into her pocket. "Let's drink to it."

"Yes." As expected, Jerry followed Miriam out of the small room and into the large main room. Miriam signaled to someone, and two drinks were brought over in an instant. When Jerry had been young and stupid, she had wished she could be like Miriam, running her own business in such a way that she had everyone at her command, but the more she thought about it, the stupider it sounded. Miriam never had a moment to just be. She was always on the run from the authorities, always underground.

Even though the sun was cast in shadow by the pollution and smog, Jerry enjoyed being outside in it. Especially on her ship in the middle of the poisoned ocean where there was no one but her, the crew, and *Yarrow*. It was perfect then, the most relaxed she could ever be.

Yarrow was the first thing she owned legally, and she was never going to give her up. The ship was hers from day one until she died, and Jerry was going to make sure that no one ever took that freedom away from her.

"How's it going, Jerry?" Miriam asked, her voice deep and husky.

Jerry would have responded with a quick answer, but something in Miriam's tone told her she really wanted to know. Leaning against the wall where Miriam had been when Jerry came in, Jerry pondered what exactly to say. "We raided that ship for vestigen."

"And you didn't find any." Miriam said it as though she already knew the answer.

Jerry nodded but didn't add any more. Miriam understood the world as much as Jerry did and knew the supplies were running short.

"I don't have any to offer you."

"I figured as much." Jerry took a sip of the malt, not her favorite brand, but it would do since she wasn't paying for it. "Know of any shipments coming in soon? We're running low."

"I haven't had any vestigen in for weeks now."

"Fuck," Jerry mumbled. She wasn't going to be able to keep her crew alive and sane without it, and if anyone else came to them—as they were prone to do—she wasn't going to be able to help them either. She'd already rationed herself down almost as low as she dared to go.

"I'll keep my ear out."

"I suppose you always do," Jerry added, eyeing Miriam up and down. "Since it's good business."

"It is."

"Hear of any alternatives yet?"

"No, unfortunately. I lost three of my best whores to the virus this week alone. It's been rough on everyone."

Jerry snorted quietly, hoping Miriam didn't hear it. In some ways Miriam was like a mother she'd never had, and in others, she was not a woman she wanted to look up to any longer. Miriam was a means to an end, and Jerry had to keep reminding herself of that. Developing compassion for this woman wouldn't do her any good.

"How's being a business owner?" Miriam asked.

"Exactly what I'd dreamed, minus this fucking virus."

"Agreed." Miriam stared out at the room, lighting up a cigarette and smoking. She blew the air into Jerry's face, which Jerry resolutely ignored. Miriam was looking for a reaction, like she usually was, but Jerry wouldn't give her one.

It was a game they played. Miriam always tried to pry as much information out of Jerry as she could, and Jerry promptly shut it down as quickly as possible. She only had a few more hours until she needed to return to *Yarrow* and wait for Ursula, and unfortunately Miriam knew her so well it was difficult to lie to her. Jerry continued to sip her drink, hoping the alcohol would loosen the tension in her shoulders. It wasn't helping.

"Do you need any more jobs?"

Jerry pursed her lips. She would always take a job here or there, especially if it was for Miriam and asked as a personal favor. She did it out of kindness but also to keep the lines open. She would need Miriam sooner or later. "If you have one needing run, I'll do it."

Miriam canted her head to the side, studying Jerry up and down. "I don't, but I can always find something."

"I'll stick with salt for now."

"Pity." Miriam raised her eyebrows. "Next time then."

"Yup. Next time." Jerry downed her drink but waved off the barkeep when he tried to offer her another. She had spent enough time in the bowels of Raegina for one day. "Until then."

Bowing, Jerry walked herself out of the underground and up to the surface. She drew in a deep breath, regretting it instantly and sputtering. Still, it was better than breathing whatever the hell smoke was down there. She walked her way to *Yarrow* but stopped as she reached the docks.

She'd spent so much time running up and down the streets as a child when her mother would let her loose if they hit land. Now there were no children. People only walked when they had to, no one going out for pleasure or to run errands unless they were absolutely necessary.

The air was still, no breeze to it, which was odd this close to the sea. Jerry had rarely experienced it even growing up, but she knew from what the old sailors had said when they thought she wasn't listening that it never boded well for anything. Straightening her shoulders, she stepped up to the pier and walked down to the end, past *Yarrow's* slip, until she could stand at the edge of the water.

What would happen if she did jump? Who would even claim her ships? She supposed Yafe and Azar should get them, since they were her most loyal crew, but she had no one left in her life. She was alone, cast out of whatever family she did have and right back into the family she didn't want. Even her own mother hadn't been able to survive it.

There was nothing for her in this world anymore.

Arloa's steel-blue eyes flashed before her, that serious yet flirtatious look she had given Jerry on more than one occasion. For something that was only ever a quick fuck and never lasted long, Jerry couldn't figure out why she couldn't ever get Arloa off her mind. The curly blonde-haired beauty had completely entranced her. They'd both known from the start what they would get out of each other.

Arloa was a Kauket, from one of the richest families in all of Raegina, a family that not only held wealth but influence. Even if Arloa didn't like her family name, it was tied to her no matter what she did or where she went. Jerry, however, was no one, and she lived up to that title. She skated through life and got where she was solely by surviving. They were from two different worlds, worlds that never collided.

Except they had, once, collided for the briefest of times, and Arloa had given Jerry all the hope she'd needed of pulling herself up by her bootstraps and bettering her life. She didn't have to be an unsightly creature in Arloa's presence. Arloa had seen right into her heart.

Cursing, Jerry clenched her jaw and fists, digging the toe of her boot into the wood of the pier. She should never have agreed to continue seeing Arloa, and the virus had only brought the inevitable end more swiftly. Still, Jerry had to figure out something to get the damn Kauket woman off her mind. She hated the Kaukets. They were the ones who funded Joab, the prison system that was designed to torture and kill criminals but was passed off to the aristocrats and government as a rehabilitation center. The place Jerry had nearly lost her life on more than one occasion, a life she could barely remember why she wanted to keep.

She could end it right here if she wanted. Jump into the sea filled with poison and be eaten away by the acid layer by layer until she couldn't feel anything. She almost did it too, but again, Arloa's steel-blue eyes flashed at her, that cocky all-knowing look she was so fucking good at giving.

And she couldn't do it.

For no reason that she could think of, Jerry couldn't step off the edge of the pier and end it all. Straightening the sleeves on her jacket and fixing her top hat, Jerry stared out at the sea one more time before spinning on her toes and walking to *Yarrow*. She had a shipment of items to get to Miriam in order to receive her payment—and she wanted it done before the night was out.

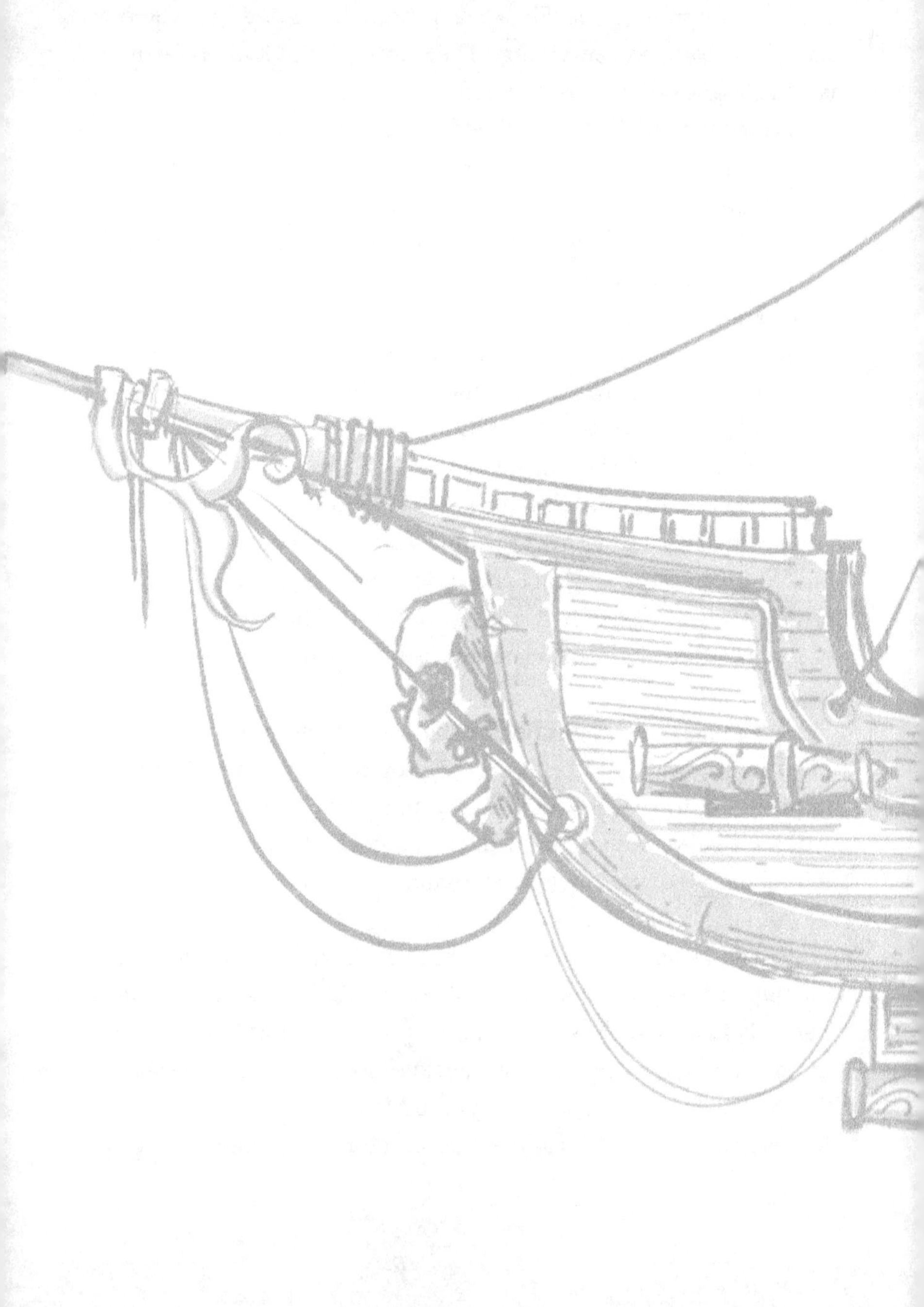

CHAPTER 3

Ursula picked her up at *Yarrow's* doors. Jerry had dressed like a proper woman that day and took an extra dose of vestigen, not wanting to draw any more undue attention toward herself when they went out. It had taken an hour, but she could already feel the drug working in her body.

Rational thought was easier.

Hiding her raging emotions was much smoother. Yafe checked in on her before she left. Ursula walked far slower than she did, and it was a struggle for Jerry to purposely slow her gait to keep pace with Ursula, since she wasn't speeding up. She kept her head down, her top hat neatly hiding most of her face from onlookers.

She didn't want them to see the crazed look in her eye, the fact that she couldn't control herself as much as she wanted to. Still, she made her way with her hands shoved into the pockets of her overcoat, following whatever path Ursula decided for them. Jerry wasn't even paying attention to her surroundings.

As they came upon the bar Jerry used to frequent, she stopped short. She hadn't been in there since she met Arloa. She couldn't. Turning to Ursula, Jerry shook her head. "We need to go somewhere else."

"We used to love coming here," Ursula urged, reaching out to grip the iron bar that was the handle.

Jerry covered her hand sharply. "No. Pick somewhere else."

"Why not? It's the only place in Raegina to get good malts."

"Then we'll drink something else."

They were at an impasse. Jerry was about to turn and walk away when a loud commotion reached them. The door to the bar opened, and two women tumbled out, dresses askew and hair a mess. Jerry jumped back, every muscle in her body telling her to be ready to fight or run, but she still wanted blood.

That was the one fucking craving no pill could get rid of. Though sometimes, it did calm it so it was bearable. She'd have to take at least a dozen of them to feel that much calm. Ursula's fists were up and ready as if she was going to join right in.

Cursing, Jerry shifted and put her arm out to stop any more brawling from happening, or at least, to stop the two of them joining in. The two women grappled, the brunette throwing a right hook and the blonde taking it like a champ. People from inside the bar piled outside to watch.

More and more of that had been happening lately, not just because of the virus, but because of the strain it had put on society. When the virus had wiped out the workers, it had put a huge strain on the economy of the planet. No one had been prepared for it. While there was work to do, no one wanted to pay, and while there were workers—they weren't going to work for free or scraps.

Jerry sucked the back of her teeth as she held her ground, still front and center for this fight going down. She had half a mind to step in and try and stop it, but it wasn't happening. She couldn't put an end to it without revealing herself as one of them. She hadn't taken enough of the drug to keep her that calm, and if she scented blood that close, she would be out for more.

Ursula growled, as if she was going to dive right into the fray. Jerry tightened her grasp on Ursula's wrist. "Don't you dare think about it."

"Why? Aren't you?" The delight in Ursula's eyes scared her.

This was what Jerry didn't want to become. Half-crazed and out for murder. She would never go back to Joab if she could avoid it, and that would certainly land her there. Grinding her teeth, she tensed as she waited for someone else to join in. The number of cases of the virus had dwindled, but she suspected it was only because people weren't reporting. If they did, it was their own death sentence. Everyone she knew who had reported had disappeared—most likely eaten away by the water she flew over daily. That's why she never had.

Cheers and encouragement echoed from the crowd. Jerry had to shut them up. She had to make them stop just so these two women would stop. She had no idea why they were even fighting anyway, but surely nothing would be worth a trip to Joab.

Just as she was about to step in, the brunette straddled the blonde, her hands around the blonde's neck as she squeezed and pushed hard. The crowd went wild, as if this was the most entertainment they had gotten in decades, but she was sure it wasn't. Anyone could see the fights in the streets, the death that always seemed to result from it.

Bodies had been strewn about on the cobblestones during the height of the virus, but Jerry was pretty sure it would come back around. They weren't done with it yet. Nor did she think they would ever be at this rate. Focusing in on the fight in front of her eyes, the brunette stayed put as the blonde's life drained from her. She stopped moving, her feet slowing. Her eyes rolled back in her head, and the hands she'd tried claw into the brunette dropped to the ground.

No one had tried to stop it. While Jerry hadn't cheered it on, guilt flooded her. Before the fucking virus, she might have stepped in. But also before the fucking virus the authorities would have been there in two seconds flat.

As soon as it was clear the blonde was dead, two people moved in slowly to pull the brunette off. Jerry watched from a distance, not sure what to say or do. Ursula stood next to her, in the same stunned stupor. No matter how many times they had seen something similar, she never got used to it.

The crowd cleared out, but Jerry stayed put, just staring at the death, the fear, the rage before her. She couldn't tear her eyes from the woman. Ursula drew in a ragged breath, but Jerry didn't even look at her. Her gaze was glued to the blonde, images of Arloa's face, the curly mass of blonde hair she always managed to pile on top of her head.

Swallowing hard, Jerry stepped forward carefully, her boot echoing in the square as she went. She inched forward, no one else around, as she moved in to see her face. She had to see her face, make sure it wasn't Arloa. Her stomach plummeted as she got closer.

They'd met at that bar. What if…?

She couldn't even finish the thought, fear running through her veins as she took another step. The woman's dress was torn from the tussle. Jerry bolstered herself, ready to see the woman she loved—she stopped that thought in an instant. She couldn't love Arloa. That had been a decision she'd made since the last time they had seen each other, and one she would hold true to.

She wouldn't give in on that one decision no matter how difficult it got.

Kneeling against the cold cobblestone square, Jerry reached out and pressed two fingers to the woman's cheek, brushing her curls from her face. Relief flooded her. Her shoulders dropped, her heart finally beat again. She moved her hand down to the woman's neck, feeling for a pulse and finding none, but the skin against her collarbone was rough and patchy as if it had been burned and dried several times over.

She was infected. Jerry jerked her head back around to Ursula, ready to explain, but instantly she was caught on the side of her head by a hand, dragged down to the ground so her face smashed against the cobblestone. Crying out, Jerry cringed as she tried to catch her bearings. Her head spun from the hit.

She couldn't see straight as she blinked her eyes open, the light reflecting off the damp stone blurring her vision. Her head pounded. A scream pierced her ears, forcing her head into another tailspin. Weight hit her, dropping her fully onto the ground. She couldn't get it off. Bucking her hips and her arms, flailing as best as she could, Jerry tried to save herself.

Panic swelled in her belly, into her chest. She couldn't breathe. She was going to die. Right then and there she was going to die. Then it hit her. She couldn't die. At least not by anything this maniac had. Clenching her jaw tightly, she jerked her elbow back, making contact with something hard. The thud and grunt that resulted were exactly what she wanted to hear, and the weight fell off her.

Twisting so she was on her back, Jerry stared up at the sky. Perhaps it was a good thing she'd deprived herself of vestigen for so long. She would win this battle, no contest. Climbing on top of the woman, she fought off her hands as Jerry tried to strangle her, much like the woman before.

She shifted, pushing her knee right into the center of the woman's chest until she could get a hand around her neck. Cutting off her airway, Jerry leaned in. "Don't fucking touch me."

The woman choked and gagged. Jerry added her second hand when she could, increasing the pressure. Nails dug into the skin at her hands, cutting her flesh and ripping chunks away, but Jerry held on tightly. The salt would sting it tomorrow, but she could deal with it, so long as she could get this one thrill.

Gasping, the woman breathed out the words, "Help me, Jerry."

She jerked back. Falling off her, Jerry skittered away. With a scream, the woman pounced up and flung herself in Jerry's direction. Ursula tackled her to the ground, bashing her head against the stone three times before the woman settled beneath her hands.

Ursula and Jerry sat, breathing heavily as they waited for the inevitable to happen, for the woman to wake up again. Yet the scent of her blood, of her head bleeding called to Jerry so strongly. She fought against it, but she couldn't stop herself from getting onto her hands and knees and crawling over to where Ursula tied her up to confine her.

Jerry reached out, touching her fingers to the side of the woman's head, where the blood was, where chunks of red sticky matter were. "Are you sure she's alive?"

Ursula shook her head. "She'll be lucky if she is, but I don't want to test it out."

Jerry frowned and brought her fingers to her mouth unconsciously. Ursula moved to slap her hand away. "Don't do that!"

Saying nothing, Jerry stilled. They waited another minute before they really had to make a decision. They could leave her for the authorities and her own death, or they could bring her back to the ship. Ursula and Jerry shared a look.

"Your choice, Cap, but she did ask for help."

"She asked for me by name."

"Word is getting around."

Jerry snorted. "It'll be the death of me someday."

Ursula raised an eyebrow. "Are you willing to take it?"

That was a question Jerry didn't have an answer for. She always figured she would die by her own hand as she avoided going back to Joab. Would this be any different than that? Sighing, Jerry nodded her head toward the woman. "Let's take her back."

"Good choice." Ursula clapped Jerry's shoulder. "Better move quick. I bet the authorities are coming out for this one."

"Maybe," Jerry mumbled.

Ursula was on her feet before Jerry was, not having endured as much in the last twenty-four hours. She tugged at the ropes circling the woman's wrists, and Jerry frowned.

"Where the fuck did you find rope?"

"Stole it."

Jerry groaned. Of course Ursula stole it. That was her one downfall. She stole everything whenever she had a chance. It was partly why Jerry hated going out with her. Pushing herself to stand, Jerry stumbled slightly. Ursula caught her, but eventually she righted herself.

Her head spun. She was going to need to lie down and get a hold of herself when they got back, and so much for a relaxing night out like Yafe wanted her to have. Grimacing, Jerry squared her shoulders and stared down at the woman.

"You're going to have to lift her."

"I figured that, Cap."

"Good."

It took the both of them, though Ursula did get the woman upright by herself. They each wrapped an arm around her back and dragged her down toward the dock. Jerry prayed no one found them. It would be the oddest sight around, a dead woman being dragged between two very strong women, one quite beaten up. They would no doubt be stopped by the authorities.

They got to *Yarrow* first and stopped there. It was closer. Jerry pressed her palm against the sensor to unlock the exterior door. It came down, landing on the dock so they could drag the woman across it. They shut it quickly. As soon as the interior door slid back, Azar and Yafe were there to greet them.

"I send you out for a drink, and you bring home this?" Yafe put her hands on her hips.

Jerry shrugged. "What can I say? I'm a magnet for chaos."

"That's the truth if I've ever heard it."

Ursula grunted. Azar took the woman in one fell swoop, and as soon as the weight was gone from Jerry, she collapsed into the wall, barely holding herself up. Yafe stepped in, helping her to her cabin. As she lay down, Jerry closed her eyes, Penum spinning in circles.

"She got you good," Yafe murmured as she checked the wound on Jerry's head.

"Get the aid kit, will you?"

"Yeah."

When Jerry was finally alone, she raised her fingers to her nose, sniffing the blood and brain on it. She'd never done it before, though she'd been tempted many times over. The thought had always disgusted her to the point of revulsion, but she'd almost done it out in that square, without even thinking. *How fucking desperate was she?*

Dashing her tongue out against her fingers, she hummed at the taste. It was the texture that got her. It made her gag, nearly vomiting all over herself. She couldn't fathom doing it, and yet, she swallowed it down. Within a minute, a rush hit her. The same rush she got when she took multiple pills at the same time —except this was from only a small amount of brain.

"Oh fuck."

Jerry wiped her hand on the blanket, cleaning it of any evidence of what she'd done. She couldn't tell anyone. It would be the end of Penum if they figured that one out. Her best guess was that before it ever got to that point, whoever was infected had already been put down, murdered. That they were so out of it, they couldn't even begin to explain what it was they craved.

Hell, it had taken her just over a year to figure it out. Clenching her eyes shut tightly, Jerry threw her hand over her face, cringing as she hit her open wound. Yeah, that one was going to bruise and be a bitch. Probably going to take stitches.

Yafe came back in and kneeled next to the cot. "Did you happen to get a name before you killed her?"

"No," Jerry murmured. "And I didn't do it."

"She got the best of you?" Yafe's eyes widened. "I've never seen that happen before."

"Trust me. It happens."

Yafe hummed but didn't respond. "So what are we going to do with her?"

"She's here only because she used my name."

"She knew you?"

Jerry shrugged. "She knew my name. I don't know if she knew who she was talking to or if she was trying to get my attention."

"I told you people were asking for you."

Jerry kept her mouth shut as Yafe dug the needle through the skin in the side of her head, slowly sewing the opening closed. She'd had so many injuries throughout the years that this would only add to the scars.

"We'll keep her here and not send her with Ursula."

Jerry hated that she'd seen so much violence and death in the last year. Even at Joab there wasn't this much. Or at least then it had been behind closed doors where no one saw it or heard it. This virus had done a number on her world, and she was pretty sure Penum would never be the same. The trauma from it all was too real.

"There, all done." Yafe's voice was so soft, as if she was a dream.

Jerry must have fallen asleep, or at least gotten seriously lost in her thoughts. She rarely found the time to sleep, but having been away for the better part of two days, she was sure it was her time—and yet, she felt so calm. Calm in a way she hadn't felt in the last year. There was only one difference that she could pinpoint, and she did not want to think about what she had done. Not to mention, she would never dare confess that to anyone. Not to Yafe or Azar. Not even to herself—except she had to.

Reaching up for Yafe's hand, Jerry held it firmly. "Thank you."

"Any time, Cap. Azar is going to stay up with her tonight and start the regimen, but I'll be back up. I think you need to rest."

"I concur with that appraisal," Jerry mumbled, trying to be funny, but she knew it came off depraved instead. "We'll leave before first light to make less of a commotion."

"I'll set the ship to wake you."

"Thank you."

As Yafe left and Jerry was plunged into the darkness of her small cabin with the one window out to the starry sky above, she released her pent-up tension. The only thought that came to mind, the only question, was when would it stop?

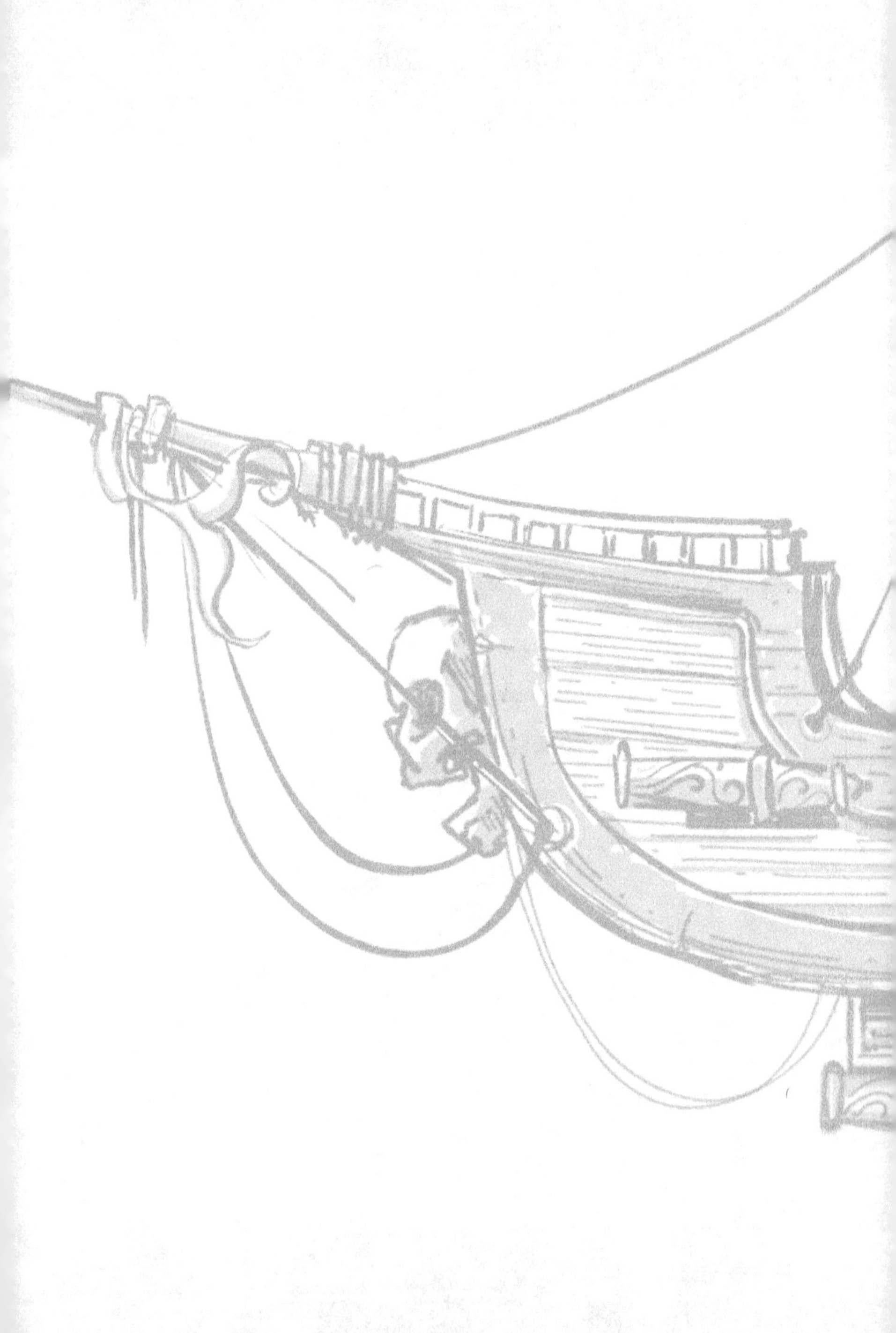

CHAPTER 4

Jerry's head still pounded when she woke up in the morning. Azar stood in her doorway, arms crossed, leaning against the frame as he all but glared at her. She rolled onto her side, holding in the nausea threatening to take over all her attention. She really should have eaten something. Not only had their drug supply gone scarce, but so had their food supply.

Morty paid fairly, but with the market taking the turn it had, even though salt was in high demand because of the frequent deaths, the pay had decreased from when they'd first started. Clenching her eyes shut, Jerry attempted to regain her composure, needing to at least look and feel decent before she could drag her sorry ass up to the wheelhouse to fly them back to Beren Island.

"It's not a good idea."

"What's not?" Jerry mumbled into the cot, trying to process what he said while at the same time not showing how awful she felt.

"Bringing her on here."

"Is she too far gone?" Jerry asked, still keeping her eyes closed. She couldn't stand to look at him—the disappointment in his voice, the anger just under the edge of it.

"It's not the right place, and there are too many. I told you this yesterday."

He had. Yet Jerry had ignored him because the idea of funding a house for removing viral infections was too much. There would be no way, that she could figure out, that they could do it without tipping off the authorities. Not to mention, it was better if the newly infected were nowhere near each other. The lack of control they had would only feed off each other to the point that it caused disaster and blood.

Jerry stayed put, soothed by the gentle rocking of her boat as the waves moved underneath it even though they hovered over the waters. It had been one of the only constant things in her life growing up, the calm in the storm of her life with her mother aboard several ships.

"Jerry."

"I heard you," she muttered. "I don't know what you want me to do about it."

"We need a place to put them, somewhere not here."

She sighed. "They need to work to learn control again. The hard labor is good for them."

"If it doesn't kill them first, you mean."

Jerry snapped her eyes open, pushing herself to semi-sit up in the bed. "I can't save every single one."

"No. But you try. Don't you."

"Is she still alive?"

"Yes, and doped up enough to find some semblance of control when she wakes."

"Ursula brought over the regimen?"

Azar nodded. "We need a healer who is willing to work with them."

"None of them are. They stand to lose their licenses and cards, remember? The threat is clear. Those who are infected must die."

"Then I suppose we're all doomed."

Jerry sighed, rubbing her fingers over her eyes and her palms over her face roughly. "We were doomed the moment we were born."

"Maybe you were."

"Oh, yes, forgive me for not being born with a penis." Jerry shot him a glare. "Are we ready to set sail?"

Azar gave her a hard look, probably trying to push her back into the argument, but the last thing Jerry wanted was to fight. She just needed to get up the two levels to the wheelhouse so she could grip onto the wheel like it was her lifeline as she took them out of the harbor. As soon as they were on open water, she could set the ship to run itself and sit down, wallowing in her own self-pity.

"We are," he grunted in response to her.

"Good. We're leaving shortly."

Azar took that as his sign to piss off, though he still wasn't wrong. Ursula's ship was close to overrun with crew. It seemed that once Jerry and Ursula helped them recover from the virus and find some sort of balance—if they survived the initial change—then they didn't want to leave. Granted, Jerry also typically offered them some kind of work for pay, which for their class of people was difficult to come by.

Proprietors didn't want to work with them. The aristocrats had found new workers to come in when they had to, workers from a higher class, and the jobs had become even slimmer for a decent wage that would support an individual, not to mention a family. Jerry sneered at the thought. The vicious cycle of shit rearing its ugly head again.

Yet the aristocrats, those like Arloa, were doing well enough they would survive into the next century, of course. Her fingers curled tightly around the edge of her cot, and she gripped onto it hard. She needed the feel of the wood under her hands to center her. She had to get out of her room, make it up the two levels to the wheelhouse. That was her one goal. Get them to Beren Island. She could find a healer, of course, but then questions would be asked, and the last thing Jerry wanted was for authorities to show up on her ship. She had too many secrets she needed to protect for that to happen.

It took monumental effort, but Jerry dragged her sorry ass up. She cleaned up in the small washroom off the side of her cabin and made sure to get the dried blood off her face. The stitching looked good, and she was pretty sure no one would even notice the scar through all of her hair.

Getting to the wheelhouse proved to be more difficult than she had anticipated. Climbing ladders with a splitting headache and no balance was probably the worst way to begin her day. Her stomach roiled in protest as she pulled herself up rung by rung, slowly making her way straight to the wheelhouse. She bypassed the galley, needing nothing from there.

As she made her way to the top of her ship, she leaned against the wheel as she pushed the vessel into engaging and prepared it for flight. All in all, it took her three times longer than it normally would have, but no one else could legally fly *Yarrow* either—at least no one currently on board.

After she pulled out of the harbor, Jerry got to the open waters and started her next task. She hated to admit it, but Azar was right. They needed a better solution to finding other victims of the virus and bringing them on board. It worked, for now, but in the long term, it was too taxing on their systems and processes to put all the weight on them. Still, the one idea Azar hadn't come up with was a ship, a vessel, that wasn't in harbor.

They could transport those needing help from Raegina to the vessel, and they could stay there until able to return to society. It would mean some crew would have to stay on the ship and never come inland except for special occasions and short breaks, but it could be manageable. She wondered if some of those they'd helped would even be willing to come back and be the front runners on it.

If they were out at sea, beyond the border, then the authorities would have nothing to do with them, and the laws couldn't interfere. Equally, however, the laws couldn't protect, so they'd have to be equipped against pirates who would no doubt attempt to find them. Perhaps a static place wasn't the best option, but it was a start of an idea.

Jerry skimmed through the manifests of the docks, looking for a ship that would be perfect for her idea. She might have to take out a loan to have enough credits to purchase it, which worried her. With the lack of income, or at least seeing it dwindle slowly, and the extra cost of not only the ship, but the crew, the necessities, and the drugs needed in order to help along the change, Jerry wasn't sure they could actually afford it.

Perhaps starting small and working her way back up would be best. Equally, if she purchased a ship legally, it would be registered with the authorities, and they would then know about it. Cursing her pounding head that was keeping her from thinking clearly, Jerry closed her eyes and winced. She just needed an easy solution.

Giving up on legal avenues of obtaining a ship, she turned to some of her seedier underground contacts. It had taken her a few months of being owner and operator of *Yarrow* to admit that she needed to revive those old relationships, but she had. And it had served her well in the past. Running both legal and illegal work was a risk, but it was one she'd had to take in order to survive the pandemic the virus had caused.

At least she could think far more clearly than the day before, that small dose of brain matter from the new one keeping her emotions calm and collected. Jerry scrunched her nose at the thought. She was going to have to figure out why that happened and if it was something they could capitalize on—although the mere thought churned her stomach.

Yafe came up the ladder, water and breakfast on a plate in her hands. Jerry kept her grip on the wheel until they reached the border and then set *Yarrow* to fly on her own most of the rest of the way to Beren Island. Jerry took the food and moved out onto the deck with Yafe, sitting down and relaxing into it.

The thought of food was the last thing on her mind, but the

water was readily accepted, and the coolness on her tongue helped ease her stomach. She narrowed her gaze as she stared out at the sea, the wind whipping in her hair.

Yafe sat next to her and picked small pieces of dried fruit off her plate, popping them in her mouth. "How's your head?"

"Hurts like a bitch."

Yafe gave a wry smile. "Figured as much. There are painkillers—"

"I'll pass. Thank you." Jerry reached over and touched Yafe's thigh lightly before looking down at her food. "Azar wants me to build a house for those recovering."

"I've heard."

"What do you think?"

They fell into a quiet silence that lasted for minutes. Jerry was comfortable with it. She grew up learning how to listen to what wasn't being said in order to survive. It was the only reason she made it through Joab, she was sure. All those years, trying to live through the atrocities that happened there. Shuddering, she thought of the one family she hated, the family who funded most of the prison—although they played it off as a rehabilitation facility. That was a lie.

The Kaukets—a family of money, but a family that kept equally quiet. They had their hands in just about everything, but most of their funding—or at least a large chunk of it—went to Joab. Jerry had never been able to figure out why, no matter how much she had dug. And she had looked. She'd wanted answers as to why someone would continue to fund a death trap for other people.

But thinking of the Kaukets made her think of one Kauket in particular. Arloa. The one who didn't seem to fit in with the family, a beautiful woman in her own right, someone who wouldn't be beautiful to many, and yet Jerry had found it, drinking in a bar at the edge of town one night over a year prior. They had found each other, started fucking whenever they got the chance, and then Jerry had gotten sick.

"Jerry." Yafe's voice was quiet but distant.

It dragged Jerry back to present reality. Right, she was supposed to be eating, and if she didn't at least eat some food and drink all her water, Yafe would be worried and continue to watch over her like a mother hen.

"What are you thinking about?"

"Nothing," Jerry mumbled, popping some sort of red fruit between her lips. She'd certainly enjoyed being close enough to Raegina to have fresh food daily instead of living off what she'd grown up on. It was such a treat.

Yafe knocked their shoulders together. "Don't do that. Don't shut me out. You were thinking about *her*, weren't you?"

"So what if I was?" Jerry frowned. She hated that Yafe was so good at reading her. They had known each other too long, and in their line of work, that was rare. She'd grown up watching people die or go to Joab and never seeing them again. Long term relationships, friendship or otherwise, were not something Jerry was used to forming.

"Nothing is wrong with thinking about her." Yafe had a serene smile on her lips.

Jerry envied it. Everything was so temporary in their lives, but Yafe always seemed to have a light to her that very few of their class did. She was a hard worker, but she never let the society or the systems in place get her down. Not like Jerry did, constantly.

"I think you should find her."

"No. That would be an awful idea."

"I disagree."

"Disagree all you want. The decision is mine to make." Jerry settled the plate onto the deck, not wanting to eat anything else. What little appetite she did have was gone, and she wasn't in any mood to try and get it back.

Yafe stayed quiet for some time, before tentatively starting again. "The decision is yours to make. I'm telling you, I disagree with it."

"You want me to expose her to all of this?" Jerry flung her hand out. "This is not the kind of life she wants or can even have. Trust me. I've thought about it since I met her, and I knew it wasn't going to work out from the start. At least this way, we both retain some dignity."

"Take it or leave it, Cap. But life is short, and when we find love, I believe we should run toward it."

"Then where is your love? Hmm?" Jerry knew she was getting nasty in her defensiveness, and she equally knew Yafe would sit there and take it.

Yafe sighed. "He died, and I haven't found it again since."

Guilt stabbed through Jerry's stomach. She'd forgotten. Yafe had fallen in love while at Joab, where they met nearly five years prior, and she had fallen in love with one of the other inmates. She'd nearly forgotten it had been so long ago, and life was so quick to change and so insignificant in some ways.

"I'm sorry." Jerry leaned her head on Yafe's shoulder. "I shouldn't have said that."

"Thank you." They fell into another lull in the conversation, rarely needing to fill the silence with irrelevant talk. Eventually, Yafe shifted. "When did you say that shipment of drugs was coming in?"

Jerry closed her eyes, trying to remember through the pain in her head. "Tomorrow. I gave the task to Ursula."

"Do you think they're prepared for it?"

"Probably more than we are, with me down and the new one on board."

Yafe raised her eyebrow at Jerry.

"What?"

"I think that's the first time I have ever heard you admit you couldn't do something because of being injured."

Jerry snorted. "I must be getting soft in my old age."

Yafe laughed loudly. "Yes, all twenty-three years makes you so old."

Jerry grinned but regretted the movement instantly. It hurt

the muscles in her face and head to move that way. She cringed and lifted a hand to her head. "I'm used to healers. But you know why we can't go to them."

"We should try to find at least one who is willing to work with us."

"True." Jerry sighed. "Maybe that can be our next task before we take on this monumental idea from your brother."

"Yes. A safe house of sorts. They used to have them when I was a kid, you know."

"They were all outlawed by the time we came to Raegina. I've seen a few in different cities, but none to the extent that Azar wants."

Yafe's lips twitched. "We stayed at one when we were little. Mama brought us there when our father—it was the only way we were able to get out, but they lost funding when the laws changed and weren't able to stay open."

"Of course they did. Nothing for the women and children in society, right?"

"Nothing," Yafe agreed. "Azar was able to go to school to get his engineering certificate, but there were no programs for women."

"There never are." Jerry had long lamented that fact. It had been what had turned her mother to the life she'd grown up in. Being so young, pregnant, and needing to work, she'd turned to the seedier side of life. She'd found the illegal to be the only way to survive as well as to keep Jerry and raise her. Otherwise the two of them would have been torn apart. If it had been discovered what was happening, that still would have very likely been the option the authorities took.

"So let's do something for the ones we can, okay?"

"I've already agreed to it." Jerry groaned. "But figuring out how to get it past the authorities and fund it is a different problem."

"Perhaps *she* can help."

Jerry stilled. Had that been the underlying point of Yafe

bringing Arloa up? Had that been the entire reason for this conversation? The Kaukets had money, there was never any doubt of that, but Arloa didn't. She wasn't the head of the house, she didn't make the decisions. Yet she did work in the government.

"No," Jerry stated firmly. "And you should be appalled to have even suggested it."

"It was only an idea, perhaps an easy solution to a problem."

"Nothing about this problem, a safe house or the virus, is easy."

Yafe couldn't deny that one. Jerry tilted her head back and drank her water. Eventually, she stood up and walked back into the wheelhouse to check the systems and see how far they were from Beren Island. She didn't want to have to worry about *Yarrow* going off course. She didn't want to think about the woman belowdecks, the one who looked so much like her Arloa but was nothing like her at all. She hadn't even bothered to learn her name yet, something she would have to rectify soon even though something inside her told her not to.

She rolled her shoulders, shifted the direction of the vessel, and pushed onward. They were going to have a long day of work ahead of them, and with Jerry's injuries, it was going to mean she was going to be dragging her feet when they finished.

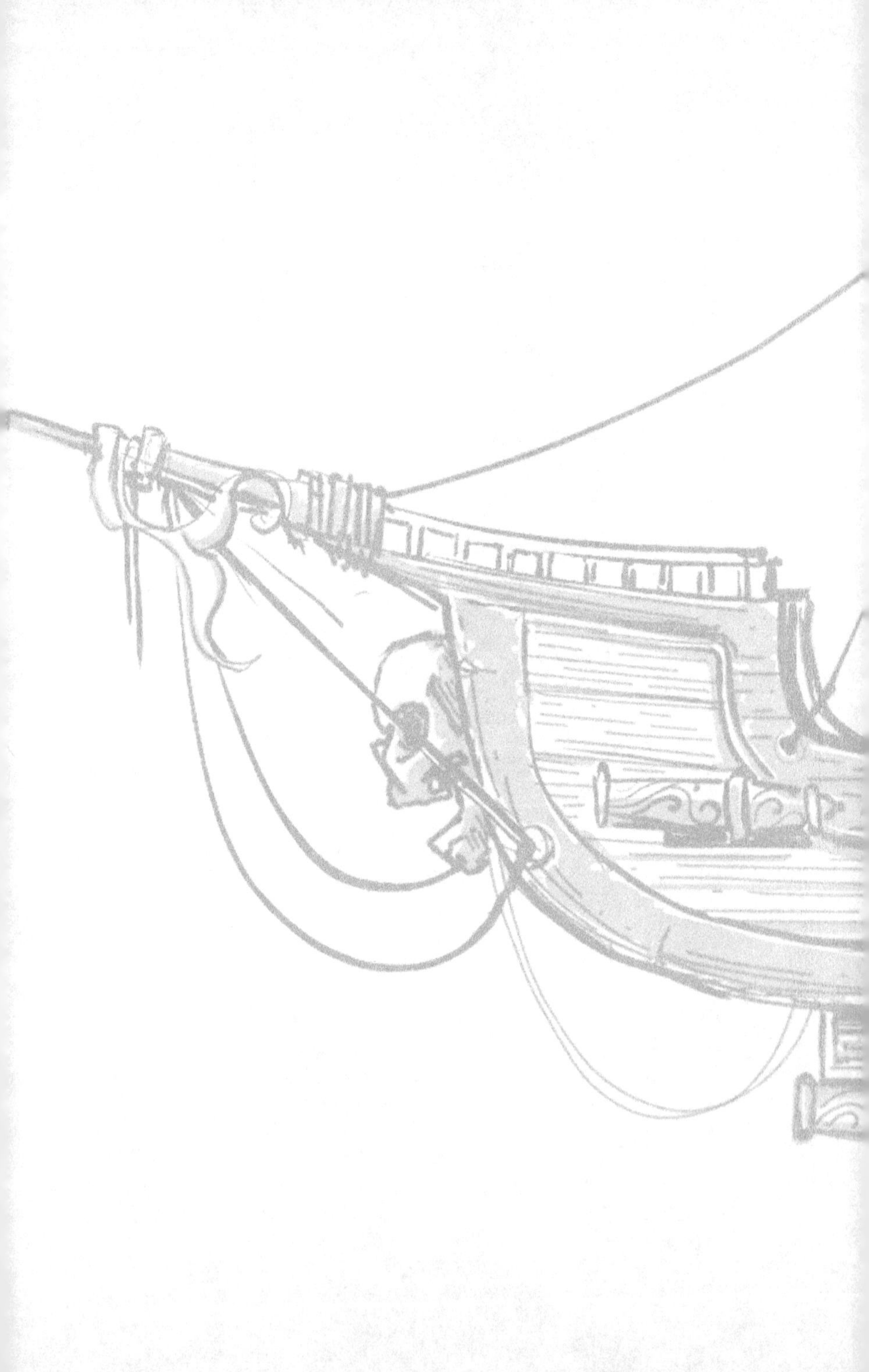

CHAPTER 5

Jerry dug the shovel into the salt mound and lifted it, dropping the precious cargo into the crate she would eventually drag to her ship. Every time she did it, all she saw was Matty's sweet face—thankfully his alive face compared to the dead one when she'd killed him. Their introduction to each other hadn't gone well the first time, but when Ursula had introduced them a second time, he had grown on her.

She dug another scoop up. She hadn't been lying to Yafe when she said she was hurting and felt old. The last year had aged her more than usual, as did life in the lower class where she'd grown up, or rather no class. Rolling her shoulders, she stretched her muscles as she dug another shovel of salt into the crate. They'd been out there four hours already and had another two or three to go, depending on how the new girl helped or didn't help.

So far, she'd been semi-useful, but she also didn't really come off as someone used to hard labor of any sort. Jerry glared at her as she took yet another break, leaning against her crate. Yafe continued to dig. Azar was checking over the systems on the ship while also watching *Yarrow*. With the way the world had changed, Jerry was loath to leave her vessel unattended if she could avoid it. While his muscles would no doubt be helpful in the labor they were doing, she wanted him on *Yarrow* in case anything went wrong. Though she might switch out with him soon since she was running up against her own limits.

Fuck her for wanting to keep a legal job to play the good citizen while also starting a whole underground operation at the same time. It was probably too much for all of them, but she wasn't going to break her contract with Mortimer Blair before it was up. She needed that connection, to keep roots in what she had originally wanted from life. For some reason, she still had a tiny bit of hope she would get there eventually.

All they had to do was find an actual cure to the virus. That would solve nearly all of Jerry's problems. As she filled her crate, she stepped over to Sacha's and started to fill it. While their newest recruit, willing or not, might not care about being out there until dawn the next day, Jerry sincerely hoped they were already on their way back to Raegina by then.

Jerry glared at Sacha, those curls falling over her shoulders as sweat glistened on her skin. Once again, very much unwelcome, the image of Arloa appeared naked, sprawled on her huge bed, her back arched in pleasure as Jerry manipulated her body, sweat along her skin tasting of pure salt and wonder. Shaking her head, Jerry focused on shoveling. She had to stop that, except it had only been getting worse, and since Yafe had dared to prod Jerry about contacting her, just about every other thought Jerry had was of Arloa.

A soft hum caught Jerry's attention. Her head pounded still, but she straightened her back, listening carefully beyond the digging of salt, beyond *Yarrow's* own engines that were still running. Shielding her eyes, Jerry stared out at the sea toward *Yarrow*. Surely Azar wasn't taking off with *Yarrow*, though he could be doing a few test runs with her since he was tinkering on her systems.

"Do you hear that?" Jerry called to Yafe.

Yafe caught sight of Jerry, and her spine straightened immediately as she spun to look in the same direction. "I do now."

"What is it?" Sacha said, as though bored with the entire situation.

Jerry really could do without her attitude, but she was coming down from the chaos of emotions the virus caused, so it would take a while for her to even out like the rest of them, if they could even be called even-keeled. With as much as they had cut down on vestigen in the past few weeks, their own moods were typically all over the place.

"I think it's a ship," Jerry murmured, narrowing her gaze to try and see beyond the bright horizon, but the sun wasn't giving any quarter and she couldn't make anything out.

"It's just *Yarrow*," Sacha grumbled.

Jerry shook her head. "I don't think so. It's too pure a tone."

Yafe tilted her chin up and spun around in a circle, looking in much the same manner Jerry was. Jerry stopped sharply, sliding her head to the side as she half bent over. "Fuck, it's right in front of *Yarrow*."

She dropped her shovel and raced through the salt, her heart thrumming. It was so hard to run through the salt, her boots digging into the ground as though she ran through sand. She had to get there. If they took *Yarrow* with only Azar on board, she would never get her back. She didn't even look to see if Yafe and Sacha followed, assuming they were running with her.

Jerry had never run so fast in her life. Azar was lifting *Yarrow* from the dock right when Jerry and Yafe got there and jumped into the open doorway. They left Sacha on the ground, at least twenty meters behind them. Jerry didn't even give her a second thought as she slammed her palm against the sensor to shut the exterior door.

Yafe's eyes were wide as they spun and raced toward the ladder. As they got to the second level, where the galley and office were, Jerry pointed. "Grab the weapons."

Yafe took off as Jerry headed up to the wheelhouse, shouting as soon as she could see Azar's feet. "What's going on?"

"They came out of nowhere."

"They didn't come out of nowhere." Jerry stood in front of the wheel, gripping the wood tightly as *Yarrow* rose higher. She took over control of the ship. "They're not doing anything."

"I'm sure they want to board us."

"Of course they fucking do. We were sitting there doing nothing. Easy pickings." Jerry's heart thumped hard as her eyes adjusted to the light in the wheelhouse from being outside in the sun and salt.

"Where's Sacha?"

"Left her on the island."

"You're shitting me."

"She didn't run fast enough." Jerry took *Yarrow* even higher. "We'll come back for her and the rest of the salt once we run these assholes off."

"They're twice our size."

"Watch me sink them."

Glaring, Jerry pushed forward on the thruster, taking *Yarrow* swiftly over the top of the other vessel. If they wanted to board them, they had missed a golden opportunity. Jerry wouldn't let them get control now.

Unfortunately, Beren Island was quite isolated, and she'd have to fly hours to find anywhere to hide. She was only half a kilometer away when she checked her sensors. The ship had followed them.

"Fuck."

Yafe showed up, loaded down with guns. She handed a few to Azar before bringing Jerry her favorite weapon, a small pistol. She'd been stupid not to bring it with her while they were filling crates with sand, but the virus made her do stupid things sometimes. It took away her ability to think clearly, and she didn't have a pill to swallow like she did the last time. Every pill of vestigen they had on the ship they had given to Sacha, and they weren't going to get any more until they returned to Raegina.

"What do they want?" Yafe asked, her voice strong but with an undertone of worry.

Jerry shook her head. "They haven't said."

"But they're following us?"

"Yup." Jerry turned *Yarrow* hard to starboard, pulling the ship in a steep one-eighty so they were now facing the other vessel. "You ready Azar?"

"Always ready, Cap."

Except he hadn't been, otherwise they wouldn't be in this situation. She'd talk to him later about what happened. They had bigger fish to fry for now. "We're going to let them board us."

"What?" Yafe screeched.

Jerry shook her head slowly as she glanced over her shoulder. "It's the only way to get them."

"I'll trust you, you know I do, but I don't get it."

"There's no place to hide, Yafe. It's either we let them board now and take them out as they come over here, or we get taken. We can't go back and get Sacha if they're following us."

"But what if there's too many of them?"

Jerry's lips pulled up on one side. "That's our specialty, isn't it?"

She looked from Yafe to Azar, seeing the resignation that this was the battle they were going to fight. When each of them nodded at her, Jerry grabbed her gun and swung out onto the deck, the wind pushing against her as she went. That was going to add an extra special element to this battle.

Excitement raced through her, raising goosebumps on her arms, kissing her cheeks and landing in the pit of her belly. She was made for this. In all the years in Joab and trying to live the legal life, Jerry had forgotten how exhilarating this could be, and it was only in the heat of the moment that she remembered.

She gripped onto the rope on the edge of *Yarrow* and leaned over to see where the other vessel was. Right on time. They maneuvered right up behind them, Azar making it seem as though they were trying to outrun them. They wouldn't. *Yarrow* was half the size and a hundred years old. It was going to take a miracle for them to outrun, but Azar knew what Jerry was planning, so they worked in tandem.

She pulled back from the edge, and raced to the back of the ship, climbing the ropes until she could reach it. Jerry crouched down low, wrapping a rope around her wrist after tying a quick slipknot in it. She gritted her teeth as she waited for them to board. They'd come in from the side, just off the stern. They always did. It was the best way to "surprise" whatever ship they were following. Jerry had used that same tactic many times throughout her years as a pirate.

She waited to see if they were coming starboard or port, so she would know which direction she had to run. Yafe was no doubt setting up somewhere near the wheelhouse to protect Azar and make sure he maintained control of the ship. They'd run practice drills hundreds of times and done this dozens more than that.

The first boot that touched *Yarrow* was on the port side. Jerry swung around and held the rope tightly in her fist. She was going to catch herself a pirate.

"Hello, mate," Jerry chimed as she stood up, half-scaring the idiot who was attempting to take over her vessel. She flung the rope over his head, pulled tight and kicked against his knee until he fell down, the rope pulling tight. Jerry circled it around the cleat to keep his body right where she wanted it.

It would be good for the rest of the crew to know what was headed their way.

As the second one came aboard, Jerry turned toward him, her gun in hand as she put it in his face and held firm. "One more step and I'll blow you back into the sea."

He put his hands up, then in an instant slammed both his palms against her wrist and tried to bend the gun out of it. Jerry kicked at him but didn't manage to knock him over. Instead, he pushed at her, forcing her to fall back onto the deck, her head spinning when it collided with the hard shellacked wood, reminding her sharply of the injury she'd already sustained.

She groaned in pain as he lifted his foot to stomp on her. Jerry rolled out of the way, barely managing to make him miss. She raised her hand, weapon still in her fingers, and fired—but she missed. Cursing, she bit her cheek and dragged herself up. She couldn't waste bullets like that–they were too scarce. He came at her again, and this time she pulled her short sword from its sheath and shoved it in his direction to defend herself.

More pirates came aboard *Yarrow*, running right past her and toward the wheelhouse. She was going to have to stop them. She counted four or five at least, but her head was still spinning, so it was hard to see.

She pulled her knee back and kicked, shoving her boot right into the man's dick. He crumbled to the ground. Jerry snorted as she reached down and put a bullet through his head. It was the only way to kill them, that or she had to have enough strength to take off his head and throw it overboard.

Bolstering herself and trying to find her balance as Penum spun under her feet, Jerry ran toward the wheelhouse. They mustn't have that large of a crew. She'd already killed two, and she only saw four more, no one else was coming to aid. Yafe stood with her back to the wheelhouse door. Azar turned *Yarrow* hard, making everyone have to brace or fall. Jerry gripped onto the boom to hold herself in one spot until Azar evened them out.

Next time, she wanted to fly and let him do this part. Jerry gritted her teeth and charged forward. Fist first, she pounded into the right temple of one, knocking him down while another grabbed her from behind. Jerry made eye contact with Yafe, hoping she understood the silent message.

Yafe blocked a sword slash from another before Jerry lost track of her. Jerry loosened all her muscles, becoming as dead a weight as possible. The man dropped down, unable to keep holding her. Twisting swiftly, Jerry lay below him, a smirk on her lips, and she eyed him up and down.

"In for a penny?" Raising her weapon, she fired and missed again. "Fuck it."

Her gun jammed, and she shoved it into the holster at her side. She wasn't going to lose that gun if it was the last thing she did. Yafe grunted, and Jerry jerked her head back to see what was happening. She had to narrow her eyes against her blurred vision, but Yafe looked as though she was going down.

Not playing around, Jerry grabbed her sword and shoved it into the man's stomach, jerking it hard to the side so he would have a difficult time surviving that one. She pulled it from him and dragged herself to her knees as he dropped to his. She shoved it into his throat, ripping out half of his neck. The scent of blood hit her fast.

Her stomach rumbled, that same freeing moment when she'd tasted Sacha's blood on her fingers, coming right back to her. She wanted him, and not in any sexual way. She wanted to lick all the spilled blood from him, see what his brains tasted like. Shuddering at the thought, Jerry stood up and stabbed her sword straight down into his head. She left it there as she went for the next, but they were already retreating.

Azar had come out, fists clenched and taking swings. Jerry pulled her sword from the one remaining and raced to the edge of *Yarrow* where the other ship was docked. Those who had boarded *Yarrow* looked at her with fear. She laughed, the sound boiling up from the pit of her belly and leaving her lips. It felt so good, and so fucking awful at the same time, but she couldn't control it.

She couldn't control anything.

As the ship flew off, Jerry grabbed another rope, tying it like a noose around the second one she had killed and tossing him overboard on the other side of the ship. The third one she didn't even bother with as she threw him overboard. She had her trophies for a little while, and she would let *Yarrow* wear them with pride.

Yafe stood a few meters from the door to the wheelhouse and Azar took them back. When Jerry approached, Yafe shook her head slowly, disappointment filling her eyes. "You shouldn't have killed them."

"They would have killed me. And frankly, it was a mercy. No one wants to live with this fucking virus."

"Then why are you still here?"

The question stung, because Jerry had no answer for her. Some days, like the day before, she wished she would just die, that she could dive into the sea filled with poison water and end it all—although she wasn't sure that would even work anymore.

Not answering, Jerry walked around her and stalked belowdecks to her cabin. She pulled out her gun and flopped it onto her cot before lifting the sword she still gripped. Blood covered the metal with a dark sheen, but there on the edge was exactly what she was looking for, a taste of what she couldn't get off her mind—other than Arloa that was.

Picking the small piece of brain off her sword, Jerry popped it between her lips and sighed as soon as the flavor hit her tongue. It didn't taste good by any means, but the relief it fed her mind was what relaxed her. She swallowed quickly and waited for the high from before to happen again.

In the meantime, she cleaned her sword and her gun, making sure it worked again before sliding it into her holster. She wouldn't be caught without it again. Climbing the ladders back to the wheelhouse, Jerry took over while Azar went belowdecks. Yafe came to stand next to her, putting a hand on her shoulder.

"I wish you wouldn't kill them."

"It's a mercy, I promise. If it wasn't, I wouldn't."

"If it wasn't, we wouldn't be in this situation."

Jerry had to agree with her. If it weren't for the damn virus, they wouldn't be in the situation they were in.

"What do you suppose they were after?" Yafe stared out the front window.

Shrugging, Jerry didn't look at her. "The same thing we are."

"What are we doing next, Cap?"

"The same thing we do every day, Yafe. We're going to go back to Beren Island, finish filling *Yarrow*, and collect Sacha if she's not dead, and then we're going back to Raegina. Maybe after this shipment, we'll have enough to buy us vestigen if we can find any."

"That's the problem, isn't it? We can't find any."

Jerry sighed. "No one can."

Her thoughts turned to the small bit of brain she'd tasted, the high already working into her veins. She was feeling much better, much more in control, more sane. If only she could figure out why the hell that was happening.

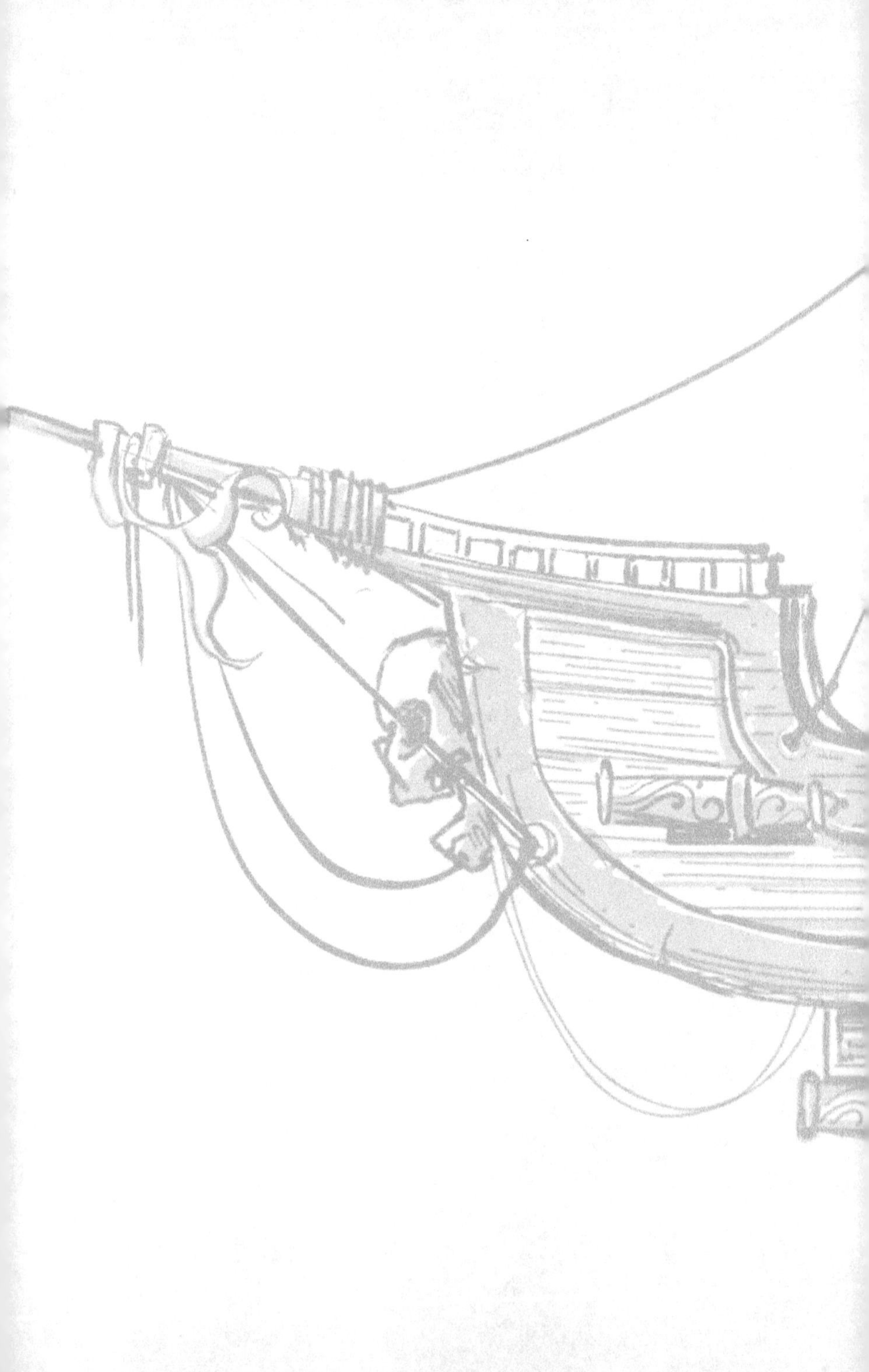

CHAPTER 6

Azar held onto the frame of the door as he leaned into Jerry's cabin. She lifted her gaze from the personal device she'd been staring at and raised an eyebrow at him, waiting for some kind of explanation as to what he wanted. If she hadn't eaten that small piece of brain, she would have barked orders at him to leave already.

"Have you thought more about my idea?"

Jerry pursed her lips, then nodded her head, indicating he should come in. "First, how's Sacha?"

"Fine. She's taking the regimen like she's supposed to and is calming down."

"Good. She said she was on something similar before?" Jerry settled the personal device into her lap as she stretched out her legs. They'd unloaded the salt hours before and were finally sitting in the harbor relaxing for once. She'd wanted a few hours of rest before she took *Yarrow* back out. Something in the pit of her gut told her to do it.

Azar nodded, sliding onto the edge of her cot to join her. "Vestigen, but when the drug became scarce…"

"She resorted to the same thing we did and ran out faster."

"Exactly."

Jerry gritted her teeth. Azar had become one of her closest

friends in the past year, one of the few people she felt she could rely on. He and Yafe were her family, the only family she had anymore. They'd been through hell and back to get where they were, and she wasn't about to do anything without their approval. "What does Yafe think of her?"

Azar shrugged.

"No opinion or is she lacking in giving it?"

Azar's dark eyes locked on Jerry's. "She wants to wait and see."

"Of course she does. She's always had the sweetest heart when it comes to lost souls."

"Probably why she likes you so much."

Jerry snorted, although Azar was likely correct in that assessment. It had been what got Yafe thrown into Joab to begin with and how they had met. A few people—not that Jerry would ever name them—would say Jerry had the exact same problem. "The feeling is mutual."

Azar folded his hands and leaned over his knees. "Will you keep her on board?"

"Who? Sacha or Yafe?"

His look told her exactly who he meant, although Jerry had known already. She'd never question whether she wanted Yafe on board—the answer would always be a firm yes.

"If you're both amenable to it, and she is, I don't mind. She needs to learn to work harder and run faster, but as soon as she's done with the regimen, she might be better able to do that."

Azar raised a dark bushy eyebrow and ran a hand over his curly black hair. "She's cute."

"Please don't." Jerry frowned. "We don't need unnecessary drama."

"A man's got to get laid at some point."

"You don't think women have the same needs?" Jerry pushed back, because she did have those needs. And the number of times she'd thought of Arloa while she cried out from her own fingers were far too many to count. When Azar didn't answer, she had mercy on him. "Find someone else, someone who is infected who you can't kill by fucking, and someone not on either of my ships."

Azar glowered, but he did nod his agreement. Satisfied, Jerry pulled up her personal device and slid it over to him so he could see what she'd been looking at.

"Thinking of buying another vessel?"

"Contemplating it."

He swiped his finger along, looking at all the ones she had pulled up with their prices. He stopped after the fourth or fifth one. "These are passenger ships."

"They are."

"Are you taking my idea under serious consideration then?"

Jerry wrinkled her nose. "I'm working through some of the logistics. Buying a passenger vessel right now would be suspicious, especially if I don't immediately start running it anywhere."

Azar's face pinched. "I suppose you're right."

"I am right. I could steal one—" His gaze cut to her. Jerry shrugged. "I am a pirate."

"Only by night."

"No, by birth." Jerry cocked her head at him. "And I'm ready to live into that birthright."

"What do you mean?"

Jerry paused, hearing feet scuffling along the floor. She focused on the sound, trying to discern who it was, and once she figured out it was Yafe, she waited for the younger woman to join them.

"There you are." Yafe smiled, her northern accent far less pronounced than her brother's. She had a better ear for listening than he did, and being a woman, had to learn to conceal her true identity to get anything done in the society they lived in. Men didn't have that problem even though legally they were all equals.

"Right here," Azar answered, the smile on his lips he

reserved only for his little sister. "I was talking to Jerry about Sacha."

Yafe quickly looked over her shoulder before scuffling into the room and shutting the door. She sat on Jerry's clothing chest, eyeing both of them. "And have you made a decision?"

"No," Jerry responded quickly. "We haven't, and we won't without your opinion on her."

Yafe visibly relaxed. Jerry knew her well enough to know that Yafe routinely felt as though her voice wasn't heard, so any chance she had, Jerry made sure that Yafe knew she was being listened to.

"So what is your opinion?" Jerry prompted.

Yafe pressed her lips together. "She's new to vestigen."

"She's had it before," Azar stated.

"Yes, but not for long. I don't know where she got it."

"We should ask." Jerry folded her hands together. "She may know where to get more, or may know where to get more without knowing that's where to get more, if you catch my drift."

Yafe nodded her agreement. "I think she needs to open up before I'll know her well enough to want her on *Yarrow*. But for now I'm comfortable with her here."

"Having a fourth for the salt runs will be very helpful," Azar added.

"It will." Yafe's eyes softened any time she looked at him. He held such influence over her, something Jerry tried not to use when she didn't have to.

Jerry ran her fingers over her thin lips as she contemplated. She'd felt much the same. It had been a short period of time since Sacha had come aboard, and she had missed the battle off Beren Island, so that hadn't helped Jerry figure out where her loyalties were. But she had been diligently waiting for them to return, happy to see them. Then again, who wouldn't when they were stranded on an island.

Holding to her silence, Jerry waited for either of the others to speak. It seemed, though, they were at an impasse with the decision. Changing topics, Jerry said, "I'm thinking of funding a ship as a safe house. I've already started to look into it and see how we can manage. If Ursula picks up a secondary contract with Morty like we have, we may just be able to."

Yafe shook her head. "No. Ursula won't do that."

"She'll do what I tell her to."

"She won't, Jerry."

Resigned, Jerry crossed her arms. "Short term she will."

"Yes, but not long term."

"I know." It had been the one wrench in the plan she hadn't been able to figure out. If she was going to keep up the legal side of things, the front for all the illegal pirating work she did, she was going to have to do a better job at it. She would need that facade to keep up the income and the papers she would need to fund the rest of what she wanted to do. It was really all a mess, and nothing she would be able to figure out in such a short period of time. "It was just a thought."

"A good one. But we'll work it out." Yafe leaned forward, pressing her palm on Jerry's arm in comfort. "I trust you."

"You might be the only one." Jerry gave her a wry smile but didn't continue the conversation.

"You can always ask—"

"Don't say it," Jerry cut her off with a glare. She didn't want to hear Arloa's name, and she was certain that was the direction Yafe was taking. She'd already mentioned Arloa once before, and that had been enough.

Yafe raised her hands up, trying to look innocent. "She has the funds."

Jerry drew in a sharp breath through her nose. "No. I won't—"

"You can't stop thinking about her. I know you can't."

Her cheeks heated because she had no comeback. She thought she'd been able to hide it, but Yafe knew her too well, she was too much of an observer in their world. "It doesn't matter."

"It does!"

"It doesn't, Yafe. And I said enough." Jerry swung her legs over the side of her cot. "I'm going to check on Sacha and see how she's doing, and then I'm going to check with my contacts and see if we have a lead on where we can get some more vestigen, which I'm sure we're all going to be desperate for soon."

She didn't wait for an answer as she opened her door and walked into the corridor, the air so much cooler out there than in her cabin. Yafe was right though. Arloa would have the answers, the connections, and the money to tell Jerry how to run something like that—except Jerry didn't know her well enough to know if Arloa would even do it. The one time she had asked Arloa for a favor in their very short courtship, Arloa had come through, but it was all legal work, nothing underground. She couldn't bring herself to do it. Not yet at least. She wasn't that desperate.

Sunset had fallen hours before, and Jerry's personal device dinged a notification at her. She rolled over in her cot, staring at it, bleary-eyed. She'd wanted to rest, not be woken up by pointless notifications. She debated whether or not to even answer it, but she had to. She had to know if there was any hope of finding vestigen in the next few days.

The message on her screen was from Miriam, which wasn't all that surprising. Jerry had told her several times they were looking, but she was equally sure everyone else Miriam bought from and sold to told her the same. The virus had swept through the underground and the poor in waves, and just about everyone had it. Yet hardly any aristocrats did. Jerry still hadn't figured out why, but she'd stopped paying close attention to it when everything had concentrated on surviving into the next day.

Focusing on the message, Jerry read it quickly. It was a time, place, and amount. The sum was higher than anything Jerry had seen, but she knew it was vestigen. There wouldn't be any other reason Miriam would be contacting her in the middle of the night with such vague information. The amount of pills given would help her crew survive for one week. It seemed they could never get enough to last any longer than that lately.

Dragging herself up, Jerry pushed her long black hair behind her ear as she stared at the information again, processing it, debating whether it was real or rumor. Miriam didn't usually come to her without verified information, but everyone had been so desperate lately. She couldn't trust Miriam hadn't also given the information to someone else who would steal it out from under her before she even got there.

Frowning, Jerry shook that thought from her head and reached behind her head to weave her hair into its standard braid. She dressed quickly, grabbed the illegal weapons that she concealed under her large leather jacket, and prepared to leave *Yarrow*. She snuck into Yafe's room, rousing her from a light slumber.

"Hey, I've got a tip. I'm going to check it out."

"I'm coming with," Yafe whispered.

Jerry shook her head and put her hand on Yafe's mouth to quiet her and stop her. "No, I don't…I'm going to do this one by myself. It's only a small amount. I can handle it."

"Do you know what you're walking into?"

"No, but if I die, you get everything." Snorting, Jerry walked out of the room and quickly left the ship.

It didn't take her long to find the location, and she leaned against the stone wall of a building while she waited. There was no further information from Miriam. Nothing to tell her who or how many people might be coming, or if she was supposed to go inside the building or not.

She stood there for fifteen minutes before she heard footsteps. Jerry's heart raced, her stomach twisting with excitement. She was actually going to get her hands on some vestigen this time. It was going to work, and she was going to be able to continue living, continue keeping her crew alive, and—she stopped short.

The dark curly hair surrounding the beautifully dark-skinned face was a dead giveaway that her vestigen had not arrived. Cursing under her breath, Jerry stepped out of the shadows, grabbed Yafe's hand, and jerked her against the wall. Jerry covered her with her entire body.

"What the fuck are you doing here?" Her breath was hot against Yafe's cheek as she whisper-screamed.

"Do you really think I'd let you come out here alone?"

"You're an idiot."

"No." Yafe looked at her firmly. "You are."

Jerry growled low but settled into the quiet when she thought she heard someone coming. She put a finger over Yafe's lips, telling her to shut up, before turning so she could look out onto the barely lit cobblestone street. She'd been down this road so many times she couldn't count, and in the last year, the lamps had gotten dimmer by the night. No one cared about them anymore, not even their own people.

Yafe grabbed Jerry's hand, twining their fingers. Boosted by the show of support, Jerry waited until two men stepped under the streetlamp. They weren't fierce looking, and one was rather short. Gritting her teeth, Jerry made the decision, and she took a leap of faith that what Miriam had told her was correct.

Screaming, she caught their attention as she flung out of the shadows and into the light, her fists raised and ready for a fight. She caught them by surprise enough that they stepped back. Jerry took the bigger one, shoving him against the wall before spinning him and pressing his face into the cold stone. She punched him hard in his kidney, hoping that it would be exactly what she needed to disarm him enough to check his pockets.

He grunted and tried to shove backward, but she pressed her knee into the back of his, collapsing him to the ground before she wrapped her arm around his neck and held on tightly to cut off airflow. He fought her, his body jerking as he tried to gain control. Turning her head, Jerry watched as Yafe took down the much smaller and weaker man.

She had no idea if these two were the ones she needed, the ones who had the drugs, but if they weren't, they'd just given up where they were hiding. Jerry clenched her arm tighter until he fell unconscious at her feet. Dropping him, she spun and decked the man Yafe was fighting right in the temple. He staggered as he tried to catch his bearings.

"Where is it?" Jerry barked.

He shook his head, but she wasn't sure if he understood her.

"The vestigen. Where is it?"

"We—we don't have it." He could barely speak.

Jerry frowned, but she didn't let up. She shoved him against the wall, her hands around his throat as she strangled him. "Tell me where it is."

"We don't have it."

"Where is it?"

"We sold it!"

"Fuck." Lifting her knee sharply, she caught him in the groin and dropped him to the ground. She grabbed Yafe's hand and booked it. Their footfalls were heavy as they ran from the building, sticking to the shadows as much as they could. Jerry turned a sharp corner, hiding against a building in an alleyway. Her chest rose and fell heavily as she tried to catch her breath, Yafe doing much the same.

They waited to see if they were followed. Although with one down for the count and the other in pain, she was pretty sure that they wouldn't be. Still, authorities were around, and they could have already been alerted. There were recordings that could have caught everything.

"You okay?" Jerry whispered.

"Yeah. You?"

"For now." Grumbling, Jerry took Yafe's hand and walked the opposite way from how they had come.

She walked as quickly as she could while still moving slow enough that she wouldn't alert anyone. Instead of going straight to *Yarrow* like she wanted to, Jerry took a very roundabout way to get back. She wanted no one to find out who they were if she could avoid that. They had touched without express consent, they had jumped two men in the middle of a street, they had broken so many laws in the last few minutes that Jerry couldn't begin to think about how many years it would land her in Joab if they were caught.

But she wouldn't be caught.

She would jump off the side of the pier before she allowed herself to go back to Joab. But she had no idea if Yafe felt the same, or if Yafe would come with her, and she didn't want her to go to Joab alone. The fear of the possibility of returning there made her take as many steps as possible to avoid the authorities figuring out who she was and where to find her. She hoped the men either didn't report because they were equally guilty of crimes or that no one else had seen them.

There was one thing Jerry knew thoroughly. They needed to find more vestigen, and they didn't have any more time to wait.

CHAPTER 7

The message from Miriam was suspicious, but Jerry wasn't sure she had any other option. Dawn was around the corner when she slipped from *Yarrow* and headed down the dock. So far no authorities had come to find her and Yafe, and considering they knew where she lived because of previous incidents with them, she suspected they weren't going to come at all.

Jerry tugged the tip of her top hat down to shade her eyes as she stepped off the wooden dock and onto the cobblestone street. Her jacket kept her warm in the chilly early morning air, but she was determined to get vestigen and keep her crew alive and well. She didn't want them to tear each other apart when the withdrawal from vestigen hit.

The weight on her shoulders had grown exponentially in the last year. At first it was just her crew's livelihood, but then it was their lives. Now she was thinking about adding a new vessel to her fleet, one that would specifically be there for helping the newly infected recover or helping those who ran out of drugs. She was insane. But with how hard it was to find vestigen lately, she wasn't sure there would be any need for a safe house. If someone didn't start making more of it, there would be no reason. They'd all be dead.

The bar was nearly empty, save for a few patrons at tables, one at the counter, and the barkeep. Jerry nodded to him but kept her chin down. She didn't want to be made a spectacle of and she didn't want to raise any alarms about her presence there. She made her way down into the underground, where Miriam hid out most days. She'd never questioned how Miriam had managed to stay in one place for so long, to keep her reign concealed and yet—perhaps it wasn't.

Jerry mulled that thought. Perhaps Miriam had an in Jerry hadn't thought about. She would need it, for sure. They all did, especially the higher up the food chain one went in the underground. It would make perfect sense. Yet the question remained, who would give such protection to Miriam and her thugs.

"Jerry," Miriam's voice was gentle, serene. "I'm glad you could come."

Jerry had to force a smile on her lips. She needed to play the perfect daughter Miriam never had. That had been her role since she was a small child. Miriam had been the mature parent, like an auntie she looked up to, who watched over her because her mother lacked the ability to do so. Leaning in, Jerry pressed her lips to Miriam's cheek. "Morning."

"Not quite yet."

Jerry snorted lightly. "I suppose. But it's been a long night, and I'd prefer it to be morning already."

"I think that can be arranged." Miriam threaded her arm through Jerry's and pulled her toward the same back room she'd been in before.

Jerry followed, willingly, curious as to where this conversation was going. Miriam had been vague in both her message earlier in the night and in her message recently, though that was the name of her game. Jerry always had to read between the lines to figure out what was going on and what was expected of her.

Inside, with the door closed, Miriam turned to Jerry and slid a leather pouch into Jerry's hand. Staring down at it, Jerry pursed her lips. She untied the top and dumped a handful of pills into her palm. Raising an eyebrow, Jerry stared directly at Miriam.

"I thought you didn't have any."

"I came into some recently. Would you like them?"

"How much?" Jerry's stomach twisted at the thought of paying full price for vestigen. She'd had to do it before, and it had wiped out a lot of the credits she'd stored up for other things. Still, she had a responsibility to her crew, to Yafe and Azar and Sacha and everyone on Ursula's vessel. She'd promised them she would take care of them. Sure they found their own vestigen on occasion and helped her steal it more than once, but she was their captain.

"Five."

"No." Jerry blanched. "I can't do that."

"Then I'll give you the friends and family discount." Miriam's lips curled upward, the smile sickening.

Jerry knew what that meant. It wasn't just because they'd known each other, it would mean Jerry owed Miriam a favor that she could collect at any point, one that would either be simple like getting Miriam off or massively complicated and risk not only her life but the lives of her crew.

"What do you want for it?"

Miriam stepped in close, trailing a finger over Jerry's shoulder. "I miss your mouth sometimes. You've gotten soft in your age."

At least Jerry knew by that comment what Miriam was expecting. She'd done it before, and she never quite considered it the same crime her mother committed. This was never solely in exchange for credits.

Miriam must have seen she'd made her decision because she leaned back against the desk and pulled up her skirts. Jerry got onto her knees, shuffling forward and positioning herself as she ran her leather-gloved hands up and down Miriam's creamy thighs.

"I will give you two for the vestigen with this, no more."

Miriam moaned, her hips already moving in anticipation of what Jerry was about to do. "Agreed."

Jerry clenched her jaw. Two was under the market value, probably saving her one thousand if she was lucky, which would buy her the time she needed to find another supplier. If Miriam was going to take this every time she sold Jerry some vestigen, then she was going to have to find someone else to go to.

Not hedging, Jerry moved straight in. She latched her mouth against Miriam's clit, sucking and swirling her tongue. Heat pooled between her own legs as she dragged in a deep breath, Miriam's scent hitting her hard. She'd done this more times than she cared to count with Miriam, but Jerry was hitting her limit. She didn't want to anymore.

Miriam's long fingers flitted through her hair, holding on tightly and tugging sharply. Jerry refused to thrust a finger inside her, refused to do any more than what she knew was required. She kept her pace, kept the pressure, increased it when Miriam seemed to be getting close.

The door suddenly opened, a rush of cold smoky air filling the room. Jerry tried to move away, but Miriam held her firmly and dropped her skirts over Jerry's head to semi-protect them. She hated having her back to the door, unable to see who it was or what was going on. Miriam's breathing quickened.

"I'm so sorry."

The soft but confident voice, precise in its tonality and pronunciation, and with an edge to it, sent a shiver down Jerry's spine. She recognized that voice. For the first time that night, she was glad her face was plastered between Miriam's thighs so the woman wouldn't be able to see her.

"I'll be out in a minute."

"Yes." The door clicked shut again.

Jerry resumed, trying not to let on to the fact that she knew who was there, that her heart was no longer in it, that all she wanted was to get Miriam off and escape unseen. Miriam keened as Jerry brought her up again, the pulsing between her own thighs no longer because of Miriam but because of that majestic voice. Fuck, she hadn't even spoken to Jerry and all Jerry wanted was to run out of the room, find her, and fuck her into oblivion.

Miriam cried out, her nails biting into Jerry's scalp. Jerry slowed her movements, licking slowly and more fully to clean Miriam up before she shifted down on her heels and lifted Miriam's skirt from her head. She raised an eyebrow in anticipation of what was to come next.

"You're always such a good pet," Miriam murmured as she reached behind her, grabbed the small sensor for Jerry's finger, and allowed Jerry to transfer the credits for the vestigen.

After the exchange was made, Jerry stood up and brushed her hands over her pants, straightening the wrinkled material. Miriam followed her pattern and wiped her fingers across Jerry's mouth, taking the excess juices still lingering and wiping them on the cloth of her outfit.

"I always love it when you do that."

Again Jerry wasn't sure what to say. She'd never hated going down on Miriam so much as in this moment. When she was a teenager, she'd found a thrill every time they were together, Miriam teaching her the ways and wonders of women. But now? Jerry had outgrown her, and it was high time she put a stop to it if she could.

Though telling the underground boss "no" could easily be the death of her as well. Jerry squared her shoulders and waited for the inevitable dismissal. She couldn't ask to use the secret door. Then Miriam would know Jerry was aware who had interrupted them, she would put the pieces together and could easily make her life even more of a living hell than it already was. Not to mention Arloa's, although what the hell was *she* doing there to begin with?

Surely she wasn't...

Jerry slid her gaze to Miriam, wondering if Miriam required

the same payment from Arloa. Shaking that thought, Jerry kept her mouth shut. She would not reveal she knew who Arloa was in any fashion. "Thank you for the vestigen."

"Come back when you need more. I'll try to keep my thumb on some just for you."

"Right." Jerry nodded, embarrassment hitting her cheeks. Would she even have an option down the road if she needed more vestigen, which she no doubt would. They all did. She was sure Miriam had taken some of whatever shipment she'd gotten and kept it for herself, so she had her own stash for when she needed it.

Jerry tightened her muscles as she dropped the leather pouch in her pocket and headed for the door to the office, but Miriam's hand on her arm stopped her. Turning back around, Miriam had a soft look in her gaze, one Jerry hadn't seen in a very long time.

"I mean it, Jerry. I will always find what you need, no matter what."

Jerry's lips quirked up. That was the Miriam she'd known and loved for years, the one who had taken care of her when her own mother couldn't or was busy. Nodding sharply, Jerry relaxed. "I know you will."

"Anything for my little pet."

This time it did come off as a term of endearment, one that Miriam had called Jerry for years when she'd grown up. She'd hoped at some point she wouldn't have to fall back into this line of work, but perhaps she was born for it. She had been an unsightly creature as a child, always hiding in the shadows from the men and women who wanted to fuck her mother to get it out of their systems, and yet somehow, Miriam had always seen her.

"Thank you, again," Jerry finally stated, her tone softer than before. "I appreciate it."

Even if Jerry had questions as to where Miriam had gotten the vestigen, if she had bought the drugs before she'd sent Jerry out to attack two men who didn't have vestigen.

"Out of curiosity." Jerry spun on her. "Where did you get the information about the deal tonight?"

"What deal?" Miriam canted her head to the side. "I bought this vestigen yesterday."

Jerry's face pinched. "But what about earlier tonight?"

Miriam shook her head. "What are you talking about?"

"You sent me a tip about some vestigen—"

"I didn't."

Jerry pressed her lips firmly together. That was another problem she was going to have to figure out, but at least she had some answers. She needed to be far more careful in figuring out where her information was coming from and if it was authentic. Although, the two men she and Yafe had jumped did have vestigen at some point.

"All right." Jerry nodded. "I'll see you soon."

"Please do." Miriam's cheeks flushed. "Perhaps we can come to another arrangement."

"Perhaps we can." Jerry's stomach fluttered, and not pleasantly. Saying no to the boss of the greatest crime syndicate in Raegina would likely result in her death, no matter how much they were on friendly terms.

With her hand on the doorknob, Jerry sent one last look over her shoulder at Miriam before stepping into the smoke-filled room. She didn't dare draw in a deep breath, even though she wanted to. She rolled her shoulders, tried to grab the edges of her jacket to tighten it around herself, but she stopped sharply when Arloa's steel-blue eyes locked on her from across the room.

"Fuck," Jerry mumbled. She'd hoped she could slip from Miriam's office out of the underground without being noticed, but she should have known better. If there was one person who would notice her, it would be Arloa.

Dipping her chin, she turned on her toes and started toward the door, but Arloa was quick. She moved in, blocking Jerry's path. Jerry had to work hard not to reach out and touch, not to do anything that would incite. She'd ended it with Arloa over a year ago, and she meant to stick to that. She meant to never see her again.

"What are you doing here?" Arloa firmly whispered.

Jerry jerked her head and raised an eyebrow, leaning down so she towered over Arloa's much shorter frame. "I should ask you that. This is my family, not yours. You don't belong here."

Arloa's eyes widened with surprise, and Jerry knew why. In the short time they had known each other, Jerry had never once spoken to Arloa like that, but she had to this time. It was for her own self-preservation.

"Jer." That soft imploring tone irked Jerry.

She twitched and shook her head, hardening her gaze. "Don't fucking call me that."

Arloa's lips parted in surprise, her beautiful blue eyes widening. Her chest rose and fell sharply, her breasts pushing against the edge of her corset. Jerry wanted to bend her neck, run her tongue right along the edge of her dress. God, she wanted to take Arloa outside and fuck her against the alley wall, but the lingering flavor of Miriam on her tongue told her that would be the worst decision yet.

"What would you have me call you then?" Arloa's jaw clenched.

Reaching up, tears stinging at her eyes, Jerry cupped Arloa's cheek so tenderly without actually touching her, ghosting her fingers along Arloa's smooth skin. So much for not alerting Miriam to their former relationship. Jerry dashed her tongue against her lips, cringing when she did taste Miriam instead of sweet Arloa. "You shouldn't be here."

"And why not? Is this your bar?"

"No."

"I didn't think so." Arloa didn't move, standing stoically still while Jerry dropped her hand.

"Why are you here?" Jerry softened her tone, hoping it would get her an answer, but there was a war waging inside her. One side told her to run for the seas and get out of there as soon as possible while the other part told her to tell Arloa everything. "You can't be here."

"Why not?"

"You'll get infected."

"How do you know I'm not already?" Arloa raised an eyebrow in defiance. "What if you—"

"I didn't. You told me I didn't."

"So you did read my messages."

Cursing inwardly, Jerry clenched her fist. She had walked right into that one. She couldn't deny it now. She hadn't responded to the majority of them, and none since that first week. She hadn't the heart to die and leave Arloa wanting. Jerry put her hand on Arloa's waist, but Arloa flung her hand off in anger.

"Don't touch me."

Jerry moved her arms back to her sides and held as still as possible. "What are you doing here?"

"It's none of your business. You lost that right."

"Did I ever have it?" Jerry fired back, regretting her anger instantly. Perhaps she wasn't as even-keeled as she had hoped. She should take one of the pills in her pocket to balance herself out even more. Or maybe this was what true anger felt like, something she hadn't felt in over a year since all her emotions had been masked by the virus.

Arloa tilted her chin up, staring straight into Jerry's eyes. "You were well on your way toward earning it."

Sadness filled Jerry's chest. "Well, then I suppose we're done here."

"Are we?" Arloa stepped toward her, but Jerry moved back.

She wasn't going to take any chances. She wanted to leave, to run—that was the side that had won the battle inside her. Shifting around Arloa, Jerry stalked toward the main door, wrenching it open. Arloa stayed perfectly still where Jerry had left her. One last look over her shoulder, and Jerry left.

Her insides were a mess of emotions, ones she hadn't been

able to deal with or feel in over a year with anger and impulse taking front and center. Perhaps she did have more control than she had originally thought. Jerry climbed the stairs and walked into the main bar. She ordered a malt and waited while it was brought over to her.

As soon as the permanently frozen metal mug was set in front of her, she chugged it, barely tasting the flavor. She set it down, paid for her drink with a press of her finger against the sensor, and stood up. Nodding at the barkeep, Jerry straightened her shoulders, bolstered herself to go back to *Yarrow* with her goods in tow and make a run for Beren Island as planned.

Screw Arloa.

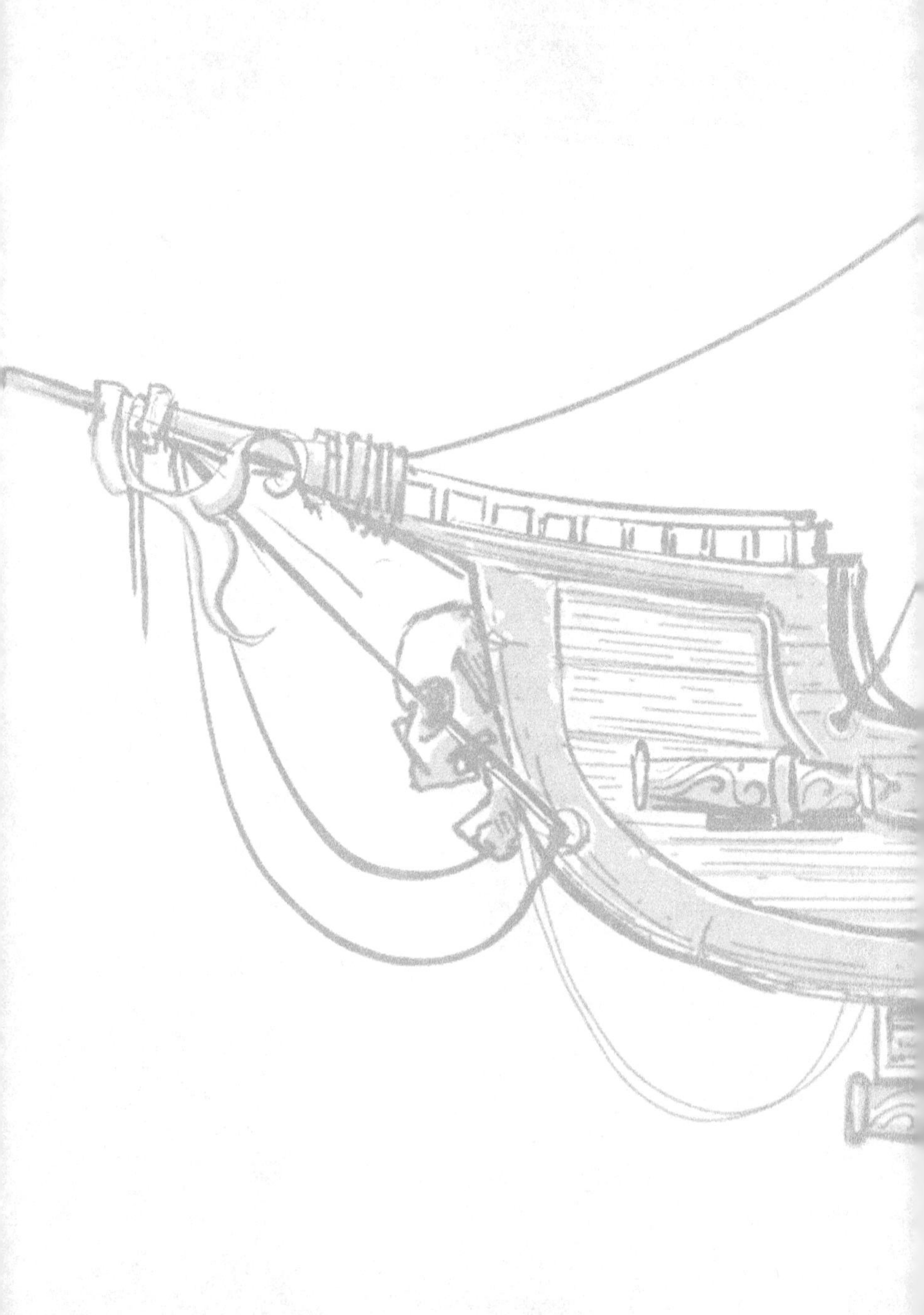

CHAPTER 8

The air was cold as it passed through her lips once she was outside. Jerry's heart thundered, every thought in her head of Arloa and what the fuck she would be doing with Miriam—hopefully nothing of what Jerry had just done. She shook that image from her mind. Arloa would never be so weak as to give in to that.

The first blow to her head was unexpected, landing right where Jerry had her previous injury, so her head spun, her vision blurred over, and she wasn't able to see anything but darkness clouding her eyesight. The slam against her back was expected, and she collapsed to the ground, her knees giving way.

The cobblestones were cold against the side of her face as she was dragged by her ankles. They were moving her out of sight of the recordings, where it would be far easier to do anything to her without anyone else seeing. Cracking one eye open, Jerry caught sight of the sea in front of her. She had been so close to home.

Her heart sank. She let them pull her wherever they were going, no energy to fight, not after the day and night she'd had. She would just let them do what they wanted to her and crawl her way back to *Yarrow*. Except—Jerry tightened her jaw as they dropped her and clenched her fist to prevent herself from reaching for the vestigen. She couldn't let them have it.

Curling into the fetal position, Jerry protected her ribs and stomach the most. Whoever was above her kicked hard, the steel toe of their boot slamming into her back, her hips, her head. She whimpered as pain ricocheted through her body, unable to prevent it from continuing. She was too weak. She'd been awake too long, she'd fought too many battles that day, and she couldn't bring herself to try anything.

When they tired of kicking her, one of them flipped her over onto her back. She stared up at the lightening blue sky, the pink and golden hues mixing, and immediately she thought of Arloa and her hair, the way the colors and strands twirled together, creating a masterpiece. The man on top of her dug into her pockets, bringing Jerry back to reality.

She would be better off dead.

She just wished she could die. The man stalled when his hand found the small pouch in Jerry's pocket. Moving swiftly, Jerry gripped her gun and pointed it directly into his belly and scrunched her nose. "Drop it, or I'll shoot."

He laughed, half his teeth missing. "Why? Got something good in here?"

"Drop it. Last warning."

He didn't, so she pulled the trigger on her gun, sending a bullet straight through his belly and through his back. Warm blood seeped onto her, coating her shirt and covering her skin. She ignored it as she cocked the gun again.

"Drop it."

He didn't. His friend grabbed him by the shoulder and dragged him off. Jerry drew in as deep a breath as she dared before shifting to lean up and aim the weapon at both of them. The injured man cowered as he dragged himself up to his feet, but the other one charged forward and kicked the gun right out of her fingers.

Fuck, she hurt so bad. Her head spun. She could barely make

out the two of them anyway that she probably wouldn't be able to hit them. The blow to her head this time knocked her right to the ground. Searing pain flashed through her skull and down into her neck, her ears ringing. They could kill her. She'd let them. So far they didn't seem to know how to kill her properly and she'd just come back to life eventually.

Wincing when he smashed his boot onto her ear, squeezing her head between his heel and the cobblestone alley, Jerry waited for the inevitable. It wouldn't be the first time she had died, and she knew without a doubt it wouldn't be the last. She couldn't die yet. The fucking world wouldn't allow it. Another slam of his foot against her, and the dawning sky went black.

Gasping, Jerry pressed her palm against the cold stone and sputtered blood from her mouth. She had no idea how long she had been down, but when she opened her eyes, her vision was clear and she could see again.

"Jer, hold on."

Soft fingers brushed against her cheek, such a damn contrast to the steel boots. Jerry closed her eyes again, reveling in the sweet touch, one she trusted. That voice brought her so much warmth and hope no matter if she didn't want it.

"Do you think you can get up yet?"

"How long?" Jerry mumbled, keeping her eyes clenched shut.

"Twenty minutes, but we don't have much time before the authorities come. You weren't exactly quiet."

"I shot him." Prying her eyelids open, Jerry stared into the blessedly beautiful eyes of none other than Arloa.

"I heard it. That's how I found you."

"Great." Jerry shifted and put her palm against the cold ground, pushing herself up slightly. Arloa helped, and soon enough she was leaning against the wall of one of the buildings. "Twenty minutes?"

"Yeah."

"Faster than last time."

Arloa's brow drew together.

"The last time I died."

"So you are infected," Arloa stated, so matter-of-factly.

"I thought we established that. You shouldn't be near me if you're not."

"I'm immune."

"What?" Jerry's head still spun, and she was having a hard time tracking the conversation, but she wanted to. Immunity was not something anyone had mentioned in about a year. They'd thought there would be possible immunity at one point, but then everyone had forgotten about it as they just tried to survive.

"We'll talk about it in a bit. I need you to stand."

"I don't think that's happening. Just leave me for the authorities. You don't need to be here when they find me."

"I'm not going to let you die."

Jerry gave a wry laugh. "Too late for that."

Arloa glared.

"What?" Jerry shrugged. "I've died so many times I can't even count them anymore."

"Then how are you still alive?"

"Regimen of drugs keeps me from spiraling out of control."

"Hmm, we'll talk about that too. Come on. Up you go." Arloa put her arms under Jerry's and dragged her to stand.

Jerry leaned against the cold stone wall, not wanting to move. Her stomach revolted, nausea coiling like a snake ready to strike. She had to keep it under control because the last thing she wanted was to ralph all over Arloa's pretty skirts.

"I'll get you to a healer."

"Don't bother. They won't see me."

"I think I have one who will."

"They won't. Trust me."

"Well, I'm not leaving you on this fucking street, Jer. So what do you want me to do?" The bite of anger in her tone along with the curse was striking. Jerry wasn't sure how to answer, because the first thought that came to mind was to throw her into the sea. She'd not only spent more than she wanted on the vestigen, but then she'd lost it—not that she was about to tell Arloa that had been what she was doing with Miriam. "Jer."

"What?"

"Where do you want me to take you?"

"Just kill me," she murmured, her voice so quiet that she hoped Arloa didn't hear. But she knew she wasn't going to be graced with that gift. She never got something she wanted.

Sighing, Arloa curled an arm around Jerry's waist and pulled her off the wall. They started walking, but instead of moving east toward the pier, Arloa took her west toward the center of town. "Where are we going?"

"To my apartment. I'm not going to kill you. That's just ridiculous."

Grinding her teeth, Jerry tried to fight back, but she had so little resolve. She'd tried to kill herself several times in the last year and she had never been able to manage it. Tightening her muscles, she tried to walk as best as she could, taking some of her weight off Arloa so it was easier to move. With dawn already breaking the horizon, they didn't have much time to get to Arloa's before the world would see them, and if they saw her— well, Jerry could only imagine how it would go.

The walk was slow, but eventually Jerry found herself in front of Arloa's building. Arloa pressed her palm against the sensor, the door sliding open so they could walk inside. The stairs were the hardest part, and Jerry tried her best not to get any blood on the pristine whitewashed shiplap walls. Fuck, she was so out of her league. What the hell was she supposed to do in the rich woman's home?

They got to the door and Arloa unlocked it with a key. Jerry frowned at it, not sure when they'd added in that, but it seemed so antiquated. She'd have to ask. Arloa always seemed to have the newest technology when it came to her home, and Jerry was always the last to get anything new. By the time it landed on *Yarrow* it was already outdated by most of Penum's standards.

Arloa helped Jerry to walk straight to the bedroom, flopping her onto the large mattress that would easily fit three people. Jerry had only slept on it once, and it had been glorious. Like before, she sank into the fabric as it cradled her back. Arloa ditched her jacket, tossing it over the brass footboard as she moved to help Jerry take hers off.

"Come on, Jer. I can't do this all on my own."

Jerry grabbed her wrist to stop her. "You shouldn't be so close to me if you're not infected."

"I told you. I'm immune."

"What does that even mean?"

Arloa sighed but moved her hands away, staring down at Jerry. "It means I can't get it."

"Anyone can get it."

"No, actually, not everyone. I'll explain it later, just let me help you."

Jerry licked her parched lips and shook her head. "No. I don't need your help."

"Obviously you do." Arloa's voice rose, anger pushing it out tersely. "I'm sorry."

"Don't be." Jerry wished she could move, that she could get up and walk away. She shouldn't have allowed Arloa to bring her there, but she'd always been so weak against her. If Arloa wanted something, told her what to do, Jerry found herself unable to resist.

"Let's get this off you so I can see the extent of your injuries."

This time, Jerry allowed Arloa to help. It took more maneuvering than she expected, and every time she shifted, her ribs ground together as the broken bones shifted. They must have snapped all of them. As soon as they had her jacket off, Arloa moved to unlace the ties of Jerry's tunic, but Jerry quickly grabbed Arloa's hands and stopped her.

"Don't do that."

"I need to see—"

"No. I don't want you to see that." This was one thing Jerry wasn't going to give in on.

Arloa sighed heavily and stepped back. "Fine. I'm going to get the healer. I'll be right back."

Finally cast into silence and alone in the room, Jerry lifted her hand to her face. She didn't have to see a reflection of herself to know that her face was badly beaten. Her entire body was. She likely needed a healer to be able to function anytime soon, but she would never be able to afford one.

Arloa came back in, a basin and washrag in her hands. She eyed Jerry carefully as she settled onto the edge of the bed and started to wipe the blood from Jerry's skin.

"What are you doing?" Fear made Jerry's voice waver.

"I need to clean you up. The healer will be here shortly."

"They'll kill me." Jerry swallowed hard. "That's what they do, Arloa. Surely you know that."

"This one won't."

"How do you know that? Since all of this started, anyone who is found out to be infected dies. You know that, and I know that. If a healer finds someone—"

"This one won't." Arloa stared at her, holding still before she reached forward and cupped Jerry's cheek again, those soft fingers just the balm Jerry needed. "I promise you. Trust me. Please."

Jerry wanted to tell her that no matter how much she didn't want to trust Arloa, she did. For some fucking reason, Jerry had always trusted her, and she couldn't put that thought from her mind. She'd grown up to rely on no one, and yet, here was Arloa, caring for her when she didn't have to.

Nodding, Jerry let Arloa wring out the cloth and wipe away the stains on Jerry's skin. They stayed silent through most of it, until the artificial intelligence alerted them that someone was trying to get in to see them. Arloa went to open the door, and Jerry remained where she was, still broken as fuck. She wasn't even sure she could make it back to *Yarrow* if she tried.

"This is Maisie. She's here to heal you."

The woman was the complete opposite of Arloa. She was dark-haired with bright blonde at her curly tips, her dark eyes holding a depth Jerry wasn't sure she had ever seen before. They eyed each other, as if to weigh the options.

"She's infected," Maisie stated.

Jerry's heart thundered. She was about to be caught, about to be thrown back into Joab in order to be murdered in a mass killing.

"She is, but I know you can't heal that. Heal her other injuries."

Maisie's lips thinned, and she took up Arloa's abandoned spot on the bed. "How did you come by these injuries?"

Again, Jerry didn't know how to answer. Arloa spoke for her. "She fell."

It was the stupidest excuse Jerry had ever heard, but it wasn't too far from the truth. She had fallen, right onto some very swift moving steel-toed boots. Jerry stayed still, waiting to see if Maisie would actually heal her or not. Finally, after what seemed like an eon, Maisie moved forward and held her hands over Jerry's ribs.

"May I touch you?"

"For the purpose of healing or killing?" Jerry asked pointedly.

Maisie's dark eyes locked on hers. "Healing, of course."

"Then yes." Jerry waited. It had been a long time since she'd been to a healer, never trusting them not to reveal who or what she was. They had turned on people like her when the virus struck and refused any sort of healing even for the injuries they could resolve.

Maisie's eyes glowed a golden color as her power worked through her body and into her hands. They all heard the cracks and pops as Maisie's ribs broke and healed, right along with Jerry's. She then moved her hands to Jerry's face, the injuries slashing across Maisie's perfect skin before vanishing on both of them. Jerry kept as still as possible, always amazed by the magic healers held. There were only a select few in all of Penum who had been gifted with that power, but Jerry could easily see that Maisie's went beyond the rest of the healers she'd ever met. She was powerful.

As Jerry was healed, she stayed put, giving her entire body over to Maisie and all she could do for her. When Maisie finished, she held on tightly to Jerry's leg, as if to hold herself up. Her skin was ashen in the bright morning light, the healing no doubt having taken a lot out of her. They stayed quiet until Maisie opened her eyes, the same dark color reflecting back as they were when she'd come in.

"Your injuries were extensive."

"Well, they did kill me."

Maisie hummed softly. "Explains something."

Arloa shifted awkwardly as she stood next to Jerry. "Thank you, Maisie."

"For you, anything. You know that." Maisie's smile was soft and sweet.

Jerry flicked her gaze from one to the other, back and forth, as she tried to read the subtext of that comment, but she didn't know either of them well enough to make any determination. Which had been her problem with her obsession with Arloa from the start—they didn't know each other. A few weeks spent together should not lead to her continued thoughts of fucking Arloa senseless or being around her or seeing her. Pulling all those stray emotions back in, Jerry waited to see what would happen next, but Arloa just escorted Maisie out, talking about extra credits she would send her way for the silence.

When Arloa returned, she sat next to Jerry, but they didn't touch. "I wish you would let me clean you up."

"I'm healed now. I can do it."

Arloa frowned, and Jerry couldn't get a read on why. It seemed as though the beatings to her head did a much worse number than she expected them to.

"You need to rest for the entirety of the day, but Maisie said you can leave when the sun falls."

"Of course. So I'm stuck here for the rest of the day. How convenient for you."

Arloa cut her a look. "Is this how it's going to be, then?"

"How what's going to be?" Jerry crossed her arms. "I'm pretty sure I told you to leave me there."

Arloa angrily stood and grabbed the basin of water. "You know where the washroom is."

"Right." Arloa left, and Jerry followed, stalking right into the washroom. She cringed when she looked at herself in the mirror. While her face was healed, and the injuries were all gone, the dirt and grease still coated her skin. The blood that had covered most of her shirt was there. Jerry must have looked absolutely awful beforehand—and she was glad she hadn't seen herself.

Stripping down, she stepped under the spray of hot water and cleansed herself from death—well, as much as she could. She would always be close to it. She took the bar of soap and washed her hair, threading her fingers through the strands to untangle it, remembering the one time Arloa had done that for her.

Sighing, she released the thought from her mind. She finished quickly and let the machines absorb the water as they always did. Then she stared down at the clothes that she couldn't wear again. She would be marked as an unsightly creature in seconds if she put them back on. The knock on the door was startling.

"I have something for you to wear," Arloa's voice was soft.

Jerry opened the door boldly, displaying her nakedness to the woman before her in an attempt to shock her. But the response she got was nothing. Arloa held her own as she handed over the thin chemise.

"I didn't think you would want to wear those."

"You're right about that."

Arloa's gaze dropped down Jerry's naked form, her eyes flitting from one scar to the next. They were new, and Jerry realized far too late that Arloa hadn't seen her since she'd gotten them. Arloa stepped in, not touching, but ghosting her fingers along the healed injuries. "Where did you get these?"

"Doesn't matter."

Arloa turned her gaze up to Jerry's, longing in her eyes. "It does to me."

"It doesn't." Jerry pulled the chemise over her head and let it drop. It was short, but it was also clearly Arloa's, so the fabric stopped on her upper thigh. "I'll rest for now."

Arloa stepped aside, and Jerry made her way into the bedroom. She found Arloa had changed the bedsheets while she'd cleaned herself up. Sliding onto the mattress, Jerry curled on her side and closed her eyes. As much as she didn't want to trust Arloa, she did, and she knew she would be able to sleep for a few hours without being disturbed by nightmares.

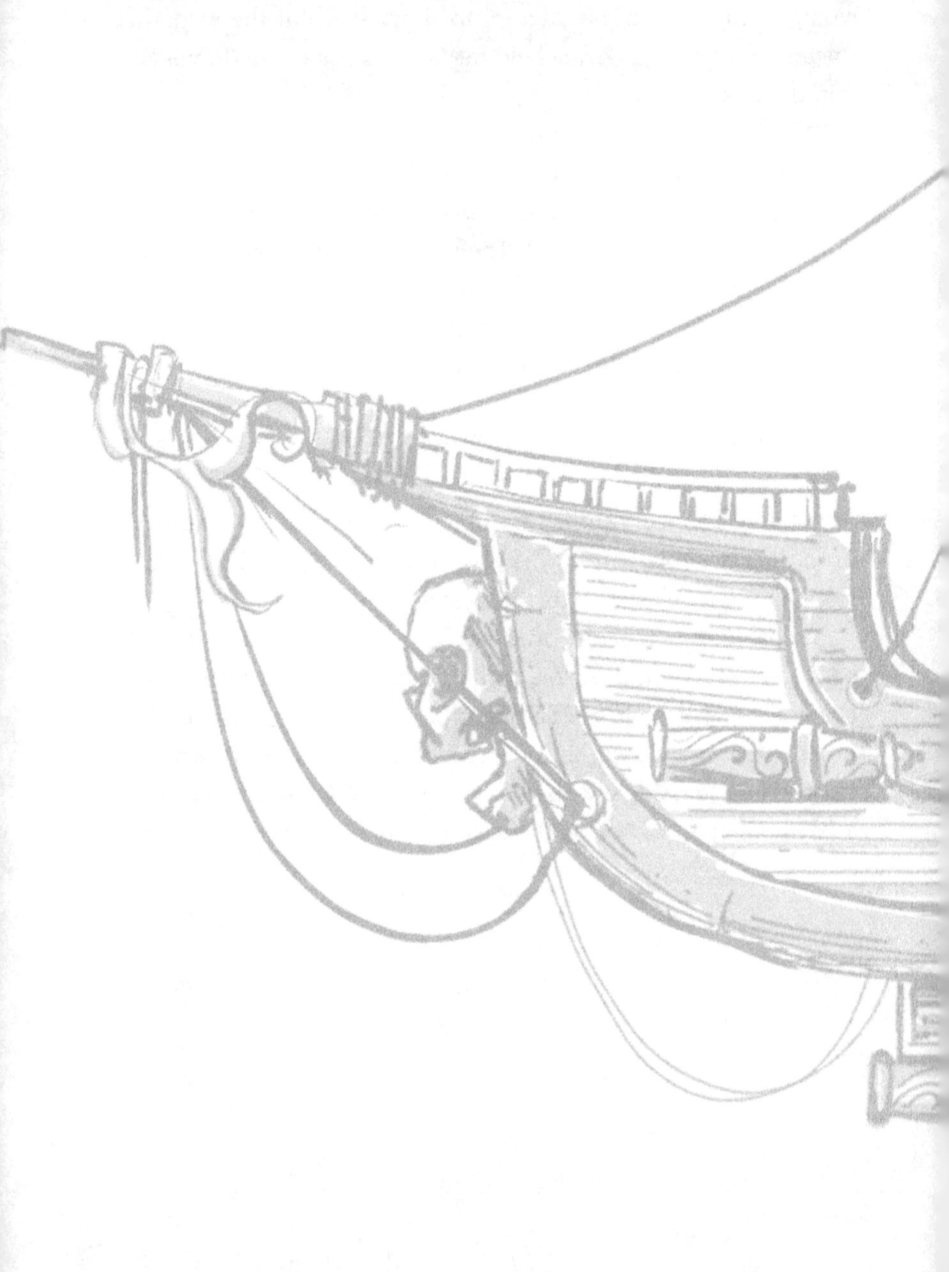

CHAPTER 9

When Jerry woke up, she was alone in Arloa's bedroom, as she expected to be. The sun was low in the sky, but it meant Jerry had slept most of the day, and she wasn't sure what that meant. If it was good or bad. Pursing her lips, she stretched her muscles, stopping when she saw her clothes neatly folded at the bottom of the bed.

Fuck, she slept hard. Sitting up, Jerry pulled the clothes loose from the pile and checked them over. Surprisingly, they were clean, and there was no sign of blood anywhere on the cloth. In fact, it looked nearly pristine, cleaner than it had been in months. Jerry stood up and dressed in silence, wondering how awkward it was going to be for her to just leave and avoid any conversation with Arloa.

It wasn't that she didn't want to talk to her, but she did not want to open that box if she didn't have to, and it had already been cracked. As she tied the laces to her boots, Jerry stared at the closed door and wondered what the hell she was going to say when she went out there. The thought of making more of a fool of herself ate away at her stomach, but she had to go that way to leave. There was no other exit.

Finally getting up the courage, Jerry opened the door and stepped out into the main living area. Arloa was propped up on the couch, her legs curled under her as she sat with papers strewn all over her lap. When she heard Jerry, she looked up, but barely moved beyond that. Her curly hair was tousled and thrown over her shoulder as she relaxed while she worked.

Fuck.

Jerry was so fucked.

All she wanted to do was fuck her senseless.

Words tumbled through her mind, and she couldn't make them either stop or come out, not that they would make sense to anyone if they did. Arloa raised her chin, eyeing Jerry. "I see you found the clothes."

"Yes, thank you. I didn't think…I didn't expect to sleep so long."

"You were quite injured."

"Yes." Jerry paused awkwardly in the vertex of the hall and the large open room, her escape on the other side.

Arloa glanced from Jerry to the door. "You're free to leave if you want. I'm not holding you hostage."

Jerry was about to leave, but something stopped her. Maybe it was the way Arloa looked at her, or the resignation in her tone, but Jerry couldn't make herself take the few steps to the door, turn the glass doorknob and leave. Instead, she stepped around the couch and settled next to Arloa, remembering the way they had fucked right on the back of it against the window for all the world to see.

"Thank you," Jerry choked out, trying not to let Arloa see her flushed cheeks.

"Are you sure you're all right?" Arloa cocked her head to the side, studying Jerry deeply.

"I'm fine. Thank you for asking."

"I realize you were in pain before, Jer, but this is quite the change and still very unlike you."

"Hmm. I know. What were you doing at Miriam's?" Jerry locked their gazes, not willing to break eye contact until she got a fair and honest answer.

Arloa moved, setting the papers onto the floor next to the sofa before she put her feet on the floor. "I suppose the same thing you were."

Flashes of Miriam's legs spread, Jerry's face in her pussy, her nose pressed against her as she made her come echoed in Jerry's mind. "No, I don't think so. What were you doing there?"

"I was looking for vestigen."

Jerry's stomach plummeted. "What the hell for? You don't need it. Not if you're actually immune."

"Correct." Arloa eyed her carefully. "I assume Miriam sold you some."

"Yes, and I lost it when I was jumped."

Arloa stood up, her skirts swishing in line as she moved, trailing behind her. She walked to a small shelf and came back with a pouch that looked very similar to the one Jerry had taken from Miriam. She untied the knots and dumped a small amount of pills into her palm. It wasn't as much as she had purchased, but it was at least half as much.

"Why did you buy this?"

"That is a story for another day, but you are free to have it if you need it."

Jerry's lips parted as she stared up at Arloa. "I can't just take this from you. Not if you—"

"I told you, I'm immune. I've been exposed many times in the last year and I've never been infected."

"But how?"

"I don't fully understand it." Arloa sat next to Jerry, this time closer than before. "But I have yet to be affected by the virus."

"How's that possible? It's highly contagious."

"I don't know." Arloa looked nothing but honest.

Jerry rubbed her temple, a headache working into her skull and pounding.

"Does your head hurt?" Arloa asked earnestly.

Giving in, Jerry nodded. "It's a side effect."

"Of what?"

Holding up the small pouch, Jerry wiggled it back and forth. "Lack of this."

"Oh. Then why don't you take one?"

"My crew needs it more, and since this is about half of what I purchased…I'll let them have it."

"Jer, you can't be a captain if you can't function." Arloa's hand hovered over Jerry's before she dropped it between them on the cushion.

Guilt stabbed at Jerry's chest. She'd told Arloa she didn't want to be touched, and Arloa was fastidiously respecting that. She had to admire that at least. "Why did you need this if you're immune?"

"I thought I could try to manufacture more of it, but that will take a lot of time and a lot of credits."

Jerry kept her mouth shut. Credits were something Arloa was not shy on. She had them in spades, more than Jerry had anticipated if that day was any indication. She should have known that, however. Arloa Kauket was part of one the richest families on Penum, the people who funded Joab, the people who helped fund the government. While Arloa might not like her family name, she was still one of them, no matter how much distance she tried to put between them.

Frowning, Jerry held the leather pouch tightly in her hand. "I'll pay you back for the healer."

"Don't think anything of it, Jer. I've been looking for a healer who would work with those infected, and it was a good test to see if she would come through."

"So now I'm just an experiment?"

Again Arloa's hand hovered over Jerry's. They had gotten so used to touching each other in the short time they were together, and even a year later, they were both struggling with it. Jerry could see the back and forth in Arloa's eyes before she dropped her hand again. "You were never an experiment."

"How will you get more vestigen if you give it all to me?"

"I was hoping you might help with that, actually."

"What do you mean?" Jerry narrowed her gaze.

Arloa's lips quirked up. "I heard a rumor about a large store of vestigen in Potelia, except I lack the skills necessary to get it."

"Potelia?" Jerry's mind flashed to Whitney, the young woman on the medical ship she'd left stranded. "That's a week's flight from here."

"It is, and it's only rumor right now. I haven't been able to verify any of the information I've received."

Jerry ran her hand over her dark hair, realizing too late she hadn't put it back in its braid. Arloa must have noticed as well because she rubbed her thumb back and forth over her fingers as if she was itching to reach out and touch.

"And you want me to help with what, exactly?"

"I want you to find it, steal it, and bring it back to me."

"All for you?"

"No." Arloa's lips thinned. "All for you, save for a small handful like right there."

Jerry stared at the pouch. "And so what I get out of it is a large sum of vestigen and nothing else?"

"Do you want payment?"

She hadn't honestly thought about that. She would do it just for the vestigen, but if Arloa was offering to pay her for the work, for the travel, for losing out on a legal job with Mortimer Blair. Her stomach sank. Fuck. She hoped Yafe and Azar had gone out without her. She stared out the window sharply. "Did you contact *Yarrow*, by chance?"

"I told them you were injured and healing, yes."

"Did they say they were leaving for their run?"

"Yafe confirmed that."

Jerry clenched her jaw. If they were gone, she had nowhere to go except to Ursula's ship, and all her belongings were gone with *Yarrow*. She didn't want to stay with Arloa another night. Being in this part of the city made her twitchy.

"Thank you for the vestigen." Jerry didn't turn to look back at Arloa. She wasn't sure she could, because if Arloa asked, she would go to the ends of Penum for her.

"Will you go then?"

Jerry didn't answer.

"Jer, will you go to Potelia?"

Facing Arloa fully, Jerry observed her carefully. There was nothing hidden in Arloa's gaze or movements, yet something Arloa had told her the last time they had seen each other in person stuck out to her, and she couldn't shake the thought from her head.

"What did you mean, a year ago, when you said I didn't know you?"

Arloa's lips parted in surprise, but she smiled, her eyes lightening. "I meant that we didn't know each other well. We'd only just started, and I wanted to continue that."

Leaning in, Jerry pressed close to Arloa, her breath hot on Arloa's cheek. "I think that's the first time you lied to me. What did you really mean?"

Arloa drew in a shuddering breath, turning her cheek so their skin barely brushed against each other. "I know my family well, Jer. I know what they do and what they don't, and I know what they expected of me. I'm not what they anticipated, but I am exactly who I want to be."

"And who is that?"

"Someone completely enamored with you." Arloa's voice was so soft, Jerry almost didn't catch what she'd said.

She didn't move. As tempted as she was to turn just the slightest, to bring their mouths together, to taste what she had been missing out on, she couldn't. Sliding away, sadness and regret overwhelmed her.

"I'll think about it," Jerry answered as she stood up. "Thanks for the vestigen and the healer."

"Jer." Arloa stood up, reaching out for Jerry's hand but stopping herself before she touched without consent. "Jer, please."

"I told you, I'll think about it. I need to talk to my crew first."

"They left. Where will you stay tonight?"

Jerry cocked her head, her eyes lighting up. "Did you think I only had one ship?"

Without another word or answer, Jerry grabbed her top hat from the table and plopped it on her head. She walked out of Arloa's apartment and into the dimly lit sky. It was earlier than she had wanted to leave, but she couldn't stay any longer. The streets were relatively empty, something Jerry suspected had become the norm since the virus hit. Quarantine was the name of the game for the aristocrats, mostly because they could afford to do it.

When she got to the docks, Jerry went to pier twenty-one instead of her normal pier and found the second vessel she had purchased six months prior. *Calluna.* Jerry pressed her palm to the sensor to bring down the door and let herself inside. As soon as she walked across the deck to the interior door, she shut the exterior one.

Finding her way to the wheelhouse wasn't difficult, and Ursula was sitting in the captain's chair. She raised her eyebrow at Jerry as she came up from the ladder. "Fancy seeing you here."

"*Yarrow* left without me."

"I know. They took two of my crew."

Jerry pressed her lips tightly together and tossed the small leather pouch to Ursula. "I had an interesting night."

Inspecting the goods, Ursula raised an eyebrow. "I thought you were getting twice this much."

"I did. Like I said, an interesting night. Have you heard any rumors about a large store of vestigen in Potelia?"

Ursula shook her head slowly as she counted the pills in her hand. "Can't say I have."

"I have."

Jerry jerked her head up at the voice, not realizing that someone else had been in the room. Perhaps she was still out of sorts with everything that had happened and being thrown back into Arloa's presence. The young woman had stringy black hair that fell around her face, her eyes dark with large purple circles around them. She was the newest intake. Ursula must have been watching over her while the others rested.

"Tell me more." Jerry put her hands on her hips as she stared the woman down.

"I don't even know who you are." The woman's eyes narrowed.

"I'm Jerry Adelric, and I own this vessel. I pay for your room and board and the vestigen you've been taking so you'll be normal."

Her eyes widened. "My apologies. I'm Vivian. Yafe found me."

"She likes strays. What did you hear about Potelia?"

"Just what you said, that they have a large store of vestigen. My…boyfriend, though I'm not really sure I can call him that anymore…said he was going to go up there. Said they hand it out like prizes to all the residents."

"I haven't heard any of that before." Jerry flicked her gaze to Ursula, who looked equally confused. Surely if there was a country handing out vestigen freely, she would have heard about it, and surely everyone who had been infected would be flocking there.

Vivian shrugged. "It's just a rumor. I never believed it."

"And how did you come by vestigen before we found you?"

"My boyfriend got it for me, but it was never enough."

Jerry wasn't surprised to hear that. It had taken her time and research to figure out the formula for the regimen they were all on, and since no healer or scientist wanted anything to do with it, the exact dosage remained unknown to many people. Which left them to flounder and die or kill someone in the process, until the authorities showed up and killed them in retaliation.

Pointing at Ursula, Jerry raised an eyebrow. "Want to do a bit of research?"

"On it, Cap."

"I'm going to the galley, but I'll help out in a bit." Jerry left the leather pouch with Ursula, knowing she would distribute it and lock up the rest, and headed down the ladder to the galley.

She ripped open a water packet and chugged it, needing the cold liquid for her parched tongue. She'd forgotten when she last ate, but for some reason since the battle at Beren Island when they were boarded, she hadn't wanted any food until then. Even after being beaten to a pulp.

Jerry crossed one ankle over her knee and waited in the silence as she slipped a small piece of food between her lips. Arloa had known more than she'd let on, and Jerry had left before she'd gotten all the information. Everything she felt when it came to Arloa was mixed up to the point it clouded her judgment. She couldn't separate work from personal when it came to her, and she so desperately wanted to. She would need to, especially if she started to work with Arloa on whatever this rumor was.

Forcing herself to take another bite, Jerry thought through the last night. Arloa had been nothing but kind to her, and she'd left with barely a mention of thanks. But she had to maintain the facade that she was angry, otherwise Jerry was worried about what she would give in to, that she really would do anything for Arloa.

Still having no information beyond a rumor, confirmed by another far more outrageous rumor, she knew if Arloa contacted her again and asked her to go that she would. She had no self-control when it came to that woman. Since the virus had attacked her, she had very little self-control in general, but add Arloa into the mix, and Jerry was done for.

After eating a small something because she should have wanted food even if she didn't, Jerry wandered to the lower decks where she knew there were a few cabins free. She picked one and flopped onto the cot after locking the door behind her. Ursula would be doing research for them, and Jerry would do more in the morning, getting hold of what contacts she still had who might know something. Unfortunately that could mean going back to Miriam—an idea Jerry wasn't particularly fond of.

As exhaustion stole through her muscles and her mind again, Jerry closed her eyes. She was going to need to figure out what her next move was. She couldn't buy vestigen from Miriam forever. It would be nice, but there was no way she could afford it, even with the sexual favor discount. Groaning, Jerry turned onto her side and tried to flush all memories of the last day and a half from her mind. She managed all of them except the ones involving Arloa, and the fucking request she'd made.

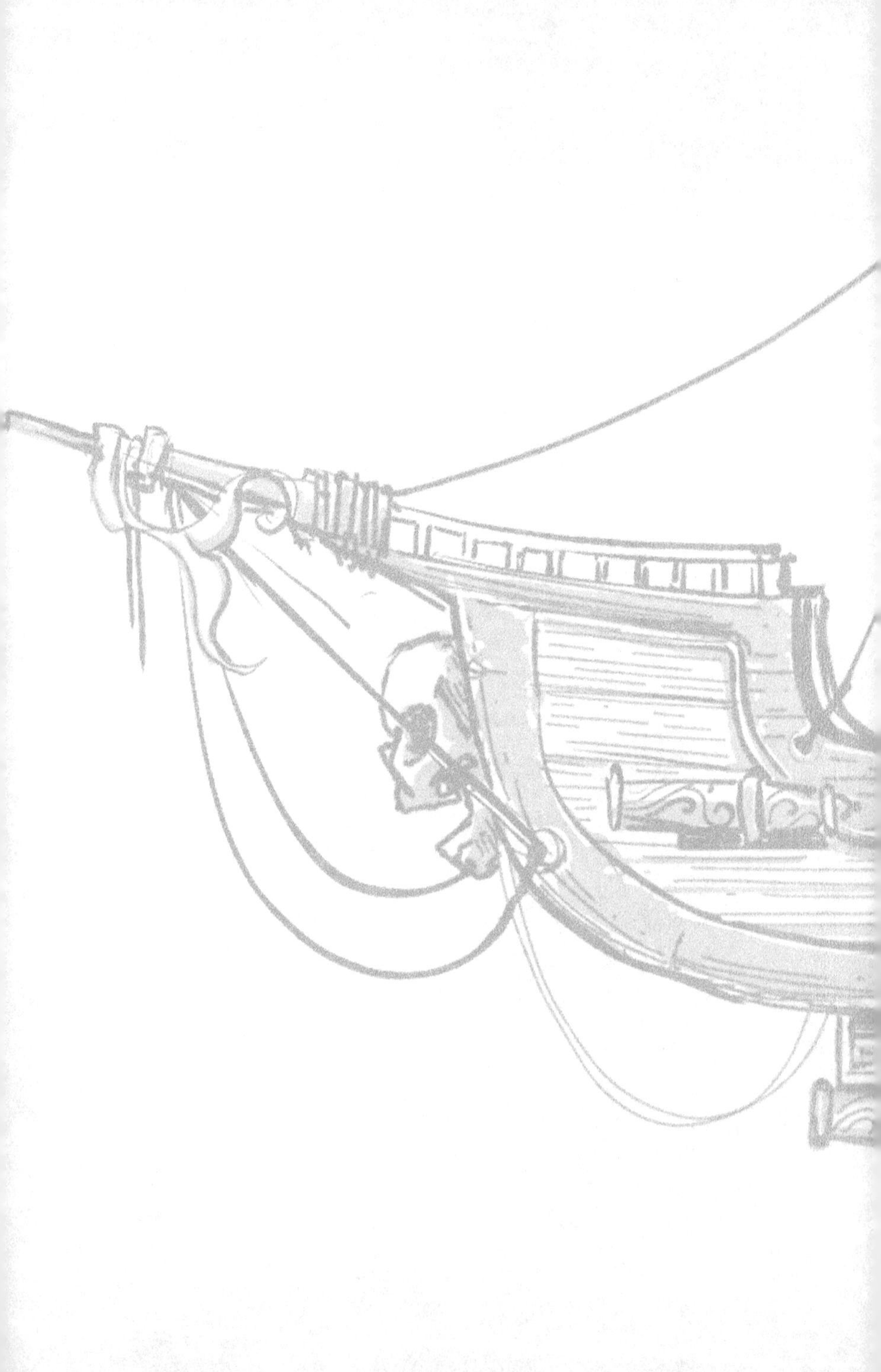

CHAPTER 10

Waking up at dawn was a new experience—especially after an entire day of sleeping. Jerry felt refreshed for the first time in ages. She didn't have a lingering headache, her body felt as though she were ready to run a long race, and her mind was thinking clearly. She stretched on the small cot, putting her hands over her head as she tightened and then eased her muscles.

She'd fallen asleep with a device in her fingers, trying to digest as much information as possible about this potential store of vestigen. Jerry had her ear to the ground and she had never heard of it before, so to have two people say they had was surprising. She wasn't sure whether she should believe them or not.

Granted, Potelia was an entirely different country, one where Jerry had very few connections. She knew the laws of each country, working hard to avoid breaking them when she could and blatantly ignoring them when necessary. Potelia had laws far different from Raegina, but from her experience law and practice were never the same.

Jerry turned on her side and grabbed her device. The rest of *Calluna* was likely not awake yet, since Ursula didn't keep as tight a schedule as Jerry did. She could afford not to since her work wasn't as legal as Jerry's. That had been Jerry's entire purpose in purchasing a second vessel when the market crashed. Buy a ship she could use for her illegal ventures, and Ursula was the perfect person to run it.

She stayed there for an hour, skimming through different reports she could easily access in the government system, but reports on the Omar Region—where Potelia was—were slim. She'd expect a bit more, honestly, but Potelia was equally known for staying out of conflict and Raegina's government was known for controlling information to the detriment of its people.

Dragging herself up, Jerry went to the galley and grabbed some water and food packets before climbing topside. The gentle breeze in the air brushed against her cheeks. It was chilly outside, frost on the surface of the vessel since they were in the early stages of winter, but Jerry ignored it as she found a place to sit in silence.

She enjoyed the quiet, and it was partly why she insisted on staying on *Yarrow*, a much smaller vessel with fewer people to annoy her. She continued as much research as she could find on the surface about Potelia and the Omar Region, and yet she still was only finding that they were in the same situation as everyone else on Penum. That didn't mean much.

Jerry was not known for her hacking abilities, which meant she was going to have to find someone else who could help her find information the government didn't want her to have. She ran through her contacts, but she already knew who she was going to ask to join in her little information-seeking adventure. Ursula plopped down next to her, and Jerry frowned as she ripped off the top of her water packet, finally drinking it.

"Find anything interesting?" Ursula pointed to the device.

Jerry grunted as her only response.

"Same here. I talked to Brant, and he had nothing for me."

"Do you know anyone in Potelia?" Jerry finished her water and tossed the packet overboard to be eaten away by the sea.

"No. They keep their borders pretty tight and don't allow outsiders in or out often."

"That vessel we pirated the other week was coming from Potelia." Jerry stared down at her hands and the food in them, still not hungry for it. She hated that the worst part of the virus was that she lost her entire appetite for human food. She ate because she had to in order to survive, but to taste something and actually be hungry for it would be a miracle.

"That was a medical vessel, right?"

"Yes, they said they were coming home."

"You don't think...you don't think that they sent the rich who were infected there for treatment, do you?"

Jerry had been thinking just that, but she hadn't wanted to make any assumptions. Since Ursula said it out loud first, Jerry nodded slowly. "I do wonder."

"Who would know? How would we even find out about that?"

Jerry equally had a pretty good idea about that, though she wasn't going to mention it yet. She had to work herself up to that one, especially with the way she had left the night before. Jerry rolled her shoulders as she contemplated how much to share with Ursula. If she was talking to Yafe, the conversation would be entirely different. She wouldn't want to hold back, but she and Ursula had some rocky history. While Jerry trusted her for work, she wasn't sure she trusted her with Arloa. Not yet at least. And Ursula hadn't been around when Jerry had first met Arloa.

"We need more information, and we're going to have to pay some people for it."

"Do we have any credits for that?"

"We do." Jerry had kept a separate fund for bribes that she could easily access. She had known they would need it at some point, although she figured it would be to get out of trouble rather than get into trouble, but for now it would have to do.

"First we need some contacts with actual information from Potelia. We need to make sure it's valid."

Whitney flashed into Jerry's mind, and she wondered if the young girl would have any information that would be useful. She'd been the most forthcoming when they'd taken control of the vessel, and Jerry had let her loose to rescue the rest of them. That had to be some basis of a connection between the two of them.

No one had been there when she'd done it. Jerry shoved the food packet between her lips and chewed as best as she could, even if it wasn't exactly what she wanted to eat. Finishing her meal mostly in silence while Ursula worked next to her, Jerry searched through her personal device to try and find any information on that vessel they'd left stranded. She needed to know if they'd been rescued and had arrived back where the crew manifest said they all went. She didn't expect to find a lot on the general channels. Jerry was going to have to dig deeper, no doubt, to find Whitney, but perhaps she could help.

"I'm going belowdecks. I've got some things to do today."

"With *Yarrow* out? You have actual work in Raegina to do?"

"I do leave the ship, you know." Jerry gave her a mock glare.

"Rarely."

Jerry knew Ursula was right, but she didn't want to admit it. She really only left when she had to. Sighing, Jerry pushed herself up, glad that Arloa had brought in a healer, though she would never admit that to anyone. Saying nothing, Jerry went belowdecks and found her cabin again. Yarrow was due back in a few hours, so she'd have to wait for them to arrive before putting the next step in her plan into action. She needed some supplies, and she wasn't very happy about it, but it was going to be the only way to do this. She wouldn't go back to Arloa's. If she stepped foot in that apartment, then she was going to fuck Arloa and say screw the rules she'd put in place herself.

She had zero self-control when it came to that woman.

As soon as *Yarrow* pulled in to dock, Jerry went out to meet them. She would help them unload before sending Azar to find Mortimer and get their credits for the shipment. The chill air kept her wide awake as she walked, but she was feeling really good compared to the last few months. Tapering down the vestigen to a small amount took a toll on her body she hadn't anticipated, and having been healed in every other aspect, Jerry finally understood how worn down she was.

How much she craved the drug.

Glowering, she made her way to the dock where *Yarrow* was. Immediately she was on board and helping to unload. Between her and the two loaners from *Calluna*, it took them half the normal time to offload their cargo. As Azar left to go to the exchange for their credits, Jerry grabbed Yafe's hand and dragged her into her cabin.

"I need your help."

"With what?" Yafe's face pinched.

"I need to get dressed up."

"For what?" Yafe raised an eyebrow.

Jerry pursed her lips as she dug through her crate to find the one outfit she knew she had in there. "I met up with Arloa last night, and I swear on all things holy, Yafe, if you make any snide comments, I'll toss you overboard myself."

"I wasn't going to say anything, Cap." Yafe barely contained her smile.

"Sure you weren't. I ran into her accidentally. She dropped a bomb that there might be a store of vestigen in Potelia, but I didn't exactly get much information from her before I left. Oh! Here!" Jerry dragged out the dark maroon skirts, holding them up to the light from the small window so she could see how wrinkled they were. That would be the dead giveaway that she wasn't one of them, aside from the fact she absolutely wasn't.

"That should do if you're thinking of going up to the government house and finding her."

Jerry eyed Yafe over the top of the dress. "How did you know I was going to do that?"

"Because you never do things simply, and because I'm a betting woman, and I bet that you made an ass of yourself and now you have to grovel in order to pry."

Jerry narrowed her gaze and glared. "You know me too well sometimes."

"Yes, I do." Yafe stood up and took the dress, bringing it into the washroom. "Clean up, and the steam will help the wrinkles."

"It better, because that's bad." Jerry grabbed the rest of the outfit and Yafe took it from her as she walked into the washroom. She'd showered only the day before and hadn't done much to get dirty, so she turned the spray on and let the room fill with steam while she pulled the braid from her hair.

Yafe eventually pushed her way into the small washroom. "We'll have to curl your hair."

"Of course." Jerry sighed. She hated curlers, but if she wanted to attempt to pass herself off as one of them, she was going to need to blend in as much as possible. "I'll need to leave my weapons. If I get caught—"

"Do you want me to follow as back up?"

"No, I don't anticipate being thrown into Joab, but it'll make me feel naked, far more than this thing." Jerry pointed at the low-cut dress.

Yafe eyed it. "I bet Arloa will like seeing you in this."

"Who knows." Jerry leaned over to study herself in the mirror. She needed to dress herself up. While she didn't look like a run-down pirate any more, thanks to the healing, she still needed to look made up. "Got any paints?"

"Some, but none your color."

"I don't suppose Sacha does."

"Probably not yet, but I imagine she'll get some as soon as she has credits."

"Wonderful. We'll have to find something to make do."

"What about Ursula?" Yafe pressed as she checked on the dress.

Jerry grimaced. "I'd rather leave her out of this if I can. She knows about the potential storehouse and is trying to confirm the rumor through her own contacts. Arloa is mine."

"A contact, or *yours?*"

Jerry ignored her comment. It took over an hour for them to get Jerry ready, but Yafe gave her blessing and allowed Jerry to leave finally. As she stepped outside, Jerry felt so out of place. The dark maroon skirts worked off her tanned skin, and the blue ribbon around the bottom matched her eyes, but she was not a lady, and the dress gave off those vibes. However, she was a master at making people think she was someone she wasn't, so Jerry straightened her shoulders and walked with confidence.

Raegina was built around the government house, one of the first buildings commissioned when the country was established. It was set back from the harbor, up on a hill, so anyone inside could look out over the city. Since it had been built, Raegina had boomed and sprawled in every direction.

She would walk past the cutoff for Arloa's building, but it wasn't far from where Arloa lived. Men and women who saw her stared at her oddly. She knew she wasn't a beautiful woman, far too masculine looking, but she also knew she just looked out of place among the aristocrats.

Ignoring them, Jerry continued to walk forward, her pace a healthy jaunt as she made her way to the government house. The wide double doors loomed as she reached the building, a stark white stone, immediately stating wealth. Jerry swallowed the lump in her throat as she forced herself not to ogle but to move.

She had no idea where Arloa's offices were, but she did know she worked in the building. She had been a runner for some of the higher-ups when they had first met, before she was elected. Jerry straightened her shoulders and walked immediately to the artificial intelligence against the wall, searching for the name Arloa Kauket.

Finally she found it. Jerry turned on her toes and walked down the corridor in the direction the artificial intelligence told her to go.

"Who are you?" The male voice was sharp, and instinctively, Jerry knew it was directed at her.

Jerry held her own, putting her parasol point against the marble floor and holding herself regally. She wouldn't back down. She had to find Arloa, and she wasn't going to go to her apartment. "I'm here to see my contingent representative."

"That isn't what I asked." His blond hair was perfectly coifed, the tight collar around his neck indicating he was a secretary. Though she wouldn't be surprised if he talked to every woman in his life this way, his government position certainly helped with that.

Jerry set her jaw, ready to defend herself. "I told you I am here to see my contingent representative."

"You can't be here. You might infect us." The way he sneered when he raked his gaze over her body was unnerving. And Jerry wasn't even sure he could be infected, but she wasn't about to tell him that. "You need to leave, immediately."

He moved as if to grab her arm, and Jerry stayed put, willing him to touch her without express consent in front of authorities and all the others there. He likely wouldn't land himself in trouble for it, but it would be a notch in her belt if he did. Unfortunately, he stopped short of making contact.

Jerry raised her chin, staring him directly in the eye since she was so tall. When she spoke, she changed her accent, strengthened the pretentious tone so he'd more readily believe she was one of them. "I have a right to be here."

"You are nothing here," he muttered, coming closer. "You are not allowed within these walls."

Jerry's stomach boiled, and she was about to respond when she stopped. The familiar clack of heels against the floor ignited in her belly, and she knew exactly who was coming. "I most certainly am, Secretary...?"

She knew who he was, but she chose to pretend not to, and shame him that he wasn't important enough for the world to know.

"Secretary Riley!" Arloa's voice echoed through the front foyer.

Jerry's stomach twirled at the thought of Arloa coming to her rescue again.

"Secretary Riley. Good to meet you." Jerry held out her hand for him to take if he wanted it, but he didn't, as she had suspected. He knew where she was from, that she was of a much lower class. She'd been able to hide it until she came into the building, which had been her first goal for dressing that way.

He scoffed at her as he faced Arloa. "She isn't allowed here."

"She most certainly is. Are you denying our constituents the right to see us?" Arloa raised an eyebrow at him, planting her foot in front of her as if she wasn't going to be moved.

Jerry's gaze danced all over Arloa's form as she became a whole new person, someone who wouldn't back down. Jerry had seen this confidence in Arloa from the moment they met, but witnessing it in full force was another thing entirely.

"I suppose I can talk to the Grand Master about this, see what he says."

Riley stared at her for a few fleeting seconds before barely bowing his head in acquiescence. Jerry inwardly leaped for joy. "Keep it quick, Kauket. I won't have her infecting the entire house."

Arloa's lips parted, but Jerry shot her a warning look, and she closed her mouth. With the commotion fading, people moved around them again. Arloa stepped away from Riley and made eye contact with Jerry.

"This way, ma'am."

The shudder that raced down Jerry's spine had nothing to do with joy at getting her way but everything to do with lust and the way Arloa spoke to her. In silence, Jerry followed Arloa closely as they moved down several corridors, weaving through people and halls until they reached a small office in the back of the house.

Arloa spun on her as soon as the door was shut, hands on her hips, and a glare in her eye. "What the hell are you doing here?"

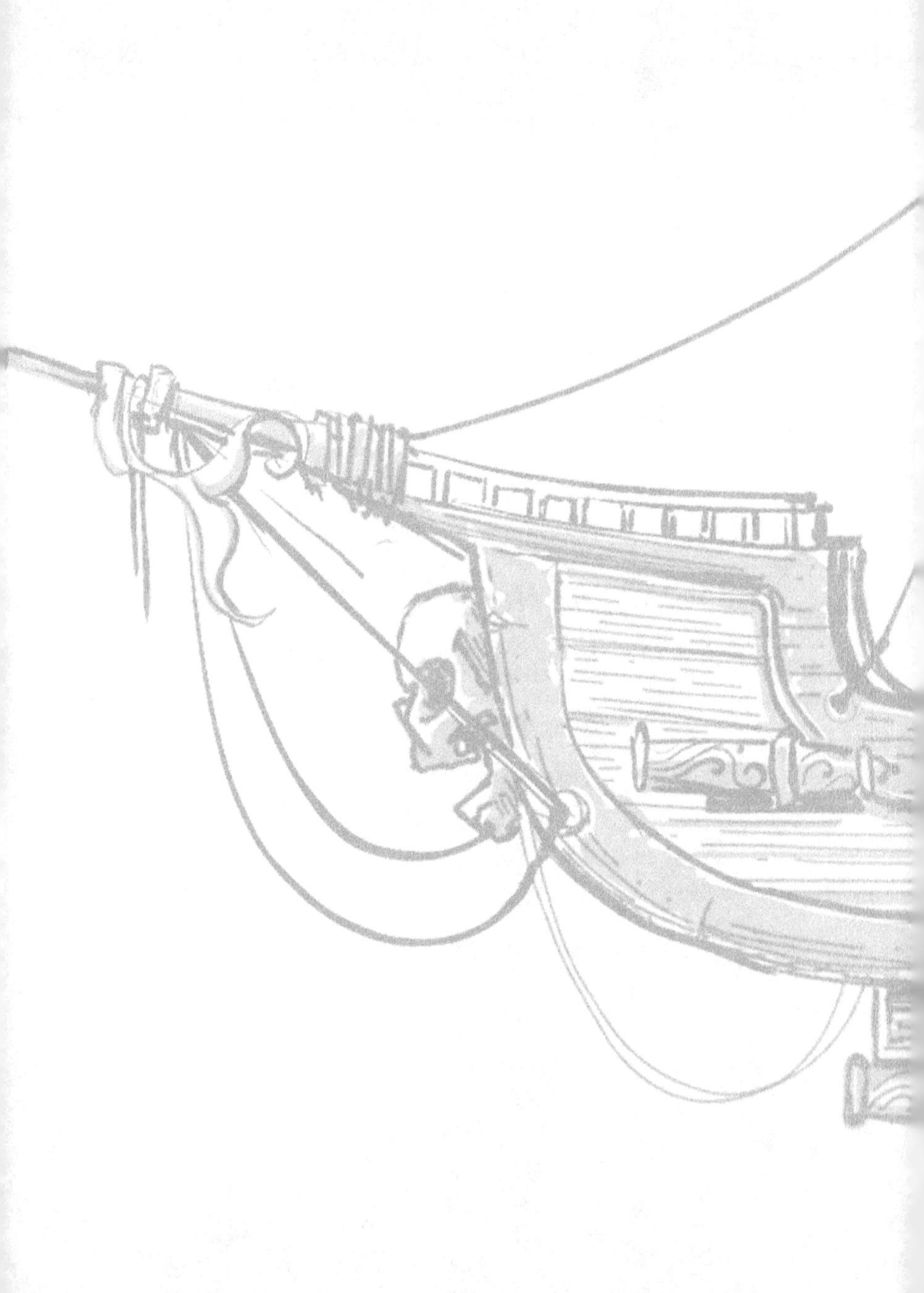

CHAPTER 11

love it when you curse." Jerry freely moved her gaze down Arloa's body and back up, enjoying the slight tinge of pink that reached Arloa's cheeks. She'd been wrong. Meeting in the office with Arloa all dolled up and professional had been a poor choice on her part.

Arloa's jaw tightened, and Jerry was satisfied to see the reaction. The window to the street outside was bright, and Jerry wondered if it was the same glass that was in Arloa's apartment, the one where people could see out but not in. Stepping over to it, uninvited, Jerry put her hand against it before looking over her shoulder.

"Is this like what's in your apartment?"

Arloa's cheeks flared red this time. "Yes."

"So I could take you right here and no one would know?"

"Jerry," Arloa said firmly. "What are you doing here?"

"Well, when someone drops live information in my lap but it largely lacks in specific information, I need to know more, and you're the one to come to for more." Jerry left the window and slipped into the high-backed carved chair behind the desk, taking over what should be Arloa's spot. She was acting like a cocky fool, but it seemed to be having the desired effect.

"I told you that information in confidence," Arloa hissed, her voice dropping so low that Jerry had to strain to hear.

"You did, and now I'm here for more."

"You can't walk into my life after a year and expect me to hand you everything again."

Pursing her lips, Jerry shook the facade she'd put on and nodded her agreement. "That's fair."

"You cut me off, Jer."

Oh, there was that nickname again. She was never going to get over it. Guilt swam in the pit of her stomach, but Jerry let it live there. She did deserve it. She'd fallen down the hole of the virus and left Arloa to figure out on her own where they stood, but again, they hadn't been together long before Jerry had gotten infected.

"I did," Jerry answered, honesty in each word. "And I would do it again."

Arloa's gaze softened. She came around the desk, sitting on the edge of it right next to Jerry. She folded her hands in her lap, her lips thinned into a line. "How are you feeling after the other night?"

"Amazing, actually. That healer of yours worked some quick magic."

"Deep magic," Arloa corrected. "She said your injuries weren't all fresh."

Jerry shrugged but kept her affect blank. She didn't want to give away just yet how tough the last year had been. She'd let Arloa into her heart once, but she wasn't sure she deserved Arloa in there again, not to mention, Arloa certainly didn't deserve her, the unsightly and now unmentionable creature that she was.

"What happened this past year, Jer?"

And that was the dam Jerry was trying not to break. Lifting her gaze, Jerry stared into those steel-blue eyes, the ones she had dreamed about most nights, even when she didn't want to. Except this person was real. This woman was standing right in front of her, opening her heart up again without Jerry even asking. Who the fuck had that amount of trust in her?

"A lot," Jerry whispered, her voice breaking. She wasn't even sure where to begin, but she knew half of her confessions couldn't really be given in the government house without her being arrested. "Is it safe here?"

"Yes. I've made sure of that."

Jerry nodded slightly, glancing around at the small room. The wood was a deep rich color, shelving lining the walls with books Jerry could only ever dream of reading, all of it there, free for Arloa's pleasure. Arloa was brilliant, and she'd been trained to restrain her intellect to make the men in her life feel better. All women were.

"I was already infected when you left. We actually traced it to Storm, a very short hire who you never met. I had already fired him when Matty took a turn for the worse."

"Matty." Arloa's look softened. "He was your friend."

"He was my crewmate, a hired man, and nothing more. But he had grown on me in the short time I knew him. We had a rough start, but we came around to each other." Jerry picked up a quill and ran it lengthwise between her fingers to distract herself. "After Matty, the others and I continued our salt mining but we searched for a cure."

"Something you're still looking for, I suspect."

"Of course." Jerry gave a wry smirk. "But in the meantime we found a treatment. It wasn't very hard, actually. It was developed when the virus first took over."

"Vestigen," Arloa filled in the gaps. "I found it, too."

Giving her a curious look, Jerry debated whether to continue speaking or allow Arloa to fill in some blanks. Silence more often than not got her more information than asking questions.

"After that night, I began working on research of my own. I suspect we ran across the same information."

"Likely," Jerry murmured. "I went in search of vestigen and found some. There was some trial and error, but Yafe and I found a regimen that will bring an infected person back from the brink of death. The only problem is we need to continue taking it in order to stave off death and destruction."

"The virus works like a blocker," Arloa chimed in. Jerry stared at her, hoping she would continue her explanation. "It moves into your brain and blocks certain hormones from being made naturally in your body. It leads to anger, violence, lack of self-control."

"It leads to more than that." Jerry scrunched her nose. "First-hand knowledge."

"Right, but vestigen is a synthetic hormone that can replace what you're missing for a short period of time."

"Makes sense, I guess. I never understood the science behind it, but that is out of my league since I didn't go to primary or grammar school like you." It was a dig at Arloa's upbringing, but Jerry couldn't help herself. Perhaps before the virus she might have been able to control her tongue, but now she had very little desire to even try.

"Jer."

The pity was too much, and Jerry stood up sharply, walking across the room and putting her hands on her hips.

"Jer, you have done amazing things with what you were handed."

Snorting, Jerry spun around and faced Arloa again. "Don't you dare think you know what my life was growing up. You have no idea."

"So tell me." Arloa's open invitation was on the table, but Jerry couldn't take it. They had to learn to trust each other again, and this wasn't the time or the place for those confessions.

"If it's a synthetic, then there can be a cure."

"Perhaps." Arloa's almost unreadable gaze moved over Jerry's form. "Did you dress like that for me?"

"I dressed like this to get in here. Seeing you was the ultimate goal, yes, but it wasn't for you."

"Good. I prefer the pants and tunic."

Heat flushed into Jerry's face, completely unarmed and not ready for that kind of comment. She shuddered as Arloa's gaze deepened, the lust behind her eyes clear.

"It's more you."

Jerry was speechless, which was rare. She usually had a comeback for everything, but this was unexpected. She had come in fighting, and now it seemed as if Arloa was going to push back.

"I don't know what to say to that." Jerry crossed her arms as if to protect herself behind the mask she'd put on.

Arloa moved and stepped in closer to her, standing only inches from Jerry. "It's a compliment. Just accept it."

"All right." Jerry looked down into Arloa's eyes. "What now?"

"You tell me more about this past year."

"You don't want to know about it."

"I do." Arloa hesitated as she reached out, her hand hovering over Jerry's arm. "May I?"

"No." She couldn't stand Arloa touching her when she talked about the last year. Nothing would disarm her more than that, and she didn't deserve it. Maintaining her distance at the moment was the only defense she had left. "Tell me about Potelia."

"You first," Arloa pushed. "I want you to help me, Jer, but I'm not going to ask you to do anything if I don't trust you."

Sighing, Jerry gnawed on the inside of her cheek. "I died. Many times over, but no one has killed me yet."

Arloa gasped. "Died?"

"We're not the easiest to kill. I've been killed many times, and yet never stayed dead. I don't know what they do with those of us they know are infected but are still allowed to roam free, the ones who don't cause problems."

"They don't know," Arloa answered. "They think everyone infected is immediately taken to Joab."

Jerry pressed her lips together hard. "Do you know what Joab is?"

Arloa paled, her gaze downcast. "I do."

"And you allow it? How could you—"

"My family runs it, not me. You have to understand that."

"You have no idea what they do to people there."

Arloa stuttered, but she finally stopped and agreed. "You're right. I don't. Not firsthand. But I have looked into it as much as I have been able to."

"And you still allow it to continue!" Jerry's voice rose sharply.

"What would you have me do? I can't fight them and win."

"Rich coming from you. You're one of them. You benefit off the money they get. You're no better than your family."

"I am." Arloa stomped her foot on the ground. "Don't you dare compare me to them. I have worked for longer than you have been alive to not be like them. You don't know what I have given up to separate myself from my name."

"But you haven't done it, have you? You're still one of them. You still benefit from it all. You're still sitting here in your office while the rest of us out there die. Repeatedly."

"It's the only way I know how to help!"

Jerry glared. "Don't talk to me about helping. You continue to live in your lofty protected homes and leave the rest of us to tear each other apart—literally."

"That's not fair. I can't be infected."

"And why is that, Arloa? Why is it that this virus has rampaged through the poor and middle class, but those of you with money and status sit here completely unaffected."

"We're not unaffected." Arloa's tone softened. "But I had wondered the same thing. I wanted to know about that, too, especially when after I saw you last, nothing happened. I should have…I should have been infected right along with you, if you were."

"But you weren't." Jerry was still very near losing every ounce of self-control she had left.

"I wasn't. And I wanted to know why, so I researched it."

"And what did you find out?" Jerry clenched her jaw tightly. "What is the magic behind being immune?"

"It's in my blood."

"What is?"

"My immunity, and Jer, it was there before the virus existed."

"How can you know that?"

"I've had the healers look. I've had scientists analyze my blood. I've had them analyze others' blood. All of us here—" Arloa spread her arms out to indicate the center of Raegina "—we're immune, at least most of us. Some have gotten the virus, but they were sick with something else first, something that compromised them usually from birth."

"What are you saying?"

"I'm saying I don't know where this virus came from, but I do know that for some reason we're all immune. I have my suspicions on why but nothing I've been able to confirm."

Jerry felt as though she'd been knocked in the chest with something. The look in Arloa's face didn't comfort her any. "What suspicions?"

"Several. Until I know more, I don't see any point in sharing my wild theories."

"That's not you talking."

"No, it's a year of being shut down and told to be quiet like a good little woman."

Jerry's lips curled upward. "Since when have you been a good little woman?"

Arloa echoed a smile. "Since you left, it seems."

They fell into a silence, the push and pull over what they needed to say and share too much, and Jerry wasn't sure where to go from there. Arloa had shared far more about the past year than she had, although Jerry had a lot more reasons to hold back. If anyone found out what she really did with *Yarrow* and *Calluna* she would be thrown into the darkest recesses of Joab or walking the plank and hoping the poisoned sea would kill her.

"Where did you go?" Arloa whispered, sliding in even closer.

"I've been here all this time. I mean, I've gone places, done things, but mostly I've been in the harbor working my loads for Morty and trying to find vestigen in order to survive."

"How did you manage that first time?"

"Well, as soon as I found vestigen, we overdosed it. Nearly died from that. Then nearly died from the crash. I think Azar was the first to kill me."

Arloa sucked in a breath, ghosting her fingers along Jerry's cheek to her lips. "Is that where the scars are from?"

"Some of them. Others are from battles we've had."

"Battles?" Arloa's gaze perked up at that bit of information.

"I'm not…I may have slid back into some old habits."

"Old as in Miriam."

"Yes."

Arloa nodded, pulling her lower lip between her teeth. "What were you doing there the night I saw you?"

Jerry narrowed her gaze. Had she not seen it? Or was she just being cruel in making Jerry confess everything? Turning her cheek into Arloa's palm, Jerry reveled in the sweet touch. Arloa was so soft with her, so loving and kind when she didn't have to be, when she shouldn't be.

"I was getting vestigen."

"That's not what I'm asking." Arloa was so close, their skirts rustling together as she listed into Jerry even more. "I want to know what you and Miriam were doing."

Jerry closed her eyes, shame filling her chest. She didn't want to have to say it. She hated that she'd done it to begin with, but before Arloa, it had been a normal payment between the two of them. Gathering her courage, Jerry dashed her tongue across her lips. She opened her eyes, staring right down into Arloa's. "I was paying her for my supply."

"That's all it was?"

"Yes. That's all it's ever been. Miriam…my mother used to work for her, when I was younger. Miriam was new to Raegina, and she gained her power by whores. My mother worked for her, and Miriam kept me out of trouble while my mom had jobs. When she could, anyway."

"She took care of you," Arloa supplemented.

"Yeah, sometimes. And when I got older, I took care of her."

"Oh." Arloa breathed heavily, her chest rising and falling, but she hadn't moved her hand from Jerry's cheek. She hadn't stepped back or looked offended by Jerry's confession. "So the other night—"

"I didn't have enough credits for the pouch."

"I understand."

"Do you?"

Arloa nodded, but she didn't say anything as they stood quietly together, staring at each other. Eventually, Arloa dropped her hand, trailing it down Jerry's arm to her fingers, twining them together. As much as Jerry wanted to tell her to stop, that she didn't have consent to touch her, she remained silent. Because, fuck, she wanted Arloa's skin against hers.

"I needed the vestigen."

"I know you did." Arloa's lips curled ever so slightly. "That's why I gave you what I purchased."

"Thank you for that."

"Anything for you." The words were said so quietly that Jerry wasn't sure she'd even heard them, and she didn't dare ask Arloa to repeat herself. She gave in and held on to the fact that it must have been what Arloa said—and meant, because if there was one thing she had learned about Arloa in the short time they'd known each other, it was she never said anything she didn't mean.

"What do you know about this stash of vestigen in Potelia?"

"Not much." Arloa sighed. "I was hoping you might know more, but it seems you didn't know anything."

Jerry shook her head. "You telling me was the first I'd heard of it."

Arloa moved away, gliding over to her desk to sit in the chair. Jerry remained where she was, leaning against one of the floor-to-ceiling bookshelves, glad for the break in intense conversation.

"I've heard rumors for months now about a special store they have, that any infected who is a member of their city is permitted to receive treatment."

"Does that mean they are manufacturing it?"

"I don't know. I'm hoping they are, because I want to see what their facility looks like, and potentially learn from them. I've been trying to lobby here, to allow the legalization of vestigen and create factories that will produce it, but I'm hitting roadblocks every direction I turn."

"They know you're partial to us, then."

"Us?" Arloa raised her gaze, confusion flashing across her eyes.

"Unmentionables. Unsightly creatures."

"You're not...Jer, you can't honestly believe you're unmentionable."

"I am. If anyone were to suspect I was infected, I would immediately be put to death. What do you think they do with those they send to Joab? Most of us are murdered. If I remained out of the line of sight of the aristocrats, then all was well. But now they won't even talk about us."

"They have been talking about you a great sum."

"What do you mean?"

"Well, they were not anticipating the economic problems that would arise from this, not like I was."

Jerry straightened her back and walked over to Arloa, joy building in her body. "Are they floundering?"

"Yes. I wonder if Potelia is not giving vestigen as freely as the rumor is, but is hoarding it for those necessary to keep the city afloat."

Pressing her lips together tightly, Jerry could see it. The government systems in each of the countries worked separately, but they were all built on the same foundation of laws. "That could be true."

"Either way, I want to confirm this rumor, and then I want you to go there and do what you do."

Jerry's stomach twisted. She'd always wanted to leave that part of her life behind her, but since she was living into it, and it was to Arloa's advantage, she would agree. She needed the vestigen anyway. "I need confirmation before I'll go."

"I'll get it. Someway, somehow, I'll find you some."

"Good." Jerry moved, sitting against the desk much as Arloa had earlier in their conversation. At this vantage point, however, she could see right down Arloa's cleavage, and she was reticent to look elsewhere.

"You'll need to take a small vessel, earn trust, find a way to get into the factory."

"I can figure out a plan, Arloa." Jerry flicked her gaze to those steel-blue eyes, acceptance settling into the pit of her stomach. She'd gone searching for vestigen with less information than this, so she didn't know why she was hesitating so much.

"Right, you can. Sorry."

Jerry smirked, dropping her gaze on purpose this time. She cocked her head at Arloa, her lips curling upward into a toothy confident grin. "While you might not appreciate me in these clothes, I certainly do appreciate a woman who has all her assets in the right place."

Arloa cocked her head to the side, slowly standing up and stepping into the space between Jerry's legs. "You wanted nothing to do with me the other day."

Jerry drew in a sharp breath. "Don't you understand what this virus is? It removes inhibitions."

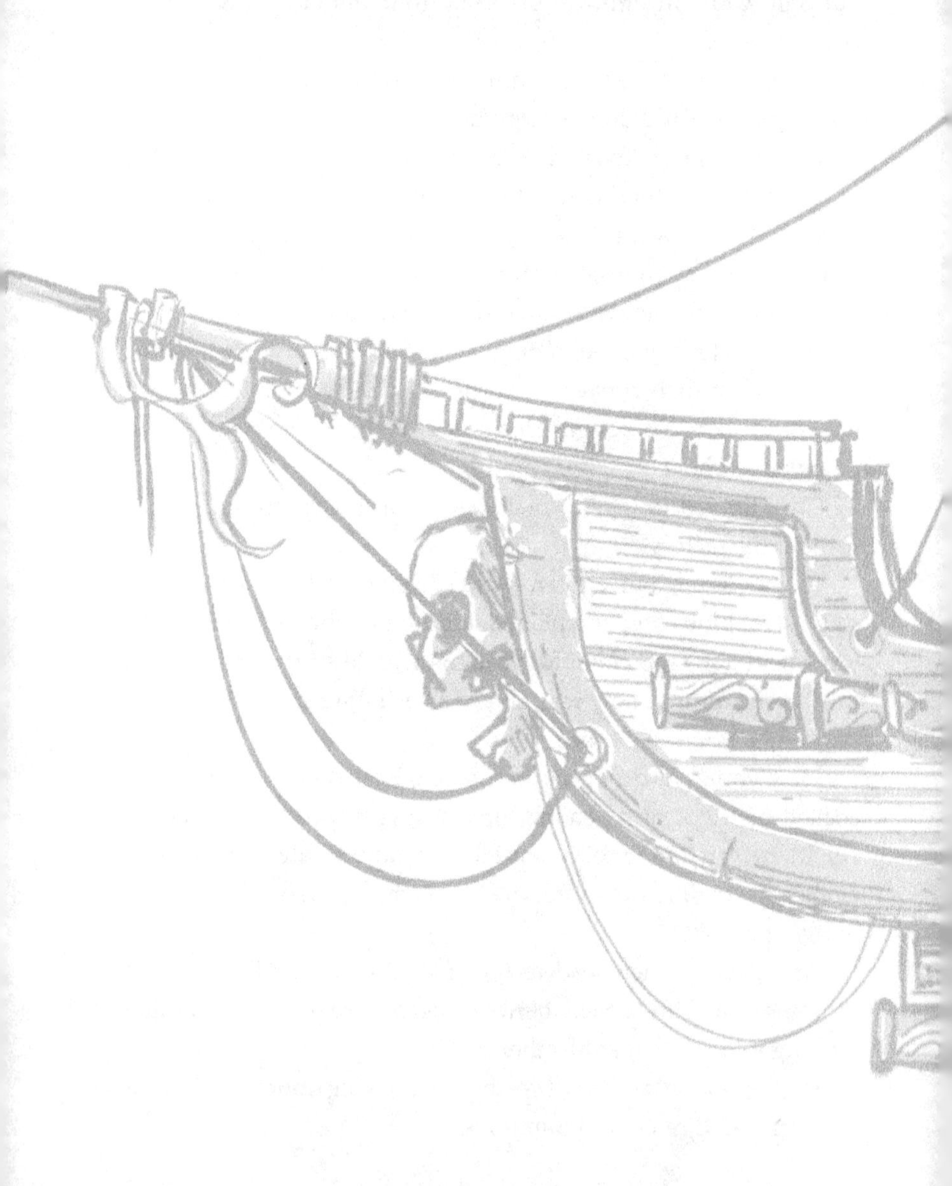

CHAPTER 12

elieve me that I understand," Arloa whispered right into Jerry's ear. "And trust me that I know you must be a woman with an amazing amount of control, considering the restraint you've shown in the last few days."

"How would you know it's been so trying?" Jerry closed her eyes, feeling Arloa so close to her, their skin barely brushing, the movement of her breath against Jerry's cheek and neck. She wanted to turn in to her so badly, wanted to move and take Arloa's lips, be consumed by her again.

"Because I've seen the way you look at me, and it's no different than it was a year ago."

Jerry clenched her jaw, Arloa's voice wrapping around her like a snake with its prey. They stayed in silence, the tension building in Jerry's chest as she waited for the moment when she couldn't hold out any longer.

"Jer, are you with me?"

"Yes," Jerry whispered, her eyes still clenched tightly. She would forever be with Arloa, as long as she could be. Somewhere in the last year, she had come to accept that, come to realize that was her fate. This woman had stolen her heart without Jerry really even knowing she'd taken it.

"Will you go to Potelia for me?"

Jerry clenched her eyes tightly, resting her cheek on Arloa's shoulder. She had to find her center again, allow her brain to move and think without Arloa's presence being such a hindering factor in it. She knew she would go. Even if she hadn't wanted more information to take such a long trip, she would go. The pull of a large stash of vestigen that would last them months if not years was far too strong for her to ignore. It was the last two words of Arloa's question that were tripping her up. She'd barely just found her again, yet Arloa was asking her to leave for who knew how long.

"Yes," Jerry answered firmly. "I'll go."

"Good." Arloa tilted her face into Jerry's neck, breathing in her scent. They were at a standstill, neither moving, neither saying anything, neither willing to take that one last step until Arloa murmured, "I want to touch you."

"Fuck, do it already." Jerry whined. She gripped Arloa's arm and held on tightly as if her body could already feel Arloa's fingers inside her, taste her once again on her tongue.

Arloa pulled away slightly, moving so their lips brushed but barely touched. "Maybe you have more inhibitions than I do."

"Doubt it," Jerry mumbled. "Just more stubbornness."

Opening her eyes, Jerry dug her hands into Arloa's curly mass of hair. She'd wanted to do that ever since she'd seen her again, take control of the kiss, extend it, keep it, never move away from her. She pressed forward, their mouths touching as they exchanged breath. Knowing Arloa couldn't be infected, knowing that she wouldn't be the death of one more person, Jerry let herself loose. She couldn't stop.

She swooped her tongue into Arloa's mouth, throwing everything she had held back into the kiss. She held Arloa's face to hers, not letting up at all. She couldn't. She needed Arloa to understand what they had been missing out on for the last year. Everything in that moment was full of passion, it was full of wasted emotion, of pain and hunger, and desire for comfort and peace.

They hadn't known each other long before, but Jerry had been able to find that home in this petite woman, in someone she never expected to meet at a bar down off the docks, in someone who shouldn't have even been there. Nipping at Arloa's lip, Jerry dove back in, unable to resist the call that Arloa was for her.

Arloa skimmed a hand down Jerry's chest, over her breasts and down to her waist. She curled her arms around her, holding on as their mouths stayed locked together. Jerry had no idea how far Arloa would take it being in her office in the middle of the government house, but Jerry wouldn't be able to resist if Arloa let her. She wanted it. She'd wanted it the day before, but she had held back, unsure if she really could trust the woman. But all her fears had been unfounded. Arloa hadn't changed. She'd been there for the unsightly creatures of Raegina from the first moment they'd met. She might be a Kauket in name, but she would never be one of *them*.

Arloa pulled away, ever so slightly, dragging in a deep breath as she pressed their foreheads together. "Normally I would never do this."

"Do what?" Jerry's heart raced, her cheeks flushed as she was so caught up in the moment, and she knew she would give in to anything Arloa asked her. It wasn't just lust at that point, it was because she wanted to give Arloa the world.

"Do you know the only distinct advantage to you wearing this?"

Arloa was already pulling at Jerry's skirts, lifting them up until she could reach the hemline of her undergarments, the white fabric stark and stiff against her skin. Jerry usually hated to wear them because they made her itch, but since she'd been trying to be a lady, she'd done everything possible to pass as one.

"That's surprising," Arloa commented as she reached the ties right at the top of Jerry's mound.

"What is?"

"Didn't fancy you one for these."

Jerry groaned as she moved her hips, spread her legs, and allowed Arloa's thin fingers to push under the fabric. Unsure of what came over her, Jerry pulled up Arloa's skirts, sliding her hands against her soft, supple flesh. She mimicked everything Arloa did to her, tugging at the short hairs between her legs, sliding one finger through her slit, teasing the small bundle of nerves that had fast become her favorite way to get a reaction.

Arloa keened, leaning into Jerry's form as they stood so close together. If anyone came in, they wouldn't even see what was happening. Everything was so subtle. Not that two women together was such a crime, but fucking in the undersecretary's office in the middle of the government house surely had to be a crime somewhere. One Jerry was willing to commit, repeatedly.

Sliding one finger inside Arloa as Arloa moved into her, Jerry groaned as warmth surrounded her. Arloa rocked her hips, and Jerry stayed still, unable to move as she sat propped against the desk. Arloa nipped Jerry's earlobe, pulling it sharply.

"You know by now not to take it easy."

"Of course," Jerry answered, jerking her wrist hard and getting a responsive squeak from Arloa. She loved that sound. She'd missed it, dreamed of it, wished she could hear it in person once again, and here she was, fucking her in the middle of the damn office. "I want to taste you."

"Not this time." Arloa breathed heavily. "There's not enough time."

"I want all night with you. Fuck, I want all day with you."

Arloa moaned, the sound reverberating around the tiny room. Heat pooled between Jerry's legs at the thought of it. She wished she'd worn her gloves, had them on her so she could fuck Arloa with them, keep her scent on them for weeks to come. Instead, she was left only with her fingers, her dull-cut nails, and her lips as she kissed Arloa's sweet neck.

"Next time," Arloa whispered. "Next time."

Jerry wasn't sure they would have a next time, but at least

this time, they would both get some satisfaction from it. However, she wasn't sure if she would ever be fully sated when fucking involved Arloa. She increased her pace, swishing her thumb back and forth, ramming a second finger in to match her first. Arloa did the same. The same rhythm. The same pattern. The same amount of fucking as each of them worked higher into their orgasm, higher into their release.

Arloa keened, her voice driving right into Jerry's soul. She had longed for that tone, for that lust to be present in her life again, and now might be her one and only chance. She would never give this up. She would never change the decisions she had made if only it brought her here again.

Jerry kissed her. Hard. She tangled their tongues as Arloa crested through her orgasm, falling into Jerry's arms as she attempted to keep her hand under control, to keep the pattern and the pleasure rolling through Jerry's body, but she didn't even care. She had made Arloa come. She could smell her on her fingers, she could taste her on the tip of her tongue, that sweet flavor that had haunted her.

"Arloa," Jerry whispered. "My sweet Arloa."

Arloa hummed, pressing her forehead into Jerry's neck. "Did you come?"

"Yes," Jerry easily lied. She didn't care if she did or didn't. All she wanted was Arloa in her arms for as long as possible. She didn't want to let up. As Arloa pressed her face into Jerry's shoulder, Jerry wrapped her arms around her back, smoothing out her hair. On a whim, she snagged the knife on the desk and cut a small lock, sliding it into the sleeve of her jacket as Arloa straightened up. "When can I see you again?"

"Whenever you want."

"Where?"

Arloa hummed. "I suppose we need to find a place, somewhere we won't cause such a disturbance."

"The bar?"

"Miriam's."

"No," Jerry whispered. "I won't meet you there again."

"Then come to my apartment."

Pressing her lips together hard, Jerry shook her head. "It's not so easy to get to your apartment without you. It's hard to get into the center of town not being one of you."

"Then the bar. We'll meet there. Night after tomorrow. I'll see what I can find on Potelia."

"Please, don't leave me there."

Arloa pulled away, their gazes locked. She shook her head and leaned in to press their lips together. "I would never leave you. You're the one who left me."

Jerry couldn't deny it. She'd known it the moment she had done it, and yet, she had done it to protect Arloa from what she could. But if Arloa really was immune, that changed everything, didn't it? Jerry kissed her, hard and deep. She lingered for as long as she could before pulling away.

"I'll see you in two days' time." Standing up, Jerry grabbed her parasol and held it tightly in her hands. In here, this tiny office, she felt nothing like the woman she was pretending to be. She wasn't the confident aristocrat she was supposed to be. Instead, she was completely lost, as if her world was slightly off axis and spinning her into the wild unknown.

Without saying another word, Jerry left Arloa's office, shutting the door behind her. She walked through the halls, having memorized them on her way in, and right to the front doors. She pulled out her parasol, shading her face from the sun as she walked through Raegina's town square and away from the center of town.

Each step she took felt heavier. Each meter she walked away from Arloa, she had to remind herself that they would see each other again, that she would gaze into those steel-blue eyes one more time. She had to, because if she didn't, she feared where she might end up, that she might not see the sun of another day. Pushing Arloa away the first time had been hard enough, but leaving her this time, when they had all but admitted their obsession with each other, was too much.

As she reached the docks, Jerry stopped by the ocean and stared out at it. This time, she didn't feel as though she wanted to jump over the edge and drown in her sorrows, in the pit of poison that would eat her alive for the rest of her days, immortal as she was unless killed the right way. She didn't want to leave Penum, not with Arloa potentially back in her life, and if anything of what had just happened meant that, she would risk staying alive just for it.

Jerry brushed her hand over her hair, the soft curls Yafe had done up to make her look feminine, to make her pass as a woman of class and status. She snorted. Of course Arloa would see right through her, though she hadn't done it to hide from her. She'd done it to hide from the world, something she was a master at.

The waves reached the pier, brushing against the dock that wouldn't disintegrate under its touch for ages to come. Jerry sighed heavily as she leaned over the railing and stared down at the sea-green color. What was she getting herself into? What had she agreed to do for Arloa? Yes, she would get to keep the majority of the vestigen for her crews, but what consequences were there for working with a woman who worked for the government?

She was still sure she would do it, but doubts crept into her mind, the fear that she was making a mistake, something that would risk her life and the lives of her crew for years to come— not just in the short term. She would have to allow each of them to make the decision for themselves, to decide whether her word was enough to warrant that they could possibly risk their lives for a flimsy rumor.

Jerry settled the parasol against her shoulder, shielding herself from the sun. Her crotch ached, thoroughly used in a way it hadn't been in months. The sweet, tender moment of fucking they had shared in her office was more than Jerry had ever hoped to experience again.

She would treasure that feeling for days and months to come, especially if they didn't get another chance to be together, ever. Drawing in a deep breath, Jerry stared down the line of vessels, finding *Yarrow* in the midst of them. Her first ship was small, barely able to hold its own, but she moved quickly, and she could maneuver sharply. It was the perfect ship for her. And it was exactly the ship she'd need to go to Potelia.

She would need Azar. If he backed out, she wasn't sure she'd be able to manage without him. He was her engineer first and foremost, and while she knew a lot about ships and how to fix them, she would need him for this. If he said no, she might have to tell Arloa to find someone else.

Ideas and plans swirled through Jerry's mind, including Arloa's suggestion, but Jerry wasn't sold on it. She needed to learn more about Potelia. She needed to find Whitney, see if there was anything she could share. She'd never met someone who had been there before. Jerry had never been. They had always skirted around the harbor town when she was a kid growing up, mostly because the laws weren't favorable to pirates.

It was easier to go elsewhere than try to fight them. But Jerry supposed there was some kind of underground there—what country didn't have an underground crime syndicate? Surely Potelia had one, and in that case, she needed to find out who was in charge and how she could connect with them, which meant she would have to see Miriam again.

Jerry stared down at *Yarrow*. She likely didn't have much more time before Yafe would start worrying about whether or not she would return and what information she had come back with, which wasn't much more than what she left with. Still, at least she knew she could trust Arloa, at least for this. It seemed as though they were on the same track—finding a treatment.

She hoped they could find a cure. If Arloa was immune, perhaps someone could find a cure, using her blood as the base.

Jerry had a feeling Arloa was already working on that, that somewhere she was hiring people who were smart enough to recreate the immunity she had. Still, that didn't leave much hope for Jerry or the people she ran into daily who were infected. Most of them were, though the authorities hadn't found them yet since they kept it hidden. That, and most of them were necessary to keep the city going. Whether they wanted to admit that or not.

Jerry glanced around the dock, finding no one within sight. She stepped away from the railing and faced north, toward the entrance for the dock to *Yarrow*. A year ago she never would have imagined her life turning this direction. Even a week ago she wouldn't have. She'd been dead set on just surviving, but now—now she had hope that there might be more, that if she could find enough vestigen to last her awhile that her life wouldn't be all about the next score she could get.

With a lighter step, she moved onto the pier and walked toward her home—a place she hadn't anticipated needing or being quite so isolated. Still with Yafe and Azar she had made it a home, and now with the tip from Arloa, perhaps she could learn to live again. Perhaps she could learn to love again.

Not sure which direction she wanted to go, but knowing she had to make plans, Jerry walked all the way to *Yarrow*. She pressed her hand against the sensor, letting herself inside. First things first. She had to get out of the awful outfit she'd been wearing for hours too long, and then she had to find Yafe and Azar. They had to make plans. She had to know if they were going to join in on this little adventure or not, and she had to know if she was going to take the risk to find out if Arloa was telling her the truth. With soreness between her legs, and sweat under her pits, Jerry went to her cabin ready to lay all her cards on the table and see where her path might take her next.

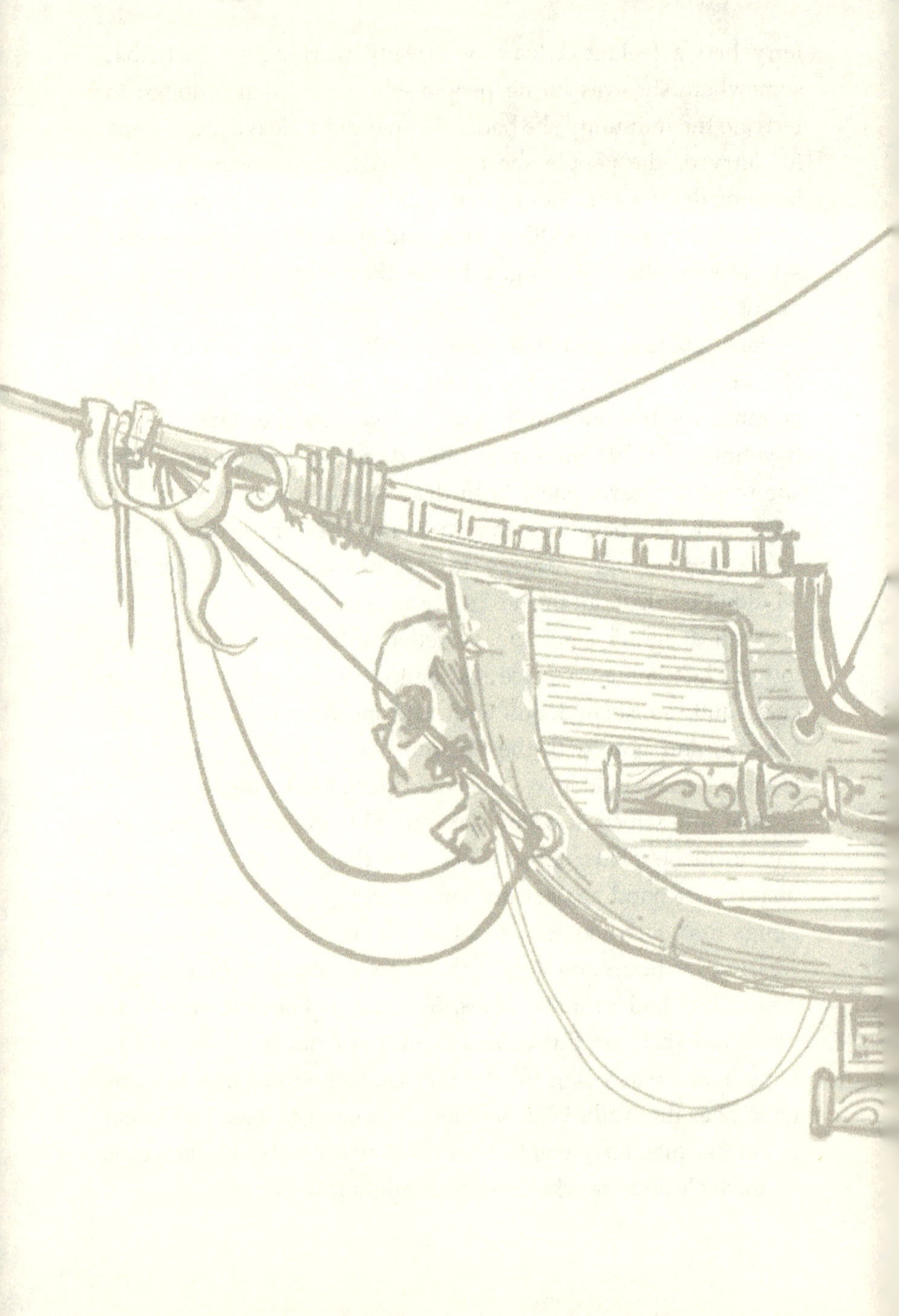

CHAPTER 13

It took Jerry longer than it should have to find Whitney, but the girl literally had no blemish on her record, and she was a minor. The government kept their records pretty tight. Jerry hadn't realized she was so young because she'd looked much older than that on the vessel.

Grabbing her brown leather jacket, Jerry threw it on and pressed her hat onto her head. They had the rest of the day before they needed to leave for Beren Island again for their regular haul, which meant time was limited for planning. And she wanted Ursula in on that conversation no matter what.

The house was one for orphans, a small building tucked away just on the inner circle of the city. It must have been established centuries ago for it to have such a location of esteem when its mission wasn't considered that by the rich. Jerry loitered outside, watching the comings and goings through the entrance, but there weren't very many people. A few deliveries here and there, but the rest of the time, the doors and windows were sealed shut.

She stalked around the side of the house, finding the stone wall that guarded the back garden. As she got into the alley, Jerry stood on a wooden barrel and small crate so she could see over it. The garden was in ruins. Someone hadn't been able to keep up through the economic downturn, not that Jerry was surprised.

Just as she was about to climb over and drop onto the other side, a movement out of the corner of her eye caught her attention. There, in the window three floors up, sat Whitney, her beautiful sunshine hair a radiant contrast to the dark, cloudy skies. Jerry cocked her head as she stared up into those baby blue eyes. She couldn't fathom why she thought Whitney looked like Arloa. They had similar coloring but nothing else, and from this angle, she could see how young Whitney truly was.

They stared at each other for what felt like minutes. Jerry couldn't decide if she was going to be turned in or if Whitney was studying her, curious as to what the fuck she would be doing there. Eventually, Jerry dipped her head and pulled herself onto the edge of the wall to sit. When she raised her chin up to check the window, Whitney was gone.

Cursing, Jerry dropped to the ground below, a puff of dirt filling the air by her boots in her wake. She had to figure out how to get to Whitney's room, because that girl likely had far more information than Jerry had about Potelia. She seemed gregarious enough to observe everything possible.

Jerry walked to the back door, and just as she was about to grab the brass handle, it clicked and opened. Her heart thudded, and she knew she was about to be caught. Instead of some old mistress' lined face, though, Whitney's sweet, full, and vibrant cheeks greeted her.

"Do you stalk all your victims?" Whitney's face hardened.

"No, actually. But I had some follow up questions to ask you." Jerry resisted the urge to shift under that confident and walled gaze.

Whitney snorted lightly. "Like were you kind enough when you shot our captain?"

"No." Jerry pressed her lips together hard.

"Or soft enough when you tied my hands and wrists."

Clenching her jaw, Jerry acquiesced. She had been hard on

them, though it wasn't out of her norm, at least not in the past year. She had to be in order to survive, to be the captain of a pirate ship. "No. I want to know about Potelia."

Whitney sighed, came outside, and shut the door behind her. "I haven't been in the garden for years."

"Doesn't look like much to see," Jerry commented wryly.

"It used to be." Whitney leaned against the brick wall of the house, her hands behind her as if she expected Jerry wouldn't hurt her or kidnap her again. "It hasn't been for years."

"When?"

"Before the virus." Whitney looked Jerry up and down. "You don't look like a woman."

"I'm not, most days." Jerry clenched her jaw. She wasn't there for small talk, and certainly not to talk about societal and cultural norms.

"You intrigue me."

"I could kill you in an instant if I wanted."

"I'm sure you could." Whitney locked their eyes together. "But I don't think you want to, or that you will."

"You assume correct. I'm here to talk about Potelia, though, not whether I might kill you."

"I've only been there once."

Jerry shifted her stance, sliding to raise an arm above Whitney's head as she leaned in. She took over the space, but Whitney didn't seem phased by it. Then again, if she was an orphan for many years of her young life, Jerry supposed that she was used to not having space. Still, Jerry didn't touch her. She'd done that once before when the circumstances called for it, but now she wouldn't. The circumstances were different, and she wouldn't pull this information from a sweet girl when she didn't have to.

Whitney raised her chin, leaning her head against the wall so she could look Jerry in the eye. "When did you know?"

"Know what?"

"That you liked women?"

Air rushed from Jerry's lips, and she closed her eyes. "If I answer you, will you tell me about Potelia?"

"Yes."

Nodding slightly, Jerry bit her lip. "Will you permit me to touch you? Your face, I mean, nowhere else."

"Yes." Whitney looked up at her with innocent eyes.

Hesitating only another moment, Jerry brushed her leather clad fingers over Whitney's cheek and down her neck, but she stopped short of brushing fingers against her chest.

"I saw you staring at me when we were on that ship."

"You reminded me of someone."

"A woman."

"One so far above my status that we'll never be together." Jerry's mind flashed to the office, to the promise of meeting again, but she had to turn it off. They would see each other again, but she wasn't sure fucking would happen. "If you're questioning, it's likely you feel this way, but to answer your query, I always knew. I didn't have a moment of clarity that others have. I just always knew."

Whitney hummed. "I think I've always known, but seeing you—"

"Made you realize you have a type."

Whitney's lips curled upward. "I suppose, or perhaps I just like pirates."

"We're not all fun and games."

"I assume you almost never are."

Jerry trailed her fingers back up Whitney's chin, jerking her so they faced each other, staring into each other's eyes. "Do you really want to know?"

"Know what?" Whitney's chest rose and fell sharply.

"How old are you?"

"Seventeen."

"Legal," Jerry commented before she moved in, pressing their mouths together. It took Whitney a moment before she reacted, which Jerry suspected would happen. She held firm, not pushing for more but not relenting either. Eventually, Whitney reached a hand up, sliding it under Jerry's braid and into her hair, tugging sharply.

Taking that as her sign, Jerry moved in more, sliding her tongue against Whitney's lips to deepen the kiss. She stayed pressed against her until Whitney moved in closer, then Jerry pulled away, her mind swirling with thoughts of Arloa.

"Does that answer your question?"

"Yes, thank you." Whitney's cheeks were bright red, but it wasn't embarrassment Jerry read in her expression. It was unadulterated lust.

Shifting back ever so slightly, Jerry maintained the close confines she'd found, hoping it would lend itself to her getting more information. "What were you doing in Potelia?"

"Treatment for a disease I've had since I was a child. My mother died of it when I was barely two. My father took his life after that."

Jerry traced a finger down Whitney's cheek. "How long were you there?"

"Three weeks."

"Tell me about it."

Whitney's lips parted. "I spent most of my time at the hospital, but I was allowed to go into the city square occasionally."

"And is it like here? In Raegina?"

"No. It's brighter." Whitney's lips curled upward in a smile. "It's so much more peaceful there. I wish I could go back."

"Did you meet anyone with connections?"

"The dockmaster. He helped me get from the transport vessel to the hospital and back. He was so sweet. He brought me little trinkets during my stay."

Jerry moved in closer, their mouths nearly touching, but unless Whitney initiated, Jerry wouldn't do that again. "Do you think he thought he might get more from you?"

Whitney's lips parted in surprise. "I...I never thought about it, honestly. I suppose he could have."

"If you wanted a second reason to realize you like women, there's one right there for you. Not even noticing the man."

"I suppose." Whitney closed her eyes. "His name is Hobie."

"I'll remember him."

"He was sweet to me. Don't do anything to hurt him. Please."

"What makes you think I would hurt him?" Jerry raised an eyebrow, moving so she could see Whitney's full face.

"You're a pirate." She said it as though it were a curse or some secret no one else knew.

Grinning, Jerry canted her head to the side. "I am. It'll do you good to remember that."

"There was one other person, a healer. She tried…she tried to heal me but couldn't. I don't know, no one has ever been able to heal this."

Jerry kept their eyes locked. "Because it's naturally forming."

"I suppose. I don't pretend to understand much."

"Don't they send you to grammar school or primary at the least?"

"No, everything we're taught is taught here."

"Some refuge." Jerry scrunched her nose.

Whitney touched Jerry's lips, her soft fingers flitting to her mouth, then her sharp jawline. "I plan on leaving as soon as I can."

"You're legal now. Why not do it today?"

"I don't have anywhere to go."

The words were on the tip of her tongue, but Jerry swallowed them back. She wouldn't be able to support another person, especially an uneducated person, who didn't have hard hands and strong muscles. "I think you'll make it."

Pushing off the wall, Jerry took a step back and put her hands out. "Anything else to share about Potelia?"

"They're quite medically advanced."

"I assumed as much." Jerry bowed slightly. "Until I need more information."

Spinning on her toes, Jerry walked to the wall and climbed

up it, using far more strength this way than she had when she went over in the first place. As she landed on the other side, she shook out her jacket and gallivanted back toward *Yarrow*. She had a meeting of the minds to get to.

They were all crowded into the small galley *Yarrow* boasted. Jerry's office was bigger, but it wasn't as relaxed an environment, and she wanted them to be able to toss ideas back and forth as much as they could. She needed an open conversation for this. She would have preferred alcohol to loosen their tongues and brains, but Jerry didn't want to share her moonshine with the rest of them. That was something she would keep for herself when it was dark and lonely.

"Vivian," Jerry started. "You said you had heard a rumor about a stash of vestigen in Potelia?"

"Yeah." Vivian's eyes widened. "But I don't know much more than that."

"My sources tell me Potelia is medically advanced." Vivian shook her head as if she didn't know. Jerry clenched her jaw. Maybe she shouldn't have brought her to this meeting of minds. "What do you know?"

"That's it. My ex-boyfriend wanted to go there because he said they hand it out to anyone who needs it."

"I can confirm they don't," Jerry added, pointing at Vivian.

Yafe nodded. "I can as well. That is one thing I don't think they can keep under wraps from the rest of Penum."

"Agreed," Ursula answered.

Jerry shifted her gaze from Vivian to Azar. "You're educated."

His brow drew together. "That doesn't mean anything. I've never been to Potelia."

"No, but you took history, yes? For your certificate?"

"History of engineering, yes. Not political history." Azar scoffed and crossed his arms.

"I've been doing as much research as I can," Yafe interjected. "It seems Potelia has always led the world in education and in science. It's rare to find an uneducated citizen there. Everyone is given access to primary and grammar school, and beyond. Whatever they want for free."

"Sounds idyllic," Jerry muttered.

No one said anything for a good five seconds. Then Ursula pressed her palm on the small wooden table they were all crowded around. "What's going on, Jerry?"

"Well, we're going to Potelia. *Yarrow*, anyway, and I need you to take our regular runs to Beren Island."

Ursula wrinkled her nose. "Do I have to?"

"Yes." Jerry looked over each of them. Azar and Yafe were firm in her decision, but she knew they would be. They always supported her crazy ideas. Ursula would whine because she had to do something she didn't want to. Vivian didn't seem phased by the conversation. Then again, she'd known about this stash for a while it seemed. Sacha, however, chewed her nail in the corner. "Sacha."

"What?"

"Are you in for this or not?"

She shrugged.

Jerry resisted the urge to growl. "I need an actual answer. You're free to move over to *Calluna* while we're gone, or just leave."

Jerry almost hoped it was the latter. Keeping her mouth shut as she waited for an answer, Jerry eyed Sacha as silence reverberated around them.

"Fine, I'll come."

"Great," Jerry muttered. "Here's what I think we do. We go

to Potelia under the guise of escaping Raegina. The difference in communities is known, so I don't think there will be much question as to why we're leaving here."

"You'll need to get transfer papers," Ursula added. "If you want to make this look legal."

"I think I can manage that easily enough."

"Actual transfer papers?"

Jerry rolled her eyes. "No. Of course not."

Azar raised an eyebrow at them, leaning back in the chair. "I can get some to work as an engineer there. I have my certification, and it'll be another in."

"Let's try to get you a job working in a plant, a medical facility where they make drugs. I want to know what they're making and how much. Maybe we can even bring something else home with us."

Azar nodded his agreement. Yafe stepped in next. "What will I do?"

Jerry sighed. "Mostly I need you and Sacha to make sure we don't have any loose ends, and we need to find some legal work to make it look like we're not up to anything. You two are in charge of keeping up the charade."

"Makes sense. We can work on finding jobs now if you want."

"Yes, please." Jerry looked each of them over. "This might be a wild chase, but I want to go there and find out. If we can get a large store of vestigen—"

"We could survive for years," Yafe finished for her.

"We could think about finding a cure instead of a stopgap." Jerry made eye contact with Ursula. They had talked about living once, when they were in Joab, hidden under the bed when one of the guards had come by to make rounds and they refused to be discovered that time. They had spoken of dreams and hopes, living instead of just getting through the next hour. "This could be exactly what we all want."

"There isn't much to live for, no reason for a cure," Sacha

interjected. "What's the point? So we can go back to being unseen instead of unmentioned?"

Jerry shrugged. She realized it was a large jump from one to the other. It wasn't as though her life was nice beforehand, but at least she'd had prospects, at least she'd had dreams. Since the virus, since she'd killed Matty and been thrown into the deep of this mess, she hadn't once thought more than a day or two ahead. It felt good to maybe wonder if in a year they would all still be there.

They spent the next two hours working out details. Yafe filled Ursula in on the exact process they used for transporting the salt, the ways to get it in the smallest number of places, and then Jerry sent a message to Morty, explaining Ursula would be taking over their runs for the time being. Azar and Yafe started researching open jobs in Potelia, but they found the positions were not as readily available as they were in Raegina. Something in the Omar Region they hadn't noticed in the past year when they'd been distracted by survival.

Potelia wasn't exactly thriving, but it wasn't falling apart like the rest of Penum. Jerry wished she'd been able to travel a little more, see Potelia firsthand instead of having to rely on a woman who was barely an adult to tell her what it was like. She reached out to another one of her contacts to get the transfer papers made up for her, and she prayed Morty wouldn't get wind of her *searching* for another job. That could ruin their relationship faster than she could blink, which would put her out of both jobs.

As they went their separate ways, Jerry climbed to the wheelhouse and out onto the deck. She grabbed her personal device and leaned against the rail, closing her eyes. Everything in her life had become such a mess, and she had zero purpose left for her to do anything. Yet once again, Arloa had given that to her. It may have come from desperation on both their parts, but Jerry wouldn't deny it.

She had a purpose. She had a direction. She had the beginning of a plan that would hopefully lead her to finding peace.

She snorted at that thought and whipped her eyes open to stare at the darkening sky and Raegina. *Calluna* had left already for Beren Island, and *Yarrow* was due to leave in the morning.

Bringing the cold glass bottle to her lips, Jerry took a long swig of the moonshine she'd stashed for the last year, grimacing as it burned down her throat and into her belly. It went to her head, making her dizzy as she closed her eyes again. Why had she kissed Whitney? It made no sense except she wanted to not be tied down, she wanted the danger, to live her own life, and in some ways, she'd been so fucking tied to Arloa in the last year that she couldn't escape her. Even now, she was walking right into Arloa's hands, doing her bidding and nothing else.

Jerry picked up her personal device and found Arloa's contact. She'd read every message Arloa had sent, and she'd never replied to any of them. Pursing her lips, Jerry stared at the sleek bronze metal in her hand when it buzzed, telling her she had a message.

Reading the name flashing across the screen, Jerry cursed and opened it. "Talk to me."

She sent the only reply she could think of. "No. We leave at dawn."

Tossing her device across the deck and watching until it slid to a stop, Jerry raised her chin to the sky. She was in over her head, and she was drowning in Arloa, and for some fucking reason, it was exactly where she wanted to be.

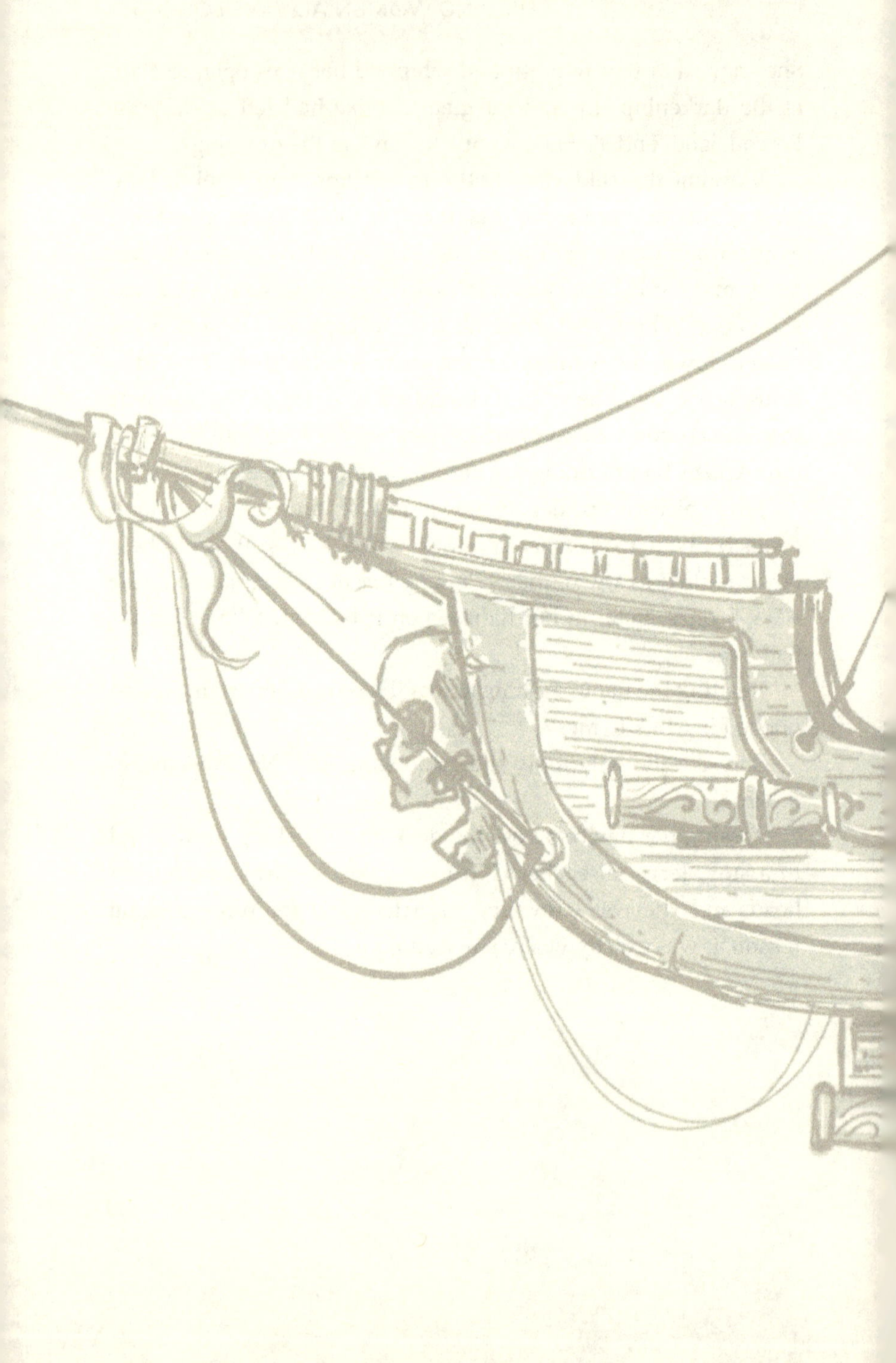

CHAPTER 14

Yarrow was still asleep when Jerry made her way up to the wheelhouse to take off for Potelia. Their plan was hodgepodged together, but the advantage was they had quite a flight time to get to the Omar Region in the north. They would go right through the Jackimore Sea and the Dead River to get to the Kigorlia Ocean and finally cross it to get to Potelia.

She couldn't imagine taking that path as an invalid like Whitney had. Jerry rolled her shoulders and stretched her back, cracking her neck from one side to the other. It was her routine when she got behind the wheel and had a few extra minutes to spare. The sun wasn't even cresting the horizon yet, but she wanted a fresh start on the day so they could make it most of the way through the Jackimore Sea at least.

She was about to reverse out of their slip when she stopped and stared at the pier. Curly blonde hair blew in the breeze, falling against pale, perfect skin. Jerry faltered. She hadn't expected this, hadn't thought she would come. Her heart thudded wildly as they stared at each other, as if Arloa could see her—not just her, but into her heart.

Jerry took a chance and settled *Yarrow* back down, putting everything on hold. They had the time. She didn't look up again as she slid down the ladders to get to the lower deck and open the doors that would lead her out of *Yarrow* and to the dock. As the door lowered, Jerry bounced in her boots, wanting it to happen faster. She didn't want Arloa to leave just yet.

As the exterior door settled, Jerry eyed the woman in question as she sauntered down the long dock toward the slip, her deep blue skirts pulling behind her as they snagged on splinters of wood. Her hair looked like a halo around her, those steel-blue eyes locked on Jerry the moment Jerry looked up. They said nothing as Arloa came closer, as she walked across *Yarrow's* lowered door to the entry.

Arloa enticingly looked over her shoulder as she stepped through the interior door, the crinkles in her eyes deepening as a slick smile warmed her lips. Jerry drew in a ragged breath as she slapped her hand on the sensor to shut and lock *Yarrow*.

What the fuck were they doing? Jerry raced after her, a lightness to her step that she hadn't had in over a year. Arloa slipped into Jerry's cabin, and once Jerry was inside, she locked the door and was on her.

Their mouths touched, their hands flitted from place to place, tugging at ties and buttons. Jerry nipped her lip, dragging cold air into her lungs every second she got. Arloa was wearing too many fucking clothes. She pulled at the buckles on her sides, jerking the material free so she could push it to the ground and divest her creamy skin of it.

"What are you doing here?" Jerry breathed into Arloa's neck as she curled her arms around Arloa's back to tug at the ties on her corset.

"I needed to see you again."

Jerry grunted as she finally got the laces undone enough to slide the damn thing off. She dragged it over Arloa's head, her hair falling around her shoulders and down her back. Jerry quickly spun her around to work at the rest of her dress. There were too many damn clothes between them. There had been the last time too, and Jerry wanted her blissfully naked.

"Fuck these clothes," Jerry growled when she couldn't get them off fast enough. "Why did you have to get all dressed up?"

"I came from work." Arloa reached a hand up, sliding it behind Jerry's head and tangling her fingers in the hairs at the nape of her neck, much like Whitney had done.

Guilt slammed into Jerry's chest, but she pushed it to the side as she trailed kisses all over Arloa's neck and shoulder, anywhere she could reach where there was skin. When she finally got the ties undone, she stripped Arloa bare and pushed her forward onto the bed so she was on her hands and knees on the tiny cot.

"Fuck, your ass." Jerry whined as she curled her hand over the gentle curve. Arloa wouldn't win any beauty pageants, but Jerry had fallen hard for her every step of the way and loved every little thing Arloa might consider an imperfection.

"Fuck me already, Jer."

Shuddering, Jerry's nipples hardened in an instant at the command and desperation filling Arloa's voice. She didn't even have a chance to take her gloves off as she rammed two fingers inside Arloa, instantly surrounded by her heat. Crying out, Arloa turned her face into the cot to muffle the sound, but Jerry wanted to hear her.

She reached forward and grabbed her hair in a fist, tugging until Arloa's face was revealed. She couldn't look away as she began a slow tedious pattern of pulling her fingers out all the way and thrusting them back in.

Arloa keened, the sweet sound echoing in Jerry's ears. She had never forgotten that noise. She'd never been able to make herself give it up. She'd craved it. Arloa pushed into her, reaching between her legs to flick her own clit as Jerry continued to finger fuck her, harder as a flush rose in Arloa's skin, covering her back.

Heat pooled between Jerry's legs, tingling through her body as though she was getting fucked herself. She could only hope she would get there eventually, but they still didn't have time.

Thrusting harder, she increased the pressure and depth of her fingers, curling them to push her knuckles against Arloa in a way that would make her delirious.

"Jer," Arloa breathed out her name. "Don't stop. I need this. I need you."

Jerry said nothing as she continued to fuck her hard, keeping time and rhythm when her own heart had faltered. *It was all sex, wasn't it?* This tension between them. In no world would Arloa, a woman of stature, education, and money, need Jerry for anything except dirty work. Cursing her own self-doubt, Jerry pressed in more until Arloa clenched around her, crying out as she collapsed onto the cot.

Jerry didn't give her a moment before flipping her over and pressing her face between Arloa's legs, licking from back to front before teasing Arloa's swollen clit. Arloa reached a hand above her head, holding herself against the wall as she touched her other hand into Jerry's hair. Her back arched, her lips parted as she groaned with pleasure.

Putting all of her concentration into what she was doing and not what she was feeling, Jerry hyper-focused on Arloa's body. On the shakes in her legs, the tension in her back, the jerk of her belly as she got closer to the edge of another orgasm. She slid her gloved hand back inside Arloa, pressing and swishing as she saw fit, any way to make this glorious woman come on her again.

Jerry had one thing on her mind. Give Arloa as much pleasure as humanly possible. This would likely be the last time they saw each other. If Jerry didn't find the vestigen, she wasn't sure she would return. She didn't know how long it would take to confirm or deny the rumor once they got to Potelia, and she wasn't going to insist Arloa wait around for her to come back. She wasn't even sure she wanted Arloa to.

Being infected with the virus meant she wasn't a safe person to be around. Unless she could keep everything under control—which the last year had proven time and again that she couldn't

—she didn't want to. It wasn't just the virus. Jerry loved living on the edge.

As Arloa crested through another orgasm, Jerry slowed her movements. Arloa would need a break, and as tempted as she was to continue, she knew Arloa well enough to know that she wouldn't allow it. Jerry kissed the crease between Arloa's thigh and hip, the tender sensitive skin, before she slipped her fingers from Arloa's body and licked them clean.

She couldn't look Arloa in the eye. Keeping her gaze down, Jerry sat up and brushed a hand through the stray strands of hair that fell against her cheek. Everything was on fire in her body. Every nerve was telling her to let Arloa take her, to fuck her into oblivion just one more time so that maybe she could forget. Because all she wanted was to forget what the world had become for her. She wanted to live in the moment they'd met, when Jerry had been innocent of the virus, free of the condemnation it brought, and striving for a better life for herself in Raegina.

Now that would never be possible.

Not even with Arloa working by her side. They were too different, from two drastically opposing worlds. Arloa had everything at her fingertips while Jerry had to fight tooth and nail just to consider surviving.

The hand on her cheek surprised her, and when she looked up, Arloa sat next to her, a look of concern flitting across her gaze. "Jer."

"Don't talk to me right now."

"Please, tell me what's wrong. Maybe I can help."

"You can't help me." Her words had a bite she hadn't intended, but it was painful. She had longed for this woman, for her touch, for her voice, for her glances for over a year, and now that she had it, she wanted nothing to do with the kindness. She didn't deserve it.

"Please," Arloa begged. "Look at me."

Jerry raised her chin, daring herself to look into Arloa's cool gaze. "You can't do anything for me."

"I *will* do anything for you. Anything," Arloa repeated. She dragged her thumb down to brush it across Jerry's lips. "When I saw you at Miriam's, I... I won't deny that I was jealous, Jer, but it wasn't because of you paying her. It was because I thought you wanted to do it."

Jerry swallowed hard, avoiding the tears that threatened to burst. She hated what the virus had done to her. She couldn't breathe without her emotions rising to the surface outside of her control, and all she wanted was to control everything around her. Arloa was the pinnacle of self-restraint. She always had been.

"I wanted you to touch me just now. I've wanted you to touch me every night for the last year." Arloa's voice was so soft that Jerry had to strain to hear her. "I can't... I don't know what the future holds for either of us, but neither do you."

"I know what my future is," Jerry said firmly, her tone deep and dangerous. "Every one of my crew understands what our future is, and if you don't understand that—"

"You don't know. There could be a cure."

She hated when Arloa spoke so much hope into her life, hope in a way she didn't want to admit existed. "If there is a cure, why haven't we found it yet? Hmm?"

"Because no one is looking. You're too busy trying to survive, and the government is too busy trying to avoid the reality of this virus. No one is looking for one."

"Except you, I suppose." She didn't mean it to come off as angry as it did, but Jerry didn't take it back after the words were out of her mouth.

Arloa's look softened, and she leaned in, pressing their mouths gingerly together. "I am. Please believe me that I am."

Jerry wanted to take that leap of faith. She wanted to, but it still made no sense to her why a Kauket would want anything to do with the poor, the downtrodden, the unmentionable creatures of Penum. Arloa had never explained that to her, never told her why she was in that bar on the edge of the harbor all those months ago, never told her for what purpose she'd submit herself to the worst of the world if only for a drink or two and a quick fuck.

"Why are you here?"

"What do you mean? I told you. I needed to see you."

Jerry shook her head. "Why are you *here*? Why were you at the bar that night? Why are you even in this part of Raegina? It doesn't make sense. You have no reason to be here. You have no businesses here. You have no family here. You're from the richest of the rich, and yet, you're *here*."

Arloa's lips parted in surprise. "I told you, I need you."

"You didn't need me a year ago in the bar, Arloa. You didn't even know I existed."

Arloa dropped her hand into her lap and drew in a deep breath, letting it out slowly. "I needed to figure out who I was. For a long time, I lived under the cloud of my family name. A Kauket." Tears gathered in the corners of her eyes, but Jerry didn't reach up to soothe them away. "I don't like what they do. I've never liked how they made their money, but also, as you pointed out once, I can't escape it. My education, my upbringing, my life—everything is because of their money and the way they got it."

"You still haven't answered my question."

"I was trying to learn who I was. And I did, before I met you, and I found I quite enjoyed being with *normal* people. People who worked for a living, who understand what labor is and what it means to be unbalanced, and not have the world at their fingertips. I enjoyed the reminder that not everyone has as much privilege as I do."

"Do you hear yourself?" Jerry's voice cut through the small cabin. "Did you honestly hear what you just said?"

Arloa's jaw dropped.

Jerry rolled her eyes and stood up, putting space between

them. "You're as ridiculous as the rest of them. Yes, I still plan on going to Potelia, and if we find vestigen, I will give you some to help with your pet project, but don't you ever use my people to make yourself feel better. We're not here for your pleasure."

Sneering, Jerry crossed her arms and glared at Arloa as she sat naked on her bed.

"You're welcome to leave."

Stalking out of the cabin, Jerry shut the door behind her and made her way up the wheelhouse. She shouldn't have stopped. She should have just left and forgotten she'd seen Arloa standing there, should have walked as far away from her as possible. Everything about their reunion reminded Jerry that they couldn't be together. Ever. It wouldn't work.

She had the systems ready to go, but Arloa hadn't left yet. *Yarrow's* doors remained firmly shut. She bounced in her boots, wanting to get moving so she could forget this morning had ever happened, though she knew the chances of that were slim because she was going to be reminded of why they were going to Potelia every five seconds.

Spinning around to tell Arloa to get out, she stopped short. Arloa stood at the top of the ladder, her hair beautifully tousled around her shoulders, her eyes wide. Every stitch of clothing back in place as if Jerry hadn't just fucked her senseless. She couldn't breathe. It hurt to draw air into her lungs. She'd been out of her mind to think anything to do with this woman was a good thing.

"You're right," Arloa murmured. "Even in my own privilege I don't see it."

"I can't walk into the center of Raegina without being told to get out. This is my *home.* I was born here, and yet, I can't even go into the government house without being told I don't belong. Do you think I don't know that?"

Arloa remained stoically still, her face not giving away any emotion, which only proceeded to piss Jerry off even more.

"You can walk anywhere you fucking want and be served.

Why? Because you're a *Kauket*." Jerry cursed her last name. Anyone who had been to Joab knew that name and cursed it. Jerry had broken that pattern because of Arloa, but she was quickly about to revive the tradition.

Arloa still didn't move.

"Get off my ship."

They stared at each other for what seemed like minutes. Arloa finally broke, her face cracking as she went to move forward, but Jerry shook her head and put her hand up to stop her.

"Get off my ship. You're not welcome here."

"Jer, please, don't leave like this."

"What other way is there to leave? Hmm? Because I don't see this resolving anytime soon, and I have a flight to run."

Arloa ran her thumb over her fingers, her only tell that she was upset. Jerry eyed her hand before flicking her gaze up to Arloa's face.

"Give me your knife." Arloa stepped forward, her hand stretched out in front of her as if she was expecting something to happen.

Jerry cocked her head to the side, taken aback by the sudden insistence in Arloa's tone. "*What?*"

"Give me your knife," Arloa repeated, her hand still in front of her. "I need it."

"What for?" Jerry found herself shifting to grab her short sword from her side before she could stop herself. Their fingers touched briefly as Jerry handed the sword over, pleasure shooting up her arm and into her chest, much like it had the very first time they had met.

Arloa brought the weapon up to her neck, and Jerry almost lunged forward to stop her before she grabbed a chunk of hair with her free hand and sliced some off. Handing the weapon back, Arloa looked Jerry directly in the eye as she held her hand out with the piece of hair between her fingers.

"For you."

Jerry understood the tradition. She'd seen other couples do this, especially those who were out at sea and left loved ones behind, but she'd never expected to be one of those.

"Get out."

"Please talk to me."

"No. I don't need you. You might need me and *my* kind to remind you of your humanity, but I don't need *you*. I never have." Jerry spun around and grabbed the wheel of *Yarrow*, ready to take off. "You can get off the fucking ship now, or I will toss you off when we're out at sea."

Arloa didn't move. Jerry could feel her presence pervading the wheelhouse. They stood like that in tense silence for too long, and when Jerry gave in and looked over her shoulder, Arloa still stood there.

"Your choice." She put the ship into gear.

"I'll leave, but please, please know that I want to take care of you."

Jerry glared at her. "I can take care of myself."

Arloa gave in and left. She moved down the ladder and out of view. Turning around to make sure she was gone, Jerry found the lock of hair on the deck, golden hues shining in the dawning light. Dragging in a ragged, emotional breath, Jerry waited until *Yarrow's* doors opened and closed, until she could see Arloa standing on the dock in the morning breeze before she grabbed it. She didn't dare look out at Arloa again, as she pulled *Yarrow* out of the slip and made her way to the open sea.

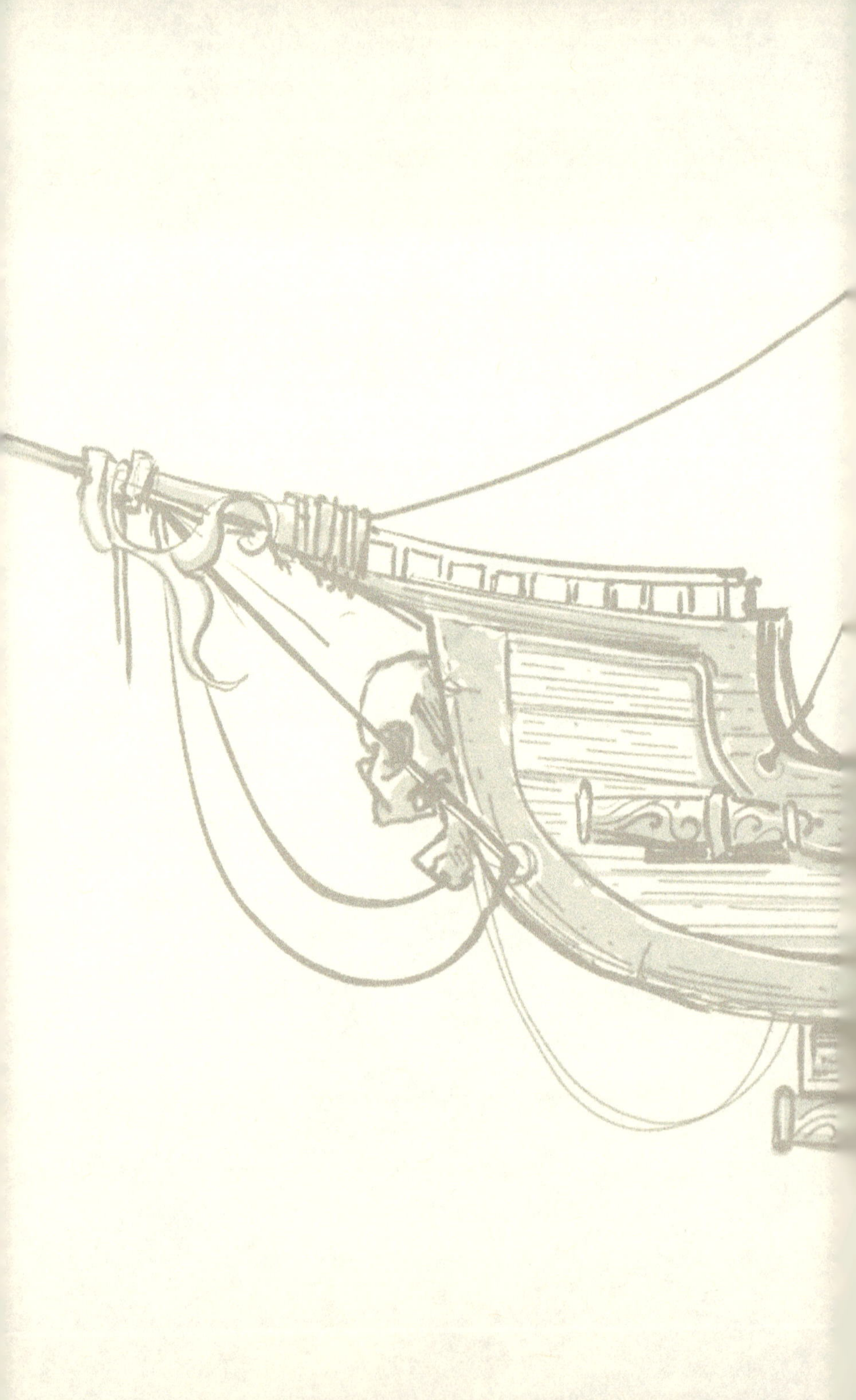

CHAPTER 15

They arrived in Potelia as dusk fell, and Jerry docked *Yarrow*. Azar and Yafe stood in the wheelhouse with her while Sacha was out on the deck, leaning over the edge of the ship to stare down at the water. Jerry rolled her shoulders and stretched her back as she turned *Yarrow's* engines off.

They were finally here.

The fight with Arloa the week before had stayed with her every moment she'd stood at the wheel. When she remembered it, one moment Arloa was sad and the next angry, then gleeful and vindictive. Jerry couldn't even recollect what had truly happened because her mind was so twisted by the argument itself. All she knew was she couldn't go back there with the way it had ended. She couldn't bring herself to face Arloa again.

Jerry was the first one off *Yarrow*, and the dockmaster strutted toward her with his large device tucked under his arm. Jerry stayed where she was and waited for him to arrive so she could exchange papers and legally be there, at least legally according to them.

He nodded his head at her. "You the captain?"

"I am," Jerry stated. "Jeraldine Adelric. I sent my papers to your foreman already."

"I've got 'em here." He lifted his device and flicked through different screens to get to Jerry's identification and *Yarrow's* papers.

Jerry pursed her lips as she waited for him to give her the okay so she could let the rest of her crew off. She looked around while he perused the documents. The dock was much smaller than any in Raegina. She hadn't rented a slip yet, though she would need to. For now she needed to get through inspections and find a contact for a slip, which was going to be rough since she knew no one there.

Even the air tasted cleaner here.

She wondered why she'd never come here before. In all her travels growing up, and all her time spent on ships with her mother when she was a kid and not landlocked at Miriam's insistence, Jerry had never made her way to Potelia. She'd traveled the world, but not here.

"We'll need to inspect."

"I figured as much." Jerry held still, giving in to everything he wanted. She didn't need him to think she was hiding anything, which she was, hiding a whole lot of things, actually.

He nodded at her. "I'm Hobert Landingham. If you have any questions about Potelia, ask away. It says in your records you've never been here before."

"I haven't. I grew up on trade ships, but I can't say we ever made it this far north."

Hobert nodded at her. "It'll get cold tonight so make sure to batten down the hatches."

Jerry curled her lips up at that. She could see why Whitney had liked him, even if he was interested in more from her. She wondered if dropping Whitney's name would be an advantage, if it would make him nostalgic enough to want to be friendly.

"I'll do that for sure. We're from Raegina in the south, so it only gets frosty in the dead of winter."

"Not here." Hobert eyed *Yarrow* as he took down more information from the ship. "You'll want a warmer jacket than that too."

"Perhaps you can guide us in where to buy some supplies then, since it seems we're vastly unprepared for a winter here."

"I can do that." Hobert squared his shoulders. "Ready for inspection?"

"Absolutely." Jerry guided him onto the ship, taking him level by level and through each room so he could give most of them a cursory glance. She remembered her inspections in Raegina, any time they'd surprise her with one or when she was required to do her annual. It was way more in-depth and invasive than here. She'd honestly thought about pulling everything from *Yarrow* each time just to make it easier.

They reached the wheelhouse, and Hobert's eyes lit up at her setup. "You have the Lamen twenty-hundred."

"I do, mostly." Jerry cocked her head at him. "Do you know a bit about them? My engineer has had to fix this one plenty of times since it's so old, but she runs well. We have a lot of mixed parts in her system now."

"It's beautiful. I've never seen one in such good condition. Most of the vessels that come through port are far younger than this one."

"*Yarrow* was my first ship, and I don't think I'd change her for anything."

Hobert ran his fingers smoothly over the brass bar in front of the command dash. He was so reverent about everything. Jerry could certainly use that to her advantage when and if she needed it. Which, given what they were there to do, would be likely.

She leaned in and showed him some of the upgrades Azar had made, allowing him to ogle every change and nuance. She promised to take him out to the open sea sometime so he could really experience how *Yarrow* moved under the slightest touch, though she never intended to follow through on that promise. It would give away too much information about her and her crew and how she flew her ship.

He eventually gave up looking at the wheelhouse, and they

moved out to the deck. Jerry had a good feeling about Potelia, about the people there, even though she'd only met one so far. Whitney had given a good report of them as well.

"Do you have any connections for jobs? My crew and I are looking. We've been out of work for a while and need someplace to settle. I've got an engineer on board who can work anywhere. He's got certifications."

"Oh?" Hobert raised an eyebrow at her. "I think I've heard of a few jobs, but you'll need to get your papers so you can work."

"Work papers? Are they not the same here as in Raegina?"

Hobert frowned. "Unfortunately no, but if you had them there, they should transfer easily enough. Once you go through the screening."

"What screening is that?"

"Just an intake exam."

Jerry shuddered at his phrase but hoped she caught it in time so he didn't see. She didn't want him to think anything of her and the crew being there. She clenched her jaw as she waited for him to finish the inspection.

"Well, I think everything is settled here." He signed something on his device and turned it off. "Do you need a slip?"

"For a bit, yes, until I can find a private holder."

Hobert shook his head. "They're all public here. You rent them from Potelia."

"Oh. Guess I have a lot to learn." Jerry knew he was telling the truth, but she also knew there were slips that weren't owned by the city. He was a city man, however, so he would want to see city revenue up. It also would mean a tighter control on what Jerry was doing. She planned for both, a private slip and a public one. It would help her maneuver that much more easily without others knowing where she was when.

"Like I said, any questions, feel free to ask. You've been approved in the system, and I'll need you to be inspected weekly for your duration until you obtain foreigner residential papers. Then we can move to monthly until they become permanent."

Jerry clenched her jaw. She hadn't planned on staying that long. Although, if Potelia was as idyllic as it was made out to be, she may just change her tune. Not to mention, it would be far away from Arloa and the toxic privilege she didn't even know she had. "Sounds great. Thank you so much, Hobert."

"Hobie, please."

Jerry forced a smile to her lips. "I know a woman I think you know."

"Oh?"

"Whitney? She said she met you when she came to Potelia for treatments. She's actually the reason I thought we'd try to find some work here. Her description of the city. I had to see it for myself."

"It's much prettier at dawn. Since most of Potelia is eastern facing, you'll see the highlights of the city as soon as the sun breaks the horizon."

"I can imagine." Jerry had to play up her fantasy of Potelia, had to build up her desire to be a tourist and hopeful worker at the same time. She'd spent most of the week preparing herself for hiding her true nature behind that role. "I'll have to make sure to set a reminder to get up early."

"It'll be worth it." Hobie grinned, three of his front teeth missing as he glanced at her. "And I do remember Whitney. Sweet little thing."

"She is. She's one of my favorite people, you know. We met when I was helping the orphanage on some outings and trans-portation issues. I used to work on a carrier line." The lie floated so easily off her tongue.

"That makes sense. I'm glad to know she made it back to Raegina unscathed."

Jerry's smile faltered slightly. "She did make it back, though I fear they had a run-in with some pirates. They were lucky they were merciful ones. She told me the whole story in vivid, excited detail. I'm not sure she's ever lived so much."

Concern flashed through Hobie's sea-green eyes. "Pirates?"

"Yes, but she's fine, I promise you. I saw her just before we left to come here."

Hobie got quiet, his lips moving as if he wanted to say something but couldn't quite find the gumption. Jerry almost reached out to comfort him but stopped herself. She didn't know how strict they were here on rules of consent for touching, and she wasn't willing to risk it. Instead, she canted her head toward him, making herself seem smaller to his short round frame.

"She's all right. She seemed pleased with the entire event, as if it was the adventure she had been waiting for."

"I hope it wasn't too frightening for her. I can't imagine—"

"I think she's fine. Really. She seemed tickled by the whole thing."

"I'll have to trust you on that. She hasn't answered any of my communications."

Jerry had to decide whether or not to throw him a bone, but she hoped it would give her some credibility as she continued to need his help. "She's back at the orphanage. They're not allowed personal communications until they leave. I can try to get her a message for you, through my contacts there, if you'd like."

"Really?" Hobie's eyes lit up.

Nodding, Jerry quirked her lips upward. "Yeah. I think she'd like it honestly. She's ready to leave that place and get out on her own. She just needs some time and credits to do it."

"I can help with that."

"Hobie," Jerry dropped her tone. "Don't come on too strong with her, all right? She's young and inexperienced. She doesn't understand the world, so she needs to figure things out on her own."

"Oh, okay."

She nearly reached out and patted his hand like a little kid, but she restrained herself from it at the last minute. "You've been such a help to me, getting Whitney a message from you is the least I can do."

Hobie grinned. "Thank you! I'll figure out what I want to say and send it to you, all right?"

"Sounds like a plan." Jerry crossed her arms. "In the meantime, I'd like to get to a slip so I can get some rest. We had a long week of travel to get here."

"Sounds like it."

Hobie followed her back inside and down the ladders to the main doors of *Yarrow*. She led him out of the ship and locked up behind him. Leaning against the exterior door, Jerry closed her eyes and released all the tension from the last hour. She hadn't known what he would find, but if every inspection was like that—she would be golden. He'd never find anything she hid on her ship, which was a lot. However, she didn't want to get lazy in her schemes, so she would keep it up as long as she could.

She was about to move and go through the interior doors when they opened. Yafe stood on the other side, hands on her hips as she eyed Jerry up and down. "I assume we passed inspection?"

"We did." Jerry remained pressed against the door.

"Why do you look like you just won a war by a thread?" Yafe raised a thin black eyebrow, her hair wild around her face so beautiful as she stood confidently waiting for an answer.

Jerry refused to answer. She pushed away from the door, instinctively reaching for her gloves to pull them off, but remembered last minute she hadn't been wearing them all week. Not since—she stopped that thought dead in its tracks.

"We'll need warmer clothes according to Hobie. It gets cold in the Omar Region."

"I remember it well."

"I nearly forgot you were from here."

"Not Potelia, and I certainly don't remember much. I was so young when we left. Azar remembers more."

"His accent proves it." Jerry took off her jacket and held it over her arm as she walked into the thin corridor of the lower holdings. "I wish you all had lived in Potelia."

"It would have been helpful." Yafe followed Jerry closely. "Are you going to tell me what's going on?"

"No."

"You can't keep it in, Jerry. That's what we're here for, to let you talk to someone other than yourself for once."

"I don't need to talk to someone." A pit grew in Jerry's stomach.

"You do. I've never seen you this tense before, not since we were in Joab together."

Jerry raised her eyes and sighed. "Arloa was here before we left."

Laughing, Yafe rolled her eyes. "I think everyone on board knew that."

"Fuck. Really?" Jerry grimaced.

"Yeah. She's not exactly quiet, but when the two of you started yelling, that was the real tip off."

"Great." Jerry made her way up to the wheelhouse with Yafe following. She put in a request with the city for a slip for at least a week and waited to be assigned one now that she had the record of completed inspection.

"Do you want to talk about it?"

"No."

Yafe groaned. "I'm not going to be stuck in Potelia with you in this mood the entire time. Own up, Cap."

Grumbling, Jerry got her slip number and pulled away from the dock they were currently stationed at. She followed the directions to the slip. "She's an egotistical, entitled, privileged bitch sometimes."

Yafe could barely contain her laughter. "Sounds like someone else I know."

"I am not privileged."

"In some ways you are. You can read."

Yafe did have a point there. While Jerry hadn't come from wealth, her mother had at one point, and she'd gotten the privilege of schooling even if Jerry hadn't. Her mother had done her best to pass that knowledge down to Jerry in an informal process. "I can teach you, if you want."

"Someday."

"Here's our slip." Jerry pulled *Yarrow* into place and settled her down to rest for the night. Once she had the systems shut down, she turned on Yafe. "She transferred thousands of credits to me after we left. I don't know what it's payment for."

"It's to help us do what she wants."

"Sure it is, and it's to keep our mouths shut about her involvement."

"Jerry." Yafe's voice was so soft, so full of pity. "From what I know of her, I'm not sure that's the reason."

"We don't know anything about her. She told me that once, and she was right." Jerry locked *Yarrow* into place. "I'm going landside. Are you coming?"

"Sure."

"Get the others and see if they want to come."

Within the hour, they were all making their way down the dock to the pier. Jerry kept her jacket buckled in the front, warding off the cold air that Hobie had certainly warned about. She would need to find a new jacket, perhaps one that was fur-lined, and she would need to give in and wear her damn gloves even though they smelled like Arloa.

She stepped up to one of the dock workers and introduced herself, working to keep her accent under control so he'd be less likely to figure out where she was from. "I'm Jerry Adelric. I'm Captain of *Yarrow*."

"Good to meet you. I'm Dash." He nodded at her and the others. "We ask that all crews staying aboard their vessels are back by the tenth bell."

"Really?"

"Unless you have residency."

"We don't." Jerry wasn't going to lie about that. It would be far too easy for him to check on it. "We might apply for it if we find some good jobs to stay up here. We're looking for work. Do you happen to know of anything?"

He eyed them up and down and shook his head. He wasn't someone who trusted so easily, which was probably a good thing, not that Jerry would tell him that to his face. It would give her away.

"Well, if you do, I'd appreciate it." She stepped around him, her motley crew following her. She would have to do better at disguising them so they could pass for people of worth. Still the entire feel of Potelia so far was different than any other place she had been. It was going to take time to get some people to trust her, which was normal, and they had the time to spare. She was as free as she wanted to make herself, which had been what Jerry had always wanted. Perhaps she wasn't as far from her dreams as she'd originally thought.

They found a tavern and ordered real warm food, something Jerry hadn't eaten since they left Raegina. As much as Yafe was a good chef, they'd kept cooking to a minimum to preserve fuel and make fewer stops on their travels. Sacha seemed far more able-bodied that week than she had the previous two, but her regimen was almost complete. Soon enough, they would be able to start weaning her down to their dosage in order to keep her as even-keeled as possible. Then she could work like the rest of them and fit right into Jerry's plan for Potelia.

CHAPTER 16

One week into being in Potelia, and Jerry hadn't found a consistent job. Neither had Azar, who was still working on getting his papers transferred—or fake ones if Jerry could swing it. Those were proving harder than she had anticipated, though Azar was currently picking up random jobs inland while she was doing random jobs with *Yarrow* in tow.

Hobie had given her a contact with a man named Jacque who had given her a few jobs, randomly. It wasn't enough credits to live on, but it was enough to pay their expenses for the jobs and a little more. That morning, as Azar left to go to a factory for a temp position he had all week, Jerry pulled *Yarrow* out of the slip and onto the open water.

Sacha stood next to her in the wheelhouse as Yafe was belowdecks, preparing the storerooms for the cargo they were retrieving. Sacha leaned against the brass bar by the dash, staring out the front windshield. Jerry said nothing to her as she maneuvered *Yarrow* through the harbor and toward sea.

"Why does he get to leave every day and I'm stuck here?"

Jerry rolled her eyes where Sacha couldn't see. She'd been whining more often lately, but at least her moods did seem to be coming off their insane binger. Jerry had taken her pill that morning for the first time in four days after staring at the small stash they still had and deciding they were going to need to cut down even more if they were going to make it.

She didn't have the contacts in Potelia that she did in Raegina in order to find vestigen for her crew. She almost regretted bringing Sacha with them because she sucked up most of those stores, but she'd wanted the extra person in case they needed a distraction the three of them couldn't handle.

"I just want to get off this ship."

Jerry rolled her eyes again, tensing her fingers around *Yarrow's* wheel as she steered her vessel. "Then get off it."

Sacha's blue eyes widened as she faced Jerry, her lips parting as if shocked Jerry would dare tell her to do what she wanted. "Get off?"

"If you don't want to be here, then leave." Anger gurgled in her belly, solidifying in its direction as she aimed it at Sacha, the only other person there who she could target at the moment. "I'm tired of listening to you bitch about everything we have given you. You don't have to be here, and if you don't want to, fucking leave already."

Sacha paled, and Jerry caught the moment she realized she needed to backtrack. "I... I don't have anywhere else to go."

"Yeah, well, you're not exactly helping much here. This mission would be easier without you, honestly. You're using up all the vestigen on the ship, and we're running low. We need to find more. Otherwise, we'll all end up like you did, and yet here you are, bitching about how you don't want to be here. The world has bigger problems, Sacha. It's not all about you."

A stab of guilt hit Jerry's stomach, but she ignored it. She would not feel bad for this woman complaining about being handed a better lease on life.

"I could fire you right now and then what? You're not my best worker. You don't help out with the rest of us. You're up here complaining while Yafe is down in the storerooms working. Did you offer to help her? No. Did the thought even cross your mind? No. You're a stuck-up, spoiled brat who has been handed everything in life and now that you don't have it, all you do is complain. Well, I'm sick of it."

Sacha paled.

"I am. So you should probably get out of my wheelhouse before I do something you will regret."

Sacha stared at her for a fleeting second before she scampered down the ladder to the lower decks. Finally alone, Jerry stared out at the sea, going to the coordinates she had been given. She hadn't heard a fucking thing from Arloa since they'd been gone, other than the large amount of credits dropped into her account.

As much as she hated taking them, it was the only way they had survived so far. Jerry rolled her shoulders. She felt in some ways she owed Arloa a response of some sort, but she had no idea what to say. Every time they'd been near each other lately, she'd picked a fight, intentionally designed to get herself and Arloa all riled up to avoid, and she really didn't want to sit in the question of why.

It didn't take them long to get to the river that split Potelia in half. Her ship was small enough to navigate it, which meant she was able to do smaller shipments daily when needed. As she flew above the water, Jerry found the right slip and set *Yarrow* down. Instantly, her system alerted her to a message.

"State your name and reason for docking."

The artificial intelligence was as cold as ever, though Jerry didn't mind. "Jeraldine Adelric. We're collecting a shipment for Jacque Kloussan."

"Please present papers."

Jerry hit a button on her dash, sending over the required paperwork to prove who she was and what she was doing there. Everything in Potelia seemed automated in this way, which was a huge change from Raegina, where far more relied on humans, which meant it was easier to anticipate human error. Here, that was far more difficult.

She waited, patiently, which was shocking considering her outburst at Sacha earlier, though perhaps that had given her enough level-headedness for this. Jerry rolled her shoulders as both Yafe and Sacha emerged from the lower deck.

"What are we waiting on?" Yafe asked.

Jerry envied her ability to always be so even-keeled. She was the master at it, while Jerry struggled every day to keep herself balanced. "Approval."

"Sacha helped me finish up, so we're ready to go whenever we're allowed." Yafe brushed her hands on her brown pants as if they were sweaty.

"Good." Jerry had taken to keeping the door to the wheelhouse closed to keep as much heat inside as possible. They had been ill-prepared for winter there, and they were in the heart of it. It was a good thing ships didn't move through the water because it was completely iced over for kilometers at that point. "Shouldn't be too much longer."

"Do you think they have vestigen here? In Potelia?" Sacha's question seemed innocent enough, but it had been the one question Jerry had wondered about.

Dashing her tongue across her lips, Jerry turned around to stare at the young woman. "I imagine it's somewhere here. The virus is, but for some reason those infected don't seem to be as much of a problem as they are elsewhere."

"They're not murdered, you mean." Sacha sneered at the thought.

"Right." Jerry's heart plummeted, reminded of the fact it was Arloa's family in charge of most of that with the use of Joab as a way to kill them off. They hadn't even managed to talk about that, and the fact the credits Arloa sent her were likely from that made her want to chuck up the meager breakfast she'd forced herself to eat.

"I wonder why that is," Yafe interjected, catching the look in Jerry's eye.

"It's a good question to ask," Jerry muttered. "But it's not really one we're here to answer."

"But if Potelia can be seen as a refuge—"

"It's not." Jerry's tone was sharp. "We're here, and while they've been amenable to us working, we're not residents. We don't have the same rights as anyone else. We don't have vestigen. We'll have to resort to the same methods of getting it here that we did in Raegina only with fewer contacts and far less market. Do you know what kind of danger that puts us in?"

Neither of them said anything in response.

"Right." Jerry gritted her teeth just as the artificial intelligence told her the papers were approved and she could begin loading her cargo. "Come on, we have work to do."

Jerry stalked her way down to the main doors of *Yarrow*, extending the bridge to the dock. They were met by one of the dock workers, a beautiful man with long blond hair plaited down his back. He had a large thick fur coat on, boots and gloves that Jerry envied. She hadn't been able to afford that for her crew, so they'd gotten thinner jackets, but warmer than what they'd come with. Still, when they were hauling items around, it helped to be more flexible with movements.

"Jeraldine Adelric."

"Jerry, please." Jerry's lips quirked as she widened her stance in front of him.

He nodded at her sharply. "I'm Milton Frazier. I work for Jacque."

"Good to meet you."

"The cargo is this way."

The three of them followed him. If a man like Milton could afford a jacket like that, then perhaps Jerry wasn't getting the full rate she could out of him. Still, she didn't have a contract, so she didn't want to push her luck. She stepped up to walk next to him. "How long have you worked for Jacque?"

"Twenty years," he grumbled, his low voice rolling through Jerry's chest.

"Wow." She resisted the urge to comment that he worked there almost as long as she'd been alive, but held the retort in at the last minute. "We're new to Potelia, but I'm loving what we're seeing so far."

"We've had a lot of people come here for work in the last year."

"Have you?" Jerry raised an eyebrow. "Do most of them last?"

"No." He eyed her up and down. "The virus."

"Right." Jerry held still on that one and its implications. It could be that they hadn't found the regimen that she had, or it could mean that vestigen was next to impossible to find up there, which would be a problem for anyone with the virus. Yet, somehow, citizens of Potelia didn't seem to have a problem. Jerry hadn't been able to figure that one out yet. Taking a risk, Jerry asked, "So how does it not get you?"

"Pardon?" Milton's thick bushy eyebrows drew together.

"I mean, if the virus is getting the outsiders, why is everyone in Potelia safe from it?"

"We treat it."

"Oh." Jerry pressed her lips together as if she was surprised. "Your government pays for that?"

"No, but the drug is affordable and made available, mostly."

"Mostly?"

He snorted. "What does it matter to you? You won't be able to get any since you're not a citizen."

"Just curious really. I have a friend who works in the government at home, and she's been trying to find a solution."

"I think the rest of the world is beyond resurrecting from this one."

"Maybe." Jerry shrugged. "I don't know. It's above my pay grade, but I do wish we could all work together to find a workable solution."

"No one works together anymore. Not unless you've got credits."

"Truth." Jerry laughed lightly.

She was starting to like him, although he seemed reserved for whatever reason. It could be that workers like her would come and go quickly, or it could just be that he wasn't personable like Jerry was to begin with. She had to work hard to keep her uneven side at bay while they chatted all the way up the dock to the pier.

He showed her into the storehouse, and Jerry sent Sacha and Yafe to work on grabbing items while she tried to deepen her relationship with Milton. She had a feeling he would come in very useful later. Still, she had to find a way to get herself some vestigen if they were going to survive there any longer.

Jerry left Milton and grabbed a small crate, hauling it onto her shoulder as she carried it back to *Yarrow*. She met Yafe and Sacha on her way back, nodding at them with a smile on her lips. She had a good feeling about Milton and about Jacque, they could certainly come in handy as contacts.

It took them a few hours, but they had two of the storage rooms filled with the small crates and were pulling away from the dock. Jerry had made as much small talk with Milton as humanly possible in her state. She blew out a breath as she took the same path back to the harbor, but to the opposite side. It was the fastest way to get a large quantity of items from one side of Potelia to the other since they weren't permitted to fly above the city, and she had taken full advantage of all those jobs that were needed.

As they unloaded, Jerry made a rash decision. She started to allow her body to feel the weariness and exhaustion and pain that the virus gave her. She took longer to get the crates from one spot to the next, she played up how awful she felt. By the time they finished the job, she was barely functioning.

She made it back to their slip and went to lie down. It took Yafe about thirty minutes to check on her, which Jerry suspected would happen. Yafe slid into her cabin and perched on the edge of the cot, cocking her head at Jerry.

"I thought you took your pill this morning."

"I did." Jerry clenched her jaw. "Mostly. I split it in half."

"Cap, you can't—"

"We don't have enough," Jerry whispered harshly. "I need you to go find Hobie and ask him for a healer."

Yafe narrowed her gaze at Jerry. "What are you playing at?"

"Trust me, will you?"

"I always trust you, Cap. You've never let me down."

"Then find Hobie, and play it up like this is the worst you've seen me in years. Please and thank you." Jerry curled on her side and rolled into a ball, her back facing Yafe.

"You're insane some days."

"Blame it on the lack of vestigen in my system."

"I wish I could, but this was you before the virus." Yafe patted Jerry's shoulder before she stood up. "Should I send Sacha? Let her make drama over it?"

"Think she'll be good for that?" Jerry turned her neck to make eye contact with Yafe.

"Oh yeah."

"Then do it."

Yafe left her alone, but she heard the exterior door opening. She imagined Sacha running down the dock to find Hobie. Her plan would work. It had to. She'd gladly poison herself to let the healers do more work on her, but they weren't stupid. Yafe came back in and handed over a small glass bottle of liquid.

"What's this?"

"Drink up if you want to be sick."

Pursing her lips, Jerry tilted the bottle up and downed the entire thing in two big gulps. It tasted rancid as it went down her throat, and she had to work hard not to gag it all back up.

"There you are." Yafe took the bottle and left the room.

As soon as she was gone, Jerry's head spun. She clenched her eyes shut, but she was still spinning even looking at the back of her eyelids. *Fuck, she was so screwed.* What had Yafe given her? She should have asked more questions, but she'd been stupid enough to trust.

Piercing pain slashed through her head, through the front,

over the top, and down into the back of her neck. She was a fucking idiot. She clenched tighter into a ball as she lay there absolutely miserable until Yafe came back in and rubbed circles into her back.

"What the fuck did you give me?"

"You're allergic to caladrine, right?"

"Fuck, you poisoned me?"

"Technically you poisoned yourself. Healer should be here soon."

"I'm going to kill you!" Jerry spouted as another lance of pain moved through her body. Groaning, she clenched her eyes shut and tried to work through it. She'd hadn't taken caladrine in years, not since they gave it to her accidentally at Joab, but that had been a small dose compared to this. The fucking liquid was a drug to get high off, and while Jerry had experimented with all kinds of drugs growing up, this was one she had steered clear of since she discovered her allergy.

"She's in here!" Sacha's worried voice broke through Jerry's pain.

Someone, she couldn't even bother to open her eyes to see, knelt down next to her on the bed and put hands over her arm.

"I don't know what's wrong." Yafe had that fake worried tone in her voice. "She hasn't been feeling good all day, but this came on so suddenly."

"I'll figure it out." The voice was deep, must be a man. Jerry kept her eyes closed and focused on the healing warmth that spread through her body. It had a bite to it, unlike Maisie's healing magic that she'd gotten in Arloa's apartment. It seemed like ages ago.

She had no idea how long it took, but slowly, the pain eased and her stomach didn't act like it was going to revolt against her anymore. Except this healer didn't fix everything. The lingering effects from the virus still pushed into the periphery of her mind, though Jerry supposed that was due to the lack of vestigen in her body.

The healer sighed and moved his hands away from her. "You should be fine now."

Jerry turned slowly, eyeing him. He was young and likely not as experienced as Maisie. Jerry nodded. "Thank you, but I think… I still don't feel too well."

"That would be the virus, which I can't heal." He frowned. "You have been treating it."

Jerry shrugged as best as she could. "I've been trying to, but we're out."

He pursed his lips and reached into a pocket on his jacket. He pulled out one small pill and handed it over. "Take it."

"I… I don't know what to say." Jerry softened her tone, as if she was a woman so thankful and weak when she actually wasn't. Reaching out, she took the pill and pushed it between her lips. "I don't know how much longer we'll be able to stay here. I don't have any more for my crew."

"That's all I have. I apologize."

"But…but where did you get it? I'll pay for it." The chalky flavor of death that moved down her throat and in her mouth confirmed it was in fact vestigen. Which Jerry again realized far too late she had trusted first. Fuck the virus for killing her ability to think properly.

"That's all I have." He stood sharply and nodded at her. "If you're healed, I'll take my payment."

Jerry's stomach plummeted, but she nodded at Yafe to allow her to make the transfer of credits. As soon as he was gone, Jerry forced herself to sit up and lean over the edge of the cot, already feeling worlds better. Yafe and Sacha crowded around her. She eyed them each.

"We're going to fucking find it. If it's the last thing I do before I die, I'm going to find it."

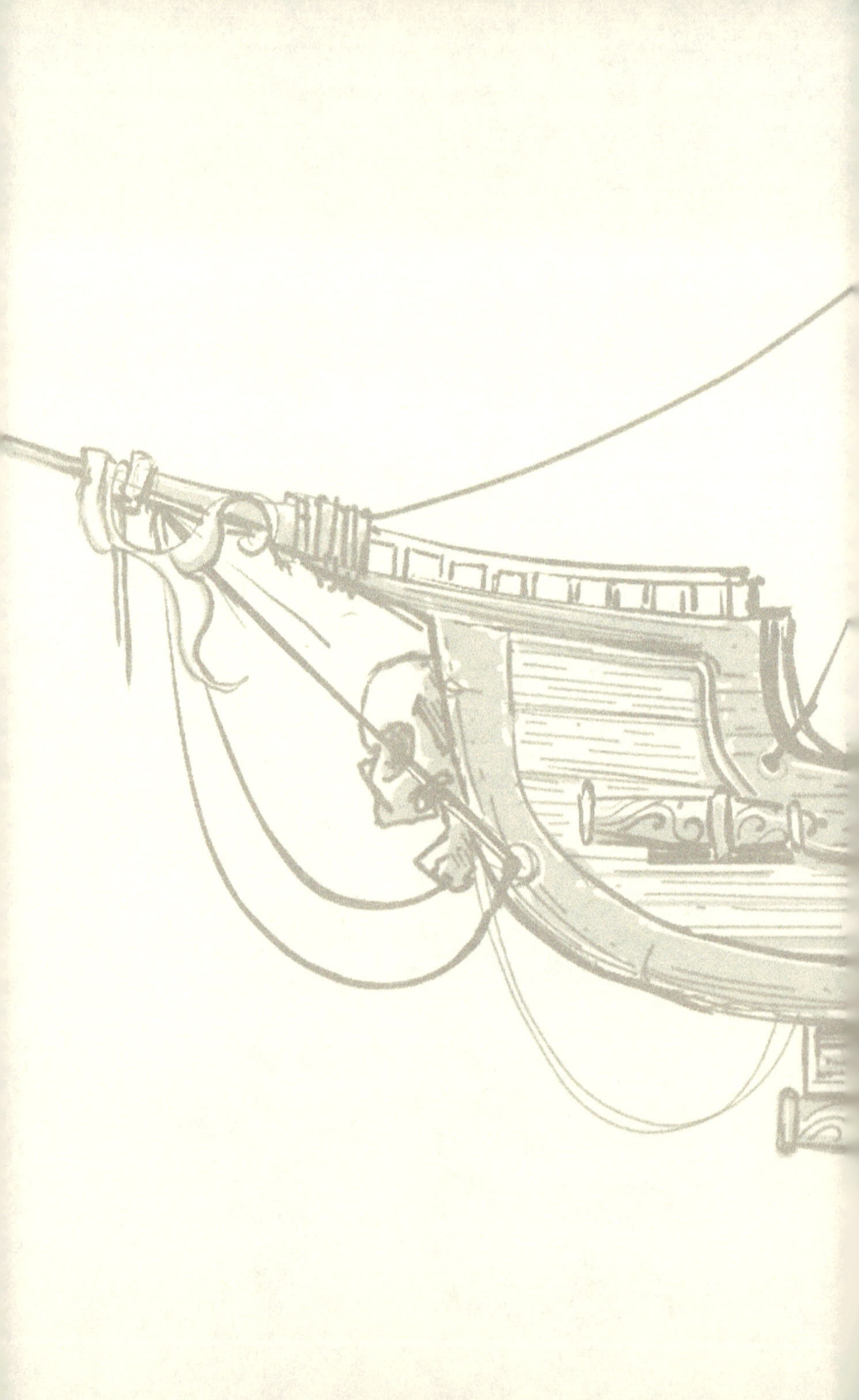

CHAPTER 17

Azar came back from his shift at the factory with a smile on his face that Jerry wasn't sure she'd be able to wipe off. If he hadn't seemed so excited about something, she may have been tempted to try at the very least. She stood with her hands in the pockets of her jacket in the galley as she forced a small piece of pre-wrapped food down her throat.

He slid onto one of the chairs opposite her, eyeing her as if he was going to burst. "Where's Yafe?"

"She and Sacha went to the bar to see if they can make some more contacts. What's going on?" Jerry raised an eyebrow at him, stilling her movements with the food packet still clasped tightly in her fingers.

Azar shook his head, his knee bouncing erratically up and down against the wood floor. "I was put in a new factory today."

"And?"

"They make drugs."

Jerry's heart skipped. "Vestigen?"

Azar shook his head. "No, unfortunately. Not from what I've seen so far. I'm hopeful they'll request me back tomorrow."

"You put on your best engineering face possible? Were the best employee ever?"

He nodded emphatically. "Yes. Of course I was."

Jerry chuckled lightly at his indignation. "Well done, Azar."

He beamed this time. "I wanted to tell Yafe."

"I understand, but we don't know anything yet."

"But we may be closer than before."

Jerry knocked her head to the side. They might very well be closer than they were before, but they still had no confirmation that Potelia was manufacturing vestigen or if they were just working off what they had in store already. Though being closer to a plant facility seemed like a good bonus to have.

"We *are* closer than before." Azar's dark eyes widened.

Jerry pressed her lips together hard. She didn't want to rain on his parade, but she was a realist, and they had no more information than they did before. All they had was access to one factory that *may* make vestigen but showed no signs of it yet. She nodded at him and plopped the last of the food pack between her lips, grimacing when it tasted like rotten corpse going down her throat.

She rubbed her temple and stretched her back. "I want you to keep working there if you can. Find out what you can about the plant, but don't put all your hope in it yet."

Azar frowned. "It's what we've been looking for."

"Yes." Jerry leaned forward. "And how many times have we found what we were looking for only to not have results in the end? Hmm?"

He frowned. She'd successfully taken his excitement down a notch or three.

"We still need to make connections here so that we can use them when we need. If not, they may come in useful in the future for some other wild chase we go on. Yes?"

"Fine." Azar pouted. She wasn't sure she could remember the last time she'd seen a grown man fully pout.

"Good. Then it's settled. Feel free to join Yafe and Sacha if you want. I'm going to stick close to home tonight."

Azar was still sulking, but he did eventually get up. Jerry

heard the exterior door open and close, and she was finally cast into blissful silence.

Now all she had to do was some good research. They'd been strategic in making contacts in Potelia, but it had taken Jerry longer than expected to find the underground here. Still, she had found it, which she maintained was no small feat. They weren't as widespread or as rich as Miriam's operation, but they were useful.

Except they had no vestigen.

Jerry frowned at that, still not sure how they were going to survive much longer without it. The small pill the healer had given her was enough to last for now, but the others on *Yarrow* didn't have that advantage.

With the ship quiet, Jerry reveled in a moment by herself. They were so rare. Usually there was always someone else there, someone coming and going who she would have to check on and make sure they were doing what they should. But for the first time in weeks, she was well and truly alone.

Jerry grabbed two packets of water as she swung by her cabin to grab the fur-lined coat she'd bought. She wrapped herself up in it, grabbed a warm hat and pulled it over her ears. She wanted the crisp air to bite her skin and remind her that for now she was still alive, no matter how much easier it would be to be dead.

Sometimes she wished she was.

All right, often she wished she was.

Cursing, Jerry climbed the ladder to the wheelhouse, grabbing her personal device as she stepped out onto the deck. She moved to the stern of *Yarrow* and leaned against the railing, hunkering down. From here she could see the lights from Potelia as they reflected off the clouds and bounced right back down to her. It was a trick, because it looked like such a warm glow, something welcoming.

But Potelia hadn't been as welcoming as she'd anticipated.

Despite Hobie's warm greeting, the rest of Potelia had been stiff when it came to outsiders. They weren't citizens, which didn't give them as many rights or privileges as everyone else. She sighed. No wonder pirates tended to stay away from there. Even the underground prioritized citizens. Not just contacts, but people who were born there—because there was no other way to achieve citizenship.

It was stuck-up in a way Jerry did not appreciate. She was so used to moving from place to place all her life that she'd gotten used to blending in wherever she went. But this time, she didn't have the right cards. It reminded her of when she was released from Joab the last time, a criminal again, never to have that record wiped from her papers.

Sighing, she opened her personal device and skimmed through the city's records. They'd already researched all the factories, and despite Azar's positive thinking, Jerry had a feeling they weren't manufacturing vestigen. Which meant, Potelia only had a store of it. Perhaps they rationed it out themselves.

She frowned at the thought.

She really hoped there was something to these rumors. Going back empty-handed would mean their deaths at that point. They didn't have enough vestigen to make it the week flight back to Raegina. Focusing on her research, Jerry pulled up the schematics for the government house. Unlike in Raegina, it was built into the side of a mountain, only the front-facing part with windows, and one entry—according to plans she could access.

However, that made zero logical sense to her, meaning there was at least a minimum of one other exit that was undesignated and hidden. If she could find it, she might be able to get in and search for a store. Equally, though, that may be too obvious a place to hide a stash of the most wanted drug on Penum.

Pressing her lips together hard, Jerry made a mental list of where else a stash could be. In some ways, the government was likely to keep it well-guarded, and in others, they'd want it as inconspicuous as possible, meaning the fewer guards the better.

But where the hell that would be, she had no idea. She didn't know Potelia well enough. If they were in Raegina, she'd know exactly where the idiotic government would store it.

That or Arloa would easily tell her.

Sighing, Jerry pinched the bridge of her nose. Arloa was working on a way to reverse engineer the pill, meaning no one else had done it. Otherwise she would fund that project and not her own, unless she wanted credits. And she didn't seem like a credit whore to Jerry at least. She had plenty and didn't need more.

Azar thought they were manufacturing it, but maybe they were just trying to get it done. Maybe they were messing with the formula much as Arloa was, but easily had a store to it. Scratching her head as she shivered in the cold, Jerry winced. She'd never felt so lost in a heist before.

She always went into them with more information, with detailed plans, but half of this heist was just gathering research, and she couldn't do that at a distance like she was used to. Potelia was too well-hidden from the rest of the world. Even Azar and Yafe hadn't known much about it, and they were from the same damn region.

Shivering again, Jerry finally got to her feet and dragged her ass inside. She made her way to her cabin and pulled out her last bottle of moonshine. She'd have to make more soon, although the laws in Potelia strictly prohibited it, and until they were out of the way of weekly inspections, she wasn't sure she wanted to risk being kicked out of the city yet.

Bringing the glass bottle to her lips, she tilted it and drank up. Being alone had her nerves on edge. When she'd first bought *Yarrow*, it had been the best feeling ever, but now that she'd lived with a full ship for a year, now that she'd been infected with a virus that caused her to be unable to control her emotions, she wanted people around, to pull her back from doing anything stupid.

She drank again, intending to get intoxicated well and

quickly. She continued her research, plotting out different places the stash could potentially be. She made a mental list of them, memorizing each location so she wouldn't forget. She would never be so stupid as to write that down in a place the authorities could find. Then they would have proof as to what she was up to.

Jerry finished half the bottle in a short period of time, her head swimming as she closed her eyes and stared at the ceiling. All her thoughts left the mission she was on and turned to Arloa. Her body was in a tizzy over the fact she had yet to get off in months, and Arloa hadn't helped that along any—not that Jerry had allowed it to happen. She'd stopped it both times.

She glanced at the device in her hand, checking the time before she made the connection. She had an hour before curfew for her crew would be called and they would be back. She'd instructed them to stay out as late as possible, making as many deep contacts as necessary. They would need all the help they could get in the end.

Arloa's sweet face lit up, holographic in nature, but steel in color—to match her eyes. It was like staring into Arloa's mind as much as looking at her face. She raised an eyebrow, her lips not moving up or down in a smile or frown. Jerry's tongue was already loose, but she'd made the call before she could clearly think about stopping herself.

"I didn't expect to hear from you before you returned."

"What makes you so certain you would when we returned?"

Arloa did frown at that. "I know you, Jer. You wouldn't break a promise like that."

"It's not a promise," Jerry hissed. "It's a fucking job."

Sitting in silence, Jerry wrinkled her nose as she turned flat on her bed. She left the device next to her so she didn't have to look at Arloa's face, didn't have to think about what it would be like to have Arloa's tongue between her legs.

"Jer." Arloa's voice was so soft, pleasant.

Jerry groaned, unable to hold it back as she clenched her eyes shut. She could hear the nonexistent whine, the pleasure curling through Arloa's tone. Her chest rose and fell rapidly as she took deeper breaths, falling into the imagery that was only a dream.

"Jer, why did you contact me?"

Brought back to reality as if Arloa had shoved her outside in the freezing cold, Jerry clenched her jaw. She turned her head, facing Arloa's steely face. "I can't find the vestigen stash you said was here."

Arloa hissed. "I swear it's there."

"Well, it's not, because I can't find it. And I'm running out of vestigen, so if we don't leave soon, we're not going to make it home." Why that last word sounded so funny but so right at the same time, Jerry wasn't sure, but she didn't want to analyze it either.

"I can send you more credits to buy some."

Hissing, Jerry shook her head. "You don't understand, Arloa. There isn't any to *buy* here, not like in Raegina, not that that is easy either. As you so well know, but it's even scarcer here. I don't know how they're surviving."

"They have to have a stash."

"I'd think so too, but I *can't* find it. I'm an outsider. I don't have ins with the government here. I don't have resources and contacts."

Arloa's lips pulled together in a pout. "I thought that's why you went up there. To make them."

"Trust takes time to build, and it has to be earned. I won't be able to do that in the short time we have left."

"That's why I sent you credits, so you could stay longer."

Jerry groaned, rubbing her hands viciously over her face before she turned on Arloa again. "You're not understanding. Without vestigen, I can't stay here. I won't survive here. This is *my* life we're talking about—the lives of my crew."

"I understand." Arloa's tone dropped, quieting. "I do. I just… I can't get you vestigen, only credits."

"Credits aren't the problem at the moment." The problem

was she wanted to live, all because fucking Arloa had walked back into her life, and Jerry couldn't even explain why. She wouldn't admit to Arloa either. A month ago, and she would have gladly died for this cause. Now? She wasn't so sure she wanted to.

Arloa sighed, the sound rushing past Jerry's ears. She reached down for her bottle and took a long swig before setting it on the floor next to her cot.

"I need some intel on where the stash can potentially be. I can't make my way through the list I have in the time we've got left."

"I'll see what I can find." Arloa pressed her lips tightly together again. "Jer?"

"What?" Jerry sounded exasperated, though she supposed she was. She was tired of fighting for everything, for her crew, for herself. She just wanted a night to relax and be wrapped in Arloa's arms and—she had to stop that line of thinking. Arloa was partway around the world at that point, and Jerry wouldn't be able to see her any time soon, and that was only if she was lucky to find this mysterious stash of drugs.

"Why did you contact me? A message would have been sufficient."

Jerry scrunched her nose. That really was the question, wasn't it? She could have left well enough alone, sent a message, washed her hands of everything, but no, she had to contact Arloa, see her face, hear her smooth and confident voice again. She shuddered, heat pooling between her legs. That's right. That had been why she'd done it this way, because her fucking body wouldn't let loose.

"It's a faster form of communication," Jerry supplied as an answer. She was right, of course, and even in her intoxicated brain, she could still spin circles around the truths she didn't want shared. "When do you think you'll know something about the stash?"

Humming, Arloa looked at something next to her. Jerry had

no idea what, but she missed that enticing eye contact. "Tomorrow at the earliest. It may take longer if I can't find anything."

Jerry sighed. "We only have a week left, at most. That's if we ration down to the bare minimum."

"A week until you run out?"

"No." Jerry shook her head, waiting for Arloa to drag her gaze back up. "A week until we're dead."

"I understand." Arloa's voice was so soft this time, as if she was as resigned as Jerry was to her own demise. Except Jerry didn't want to hear the deferential tone. She hated it. If Arloa lost hope, then what was the point of her having any. "I'll do my best."

"Your best might not be good enough."

They lapsed into an uncomfortable silence, Jerry's last comment hanging in the air between them heavily. She wanted to take it back, to make Arloa feel better about herself, but at the same time, she didn't. It was true. Even if all of them did their best, Jerry would most likely end up dead. So would her crew. If it wasn't from the fucking virus that was attacking them from the inside out, then it would be from something else they were doing.

"My crew will be back soon," Jerry whispered, finally breaking the stay.

"Do you not want them to know you contacted me?"

"Not this way. They might think something else of it." The words were out of her mouth before she could stop herself. She really shouldn't get drunk and then talk to Arloa. It was a bad idea all around.

"And they don't already?"

Jerry frowned. "We weren't exactly quiet before we left."

"We weren't."

"But I don't know what they think. Frankly, I don't much care what they think either."

"Then why does it matter if they come back?" Arloa's tone was hushed.

Jerry had to stop herself from answering. She was the one who didn't want a show of it. She was the one who didn't want anyone to know, because if they found out, then she would have to put words to what she wasn't wanting to feel. Frowning, Jerry turned on her side and planted her head on her hand as she propped her elbow into the cot.

"I'll talk to you soon." She ended the conversation without another word. She knew it was cruel, but she also knew Arloa wouldn't contact her again—at least not any time soon and not for this. She hated what the virus had done to her. Before it, she'd been calm, cool, and collected. Able to control her feelings, figure out what she wanted and needed, and she wasn't scared shitless to let anyone else see it. But since then? All she had to do was hide. Because if they found out she was infected, at least in Raegina, she'd be dead. And it took everything in her to hide it from the world.

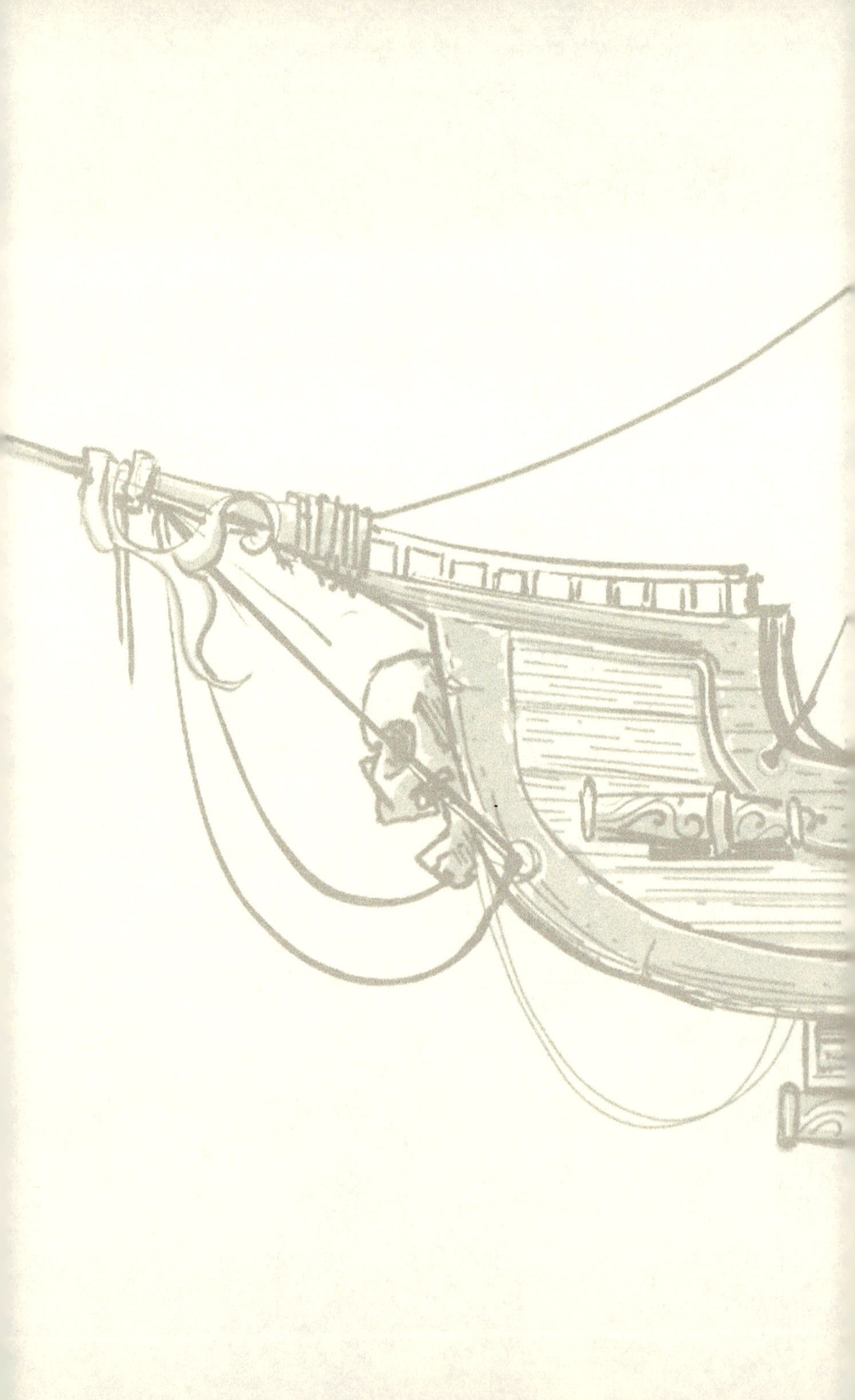

CHAPTER 18

Jerry returned from the run for Jacque only to find Azar waiting on the slip for her. He looked half-frozen, standing wrapped in his fur-lined jacket with a fur hat low on his forehead. Jerry cocked her head at him as she parked *Yarrow*, and he had the door open and was inside before she'd even shut the main engines off. She glanced at Yafe and Sacha who stood with her in the wheelhouse and shrugged.

"He did have a shift at the factory today, right?"

"Yeah," Yafe answered. "That medical one he's been going on about."

Pursing her lips, Jerry scrunched her nose and put her hands on her hips as she turned and waited for him to climb up the ladder. "All right."

It took longer than she expected, but they were all moving slower than usual. Damn them for running low on vestigen. It had taken them longer to do their run for Jacque too. Jerry cocked her head as Azar's dark face lit up the room, the smile blooming on his lips.

"There was a problem at the factory. They shut everything down." He climbed up the last ladder.

"So you're missing a day at work because...?" Jerry eyed him cautiously. They were supposed to be making contacts, not spurning them.

"Because we're waiting on a part to get in before we can fix the machine. We can't work if there's nothing running."

"So they sent you home. Without pay. Of course." Jerry rolled her eyes and faced *Yarrow's* dash, pretending that she was busying herself with work.

Azar came to stand next to her, nearly vibrating in his boots. "Yeah, it sucks."

Lifting her chin, she finally looked him over like she should have done the first time. His nearly black eyes were wide with excitement. Every muscle in his body was tense. His hand remained tightly fisted as he rested it on the brass bar in front of the dash.

Jerry didn't say anything as they stared at each other. She wanted to ask, she really did, but she feared the answer. Azar flicked his gaze over her shoulder at Yafe and Sacha, then he grinned again.

"Out with it," Jerry muttered so quietly she wasn't even sure he heard her.

Instead of saying anything, Azar lifted his hand, opening his fingers one by one. In the center of his broad palm sat a small unmarked pill. It wasn't in the shape of vestigen, but that didn't mean anything. If they were newly manufacturing it, they could make it whatever the fuck shape they wanted. Jerry stared at it, her mind swirling with ideas, thoughts, hopes.

"What is it?" she finally asked, finding her voice.

"A supersecret project I'm not supposed to know about."

"And how do you know about it?" Reaching forward tentatively, Jerry plucked the small pill from his palm and lifted it up so she could see it properly. There were no markings to identify what it was. Which could mean anything, really, and they weren't set up to run a bunch of experiments on it and find out if it was what they were hoping for.

"I stumbled across the room by accident. It's the one causing all the problems today, and since they only allow certain workers in there, they kicked the rest of us out to continue to keep it a secret."

"How did you manage to swipe this?"

"Stealth." He was bouncing again in his boots, excitement rolling off of him in waves.

Jerry faced Yafe and Sacha, holding up the pill so they could see what they were talking about. Jerry stared at it, nearly going cross-eyed from how long she held the thing in her gaze. *Could this really be it?*

"How do we know this is what we're looking for?" The question finally came out of her mouth. "If this is vestigen, or another form of it, how do we know that without a lab or scientist?"

Azar frowned. "I can try to steal the schematics for making it."

"You mean formula." Jerry sent him a side-eyed look. "How are we supposed to read that? We're uneducated."

"You can send it to Arloa." Yafe stepped in, moving closer to see the pill. She held out her hand for it, as if it was the most precious thing in the world.

Sacha moved next to her, and they all stared down at Yafe's brown hand and the small white pill. *What the fuck were they supposed to do with this?* Jerry hadn't planned on needing to run experiments, and even then, she wasn't sure she knew anyone who could in a short period of time. Definitely not anyone in Potelia. Frowning, she locked her gaze on that pill again.

"We don't have time to send it to Arloa. We need answers as soon as possible. We don't have much time left." She couldn't look away from it. This small white pill might be the answer to their problem. If they didn't have a stash, or they were running out, then perhaps they were trying to do exactly what Arloa was doing. If they were, then perhaps Arloa could just buy them out or work with them—whatever she wanted. Either way, they had an answer to a problem. But this small pill could honestly be another drug, one that had no effect on the virus whatsoever.

"There is one way to find out what it is," Sacha murmured, her sweet melodic voice carrying through Jerry's turmoil.

"What do you mean?" Jerry stared at her. "No one is taking it without knowing what it is."

"It might be the only way, Cap." Sacha gave her a firm, clear-eyed look.

Somewhere in the back of Jerry's mind, she'd already come to that conclusion, but she really didn't want to go down that road. While she was dumb and crazy enough to do it, she didn't want to put anyone in her crew in harm's way, which meant she would have to be the one to try it.

Azar leaned in. "Give me a day to try and find some information on it. The formula or whatever we want to call it."

Except Jerry knew they didn't have a day.

"How many of these do you think you can steal?"

"Without them finding out?" Azar's brow rose up, lines etching into his skin. "Maybe one or two more. They keep an impeccable count of everything."

"Then only this one," Jerry murmured, not daring to take it back from Yafe because she didn't want to accidentally drop the thing. They were going to have to find some way to keep it.

"There is a faster way to find answers," Yafe said it so smoothly.

Jerry lifted her gaze to Yafe's face, those dark brown eyes glued to the pill, her tightly-curled hair haloing her face. She was just about to object when Yafe opened her mouth and slapped her palm straight to her lips, the pill disappearing.

"What the fuck?" Jerry shouted as she gripped Yafe's wrist and jerked her hand away from her mouth, but it was too late already.

Sacha stepped away, like Yafe was about to go wild, killing everyone in a murder spree. Azar gripped Yafe's arms, holding them to her side as he ordered her to spit it out. Jerry just stared at her like she was insane.

"Spit it out!" Azar yelled again.

Jerry shook her head, gripping onto the brass bar. She couldn't lose Yafe. She was the one person keeping her sane on the ship. She was the one person Jerry trusted the most, even if she didn't trust her with everything—not yet. Tears stung at Jerry's eyes as Yafe gave a broad, sickening grin.

"It's too late," Yafe stated, so simply, so without fear or worry.

"You could have just killed yourself," Jerry murmured. "You have no idea what you just took."

"Aren't you the one who is always saying we're dead anyway?"

Fuck, why did she have to toss those words back at her? Jerry cringed. "Yeah, but don't kill yourself just to prove it."

Yafe's serious look went straight to Jerry's stomach. The number of times she had thought about jumping over the side of the dock and into the poisoned sea were too many to count, and Yafe must have known it. Azar released her, but he looked so angry. Jerry had never seen him this pissed before.

Sacha came back over now that she knew Yafe wasn't going to explode on her. "Why did you do it?"

"Someone had to." Yafe eyed her carefully. "And it can't be Azar because we need his skills. It can't be Jerry because she's captain. So it was me or you, and I didn't think you'd be so inclined."

Sacha frowned. "I might have."

Yafe gave the lightest of snorts but reined herself back in. They were going to have to watch her carefully for the rest of the evening and the night. They weren't going anywhere, none of them. They would lock themselves in—that way if this pill had any devastating effects it would only affect them and no one else.

Jerry swallowed a lump in her throat. She stepped closer to Yafe, her eyes softening and her heart nearly breaking as she curled a hand around Yafe's cheek. "If I fucking lose you, I'm going to haunt you."

Yafe smirked. "Pretty sure since I'll be the dead one that *I* get to haunt *you*."

"We'll see about that." Jerry's lips curled upward slightly. She had no idea how to even broach what had just happened. It was against everything in Jerry's gut, even though she knew this was the quickest and best way to get answers.

Yafe stepped back from them all, her hands out at her sides as she raised an eyebrow at each of them. "For anyone wondering, it tastes way better than vestigen, but it still has that awful chalky texture to it."

Jerry grimaced. As soon as Yafe had said it, she remembered the flavor and texture of vestigen as if she'd just taken a pill herself. Except she hadn't, because she was completely out of the drug. She'd given her last pill to Azar without him knowing.

She would be the first one of them to go, and they didn't even know it.

After an hour had passed, there seemed to be no adverse effects from the pill. Yafe looked and acted completely normal. Jerry wouldn't let her be alone, and most of that time had been the two of them sitting together, talking and planning. Jerry cringed when Yafe rolled her eyes after some ridiculous comment. Sacha sat in the corner, munching on a food pack while the two of them sat still.

"Before I die," Yafe said, a glint to her eye as though she were trying to make a joke, which wasn't funny. Jerry glared. "You should know that my dearest brother and that one are fucking."

Jerry whipped her head around to stare at Sacha. "Really?"

Sacha paled completely.

"How did I not know this?"

Yafe giggled. "Because they go down into the storage rooms and he gags her so she doesn't scream.

"How do *you* know this?" Jerry's brow drew together.

"I caught them by accident one time, and I can't get the image out of my head. I needed someone else to live with that scar for the rest of their life if I can't."

"Fuck you," Sacha said, maliciously.

Jerry shook her head. "I would rather that than either of you hiring a whore."

Yafe nodded. "I knew you'd say that."

Sacha wrinkled her nose. "What good are whores?"

Jerry eyed her carefully, not saying a word. She held Sacha's gaze for a long time before she focused back on Yafe. "So how are you feeling, truthfully?"

"I think this is a drug they are trying to take vestigen's place, but I got to tell you, Cap, it's not very strong. Like I can barely feel it working on the edges of the pain and hunger."

Pausing, Jerry pressed her lips together in a thin line. "But you do feel it?"

"A bit. I think I'd need a handful of those to make any difference."

"I wonder if they got the formula wrong."

"Or it just takes longer to feel the effects from it." Yafe stared at the tabletop. "Either way, it is a drug that will do what we need, we just might need more of it than normal."

Jerry sighed and rubbed her temple. "Do you know how ridiculous an idea that was?"

Yafe shrugged. "You're not the only one desperate for some relief, Cap."

And there it was, the truth in plain words. They were all struggling with an addiction they never wanted, a craving they couldn't control. The drug to medicate themselves was also a drug that could very easily kill them, especially if they didn't get it. They *had* to take it.

"So is this the drug we're trying to find?" Sacha asked the one question Jerry hadn't been able to voice.

If Potelia was manufacturing vestigen, or trying to anyway, then did they have a stash of it somewhere? She stared into her packet of water, wishing she could talk to Arloa again, bounce these ideas off her. She was smart, but she also understood governments in ways Jerry didn't. She might be able to help them figure out if they were on the right track or not, but with the way they had left the conversation—or rather Jerry had ended it—the last time, she wasn't too keen on the idea of contacting Arloa again.

"It might be," Jerry murmured. "Yafe will have to tell us if it works or not. It may just need a higher dose, which is something we can play with if we get more."

"It seems to be working, it's just not super effective."

"Maybe it's your body chemistry. I've read studies about how different drugs work differently on men and women, along with a host of other variables," Sacha stated.

Jerry spun on Sacha at that comment. She trailed her gaze over Sacha's form, stopping again as she looked into her eyes, debating whether Sacha was more educated than she'd first anticipated. "Where did you get your schooling?"

Sacha's lips parted. "I didn't—"

"There's no way you would say that without schooling. Where did you go?"

Sacha's cheeks tinged pink in embarrassment. "I never finished grammar school, but I made it through the fifth year before I dropped out."

"In Raegina?" Jerry pushed.

Nodding, Sacha dropped her gaze to the ground. "My parents paid for it, but I left when I got pregnant."

"Where's the baby?"

"He died while he was still inside me." Sacha's eyes watered. Yafe moved in and wrapped an arm around her shoulder. "I didn't have the heart to go home, so I've been living on my own since."

Jerry frowned. "I'm so sorry."

Sacha lifted and dropped a shoulder. "It was a few years ago now. I'm much more careful now. Don't you worry. Azar and I won't—"

Jerry cringed and held up her hand. "I don't make it a point to interfere in my crew's lives, Sacha. If it happens, we'll figure it out, but I don't allow whores on board either."

They lapsed into silence, Sacha gathering herself before Yafe leaned into her chair. Azar came in at some point, and they fell into a quiet murmur. Jerry wanted to start a plan, but she wasn't going to until she knew for certain that this was what they were after.

"Azar, I want you to find as much information as you can on this drug, but please don't take any unnecessary risks. I don't want to be breaking you out of jail."

He nodded at her. "I'd already planned on it."

"Good." Jerry eyed Yafe again. "In the morning, we'll talk about a more detailed plan if this is what we're after. We'll need information about shipping times, manufacturing times, and efficacy if we can get that."

Azar stared directly at her. "I'll find out whatever I can."

Sacha leaned forward. "I've been seeing the dockmaster, Hobie. I'll try to figure out something from him, too."

Azar jerked toward her, but Jerry interrupted, not wanting an argument on that front. "Good. Deepen your contacts while we're at it. We'll have a full brainstorming session tomorrow to talk about plans once we know for certain this pill isn't going to kill us."

She eyed Yafe again, up and down, trying to see if there was any sign of change in her demeanor that could be a tell for what might be happening in her body. Jerry knew it was ridiculous, but she couldn't stop herself. Yafe had been her rock throughout the entire year, and while Jerry had been Yafe's when they were tossed into Joab together, she wasn't sure she could live without her best friend.

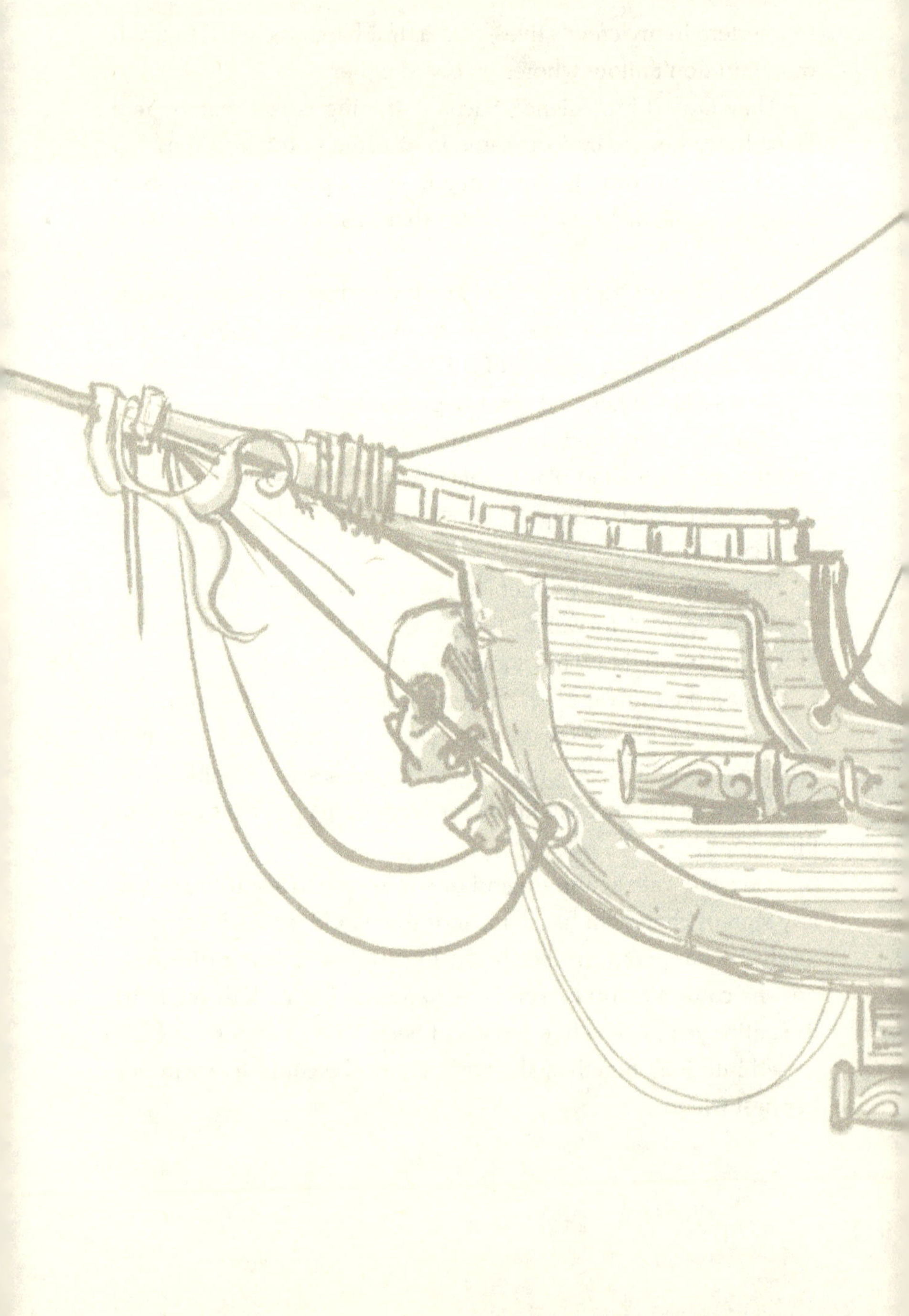

CHAPTER 19

Jerry checked on Yafe as soon as she woke up, finding Azar asleep on the floor of her cabin. She smiled at them both, knowing he'd been just as worried as Jerry had. Slipping from the room, Jerry went up to the wheelhouse, which was more her refuge than her cabin. The dock was already coming to life around her. People moving from the pier to their vessels, getting ready for the day's work. She could see Hobie, bumbling around up toward the station, wrapped tightly in his warm jacket as a breeze came off the shore. That was another thing Jerry wasn't sure she could get used to.

Her head ached, a sharp stabbing pain that sliced through her skull and down into her shoulders. A migraine from hell, though she knew what it meant. They didn't have much time left. Their connections were strong. Hobie liked her and had given her several tips about jobs throughout the weeks they'd been there. Sacha had made nice with a few of the other dock workers, most likely using her body to get what they needed, but Jerry hadn't told her to do it. She'd just done it.

Jerry pressed the button on the front of her dash and made contact with Arloa. If the heist failed, it would be the last time they saw each other, that much Jerry understood, and she hoped after their previous conversation that Arloa understood it too.

Arloa's face appeared in front of her, holographic steel at its finest. Jerry leaned over the brass bar so she got closer so she could see into Arloa's eyes. "Sorry about the other night."

Arloa's lips thinned into a line, and she cast her gaze down. "I don't have much time to talk today."

"I understand. I think there isn't a stash of vestigen here."

"I concur." Arloa looked around, then lowered her voice. "I've done as much research as I can, but I've found nothing."

"We may have found something."

Arloa's eyes widened, and suddenly, Jerry had every ounce of her attention.

"Azar came back from the factory with a pill, which Yafe stupidly took. It's like vestigen, but not. It's not as effective, but it might be just enough that it'll work."

"Are you serious?" Arloa whispered.

Jerry jerked her chin up. "Seems as though they're trying to manufacture it."

"Fuck," Arloa muttered, and Jerry grinned at the curse word. Getting her to curse was not easy.

"We're going to make a plan, but we only have a day or two to execute it."

"What do you need? I'll do anything I can to help."

Jerry hesitated before answering. Arloa didn't have anything she needed, at least not in that moment. She would when they got back to Raegina, but for now, they had everything. Well, maybe not everything, but it wasn't anything Arloa could get them. "You've done what you can so far."

"Are you sure?"

Nodding, Jerry straightened her back, catching sight of Hobie walking down the dock. "I think we're up for an inspection today."

"What does that entail?"

"Nothing we can't handle. I should be home soon." Jerry made eye contact, a brow raised as if she was flirting. But the sentiment about going home felt good. She didn't know when Raegina had become home, but sometime in the last year, it had.

"Please find me. I think we need to talk when you do arrive."

"Maybe." Jerry dropped her gaze, breaking eye contact. "I will give you what you asked for at the very least."

"But, Jer, we do need to talk."

"There's nothing to talk about."

"There is. You can't leave the way you did without talking to me. I won't stand for it again."

Clenching her jaw, Jerry had to admit Arloa had a point. Ever since she'd been infected, she'd avoided Arloa at all costs, and then when she couldn't, she left before the conversation got too personal. She didn't want to talk about feelings. She didn't want to analyze why she stopped fucking Arloa before even giving her a chance.

"I've got to go. It's time for inspections." Jerry ended the communication and straightened her back, popping her spine before she slid down the ladder right when *Yarrow* informed her Hobie had arrived.

She opened the interior door, then the exterior door, which lowered down to create a bridge between the ship and the dock. Jerry plastered a smile on her face as Hobie nodded toward her and came right inside to get out of the wind and cold.

"Morning," he grumbled.

"Inspection time?" Jerry asked with a happy tone. It wasn't her norm, but she'd learned quickly that Hobie responded to this overwhelming giddiness. So as best as she could, she tried to make all her interactions with him like that.

"Yes. Sorry to make it early, but we have an important vessel coming in tomorrow, and I need extra time to do the inspection, so I moved some things around."

"It's not a problem." Jerry stepped away from the interior door to let him in.

They walked down into the storerooms, where she had nothing, so the inspection was easy. When they got to the deck with cabins, Jerry stopped. "Let me wake them up first."

Hobie didn't look impressed, though she supposed he wouldn't be. Normally they were already starting their day by then, but since they'd had such a late night, Jerry had let her crew sleep in. She started on Sacha's door, knocking until she answered, tousled and red-cheeked from sleep.

"It's an inspection day."

"Oh." She brushed a hand over her hair. "Um, yeah, he can come in."

While Hobie was busy there, Jerry went to Yafe's room and knocked, waking both her and Azar. Yafe looked slightly better than she had the day before, which Jerry figured was a good sign. Azar blinked bleary-eyed up at Jerry.

"What time is it?"

"Just past the sixth bell."

"Fuck." He scrambled to his feet. "I don't want to be late."

He was out of the room like a shot, didn't even bother to run to his cabin before grabbing his jacket and leaving. Jerry crossed her arms and leaned against the wall while Hobie went to the next cabin to do his inspection.

She watched Hobie carefully. She'd gotten to be pretty good friends with him, but it was time to lay some new groundwork. As they made their way up the ladder to the next level, she said, "Do you have any other quick jobs we might be able to catch this week? We're trying to store up some extra credits so we can make our trip back to Raegina."

"You're leaving?" He glanced down at Sacha, who joined them.

Jerry waited until they were all standing. "Unfortunately. We're needed at home, but also, we can't handle this cold. It's too much for our weak blood."

Hobie let out a bellow of a laugh. It sent shivers up Jerry's spine. She'd set that one up right. Sacha sent Jerry a look, and

Jerry shook her head slightly at it. "I can send a few more your way."

"Thanks. I'd appreciate it."

He checked the galley and the small room behind it, then went to the wheelhouse. His inspections were never long or detailed, and Jerry couldn't help but wonder how much actually got by him. In that way, pirating from Potelia would be very easy. Except, most pirates didn't do anything on the legal side. She had found her way to the legal and was pulled back to the illegal, otherwise she would never have those contacts either.

After they finished in the wheelhouse, Hobie gave Jerry a couple contacts for jobs. As he was turning to leave, she popped her fist on her hip. "Why did you say you had to do the inspection early again?"

"Important vessel's coming in tomorrow."

"What for?"

"Shipment, I think."

"These ones don't come often?"

He shook his head. "Only once a month."

"Huh. What do they carry? I've always wanted to run bigger ships than *Yarrow*."

Hobie finished out his report on his large device and settled it next to his side. "Oh, I think this one runs medical equipment, mostly. Although when the virus first hit, it did take the dead out to sea."

"Oh." Jerry's face fell. "They did something similar in Raegina, except they just tossed them off into the harbor. Flying in during those first few months was awful."

Hobie looked as though he was going to lose his lunch. Jerry knocked her head to the side.

"I wish they could have had a proper burial," she murmured.

"Agreed." But he didn't say more on it.

"Well, thanks for the contacts. I'll get right on it. We'll probably leave before our next weekly inspection."

With the dismissal in hand, Hobie left *Yarrow*. Sacha turned on her. "We're leaving?"

"We came here for one purpose, and we've found it. We need to steal a shipment of that drug Yafe took, and then we need to hightail it out of here. If he thinks we're already leaving, there will be less suspicion when we don't return suddenly."

"Makes sense, I guess," she mumbled. "I think I might miss this place."

Jerry snorted. "I won't."

"Missing your girl?"

Clenching her jaw tightly, Jerry refused to answer. She faced the front window of *Yarrow* and stared out at the city in front of her. *Potelia.* She might have to come back and visit someday, so long as she knew she wasn't going to be hauled away into their prison system. Still, it seemed like a nice city.

"Maybe we should come back in the warmer months."

"Agreed." Sacha chuckled, crossed her arms, and stood next to Jerry. "What are we doing today?"

"We've got a run for Jacque, and I want to make maybe one more run for someone if they'll give us the job. Mostly we're waiting for Azar to come home and see what he's found out. I want to know what that important vessel is bringing in."

"It's vestigen." Yafe's voice was smooth as she climbed the ladder.

"What?" Jerry's eyes widened. "Are you sure?"

"I am."

"How?"

"I was on my device trying to get hold of Pauline, and she slipped up that they had to get in line for their drugs tomorrow. Apparently the vessel brings in a one month supply and then it's distributed to citizens. They have to regulate their own intake for the whole month."

"Fuck." Jerry's clenched onto the wheel. "We must have just missed it when we came in."

"Agreed." Yafe's eyes lit up. "The drug they're making is a poor substitute. I'm already feeling withdrawal."

"It'll work if we take more than one pill in a go."

Yafe nodded, looking toward Sacha. "Think you can get your friend to let us on board?"

"No. He won't. But I might be able to figure out when they'll be offloading it."

"That'd be good." Jerry turned on Sacha. "Do that. Then we can form a better plan. More details always work better."

Each of them went to work on what they had to do. Jerry pulled *Yarrow* out of the slip and headed toward the river so she could pick up her regular shipment for Jacque.

Milton waited for them, and they were right on time, even with the inspection. Jerry pulled up to the dock and lowered *Yarrow's* door so they could exit. Milton kept a stern look on his face as he led the way to where the goods were. Jerry shoved her hands into her pockets as she followed, keeping her fingers warm against the biting wind.

"We won't be doing many more runs for Jacque," Jerry stated, by way of small talk. "I already talked to him. Love the work, hate this cold."

Milton snorted. "You transplants never last long."

"I suppose not. We were ill-prepared for it."

He nodded and stopped in front of a large bounty of crates. Jerry eyed them over. Having Azar there that day would have been helpful. Instead she was stuck with Yafe and Sacha, and Sacha was not usually super helpful when it came to moving heavy objects. Jerry rolled her shoulders as she tugged on one of them.

"Is this the only run today?"

"Yes," Milton answered. "We're low on supplies this week."

Jerry pursed her lips. That actually worked out in her favor, not that she was going to admit that. "Great."

"Not my problem there's more for you."

"Of course it's not," Jerry said under her breath. She didn't expect him to suddenly like her. She'd only been working on it every day since they'd started working for Jacque, and had failed miserably. Milton was not someone she could turn to for favors. Luckily, Sacha and Yafe had both been working their magic back in the harbor.

It took them a few hours to load *Yarrow*. But as soon as they were on board, Jerry said goodbye to Milton with as much disdain in her tone as she could muster. He was not someone she wanted to meet up with again. With their load delivered, Jerry found her slip and parked. They went down to the bar to get some food, and something in the back of Jerry's mind told her that it would be their last warm meal for a while.

She couldn't stop thinking of Arloa the entire time they were in the bar. That had been how they'd met. Jerry had walked into her favorite bar in Raegina, sat in her favorite worn down wooden stool and right next to the beautiful Arloa.

She swallowed hard as she sucked down some of her malt. It wasn't as good as the one at her favorite place, somewhere she hadn't been back to since she'd gotten the virus and broken whatever tenuous relationship they'd started. Jerry shuddered at the memory. Arloa had been just as bold and courageous then.

Jerry had come on to her, asking to touch her, hoping Arloa would allow it, and Arloa had willingly given herself over to Jerry, multiple times. The one entire night they'd spent together had been the best marathon sex Jerry ever had.

Sacha brushed against Jerry as she leaned in to flirt with the barkeep. Jerry ignored it. Sacha had grown fond of touching her since her time aboard *Yarrow*, and each time Jerry had ignored it. She couldn't tell if Sacha thought that was what she wanted or if it was something else. She'd leave that fun to Azar—which was odd. Sacha didn't strike her as someone he would want. Then again, she had dragged them all to Potelia without so much as a warning, and when people were stuck in a vessel, shit happened.

She frowned into her drink as she guzzled the rest of it and ordered another. Yafe kept sending her worried glances, and

Jerry knew she was on edge. The withdrawal from the vestigen was already wearing on her mind, and she had to work twice as hard to manage her emotions. Drinking likely wouldn't help that situation any.

Like when she'd gotten drunk and then contacted Arloa. *Why was that woman such a weak point for her?* Jerry couldn't get enough of her. Her strength, her tenacity, her almost simplistic understanding and acceptance of whatever Jerry said and did. How could someone be so saintly and be a fucking Kauket?

It was mind-boggling. Jerry frowned as another drink was set in front of her. She hated to think of it, but at the same time, she had to. She'd spurned Arloa multiple times already, and yet, she still wanted to talk about them? It seemed unfathomable. Jerry wasn't someone Arloa could find refuge or hope in, someone she could find a wife in.

Not when Arloa was in the government. Not when Jerry was still a pirate. Clenching her jaw, she grabbed her drink and sucked down half of it in four large gulps. Jerry could never be a perfect mate for Arloa. That much had been clear from the start. It had all begun in good fun and turned into something else entirely. When had *that* happened?

Yafe leaned in and touched Jerry's shoulder, whispering, "We should go. Azar will be back soon."

Nodding, Jerry paid for their meals, and they all left.

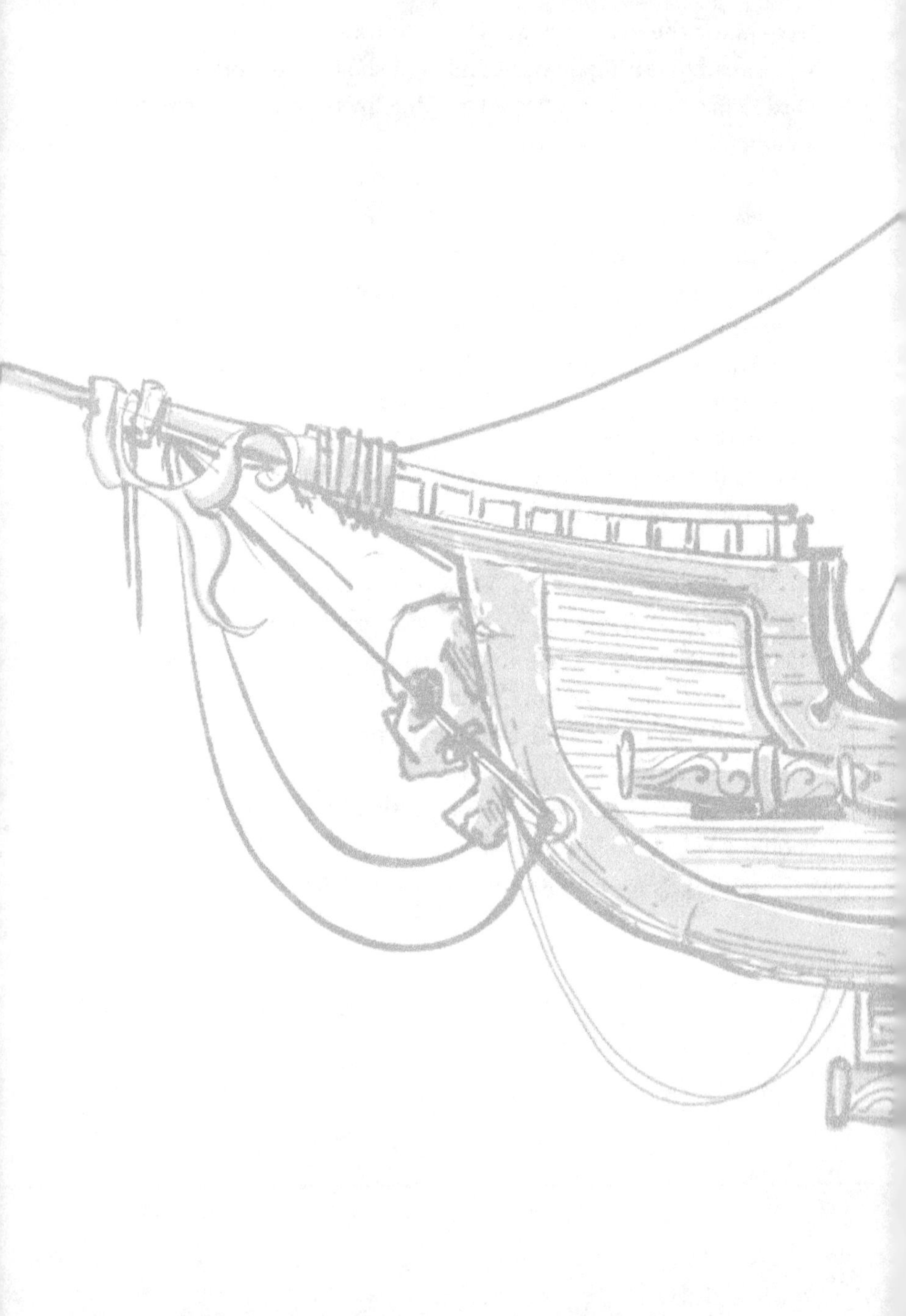

CHAPTER 20

Azar swung into *Yarrow*, making a racket as he clambered up the ladder to the galley. Jerry waited for him. Sacha and Yafe were in their cabins, but Azar was later than Jerry expected. She bounced her heel as he came around the corner, a wild look in his dark eyes.

"I have a shipment date."

Jerry pursed her lips. "Is this a drug that we really want to take?"

Azar's look of confusion wasn't out of place. They'd spent the last month trying to find vestigen, the drug that would help them survive, and now Jerry seemed as though she was backing out of the plan. Jerry shook her head slightly but could barely drag her gaze back up to look him in the eye. She'd been pondering the same question since Yafe had taken the pill, since it hadn't been as effective.

Shuddering, Jerry stayed motionless as she spun through the question again. *What was the point?* If the drug wasn't as effective, they would need more than before. She couldn't be sure how it worked with their current protocol for those coming off a new exposure or binger with no vestigen, or if it would even work for that.

Azar slid into the chair across from her at the small table. He pressed his hands flat on the smooth wood and stared at her with those deep eyes, concern filling his gaze. Jerry couldn't help but look up at him.

"I mean…this drug isn't really effective. So what's the point? Will it work?" Jerry frowned. She'd doubted the mission from the moment she'd decided to go, but she'd always thought it was simply because Arloa had been the one who sent her on it. Jerry's stomach churned. *She wouldn't…send them on a fruitless mission, would she?* The doubts had been creeping in more as the last week had passed, as her body weaned off the vestigen they had no more of.

"Cap, this is what we came here for."

"But it's not." Jerry stared at him wildly. "This isn't what we came here for. We came for vestigen, and now we're leaving with this? This drug that doesn't work right?"

Azar frowned, his gaze falling to the tabletop with nothing on it. Jerry had sat there for hours, waiting for him to return with information she wasn't sure she wanted. Spinning in her own thoughts was a detriment to her crew, but this time, she couldn't pull herself out of it.

Vestigen had been their goal from day one. Find it and survive. Yet here they were with an inferior product. Clenching her jaw and fists, Jerry finally looked up at him. "We can't do this."

"We have no choice," Azar pushed back at her. "We need *something.*"

She knew he was right. Ultimately even a drug that was a third or less effective was something they needed because thus far they hadn't found another option. Swallowing the lump in her throat, Jerry shook her head. "I don't have a good feeling about this."

"You never have a good feeling, Cap. Not since the virus—"

"This virus changed the world!" Jerry slammed her fist onto the tabletop, her shoulders curling with tension as she glared at him. She dropped her chin down as she added, "Nothing is the same anymore."

Azar canted his head toward her. "I can't believe you. If this virus hadn't infected you, I would have relieved you of duty."

Jerry stared directly at him, fury in her look. "Exactly my point. We're already dead, so why even continue?"

"Because we're not dead yet," Yafe's clear tones reached Jerry's ears, startling her. She stood in the galley doorway, leaning against the frame with her arms crossed as she eyed both of them.

Shock twisted in Jerry's gut, that same feeling of something being wrong penetrating her thoughts again. She had a crew she had to take care of, not just here but back in Raegina, and she was charged with making sure they survived. But the question wouldn't stop rampaging through her mind—*survive for what?*

"Cap?" Yafe stepped into the galley, worry etched into her features.

Jerry shook her head sharply. "I need a minute."

Pushing her way out of the room, she climbed the ladder to the wheelhouse and ignored her jacket as she walked right by it and headed for the deck. Cold air rushed over her, chilling her cheeks and drying the tears that had found their way into the corners of her eyes.

The problem wasn't that she didn't think they should steal it or that the mission was fruitless. The problem was she didn't understand why they should survive or what they had to live for. There would be no change in Raegina—or Penum for that matter. Their planet would endlessly put down her people, shunning them and forgetting they existed except when they were needed.

She shivered but not from the cold air. Jerry stared at the wheelhouse. She'd pushed through for as long as she could, and even with the crew belowdecks, she couldn't bring herself to want to care. She was one uneducated woman in a sea of misogyny and classism and sickness. She would never survive.

Jerry stayed outside for as long as she could stand it, but when her fingers were completely numb and her face hurt to move, she stepped into the wheelhouse. No matter how many times she had contemplated ending her own life, freezing to death was not the option she would choose. Her luck would have Azar warming her up and her heart restarting because the damned virus wouldn't just let her die like it should.

She stopped short when she saw the blue blinking light on the dash at the front of the wheelhouse. Rubbing her lips together side to side, Jerry debated whether or not to check it. She hadn't come to any more conclusions about the heist and had no answers for Azar and Yafe.

On impulse, Jerry hit the button. Arloa's sweet face filled the holographic communication device in front of her, the soft blonde curls of her hair against her cheeks as her eyes brightened. Jerry scowled. She should have known better. Now fate was throwing a sick twist in her direction. Arloa looked as though she was about to speak but stopped short when her gaze landed on Jerry.

"What's wrong?" Arloa's tone was precise and filled with pure concern.

"Nothing is wrong," Jerry ground out, her jaw tight as she avoided an answer.

"Please don't lie to me."

The silence was heavy. Jerry didn't dare glance over her shoulder to see if anyone was coming up to find her yet. Instead, she stared directly into Arloa's pale eyes, a blue she remembered dearly though she couldn't see it through the device itself. She repeated, "Nothing is wrong."

Arloa drew in a steady breath. "You're out of vestigen."

"I told you we would be." Jerry's fingers tightened into a fist as she stood still, every muscle in her body tight, ready for fight or flight. She hated that feeling, but she had no reason to walk away other than her own raging emotions that she couldn't control.

"You said—"

Jerry snorted, interrupting her. "We haven't found any more vestigen. There is a poor replacement being manufactured, but it's not worth the dirt on my boots."

Arloa frowned. "What do you mean replacement?"

Blinking slowly, Jerry knocked her chin up. "Meaning Yafe took it, and it barely worked."

"But enough of it—"

"It won't work," Jerry reiterated, her voice tight as she attempted to hold back.

"Jer." Arloa frowned, glanced over her shoulder at something Jerry couldn't see, then focused back on her. "I want you to come home."

That word hit her hard, but it repulsed more than anything. Sneering, Jerry shook her head. "I don't have a home."

"You do. Here in Raegina. You have people who care—"

"The people who care about me are on this ship. This is my home. *Yarrow* is my home, and if you don't understand that, then we really don't understand each other."

Arloa's eyes widened. "I understand that you're struggling without vestigen in your system."

"Do you know what it's like? To have this slow painful death that will just never fucking come?" Jerry glared. "No, you don't, because you're *immune* to it."

"That's not something I chose."

"Of course it wasn't!" Jerry yelled, her voice echoing in the wheelhouse as her movements became jerky and uncontrolled. "Because why would the government let us choose anything? You're part of it. Why can't you—"

"Jer. Stop." Arloa's soft but firm tones filled Jerry's ears and halted her in place.

Taking deep breaths, Jerry worked to calm her racing heart. A headache pounded its way in her skull, ringing in her ears. She closed her eyes as she focused on the pain, centering herself again. She wouldn't apologize. She would never apologize for being infected with death.

"Get the drug. Even if it's only partially effective, it'll help."

"It won't," Jerry answered quietly. "That's what you're not understanding. Nothing will fix this."

"Not yet," Arloa responded, coaxing. "But I have hope we'll find a cure."

"There's no fucking cure, Arloa. And there's no one looking for one but you." Jerry knew she had Arloa there. It couldn't be denied. The government didn't care about unmentionables like Jerry, the scourge of Penum that no one wanted anything to do with. She wouldn't put it past the damn government for introducing the virus to wipe them out in the first place.

"Jer, I want you to listen to me."

As much as she didn't want to, Jerry couldn't stop herself from leaning in and hanging on every word, on the soft confidence in her voice, the way her thin upper lip remained firm but her lower one quivered. Her heart shattered.

"I will find a cure, no matter how long it takes me. I have people working on it, not just manufacturing vestigen, but on an actual cure."

"I don't believe you," Jerry murmured. "I don't believe anything you say."

"I need you to push beyond the virus and what it's telling you to think. This isn't you. This isn't the Jerry I know. You had so much hope when you bought *Yarrow*, when you finally were able to redeem yourself."

Tears pricked Jerry's eyes again, and she hated herself all the more for it. Dragging her gaze up, she locked her eyes on the image of Arloa. "Fuck you."

Slamming her hand onto the light, she ended the communication. Jerry's chest rose and fell sharply as she caught her breath, staring out the front of *Yarrow* to Potelia. Where was all that hope she'd had, not when she first purchased *Yarrow* but when they'd come there? She needed it, or she needed to realize she would never have it again.

"We need to get it." Yafe's cool voice startled her.

Jerry spun around, her hands flinging out to her sides as she glared at her intruder.

"Arloa isn't wrong, Cap. Azar and I will do it without you if we have to, but we need something to buy us more time."

Pressing her lips together hard, Jerry looked Yafe over carefully. This young woman may have stood a chance if Jerry hadn't hired her, stuck her on a ship with another infected asshole. Swallowing hard, Jerry gave a firm nod. "Yeah, fine, we'll go get it."

Yafe didn't smile as she stepped in closer, but thankfully, she didn't reach out and touch Jerry either. She wasn't sure if she would be able to handle it. "Thank you, Cap."

"Don't thank me for anything, Yafe."

Yafe's thin dark eyebrow rose as she stared directly into Jerry's eyes. Jerry held still, waiting for the judgment to wash over her. "What's the plan, Cap?"

Jerry snorted and rolled her eyes. Sighing, she waved her hand toward the ladder. "Get your ass up here, Azar."

He dragged himself through the entry until he stood tall in front of her. Jerry leaned against the front dash of *Yarrow* and stared the two of them over. "When's the shipment time?"

"Three hundred."

"So that gives us less than twelve to put a plan together."

Azar raised an eyebrow. "We knew we wouldn't have much warning."

"Yeah." Jerry crossed her arms over her chest and pushed the argument with Arloa from her mind. She'd been building up to that one for a while, although it hadn't made her feel any better, not that feeling anything was something she could control anymore. "We need papers, which I'll handle. Something that will look legal enough to get them to load it onto *Yarrow*."

Azar raised his eyebrows. "I can make sure everything goes smoothly from inside."

"But once it's loaded, we're leaving, so you need to make sure you're on the ship—"

"You can pick me up on the dock."

Jerry frowned, not liking the idea of him not being with them when they first pulled away with the shipment.

"I need to be inside."

"Why?" Jerry pushed.

Azar shifted a glance to Yafe. "Because I am on the packing team, and if I am gone, they will suspect something is wrong and will delay the shipment again. That's what happened last time, at least what I've heard from rumors."

"Where will we pick you up?"

"Here?" Yafe supplied.

Jerry shook her head. "No, it's too easy for them to find us, and I don't know how long the forged papers will suffice to hide the ruse."

Azar nodded sharply. "On the river, then. It'll take me a bit to get there."

Jerry pulled her lower lip between her teeth and eyed him. "You'll need to run. If we're doing this, then I don't want to be in Potelia longer than necessary."

"I'll be there."

"If you're not, we're leaving without you."

"I understand."

Yafe stepped forward, putting her hand out. "I won't leave my brother."

"I'll be there, Yafe," Azar comforted. "There's no reason to worry."

Jerry ignored Yafe's concerns. She would try her best not to leave without Azar, but if he was caught, she would fly out of Potelia faster than he could utter *go*. "Yafe, I'll need you to keep me sane and even."

"What?"

"You heard me. I haven't had vestigen in nearly a week, and as tonight demonstrates, I'm not able to control myself as well as I should. You need to do that for me while we're doing this." Jerry gave Yafe a hard stare. She'd had the last dose of any kind of medication they had on the vessel, and she would be the best person to be front and center. However, Jerry knew it would have to be her job to pick up the shipment.

"I understand, Cap."

"Good." Jerry nodded sharply. "Tell me about shipments. Do vessels know what product they're taking?"

Azar shook his head. "It's all blind shipments."

"Even easier." Jerry rubbed her thumb over the tips of her fingers as she stared at each of them. "This may work, but if it doesn't, I trust you both know it's been an honor to have you on my ship."

Azar and Yafe said nothing as they looked her up and down.

"Let's get to work. I need to get these papers. Azar, I want you to find out who was going to get the shipment so we can derail their arrival until after we've left."

"On it, Cap."

"Yafe, start clearing the ship and making us look good. Get Sacha in on it."

Jerry rolled her shoulders as she turned back to the dash. She would have to talk to Arloa again after hanging up on her. Her heart sank. That was going to be the worst part of all of this. As she listened to Azar and Yafe scurry to their duties, Jerry hit the communications device. She leaned over the wheel as she waited for Arloa to answer.

With her beautiful face lighting the screen, Jerry raised a single eyebrow. "You win."

"You're taking the shipment?" Arloa's voice dropped to a near whisper.

"Yes, but I need paperwork."

"Anything." Jerry gave Arloa the details since all her main contacts were in Raegina. Potelia was so far out of their norm that they wouldn't have any idea what to do to forge the right paperwork. Arloa, however, had been planning on this since she'd sent them out there.

"You'll have them in a few hours."

"Thank you." Jerry rolled her shoulders and straightened her back. "And…I'm sorry about earlier."

"Jer, don't think anything of it. I understand."

Again with Arloa thinking she knew what Jerry was going through, what her crew went through daily. They were two vastly different people from vastly different worlds. Arloa would never be able to understand.

"I'll see you soon." Jerry ended the communication and stared out at Potelia's harbor again. She would be glad to never see that city again, and in a few short hours, it would all be behind her.

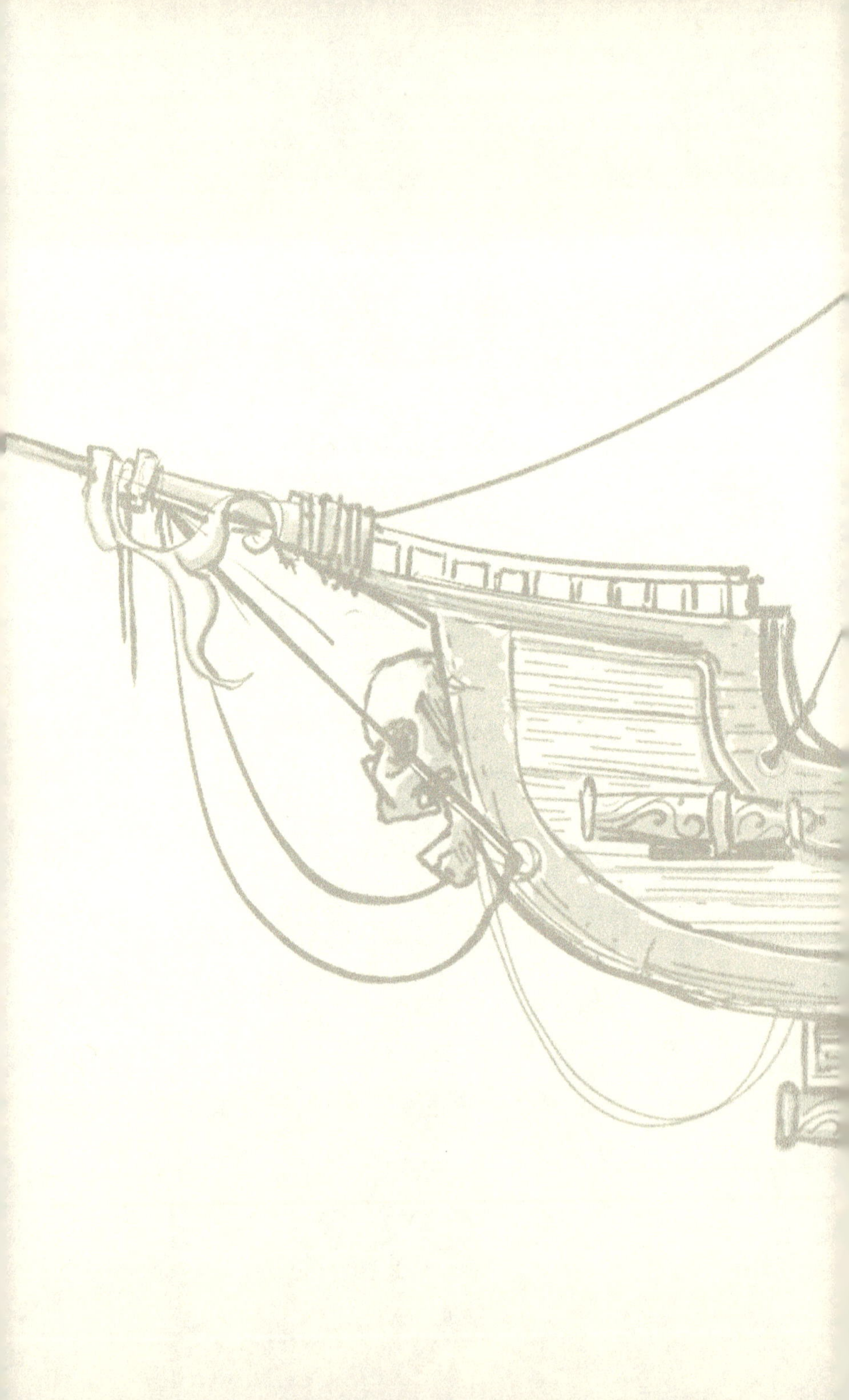

CHAPTER 21

Jerry hadn't slept all night, having spent most of it in communication with Arloa on and off while she set up the details of her plan. Azar looked a sweaty mess as he stepped into the wheelhouse, his face smeared with dirt and his dark hair covered in a fine sandy salt-dust they still hadn't managed to clean out of the ship yet.

She wasn't sure they would ever have a clean ship again after that contract. Jerry put her fists on her hips as she stared him over. "You're not going in like that, are you?"

"No. I've got a few minutes before I need to leave, but I wanted to make sure everything was in place."

Jerry jerked her chin up at him in acknowledgment. "It is. Arloa sent the paperwork this morning. It looks official even to my own scrutiny, and you know I've seen a lot of forged papers in my lifetime."

Azar's lips curled upward into a grin. "Aye, Captain."

Rolling her eyes at him, she turned around and grabbed the display that would show them a map of the city. She pointed at it. "We'll pull into this loading dock. I need you to be at this dock before the second morning bell. We can't wait for you."

"I know." Azar's voice was deep, and while he sounded confident, Jerry detected the note of fear in the back of it. If they did have to leave him, he would no doubt be arrested by the authorities as a conspirator. She wouldn't want that for anyone, and he deserved it least of all. She was the mastermind behind everything, the one who dragged them into it. Though she had given them a choice—mostly. But really, what choice did any of them have?

Clearing her throat, Jerry rolled her shoulders. "We're going to fill the hull as best as we can."

"I know," he repeated, turning to look her directly in the eye. "We trust you, Cap. You have to know that by now."

Jerry's stomach plummeted. She was no one worthy of that trust. At one point in her life she had wanted it, but after the last year with the virus raging through Penum, she knew she would never be worthy of it. Blowing out air, she shook her head. "Just don't trust me to your death."

"If I'm going to do that for anyone, it better be you." Azar clapped her hard on the shoulder before stepping away and walking toward the ladder. "I'll clean up and see you in a few hours."

"You better!" Jerry called after him, still unsure how that piece of the plan was going to work out. She supposed, like Azar, she just had to trust.

She finished prepping *Yarrow* for the transport in the wheelhouse and then headed belowdecks to help Yafe and Sacha adjust the rest of the ship so they had room for the shipment they were about to steal.

Jerry pushed her dark hair out of her face as she bent down to grab another crate. She didn't even know what was in it or where it came from. It had been so long she'd forgotten. Sacha stopped moving crates and stretched her muscles, her breasts jutting out in front of her as she pressed her hand to the small of her back.

"This better be worth it," Sacha muttered.

Jerry raised an eyebrow at her but said nothing as she grunted while lifting. She was at the main door, but caught the corner of the crate on the frame, her hand smashed between the two. Crying out in pain, Jerry dropped the box and cursed as she eyed her fingers to see if she'd broken skin.

Luckily, it didn't look like she had. Ignoring Yafe's questions of concern, she stared at her hand and then at the crate. The lid was ajar. Biting her lip, Jerry got onto her knees and opened it, glancing inside she was overwhelmed with despair. These were Matty's things. She hadn't known what to do with them, so she'd left it all up to Yafe.

She couldn't even look at Yafe. Guilt pounded into her chest and skull. Matty's dying was her fault. She had killed him. She had watched the life bleed from him. Twice over. Yafe's hand on her shoulder startled her. Jerry had known this was a bad idea from the start, that sinking feeling in the pit of her stomach only growing heavier with each passing minute.

"I didn't know what to do with it." Yafe's tone was gentle, as sad as Jerry felt.

But she couldn't let herself mourn. She had to be strong for her crew, and Sacha wouldn't understand any of it. She hadn't been on *Yarrow* when Matty was there. He'd been Jerry's first hire. Tears sprung into her eyes, as much as she didn't want them to. Clenching her jaw, Jerry shook her head. "We should have thrown it over with him."

"Thrown him over?" Sacha's higher-pitched voice nearly screeched. "You threw him overboard?"

"He was dead already," Yafe corrected. "It was a mercy since he had no family."

"You threw him over," Sacha said it as though it was the worst offense Jerry had committed.

She didn't even know the half of it. Jerry brushed her fingers over Matty's jacket before she dropped it back into the crate. "We'll do it on our way home."

"Aye, Cap."

"Help me close it up." Jerry stood up, grabbing a mallet and slamming the lid back into place. Together, she and Yafe carried it and maneuvered it up to the wheelhouse so they wouldn't have to do it later.

With that out of her mind, Jerry sent Yafe down to the hold to finish clearing it out while she stayed topside to gain her footing. That had been unexpected. Matty had been so innocent in some ways, coming from the exact situation she had. Joab. The prison of all prisons on Penum, located in Raegina, and sponsored by none other than Arloa Kauket's family. Jerry had almost ignored everything about Arloa because of that, but she was so different from her family, determined to make a name for herself despite her family's transgressions.

Shivering, Jerry planted her hands on the wheel to her vessel and closed her eyes. She needed to focus. They were never going to complete this heist without her extreme concentration on the moving parts and trying to disguise herself as one of them, as someone worthy of carrying such *precious* cargo.

They hadn't even figured out what they were doing with it or where they were shipping it off to. Potelia had been quite secretive about that. They'd been lucky enough to even find it, but it seemed to Jerry that the drug wasn't staying in Potelia. They were sending it somewhere else. Gripping the wheel tightly, she centered herself. She had to do this. They were in too deep already to give up now.

"Cap," Yafe stated, Jerry spinning around and finding her head popped up through the hole in the floor where the ladder led to.

"Yeah?"

"We're done."

Jerry frowned, not realizing how long she had been up there. "Take a nap. I want you two rested before we leave."

"You as well?"

Jerry nodded even though both she and Yafe knew she wouldn't. She didn't have the energy to try and fall asleep. Yafe disappeared, leaving Jerry alone in the wheelhouse. She ran her fingers along *Yarrow's* dash. "Well, love, are you going to see us through this one?"

Yarrow of course didn't answer, though Jerry swore she could feel the ship talk back to her. The strength in the lines of the vessel. She may be a small ship, but she was worth her weight in salt. Jerry's lips quirked at the thought as she tapped *Yarrow's* wheel. She was just about to step out on deck, when the small communication device she'd put on top of the dash blinked. Jerry narrowed her gaze at it and picked it up.

Arloa's face filled the screen, deep bags under her eyes. "Are you ready?"

"I thought you trusted me." Jerry clenched her jaw as she held the device in her fingers.

"I do. Is the ship ready?"

"She's always ready." Jerry moved to the ladder and stepped down it, carefully holding the device as she climbed to get to the level with cabins. Azar was already gone, no doubt preparing the shipment they were about to steal, and here was Jerry, stuck talking to Arloa. Again. Not that she minded, but she really didn't want Arloa to know that. Jerry flopped onto her cot after shutting and locking the door to her cabin. When she moved the device to see Arloa's face, she sighed and closed her eyes. "I'm not ready."

"Oh?" Arloa's eyes widened in surprise, but she didn't seem too worried or concerned. "I imagine that might be true for most things like this."

"Is that why you keep contacting me?"

Arloa's head turned to the side. "That, and I like you, Jerry. I want to make sure you're safe."

"I'm never safe," Jerry answered wryly, her voice barely above a whisper.

"Are we talking about us, or you being a pirate?"

Jerry raised her gaze to look directly at Arloa. "There is no *us*."

Arloa paled. Even through the blue on the communication

device, Jerry could see it. The lines in her face tightened, her lips thinned. Jerry felt somewhat guilty for putting that look on Arloa's face.

Sighing, Arloa pressed her palm to her cheek and stared directly into Jerry's eyes. "When I met you all those months ago—"

"It's been over a year," Jerry corrected.

"All those months ago," Arloa repeated. "I didn't anticipate feeling anything for you beyond simple attraction."

"There is nothing between us," Jerry reiterated. She'd maintained that for the last year, no matter how many times she had thought of Arloa while she'd fucked herself on her cot. She'd wanted to be with her again, and when she'd seen her, she couldn't resist.

"You can say that, Jer. You may even believe it, but in your heart, I'm not sure you do."

Jerry frowned. She wouldn't admit it. She would never admit it. She couldn't stop thinking about Arloa, and the opportunity for this heist had only been one more way to get into her good graces, to see her again, to talk to her repeatedly. Jerry might have told the others on her crew that she had taken the job to get more drugs to help them survive, but the reason truly was because she needed Arloa in her life. She couldn't resist her.

"Jer?" Arloa's voice was low, seductive. "What are you thinking?"

"There isn't an us."

Arloa swallowed hard, her eyes widening as she looked deep into Jerry's gaze. "I don't agree with that."

Jerry's heart pounded. "You can say that all you want, but it's true. We aren't in a relationship. I'm a pirate. You're an aristocrat. I steal. I'm a convict." *You're perfect.* The words never made it out into the open because she couldn't say them. She *wouldn't* say them.

"You are who you are, and I have never asked you to be

anyone else." Arloa's tone was smooth and confident. "I don't want you to be anyone else."

Jerry drew in a ragged breath. "I'm going to die."

"I know," Arloa whispered. "We all will eventually."

Jerry's eyes stung again. Apparently she had morphed from anger into tears and there was nothing she could do about it as the withdrawal from vestigen took over her body and left her with very little control.

"Jer?"

"What?" Jerry snapped, not wanting to admit anything that was happening with her.

"How bad is it?"

"How bad is what?"

"The withdrawal."

How the hell had she known that? Jerry cringed and closed her eyes, rubbing her fingers over her temple and then her eyes. As much she wanted to avoid answering, she knew she wouldn't be able to. Arloa had this spell she'd cast, and no matter how much Jerry resisted, she always gave in. "It's bad."

"How much longer do you think?"

"A day, maybe two, if I'm lucky." Though Jerry wasn't sure she'd call it luck in general. She'd seen so many others go through withdrawal, and the thought didn't appeal to her. She'd been through it, though she'd gotten her hands on vestigen just in time. She didn't want to experience that again.

"As soon as you get the shipment, you take some. Okay?"

"Already planning on it," Jerry muttered. "Where do you want us to bring it?"

"Anywhere. I'll meet you anywhere."

Jerry swallowed hard. They hadn't discussed many details beyond the initial heist and needing to get the shipment of drugs from Potelia. Jerry honestly had no idea what she was going to do with the amount of drugs she was bringing. "Outside of trying to manufacture it, what are you going to do with it?"

Arloa raised an eyebrow. "I'm surprised you didn't ask this before."

Jerry frowned. "I don't think straight when I'm running low on vestigen."

"I'm noticing that. I'll try to reverse engineer it, perhaps make it better. But what I don't need, I'll give away."

"Give away? Or charge?"

Arloa lifted a shoulder and dropped it. "I'll charge, but minimal."

"We can't afford it."

"I'll make sure everyone can afford some."

Jerry raised her gaze and locked eyes on Arloa. "How will you do that and still have enough to pay your people?"

"I'm an aristocrat, remember? My pockets are endless." Arloa's lips twitched upward.

Jerry loved seeing it, not that she would ever admit that, but seeing the brilliance of the smile on Arloa's face was exactly what she needed. Elation built in her chest, and before she knew it, she moved from melancholy to giddy. *Fuck, she hated not being in control of herself.*

"I want to fuck you," Jerry murmured.

Arloa sucked in a sharp breath, her gaze widening in a moment before her lips curled into a shy smile. "I wouldn't be opposed to that, but you're halfway across Penum."

Jerry could easily think of other methods of fucking Arloa, ones that didn't require them being in the same room. Though she didn't know how secure the channel they were on was, and she didn't know how alone Arloa was. Although, that could make it all the more interesting.

"Jerry." The sexy whine in Arloa's voice was almost too much. Jerry closed her eyes, focusing entirely on the tone, wanting to hear more of it. "When you get back…"

"We'll be in the same boat we're in now." Jerry clenched her jaw. They wouldn't. She wouldn't allow herself the temptation again. "I have to go, but I promise, we're ready for tomorrow. I'll see you in a week."

Before Arloa could answer, Jerry ended the conversation. She checked the time, noting that they only had thirty minutes until they needed to leave. Azar had risked a message to her, confirming the pickup time. Jerry ran her fingers through her hair and sat up. She needed to wash and prepare herself for the role she had to play.

Jerry was the master at playing roles, when she was properly medicated to keep her infected side at bay. However, with no vestigen in sight and nothing in her system for nearly a week, it was going to be tough to maintain the facade. Stripping, she stepped under the spray and closed her eyes as the hot water covered her from the crown down.

She needed this. The conversation with Arloa had put her on edge, not just a sexual edge but rather something beyond that. She wanted her ship to be ready for the heist, but she wasn't sure they were. Something in the pit of her stomach kept telling her it was all going to go awry, that she would end up back in Joab with no hope of escape. She'd spent too many years there to ever want to go back, and even Arloa with all the power she held couldn't get her out.

Opening her eyes, Jerry scrubbed her body of dirt until she was clean. Then she stepped out, dried off, and dressed in the finest outfit she had. She wore a skirt instead of pants to make herself more accessible to the men she would no doubt have to deal with. This was it. This was the day they were going to make a name for themselves in the underground. She would have Penum at her fingertips.

Because Arloa would have no idea how much she stole, all she'd have to do was hide half of it before she brought it to Raegina. She could sell it herself. She'd be rich, able to live comfortably, or even better, she could stash the drugs for her own personal use. Rolling her shoulders, Jerry finished knotting the ties to her corset. She checked over her unofficial uniform in the small mirror her washroom boasted.

"This is it," she whispered to no one but herself.

No matter what, they would survive this. No matter what, they would find a way through, and they would come out the other end as winners. They had to. They didn't have another option.

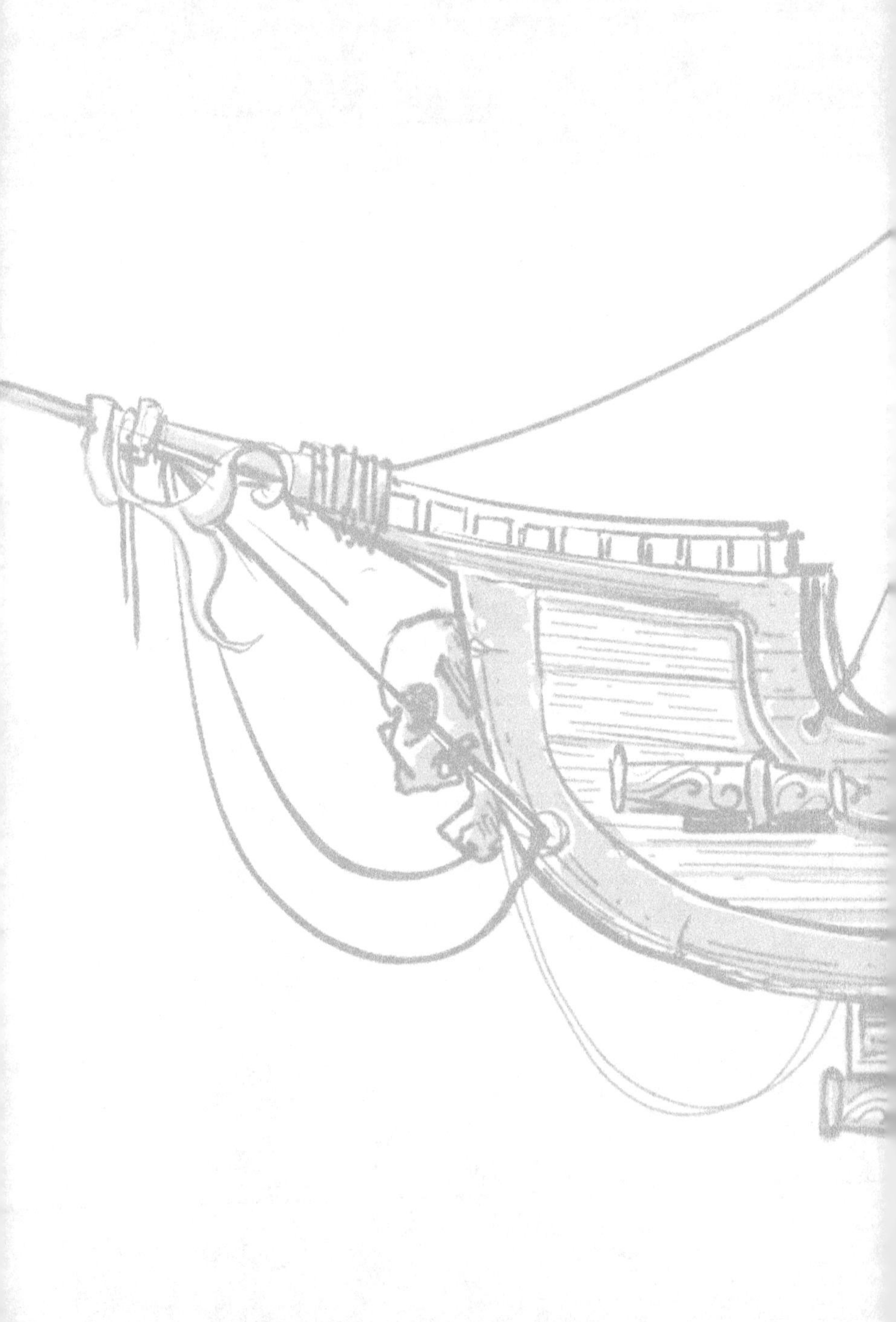

CHAPTER 22

Yarrow's engines hummed. The small vibrations echoed through Jerry's boots and into her bones. Anticipation built as she pushed *Yarrow* into gear and pulled away from the dock for the last time, the dock that had been their home for longer than she cared. As much as she was worried about the job that day, she knew she'd be happy to get back to Raegina.

Something about that particular harbor town was everything she needed and wanted. When she was younger, she used to tell herself she would never step foot there again if she could avoid it, but since she'd gone out on her own, she'd found she couldn't stay away. She wanted to be there, and it wasn't just because that's where her jobs were. Raegina was home. Arloa had been right.

Yafe and Sacha joined her in the wheelhouse, both wearing their nicer work clothes to impress the receivers and loaders they were going to come into contact with. They couldn't look like pirates when they showed up because then Jerry had no doubt they wouldn't be allowed anywhere near the loading dock.

The lump in her throat grew, and the pit in her stomach widened.

Her gut told her that something was going to go wrong.

Something was going to not go smoothly and disaster was going to strike, but Jerry had no other option. Azar couldn't risk stealing more pills to stabilize her or her crew, and they couldn't hide away in the harbor with no hope of survival.

Yafe leaned against the dash as Jerry spun the wheel to turn *Yarrow* so she faced the ocean. Flying just above the water, she guided her vessel through the crowd of ships that she'd come to know over the last month. She'd memorized every single one of them, fearing she may need a quick escape. Seemed all that work was for naught.

"I'm nervous," Yafe murmured, not looking Jerry in the eye.

"Me too," Sacha echoed. "This is huge."

Jerry wanted to say, "If we can manage to pull it off..." but she knew she needed to be the strong voice filled with confident affirmation. Yet digging deep to find that quality in herself was tougher than it had ever been before. She couldn't bring herself to say it, so instead she remained silent, keeping what semblance of control she had.

"Azar is in place?" Yafe turned to look at Jerry, asking the question they were all wondering.

Jerry nodded sharply. "He checked in once since he left for his shift. We agreed to as little communication as possible, remember?"

"I know. I just worry about him." Yafe looked out the front of *Yarrow* as Jerry hit the open seas.

She had to take them around the docks and to the river, flying her small ship through the winding poisoned waters until she reached the specific loading dock they needed. It would take a total of twenty more minutes, and she had deemed she would not arrive one minute early or one minute late. Her hands shook as she let go of the wheel for a moment. Slamming them back in place, Jerry gripped the spokes hard to rid herself of the shakes.

She couldn't let that happen. She needed to be strong and confident in their plan. They had run through it so many times in the last few hours, ironing out any kinks they could find, and yet that gnawing sensation in her stomach grew even stronger. *Fuck.* She had to put a stop to that. If this was going to be her end, then she should at least get a say in how it was going to go, and pulling off a job this big would be the perfect way to end her freedom.

"Captain?" Sacha eyed Jerry curiously.

"What?"

"I asked what you want me to do when we get there."

Jerry wrinkled her nose, squeezing the spokes hard as she leaned in. Sacha was a beautiful young girl, someone who at one point had places to go, someone to become. Then the virus had found her and she was thrown to the bottom with the rest of them. "I need you to do everything I tell you to without argument or question. Because I don't know what's going to happen when we arrive there, but nothing ever goes exactly to plan, and I need to know you're not going to fuck this up."

"I won't." Sacha's eyes widened. "We all need these drugs."

"Right. So let's get them." Jerry jerked her chin up toward the loading dock she could see in the distance. "We're almost there."

They stood in silence as Jerry maneuvered *Yarrow* through the air to set her right into the spot to receive the goods. Her stomach lifted, nausea working its way up her throat, but she swallowed it back down, the bitter warm taste lingering on the back of her tongue.

"Yafe, stay here until I get approval. Sacha, you're with me."

She was still shaking as she climbed her way down ladders until she reached *Yarrow's* main door. With her palm against the sensor for the interior door, Jerry closed her eyes and drew in a steadying breath. Arloa's voice echoed in her mind, words of confidence and praise—not for the job she was about to do but for fucking her senseless.

Opening her eyes, Jerry stared out the open interior doors and stepped into the breezeway to the exterior door. She pushed her top hat on and tightened her coat to avoid the frozen air. The exterior door to *Yarrow* lowered, connecting to the dock with a gentle thud. Jerry sent Sacha a glance, silently telling her they were about to begin.

A man walked down the loading dock, his foot clacking loudly on the wood. He had a device in his hand, one Jerry recognized as some sort of record keeping system. She'd seen them used so often throughout her life that she'd know it from anywhere.

"Who are you?" his voice boomed across the dock, reaching Jerry's ears.

Her spine straightened, and the muscles in her shoulders tightened as she clenched her jaw. This was not the way she wanted to start this job. She hadn't even had a moment to explain herself before he was already angry. She stepped onto the dock and reached into her pocket for her personal communications device and held it out to him.

"I'm here to pick up a shipment."

He shook his head at her, pointing a finger in her direction, and stopping short without even looking at the documentation Arloa had taken hours to make. "No."

"No? What do you mean no?" Jerry pushed. "I can't leave without a shipment."

"I don't know this ship."

"It's new to the fleet. Not new, obviously, but we've been having to buy older ships because of the shortages in supplies and builders."

He frowned, his bushy eyebrows drawing together. Jerry had taken a risk with that explanation, but since there were pretty much shortages of people everywhere on Penum because of the damn virus, she thought it might be a safe bet.

"I have the certifications right here." Jerry held out the device, hoping he would take it.

"I've never seen you before, and your accent—"

Jerry interrupted him, "I'm not from Potelia. With everything happening, I've had to take on new jobs in new places to keep up with paying my crew." She nodded toward Sacha. "We all have families to feed."

"Potelia isn't known for welcoming outsiders." He still hadn't taken the device to look at her paperwork.

"That doesn't mean we aren't here." That was also something he couldn't deny. Jerry had seen it and heard the dockmaster complain about it. The entire world was thrown into the virus, and they had to work together in order to survive.

He narrowed his eyes at her but snagged the device from Jerry's fingers. Her heart thumped wildly to the point it was hard to breathe as he looked through her certifications and paperwork. Arloa had done an excellent job on forging the paperwork, but Jerry still worried it wouldn't be enough, that they'd be stuck arguing with this asshole for the next thirty minutes before one of them gave up and she was forced to leave.

Sacha stayed close by, her body relaxed in a way Jerry hadn't seen before, and she was glad she'd brought her out instead of Yafe. Yafe didn't have much of a poker face, but Sacha could lie with the best of them. Jerry forced her fingers to unclench from the fists she'd found them in and relaxed the muscles in her shoulders.

She needed to appear confident, nothing of which she felt in that moment. Fuck the virus. Had she not been infected or so deprived of vestigen, she would have all the confidence in the world. The dock worker shook his head and pushed the device back at Jerry.

"You're not on our list as the pickup."

She had anticipated that might be a problem, and she'd woven an entire lie about it already. Glad to have the thread of plan in place, Jerry shrugged. "Ship's down, something about the buoyancy. It kept sinking toward the sea, which with any cargo weighing you down, you don't want that to happen."

He didn't look convinced. Jerry wished she knew his name so that she could use that to her advantage when trying to lie to him. It would create intimacy, as if she knew him, but she was left without that information. A heavy wind moved through, blowing against them as they stood on the dock.

"We're the replacement crew, also hence the small vessel. We didn't have another one to send."

He frowned and stared down at the device again with all her information—legal and forged—on it. Sacha stepped in closer, hunching against the wind as it moved up. Perhaps Jerry should have shown up early. Then they wouldn't have been waiting for this idiotic man to make up his mind, wasting precious time.

"You won't be able to hold the shipment," he commented.

"We will." Jerry's eyes lit up as she pointed to the device. "See here? We can manage. We just won't have top speeds."

His blue eyes flicked down to the device again. Jerry held her breath as she waited to see if her lie would hold. She was about to speak again when Sacha drew in a sharp breath. Another dock worker approached them, his body tightly wrapped in a long jacket that Jerry envied. She glanced at Sacha, her eyes bright with excitement.

"Garth, what's the hold up?"

Sacha seemed so excited. Jerry couldn't figure out why, but Sacha remained quiet and right next to her. However, when the new arrival arrived and stood next to Garth—finally, Jerry had a name—his gaze locked on Sacha.

"They're new," Garth answered.

"So?" The new dock worker answered. "Do their papers check out? I know they're new to Potelia and the company, but they've been here over a month now."

Jerry slid Sacha a look, raising an eyebrow in her direction but remaining stoically silent. That ball in her stomach grew even larger, although things seemed to be moving in the right direction. She couldn't quite decide why since they were making progress.

"You know Holbrook hired them?" Garth turned on this new man and raised an eyebrow.

"Yeah." He looked at Sacha, his gaze softening.

Thank fuck Jerry had brought Sacha with her instead of Yafe. The two of them must have been in town on more than one occasion, but he was about to save their hides whether he knew it or not.

"Come on, we're already late on loading and my workers are getting restless waiting for you."

Garth grumbled, but he transferred the documentation to his record keeper and gave it his approval before handing the device back. Jerry tried not to let the relief show on her face as she shoved the sleek device into her pocket.

"We're ready whenever you are."

The new man nodded sharply. "Open the holds."

Jerry turned on her heel and stalked back toward *Yarrow*. Sacha followed, and as soon as they were at the interior door, she let out a sigh of relief and leaned against the hull of the ship. "What the hell just happened?"

"That, Cap, is my boyfriend."

"Boyfriend?" Jerry glanced down at Sacha. "Seriously? I thought you and Azar…"

Sacha lifted and dropped her shoulder. "I have a lot of boyfriends, but Damon has been showing me around Potelia when we've had some spare time."

"You're ridiculous, but thank fuck for it." Jerry pushed off the wall and hit the enunciator on the wall to talk directly with Yafe. "They're letting us load up."

"What was the problem?"

"Someone is a stickler for rules. Garth didn't believe we were here to pick up the shipment." Too bad that was the only thing they were telling the truth about. Jerry wanted those drugs. "Sacha, go get the storerooms opened. I have a feeling this is going to be a tight fit with the crates."

"On it, Cap."

Jerry stayed by the door while Yafe came down from the wheelhouse to help with directing and moving crates. She went back outside and found Garth standing awfully close to *Yarrow's* exterior door. They were going to have to watch what they said before they left with the shipment, especially if he was going to keep that close of an eye on them.

Jerry swallowed hard as she watched Damon and his workers bring down the shipment from the warehouse, the carts moving along as they floated just above the dock. She would have killed for those on Beren Island. Maybe if she could make enough credits off this haul of drugs then she'd be able to buy herself a few for their salt-mining operations.

"Thanks, Damon." Jerry grabbed the first crate with her bare hands and walked it inside *Yarrow*. She and her crew would take it from the dock and down into the holds they had cleared out for it. The crates were awkward to handle, but they had no other option since the only door they had was too small for any type of moving equipment.

Yafe took the next one while Sacha stood by the door and flirted with Damon. Jerry rolled her eyes, but she let Sacha have her moment. The girl wasn't going to get another one with her boyfriend since this was likely to throw them on the blacklist for any type of work in Potelia. Not to mention, it was Damon who had ultimately convinced Garth to let them take the shipment.

She dropped the first crate in the corner of the lowest hold and stretched her back. They couldn't take more than two hours to load the vessel, so they would have to work fast. Jerry wanted to be out of Potelia just after the second bell and well on their way toward Raegina. She still needed to find a place to drop half their load and store it so Arloa wouldn't find it, but she could spend the next couple days working on that problem.

Eventually Sacha joined in the moving, and so did Damon and a few of his crew once the crates piled up high enough outside of *Yarrow*. Apparently they were frustrated Garth had delayed them so much, so they were doing it to stick it to him. Jerry had laughed at that one.

She didn't stop for a drink, no matter how parched her throat was. She'd ordered Yafe and Sacha to stop several times. Crate after crate was piled into *Yarrow's* hull until the storerooms were filled. After two and a half hours, they were finally finished, and Jerry stepped outside into the bright sun to find Garth waiting for her to sign off on the shipment. Damon and his workers cleaned up the mess on the dock, while Jerry pressed her thumb to his record keeper. As soon as they were dismissed, Jerry stood by the exterior door of *Yarrow* and closed it up, locking it in place.

They'd done it.

The feeling in her gut was wrong because they had done it. They'd gotten the drug onto her ship and there was no going back now. They just had to pick up Azar and be on their way. Giddy, Jerry climbed up the ladder to the wheelhouse, ready to set out for home.

CHAPTER 23

Jerry waited until Damon and his crew were far enough away before she fired up *Yarrow's* engines and pushed the ship away from the dock. Yafe and Sacha were belowdecks, doing a quick inventory of what they had, and in theory, opening one of the crates so Jerry could get some drugs in her system. Fuck, she needed that.

With the ship humming to life under her fingertips, Jerry very carefully eased the vessel over the waters on the river. She took it slow, not sure how *Yarrow* would handle with all the added weight, especially because she'd gone over her max allowable load. But with the illegal modifications Azar had made to *Yarrow* over the past year so she could take on more salt when she worked for Morty, she was pretty sure they could handle it.

The hull shivered as she picked up speed. Her heart raced. The farther she got from the loading dock, the more she hoped that she'd lose that feeling in the pit of her stomach, but it was still there. Clenching her jaw, Jerry moved down the river toward the harbor, keeping her eyes peeled for Azar and the dock where they had said they would meet. He should be there by then, since they were already late, but she wasn't looking forward to settling *Yarrow* down for him to join them only to have to lift her up again.

It took her five minutes to get there, and she was sufficiently out of the view of the loading dock so they wouldn't see her land so shortly after picking up the product. Jerry kept her jaw clenched tight as she settled *Yarrow* down at the end of the pier, wanting an easy escape if she had to make one. Her first priority in just about every situation was having a way to escape.

She wouldn't put *Yarrow* or her crew in a situation where they couldn't readily escape. Grabbing the enunciator, Jerry spoke rapidly. "How's inventory going?"

"Good!" Yafe seemed breathless. "I'll send Sacha up with some pills for you in a minute. We're just finishing the first storeroom."

Jerry didn't answer, ending the communication as she straightened her back. Azar made his way down the dock to the end of the pier, no one following him. She wasn't quite sure how he'd managed to slip from the production plant undetected, but she could only hope he had. It would be just her luck that someone had followed him or he'd been caught.

Hitting a couple buttons on the dash, she lowered the exterior door to *Yarrow* as soon as he was within walking distance of them. She didn't tell Yafe he was there, figuring she'd hear the door as soon as it closed anyway, and she didn't want to waste time that they didn't have a lot of.

She was up and away from the dock before Azar made his way up to her, shedding his jacket as soon as he reached the wheelhouse. "Was it a success?"

"Would we be here if it wasn't?" Jerry shot him a sharp look. "I take it you weren't followed."

Azar shook his head. "No. I made sure of it."

Something in his tone worried Jerry. She eyed him suspiciously before concentrating on weaving her vessel through the other ships coming up and down the river. She couldn't relax until they were out of the Omar Region and beyond the sea, when they would be the only ship in sight and no one would be coming for them.

She gripped the wheel hard, the worn wood a reminder of just what they were there for. This wasn't just about a job they were paid to do, it was about living—something Jerry hadn't been sure she wanted to do since she'd been infected.

"What did you do?" Jerry finally asked as Azar took up the second wheel to help guide the ship. She was grateful, since the added weight was making steering in such tight confines difficult.

"Nothing you need to know about."

Jerry snorted. "How many?"

"Two."

"Wonderful, so we'll be on the list again."

Azar shrugged as he looked at the front of the ship. "Worth it in the end, isn't it?"

"You know I don't like killing people."

"It's unavoidable in our line of work."

She knew he was right, but that still didn't make her feel giddy about doing it. In fact, her stomach churned at the thought. She'd killed before, many times, but it wasn't something she tried to remember or dwell on, and it was only ever when she had no other choice. Raising her hand, Jerry leaned forward to press a few buttons on the dash as they reached open water.

Yarrow rose higher as their thrusters lifted them so they could increase their speed. She kept her mouth shut as she focused on stilling the shakes that had returned to her hands now that she wasn't forced to move crates. It had been a perfect cover for the effects the withdrawal was having on her, but standing in the wheelhouse with no hard manual labor, she couldn't hide it.

Azar must have caught it out of the corner of his eye, because he raised an eyebrow at her, his full lips parted. "You should go take something for that."

"Yafe said she's sending Sacha up with it."

"Can you wait that long?"

Jerry growled, the sound low. Of course she could wait. It

wasn't like she was going to keel over dead in the next thirty minutes while Sacha made her way up from belowdecks. Her ship wasn't that large.

"Just a question," Azar amended. "Make sure to take it light on the thrusters."

"I know," Jerry grumbled. "This isn't the first time we've pushed the load."

"No, but it is with something we care about."

Jerry gave him a side look that meant business. She couldn't take any more comments from him and not do something she might regret later. The anger gurgling in her belly wasn't a new sensation, but it was much better than feeling like something dreadful was about to happen. She still couldn't shake that.

They hit the edge of the harbor, pulling out so they could fly over the last of the old bridges that were built. Jerry concentrated everything she had on making sure they got to the open sea. That was the first step. The next step would be to get out of the Omar Region, but that would take a few hours easily.

Once they were beyond the country's clutches, she'd feel better. That had to be it. She needed to be far enough away to know they weren't going to get caught in the act of stealing something that wasn't even supposed to exist. Jerry ground her molars together as she squinted against the bright sun as it rose over the horizon.

The enunciator beeped before Yafe's voice echoed over the line. "Sacha's coming up."

Jerry didn't respond. Instead, her nerves fired in anticipation of the sweet drug that would fill her system with exactly what she needed to survive. So she wouldn't go mad and try to kill everyone on the ship, and her reaction to Azar moments before should have told her she was further gone than she'd originally thought.

In all their time together, in all the withdrawals she had gone through, never once had she attempted to kill Azar outside of that first time. That one had been the worst because they hadn't known what to do about it or how to control it. She could smell his blood if she focused enough, and as soon as she got a whiff of it, she couldn't stop.

"Fuck," Jerry muttered. She needed that drug, and she needed it before Sacha would be able to get up to her.

Jerry said nothing as she spun around, just about to climb down the ladder and go swimming in the small pills they had stolen, but Sacha stood right in front of her, palm open, with six little pills in her hand. Jerry's heart raced, thrummed steadily as she stared at the pills, needing to know exactly how many she should take.

"We don't know," Sacha murmured. "Yafe said to try this."

"Right." Jerry reached out her hand, and Sacha deposited the pills into her palm.

They were warm, probably from Sacha carrying them up to her, the outer coating on them not smooth. Like they could ever make a pill to take that wouldn't taste like ass.

She popped all six pills into her mouth and swallowed, straining her neck against the flavor. Sacha raised an eyebrow at her. "Does it taste just as bad?"

Jerry grunted her answer.

"Yafe told me to take two."

"Do it. You too, Azar. We've all been deprived long enough, and I want us thinking clearly as we head home." Jerry didn't wait as the two of them disappeared belowdecks.

With the wheelhouse completely hers, Jerry lived into the silence. She'd nearly forgotten the noises of open sea after being stuck in port for so long. She missed it. If only the water weren't poisonous and she could go outside and feel the spray of droplets against her cheeks. That would be perfect.

Jerry picked up speed as she moved beyond the harbor and farther from other vessels. The farther away they got from Potelia, the easier the pit in her stomach became, and Jerry was finally able to let up on it, breathing fresh air and relief. They'd actually done it. They had pulled it off, and now all they had to do was fly home, stash whatever she wanted to keep with her, and send the rest to Arloa, wherever she was hiding her production facilities. They were near the end for a little while.

Hours later, when they crossed the Omar Region's borders, Jerry relaxed. It had been as far as she needed to go that day, and they'd made it before nightfall. The air was warming incrementally as they moved farther south, although she was still stuck with the jacket to keep herself warm.

Yafe was the first one of the crew to come back to the wheelhouse. With the new drug in her system, finally, she felt slightly more even-keeled, though she bet that Yafe had underestimated how much Jerry needed in order to survive. Yafe opened the door to the deck and let the cool air rush into the stuffy wheelhouse.

"We finished inventory."

"And?"

"This is going to be an excellent haul, Cap."

"If we can sell it. No one even knows about this drug other than us."

"You could give it all to the Kaukets."

Jerry sneered. Yafe had used Arloa's last name on purpose, to remind her exactly who the Kaukets were for Jerry and how much Jerry did not want to deal with that family if she could avoid it.

"That's what I thought," Yafe murmured. "Set it to run, Cap. Azar has a surprise for us."

"I'll be a minute." Jerry sighed when Yafe disappeared belowdecks again. She moved to the open door to the deck and looked out at the crate that they had brought up the night before, the one with Matty's things in it.

She set the ship to fly automatically and stepped onto the deck. With her short sword, she pried the top of the crate up and grabbed the jacket on the top. She held it tightly to her chest as she stared down at the rest of the items in it. Jerry sighed as she reached in, bringing each item to the edge of the ship and dropping it into the poison sea below them. It ate whatever she put in almost immediately. She couldn't help but remember how Matty's face had looked when he'd sunk below the surface, the flesh eaten away as soon as he hit the water.

She wiped her hand over her face as she dropped everything but the jacket into the sea. Still clutching the leather to her chest, Jerry raised her hand in a salute. It was time to give up Matty, the hurt she had caused him, the death she'd eventually given him. She needed to forgive herself for it, move on from it, then maybe she could learn to live again.

On her way back into the wheelhouse, Jerry checked her systems and let them run before going belowdecks. Yafe, Sacha, and Azar were in the galley, two bottles of moonshine sitting open on the small table as they shared sips. Jerry's lips curled upward in a smile at just the thought that she'd have someone to share this time with.

"We needed to celebrate, so we splurged," Sacha said, her voice already slurred.

"Make sure to take it easy," Jerry chided. "We are still at open sea. Could need you sober at any moment if a storm were to come up or an engine to fail."

"Shh," Azar stated, shaking his head at Jerry. "We don't need you to curse our trip home."

Home. There was that word again. Jerry let it linger in the room as she reached forward and took her favorite of the two bottles. It hadn't seemed like they'd found her stash of booze, which was something Jerry was very happy for. She'd taken great pains to hide it after their last crew member took to stealing it.

The alcohol burned her throat on the way down, and she thought far too late that they hadn't tested the new drug with liquor. But, by her estimation, they'd all mixed by that point so if it was deadly, they were dead. She took another long pull from the moonshine before setting it onto the table. She would remain the most sober of the bunch, her duty as captain.

The galley became warm as they laughed and teased for the next hour. By the time Jerry dragged her sorry ass up to check the wheelhouse and their heading, the sun was down and she had to move by feel and memory only. When she got to the wheelhouse, she let out a sigh of relief.

They had done it. There were so many times in the month since they'd gotten the tip that she thought they couldn't manage, but they had. Happiness built in her belly and worked its way into her chest, the medication she'd taken clearly having a full effect. She rolled her shoulders as she checked the systems and navigation, making sure they hadn't wandered too far off course.

When she pinpointed exactly where they were on the map, Jerry smiled to herself. They were finally going home, and she would get to see Arloa again. Though that relationship was something she was going to have to figure out. If Arloa was going to continue to send odd little illegal jobs her way, then she would have to shift into Arloa being her patron instead of a former lover. That would add a host of complications between them, though Jerry could just stop fucking her.

She snorted at the idea. She wasn't sure she'd ever want to stop doing that. Arloa had some type of air about her that Jerry was unable to resist. They were worlds apart in so many ways, but in that one, when they came together it was explosive.

Jerry was just about to reach forward and let Arloa know they had successfully moved out of the Omar Region when she stopped short. Narrowing her gaze, Jerry canted her head to the side as she stared out the front windows to *Yarrow*.

"What the hell is that?" she mumbled.

Flipping through her systems, she tried to get a reading on it, but before she could manage it, *Yarrow's* hull rocked hard as something hit it.

"Fuck!"

Alarms blared through the ship, and Jerry hit every button she could think of to stabilize their sudden descent toward the sea. *Yarrow* plummeted. Her stomach was in her throat as she twisted a knob then hit another button, trying to get the engines to restart after the shock they had received.

Jerry hit the enunciator, shouting, "Get your asses in gear. We're under attack!"

Sacha screeched back. "There's a hole in the galley!"

"Anyone dead?"

"No," Yafe answered.

Jerry didn't continue, letting Yafe handle that situation as they all got into position. She kept *Yarrow* from falling into the sea, but barely, and lifting her back up to their former elevation was next to impossible. Fuck, she hadn't wanted a second escape door in the damn galley.

Flipping switches, Jerry armed her weapons, needing to fight back. She cringed as the small light she saw in the distance earlier hit again.

"Fuck, fuck, fuck." She hit the wheel sharply, but without Azar there to help on the second wheel, she wasn't able to maneuver fast enough and a second cannonball ripped through her hull. "Fuck!"

"Where are they?" Azar asked as soon as he reached the wheelhouse, out of breath from running so hard.

"I don't know." Jerry looked out front, trying to catch sight of where that light had been, but she couldn't see it. The sirens screamed around her, so many things wrong with her ship that she knew she wasn't going to be able to fix them. That last cannon had gone straight into one of the storerooms.

"Find them," Azar ordered.

"I'm trying." Jerry cut the wheel hard to starboard, knowing Azar would follow her lead without comment. She took *Yarrow* as close to the surface of the water as she dared at their current speed. Her heart sank. If she couldn't get *Yarrow* back up, they would lose her. The shipment they had didn't matter, but Jerry couldn't lose the only home she'd had her entire life.

Another cannonball ripped through the hull.

Jerry leaned over the wheel, shouting at the top of her lungs. "Stop putting fucking holes in my ship!"

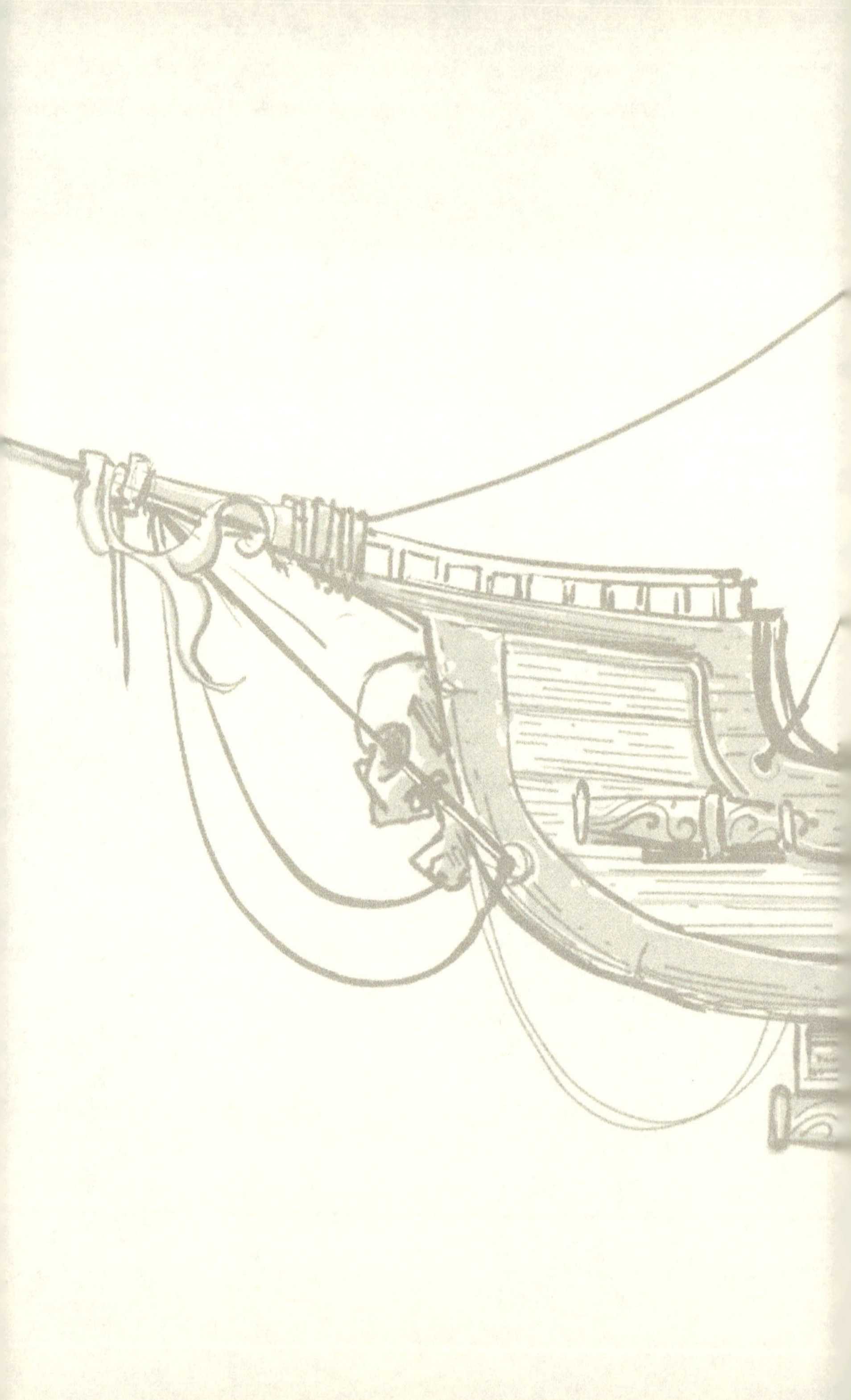

CHAPTER 24

Azar ducked down, and Jerry gripped the wheel hard as *Yarrow* tilted starboard, sending them reeling. She held on as she reached forward to hit a button that hopefully would stabilize their descent. Her heart raced as she held on, not wanting *Yarrow* to fall any closer to the sea. With the damage to the hull, they would never survive.

Yarrow shuddered, her engines trying to move according to Jerry's commands yet resisting the swift change in altitude again. Cursing under her breath, Jerry pushed the thruster harder to get *Yarrow* to react.

"You'll kill us if you don't stop!" Azar yelled.

"We don't have a choice!" Jerry pushed the throttle all the way and sent up a silent prayer that it would succeed. They needed to get some air between them and the ocean's surface.

"Where are they coming from?" Yafe asked as she raced through the wheelhouse and out onto the deck.

Jerry straightened her back as *Yarrow* lifted upward, the thrusters finally working. "Azar—"

"Already on it." He got onto his back under the dash and pulled out wires, his jaw set as he went to work in the dark, doing everything by feel.

Jerry narrowed her gaze to look for Yafe, making sure she

was readying their own cannons. *Yarrow* was too old to have weapons automatically able to fire from the wheelhouse. Jerry had always wanted to add that in, but they hadn't had the funds or the time for Azar to build it yet.

"Where's Sacha?" Azar grumbled.

"No idea." Jerry twisted the wheel hard, trying to even *Yarrow* out so they were level. Instead, she over-corrected and Azar's tools went flying across the floorboards.

"Fuck, Cap!"

"Sorry!" Jerry moved back and steadied everything. Hitting the enunciator, she spoke to Yafe. "If you see them, shoot. Don't hold back."

"Got it, Cap."

Jerry plowed forward, their speed much slower than before. She wasn't sure how long they'd be able to keep up. Her mind spun as she tried to remember where they were and exactly where they could go, where she could land. But if they landed, then she was going to be the same position she was now. Defending against an enemy she couldn't see.

Sacha finally emerged from belowdecks, blood pouring down the side of her face as she gripped her upper arm tightly. "What do you need?"

"Get Azar his tools."

She grunted as she searched around for them in the dark. As much as Jerry wanted to turn on a light so they could see better, she didn't want to give the other vessel a better chance to aim directly at her. So far all the damage was to the hull—classic for trying to run them aground.

Except there was no ground for them to find.

Jerry swallowed the bile that tried to emerge from her stomach and steered *Yarrow* in any direction she thought might be safe. When the flash of light in front of her seemed closer than before, she knew she had made the wrong decision. Jerking the wheel sharply to port, Jerry tried to evade the oncoming cannonball.

Shouting loudly into the enunciator and the wheelhouse, Jerry cried out, "Brace for impact!"

The ship rocked. Fuck, they had hit something Azar wouldn't be able to fix. The engines sputtered before dying out. The dash went dark, the ship sinking in an instant.

"Get the backups!" Jerry ordered, hoping Azar was already working on them. With their hull shattered, as soon as they hit the water, they would be dead. She'd never wanted to live more than in that moment, never wanted to survive something even when she had no idea for what.

"Got it." Azar sounded pleased with himself, and within a second, the backup lights came on and the engines hummed.

It was enough power to keep them floating, but they weren't going anywhere. Jerry reached under the dash and grabbed her gun and sword that she stored there. Gripping them hard, she eyed Azar and Sacha.

"Arm yourselves. We're about to be boarded."

Sacha and Azar moved swiftly, and Jerry stepped out onto the deck. The only way in was through the wheelhouse or through the holes they had blown in the sides of her ship. She would fight until the death to keep *Yarrow* in her possession.

Yafe joined her, two weapons in each of her hands as they all stood back-to-back and waited. The silence was unnerving. The sky was pitch black, and the only reason Jerry knew how far they were above the ocean's surface was because of the technology in her ship. The sky was clouded over, the air frighteningly bitter.

"Where are they?" Sacha whispered.

"Shut up," Jerry ordered. She needed to concentrate, and the drugs in her system weren't enough to give her the boost she really needed. And the rest was too far belowdecks for her to even consider it. Hell, they might even be losing some of the shipment through the hull breaches.

Every thump of her heart echoed in her ears. Every breath she and the others took was loud. Closing her eyes, she used her other senses to try and figure out where they were going to come from. When the loud clack of metal rang through her ears, Jerry turned directly toward it.

Racing forward, she screamed as she sliced through the rope on the hook and sent one of them plummeting to their death in the ocean. The scream when he landed was horrendous, but Jerry didn't have a moment to stop and think about it.

She didn't need to wait as the next hook gripped onto the railing at *Yarrow's* side. Azar ran to port while Jerry took care of starboard. They worked together, fighting to keep their vessel and their lives. Jerry moved swiftly, even when bullets flew around her. Yafe fired a gun as Sacha stood still in the center, aiming her gun but not firing.

Jerry took a step, her ankle twisting hard so she collapsed onto the ground. She missed the next pirate coming on board. The vessel tracking them must have been huge because they just kept coming. Jerry stood up and grabbed her small pistol, firing and hitting a man in the shoulder. He slumped to the deck hard before crying out.

Azar moved over to him and shot him point blank in the head. Jerry clenched her jaw as she pushed herself to stand and ran toward Sacha. "Snap out of it."

Sacha's eyes widened, and she ducked. Jerry was too late, the hard butt of a rifle slamming into her temple. Her ears rang, and her vision was completely black. She couldn't see or focus. Each step she took felt like *Yarrow* was going to dump her over the side.

Voices echoed in her ears, but it was so quiet compared to the ringing. She collapsed onto the ground, holding her gun close to her chest so she could defend herself if anyone came up on her. She couldn't focus, her brain spinning. Men's voices shouted, but they weren't Azar. Yafe screamed at some point.

Jerry clenched her eyes shut and begged for it all to stop. When she couldn't make it, she turned onto her side to get up on her hands and knees, trying to help out. Instead, a boot to the back of her neck forced her onto the deck and pushed against her so she could barely breathe. Gasping, Jerry closed her eyes and listened through the ringing in her ears.

There were too many of them.

They were outnumbered.

The slam of a body inches away startled her. Prying her eyelids open, she found Azar's dark gaze staring back at her. He looked afraid. She wasn't sure she had ever seen him so scared before. She wanted to tell him it would be fine, that they would make it through this, but she honestly didn't have any words. She didn't know, and in some ways, she'd rather end up dead than survive whatever this gang was going to do to them.

Sacha screamed, her voice piercing the air. The boot on Jerry's neck eased up, and she managed to look over and find Damon, holding Sacha by the throat as he squeezed her neck. Yafe fired her weapon and shot him in the side, and he dropped Sacha immediately. She was grabbed by someone else, her arms held behind her back as they wrangled the gun from Yafe's fingertips.

In seconds, the commotion on the deck calmed. Lights burst on them from the ship that faced them and one behind them. Jerry swallowed hard. That had been why. Two vessels were always better than one when trying to board. She could have kicked herself for not noticing them sooner. She should have been more on-guard. She shouldn't have let her crew celebrate.

She was dragged to her feet, a sword held against her throat and lifting her chin so the one in charge could come closer to her. He eyed her as he leaned. "I'd fuck you, but you're too ugly for that."

Jerry bit her tongue. Antagonizing him would do no one good, and the last thing she wanted was for them to torture her crew. She just wanted them to take what they were there for—the drug no doubt—and leave them the hell alone so she could limp her way back to Raegina.

"Got a bit of a harem here?" he said to Azar.

Azar had a gun pointed at his temple as they dragged him to

his feet. Jerry eyed him carefully, not wanting him to reveal anything or spook too much. They shared a silent conversation as she waited for whatever was going to happen next.

"I heard you had a large shipment of vestigen."

"We don't," Jerry answered, her voice rough from the damage they had done to it already. She eyed him, his dark eyes, the warm clothes he wore, the scar above his eyebrow. He'd had many fights like she had.

"Not vestigen," Damon answered, coming over to stand next to the other captain. "Cirax."

"Ah." The captain sneered in Jerry's direction. "I suppose it'll do."

Jerry swallowed hard. She wanted to know what they were going to do with her and her crew, but she was too scared to ask or even accidentally give suggestions.

"Tie them up," the captain ordered.

Two men grabbed Jerry roughly and ran their hands over her body, finding all her hidden weapons and tossing them into a pile in the center of the deck. The captain came back over, his face too close to hers for comfort.

"What's your name, *captain*?" he spat out the last word like it was a curse.

"Jerry Adelric."

His eyes lit up as if he'd won a prize. "I've heard of you. You weren't so hard to capture. Guess you don't live up to your reputation."

Jerry wisely kept her mouth shut. She hadn't realized her reputation had traveled that far north. That or he was making fun of her. She couldn't tell which it was. Azar hung his head, blood falling off his lip. She must have missed when he got hit, or where he was hit, but he was injured, that much she knew.

The captain leaned in closer. "I'm Blaise Lotchski, Captain of Wench's Dream."

If Jerry had it in her, she'd snort at the name of his ship. Typical of a misogynistic horny pirate. She had to keep her wits about her, all the cards she had left in her hand, not his. There were still hidden rooms and compartments in *Yarrow* that could help her out if she was left alone long enough to get there.

"You've been boarded."

"No shit," Jerry answered, her voice ringing through the cold night.

The palm of his hand to her cheek was unexpected but deserved. Jerry would be the first to admit she had a mouth on her. She straightened her back and raised her eyebrow at Blaise, daring him to do it again, but he restrained.

"Tie them up," he gave the order again.

"You two, fix the ship so we can tow it."

Jerry jerked when the hands holding her wrists twisted her arms hard to wrap rope around her. Blaise walked away. They were shoved into the center of the deck, guarded by two of Blaise's crew as the rest of them raided *Yarrow*. Violation stung in her chest as he touched *Yarrow*.

Yarrow was her home, and every hand that touched her that Jerry hadn't approved of was as if someone was touching Jerry. She couldn't stop the thoughts that ripped through her mind as they moved around.

The cold air froze her fingers and her cheeks. Jerry could barely move when *Yarrow's* engines kicked into gear. She ground her molars. She had hoped they wouldn't be able to fix the vessel that quickly, but it had only taken an hour. Jerry stared at Blaise as he gave orders from her wheelhouse.

"What are we doing, Cap?" Azar murmured.

"Waiting them out." Jerry kept her voice to a minimum. She didn't want any hint of what she was planning to get out, not that she had much of a plan to begin with.

As Blaise's crew maneuvered to Wench's Dream, Jerry and her crew stayed put, still under guard. Blaise eventually raised his hand and gave an order for the vessels to move. She held her breath as they were pulled slowly through the freezing night.

Damon walked by them, eyeing Sacha up and down. Jerry

could tell he was still struggling with the pain as much as he tried to pretend he wasn't affected. He nodded toward Sacha. "Get up."

Sacha shook her head.

Damon clenched his jaw and bent down, gripping Sacha by the arm and dragging her up. "I told you to get up."

Jerry shot to her toes, ignoring the pain in her joints from being stuck in one position in the cold temperature for so long. "You won't touch her."

Damon glowered. "I'll do what I damn well please."

"You *won't* touch her." Jerry's voice was low, a growl. She wouldn't let any harm come to her crew so long as she was alive. They had entrusted their lives to her, and she didn't take that responsibility lightly.

Damon pulled at Sacha's skirts and lifted them up, a sneer on his lips. "Do you want to watch? I know how you like your women."

Sacha whimpered. Jerry didn't dare step forward, not wanting the two guards still watching them to do anything stupid that would prevent her from protecting Sacha. Damon grabbed Sacha's breast hard and squeezed.

"I've had her before, you know."

"Doesn't seem like she wants you now," Jerry countered. She caught sight of Blaise behind Damon but didn't say anything about it as Blaise watched on. "Let her go."

Damon laughed. "She gave herself to me. She's mine to do with as I please."

"Damon," Blaise's voice was strong. "Let the wench go."

Sacha was released, and she stumbled to the deck next to Jerry. She squared her shoulders as she turned around and eyed Damon up and down. Jerry willed Sacha to stay silent and not say anything. She would have to watch out for him so long as they were stuck in Blaise's control.

"We're almost there," Blaise said to Jerry.

"Where?" Jerry's brow furrowed.

"Your new home." Blaise bowed and backed away.

It wasn't much longer before Jerry understood what he meant. The island was miniscule. There was, however, rock cover which would work for a shelter until they could get help. They were taken down to the island one-by-one, and Blaise made Damon take Azar. Jerry had to suppress the smirk on her lips when Blaise had given that order. Despite his rough exterior, he did at least seem to respect the role of women even if he worked solely with men. Jerry had yet to see a woman under his command yet.

Blaise tossed Jerry's short sword into the sand as he eyed her. "Thanks for the cirax."

Jerry glared. "You're taking my ship?"

Blaise stepped in close to her, his warm breath washing over her cheeks as he grinned. "Do I get the sense you care more about your vessel than your cargo?"

"Of course," Jerry whispered. "You would feel the same."

She knew she had him there. As the sun rose over the horizon she was able to get a good view of *Yarrow's* hull and the damage Blaise had done. It was tremendous, but not unreasonable. They could repair it with time and credits for supplies. She stiffened her shoulders.

"We won't survive here."

"We'll see about that," he grinned at her. "I don't like to kill women."

"That's what you'll be doing if you leave us here."

"True." He stepped away from her with his hands out to his sides. "But I don't have to watch it."

His crew that had brought them there clambered onto Wench's Dream. All except Damon. Blaise held his hand up when Damon tried to board and held a gun on him. "I knew there was something different about this time."

"What?" Damon seemed confused.

Jerry watched with raw curiosity, the rope around her wrists still too tight for her to do anything.

"I don't allow rapists on board my vessels." Blaise turned on his heel and stepped onto the exterior door to Wench's Dream and stood there with his gun pointed at Damon as the ship rose into the sky and left, *Yarrow* towed behind it.

Damon turned on them, fury in his gaze. Azar reached down swiftly, grabbed the sword and sliced the rope holding Jerry's wrists together. She took the sword from him, cut the ties at her feet, and stood to defend her crew. Her chest rose and fell sharply as she waited for his next move.

"Fuck," Damon muttered.

"Damn straight," Jerry answered.

CHAPTER 25

WEEK ONE

Jerry sat on the edge of the cliff, dangling her feet over it with Sacha right next to her. She hadn't let the woman out of her sight since they'd been marooned there. Damon had been under Azar's supervision. Jerry was glad it wasn't her because she likely would have killed him a thousand times over already.

She'd dreamed of it.

The night before, when the lack of water in her body had gotten to be too much, she had hallucinated what it would feel like to slide the short sword between his ribs and right into his heart, the warmth of his blood as it spilled over her fingers. The scent of it.

Shaking the thought, Jerry leaned back on her palms and looked out at the sea. It hadn't rained in seven days. Seven days since they'd been stuck there with no sign of anyone coming to rescue them, though she doubted anyone would. No one knew where they were. No one knew what they had been doing other than Ursula and Arloa.

Sacha sighed and lay flat on her back to stare up at the sky, blocking the sun from her eyes with her forearm. "What are we doing here?"

Jerry frowned. Sacha had been asking the same question all day, but she didn't seem to remember Jerry's answers. The scuffle of boots against the rock surprised her, and Jerry turned sharply to find Yafe standing above them, blocking the sun on their little spot.

"Join us," Jerry asked. "We've got time to kill."

"Nice turn of phrase," Yafe murmured as she slipped onto the rock on the other side of Jerry. "It is beautiful here."

"It is," Jerry answered. "Nice place to die, I guess."

Yafe rifled around in her pant line and pulled out two small white pills, handing them to Jerry. "One for today."

Jerry knew they were running low, but they'd also refused to give any to Damon and kept the entire stash Yafe had managed to smuggle off *Yarrow* a secret from him. If Blaise was going to ditch him, then Jerry saw no reason to help him stay alive.

She handed the pill to Sacha, wishing she could give her another one to help with the memory issues, but knowing if they wanted to survive for as long as possible, then they had to ration out the cirax as much as possible. She swallowed her pill, really wishing she had something to wash it down with but knowing water was an even rarer commodity on the island than the drug that would keep them sane.

Jerry sighed and licked her lips to try and remove the chalky flavor. It didn't work. "How's Azar?"

"Ready to kill Damon."

"I think we all are," Jerry muttered and shifted a glance to Sacha. She would kill Damon before he would touch Sacha again. "I feel a storm."

"We need it."

"We need to rig something to collect the water."

Yafe pursed her lips as she stared out across the ocean. "We don't have much by way of supplies."

"I know, but we need to try. We don't know when the rains will come, and we need to save the water."

Lack of water wasn't something new to them. The entire planet of Penum had been in a severe drought for years, but to not have access to cleansers or rations meant they were left completely deprived. "Come on. Let's figure something out."

WEEK TWO

Exhaustion seeped into every single muscle Jerry had. The lack of water was too much, and it was next to impossible to keep going. They'd caught enough rain to last a few days from the last storm, but that was over a week ago. It hadn't been nearly enough. Nothing would ever be enough.

Jerry dragged her sorry ass up toward the rocks. She kept her sword with her, never leaving it out of her sight so long as she could manage. The giant rock in the center of the island had become her new companion. The number of times she had climbed to the top and thought about jumping off were too many to count, but leaving Sacha with Damon was not an option. Even if she did trust Azar and Yafe to take care of the situation, it was her responsibility—not theirs.

Jerry found her way to the backside of the rock and etched another line to mark the day. She'd been keeping track, but for what reason she had no idea. No one was coming. They might as well just let themselves die. At least then it would be by their choice. Jerry sighed and pressed her palm to the etch marks and closed her eyes.

Arloa's steel-blue eyes echoed in her mind, that odd little smile where one side of her mouth pulled up higher than the other, the smooth sounds of her voice when she would speak with such precision, when she would cry out her release. Rolling her neck, Jerry straightened her back. Memories and dreams were all she had.

And they were out of cirax.

The end wouldn't be that far off, unfortunately. They would all go insane first. Surprisingly, Damon had managed to stay mostly sane up until two days prior. He must have had vestigen on him in order to last that long, and Jerry regretted not shaking him down when they were left there. It wasn't the first poor decision she made.

Jerry found the tree they had been carving out day by day in order to fashion something better to capture water with. She set to work, wanting to make sure they were able to hit the next storm, but mostly to keep herself occupied. She couldn't stand to be in silence because all she did was think of Arloa.

The shuffling of feet behind her startled her. Jerry spun around and came face-to-face with Damon. He had a wild look in his eyes, one that told her the drug was completely out of his system. Jerry's heart rate skyrocketed, and she gripped her sword tightly, prepared for anything that might happen.

"Water." He grunted at her.

Jerry shook her head. "We don't have any."

Damon's nose wrinkled up, and he leaned over her. "Water."

"We don't have any," Jerry repeated. "And you need to back up. I have no problem killing you, and if you don't move, I will."

Damon reached forward, skimming his hand down her cheek and over her breasts. Jerry held her ground, no matter how tempted she was to chop his hand off. The arm he'd been shot in was completely useless, but his side had healed up—kind of. Yafe had tried to tie up the wound with fabric, but she couldn't do anything to fix the damage since she wasn't a healer. Jerry clenched her jaw and straightened into her full height.

"Step away from me."

Damon didn't move. Jerry reached forward and shoved his shoulder so he had to move away from her. Instead, he jerked forward swiftly and wrapped his fingers around her throat. Jerry gasped for air as he cut off her supply. She dug her nails into his bad side and rode the thrill of success when he cried out and let go of her.

Stomping on his foot, Jerry jerked her elbow into his nose, snapping it. Blood poured over his face. The scent hit her harder than she had ever thought possible. All she wanted to do was reach forward and smear her fingers in it, bring it to her lips so she could taste.

Fuck, what was she doing?

Snapping to attention, Jerry pulled herself together and glared at him. "Don't fucking touch me again or I will kill you."

WEEK THREE

Jerry's head pounded. The dull ache that had started over a week ago was now full-on rage every time she opened her eyes. Well, and even when she had them closed. She hadn't slept in days because of it. It hadn't rained. They were desperate. Jerry went to work on the tree, begging for rain to fall.

Azar, Yafe, and Sacha lay sleeping in the shelter they had built, but Jerry couldn't watch them any longer. She made it to the tree and started digging into the trunk so that it would hold water when it did rain. She was there until the sun rose in the sky before she realized that when she had left, Damon wasn't anywhere near them.

Stopping her work, Jerry stepped out from under the shelter of trees and looked around the shoreline to find him. He stood dangerously close to the water's edge, sticking his bare feet into the poisonous water before jumping back and laughing like an idiot. Jerry carefully watched him do it three more times before she decided she had to take action.

She really didn't want to.

Stumbling out from the tree line, she moved onto the sandy shore and covered her brow with her hand. "Damon, stop that."

He stilled and looked over at her, his eyes wide and red-rimmed as if he hadn't slept in days. Though to be fair, she had barely slept in the last few days, the lack of cirax finally catching up to her. She'd given Sacha the last dose.

"Come on in. The water feels so good."

Jerry wrinkled her nose at his burned feet. There would be no healing on the island without supplies. He was as good as dead now. Still he stood, facing her, glee written all over his face as he held his hand out to her.

"Come on."

"I don't think so," Jerry answered, staying put twenty feet from him.

She didn't want to get too close. Didn't want him to do anything stupid like try to drag her in, and she'd seen the virus consume enough people to know there was no telling what he might do. Though she was just as infected as he was and there was no telling what she would do either.

"Let's go back to camp."

Damon shook his head, his dark hair flying out around him. He stripped his jacket off and threw it into the water. Immediately, it was eaten away until she couldn't even see it anymore.

Jerry held her tongue, not sure what she wanted. If he killed himself, she wouldn't feel bad.

She was just about to walk away when Damon screamed out in pain. Jerry jerked her chin up as he jumped out of the water, his bare feet plunging into the sand as he covered them in mounds. Jerry didn't understand what he was doing or why, but that was the nature of the virus. Nothing Damon did was going to make sense to anyone but him—if he was even lucky enough for that.

Slowly moving forward, Jerry touched his shoulder to settle him. "Come on. Let's go back to camp."

Damon nodded up at her like a lost puppy. She helped him to stand, making sure to hold his hand so he couldn't suddenly grab her sword and plunge it into her back. They walked together to the camp where she sat him on a rock and bent down to grab the grubs they had dug up from under the rocks in the center of the island. It was what little protein they had to eat.

"You need your strength," Jerry said, not that she believed it, but at least it would keep him occupied for a while. The others were still sleeping. They had been doing more of that while she had been doing less. Sighing, Jerry left Damon alone and walked to the rock where she kept track of their days. Etching one more line into the hard stone, she started work on the tree trunk again.

WEEK FOUR

Damon had his fingers wrapped tightly around Jerry's throat

as he pushed her into the side of the rock. She hadn't even heard him coming up behind her until it was too late. He leaned in, his mouth open as he sunk his teeth into her neck.

Crying out, Jerry tightened her grip on his side as she hoped to knock some sense into him. She was blinded by pain, unable to control anything about the moment. Azar and the others were on the other side of the island, and it would take too long for them to get to her, to even hear her over the raging storm.

Jerry's back was cold against the stone wall as rain pounded down on them. She cringed and brought her knee up to hit Damon right in his groin. He didn't budge. Swallowing hard, Jerry reached up and pressed her thumb into his eye socket, hoping that would be enough pain to get him to stop, but it didn't.

He bit down hard, his teeth slicing into her skin and ripping the flesh. Heat swelled in her head, blood pouring down her neck from the injury as he backed away, happily eating her flesh as he grinned while towering over her. Jerry reached up to touch her neck, stunned into silence.

When she raised her gaze up at him, she didn't know what to do or say. The scent of her own blood was intoxicating, and she brought her blood-soaked hand to her lips, tasting. Flavor bloomed on her tongue. She'd never tasted something as good as that.

Raising her gaze to Damon, she looked him right in the eye as she pushed him backward. He stumbled, falling onto the hard ground, his head smacking into a rock. Jerry straddled him, wrapping her hands around his large neck and pushing against his jugular to rid the remaining life from him.

Azar grabbed hold of her, pulling her off. Jerry kicked and screamed as she tried to get back to Damon, needing to feel his life-force leave his body by her hand. She scratched Azar as she tried to get loose from his grasp.

Jerry reached around for her sword, but it was gone. Panicked, she stopped fighting Azar and looked for her precious sword. She needed it. That was *hers*. Rifling through the dirt with her hands, brushing it aside, she looked for it. She couldn't give up. She needed that fucking sword.

Crawling back to where Damon lay on the ground, Jerry tried to find it, but she stopped short. Bare toes that were black from frostbite pressed into the rock, the sword right between the legs. Jerry raised her gaze, her chin tilted back so she could see Sacha, standing there, the sword in her hands as she cocked her head at Jerry.

"Take it," Sacha whispered.

Jerry gripped the sharp end of the blade with her bare hand, pressing until it pierced her flesh and sliced her fingers. Sacha let go, and Jerry pushed herself to stand. Damon still lay prone on the ground, blood pooling behind his head.

Sacha touched Jerry's shoulder lightly. "Be done with him."

Jerry didn't hesitate this time. Getting on her knees, she straddled Damon and put the sword to his neck. She sliced swiftly, cutting his skin, his muscle, everything between her and the ground. In one deliberate motion, she decapitated him.

The smell was overwhelming, and it made her mouth water. Without thinking, Jerry took her sword and slammed it down into the front of his skull, splitting the bone until his brain was revealed. She dug around with her finger until it was covered, and then plopped it between her lips, sighing as the flavor hit her.

This had been what she needed. This was it. She did it again, her mind shifting back to where it once was, to who she was. Sacha bent over Jerry and did the same thing, breathing heavily as she sucked down even more than Jerry had.

Stopping herself, Jerry leaned against the base of the trunk she'd prepared for rain and closed her eyes. They had to save some of it. As much as she hated to admit it, Damon could very well allow them to last even longer.

WEEK FIVE

Jerry sat on the topmost rock on their little island, her mind clearer than it had been in months. Damon had come in handy for something, she supposed. Though she didn't want to admit it to anyone. Except her crew stranded with her had done the same thing. She had willingly eaten him.

The thought repelled her as much as it intrigued her.

Leaning back and holding herself up with her hands, Jerry stared at the far horizon. They didn't have much longer. Each of them knew that. They had done their best to survive for as long as they could, but Damon's brain and body were deteriorating quickly, and they would all slide back into the insanity the virus caused.

She heard it first. Popping her eyes open, Jerry shielded her vision from the sun so she could look around. She turned left and right, searching for the cause of the rumble. There wasn't a cloud in the sky and the air was dry as ever, so it wasn't a storm.

Standing up, Jerry lifted up on her toes when she saw it.

White sleek lines.

A ship.

ABOUT THE AUTHOR

Adrian J. Smith has been publishing since 2013 but has been writing nearly her entire life. With a focus on women loving women fiction, AJ jumps genres from action-packed police procedurals to the seedier life of vampires and witches to sweet romances with a May-December twist. She loves writing and reading about women in the midst of the ordinariness of life.

AJ currently lives in Cheyenne, WY, although she moves often and has lived all over the United States. She loves to travel to different countries and places. She currently plays the roles of author, wife, and mother to two rambunctious youngsters, occasional handy-woman. Connect with her on Facebook, Twitter, or her blog.

SCHEMING WOMEN SEEK REVENGE

Never piss off a woman.

A captain without a ship isn't a captain at all. Rescued from the island she and her crew were marooned on, Jerry wants nothing more than to exact her revenge on the Wench's Dream.

Shipless, penniless, and stuck, Jerry scrambles to form a plan. With the virus taking a severe toll, her resources are thin. She has a crew to feed and responsibilities to live into. But she's consumed by her obsession with her ship—the only home she's ever known.

Calling in all the favors she has, Jerry sets on a quest to rescue her ship from a band of pirates.

Releasing spring 2023